DANG

Three men hurried toward me, indistinct because of the driving snow.

My spacer's instinct registered danger immediately. They spread out, coming around one side and herding me toward the edge of the landing. Clearly, their intentions were to force me over the side.

So I turned as if to run, continued the turn building momentum, and nailed the short one on the far side with a slicing kick to his right knee. It buckled and he went down. I began to lash out at number two, the one in the middle, when he produced a stunner and I hit the landing on my shoulders to avoid the beam, rolled in the snow, and came up running. My breath exploded into puffs of steam.

Off to the side in the snow and gloom, I glimpsed a dark presence. I had time to see him drawing a weapon, too. His compact, muscled frame was already in motion. This fourth man had the air of command about him.

I feinted past him and ran for an aircar.

An energy beam sizzled the snow behind me.

Now I was under the overhang and protected from the snow. I dove into an aircar, slapping the "MANUAL LAUNCH" button. Shrouded by snow, the man with the dark presence stood and watched me.

I'd gotten somebody's attention.

A WORLD LOST

JAMES B. JOHNSON

DAW BOOKS, INC.
DONALD A. WOLLHEIM, FOUNDER
375 Hudson Street, New York, NY 10014

ELIZABETH R. WOLLHEIM
SHEILA E. GILBERT
PUBLISHERS

First Printing, August 1991

1 2 3 4 5 6 7 8 9

DAW TRADEMARK REGISTERED
U.S. PAT. OFF. AND FOREIGN COUNTRIES
—MARCA REGISTRADA.
HECHO EN U.S.A.

PRINTED IN THE U.S.A.

Dedicated to my father James. Thanks for your long-time support. Also, please note that the term ''seems like'' does not appear herein.

Contents

1: SEARCHING

When I popped out of transpace, Roanoke was gone. The whole planet. My home. My girl waiting for my return. My family.

The entire planet had disappeared.

Then I got my brain in gear. I could just hear my betrothed now. "Rusty Wallace," she would say, "you simply missed a few calculations."

Me?

I admit that not many people bothered to chart their own starship courses any more, what with the Plex Net and all. For that matter, not many people went into space any longer, not when the Plexus could send 'em to any settled planet in the galaxy—plus selected asteroids, moons, wherever the folks at Plex Central had set up Plex stations or beacons.

My brain reengaged and I queried the ship. "Run over those figures again, will you, Betsy?"

"Which figures, Rusty?"

I sighed. "The ones we used to get here. When Ginny and I get married, she's gonna de-humanify you."

"Yes, Rusty. I confirm the data."

I gulped and looked out the viewer where Roanoke should be. This funny feeling began way down in my scrotum and climbed through my guts and palpitated my heart and constricted my throat and fuzzed my brain and threatened to blow off the top of my head.

Nothing.

"Search for debris." My voice was harsh.

"Searching," said Betsy. "Nothing."

There was no reason for an entire planet to explode, but it was all I could think of. The fact that I could find no debris was heartening.

While trying to think it all through, I ate some chunky peanut butter and jalapeño pudding I'd made as an experiment. The peanut butter pepped me right up.

Something had been tickling the back of my mind. "Perhaps we're on the wrong side of the sun, a transposition of one figure." My voice was hopeful, but I knew what was wrong as soon as I said the words.

"The sun is gone, too," said Betsy.

"Uh, oh." My gut was churning like Roanoke rapids. Zira gone, too. My grandfather had named the star after his wife. "When I first saw the star out there all alone pulsing heat into the void, it reminded me of your grandmother, she was so hot all the time—may her soul rest in peace."

Not only do planets not vanish, but suns don't vanish more than planets don't vanish.

No debris, no sun. Checking—nope, no moons, either. Roanoke has—had?—a couple of small chunks of asteroids we called moons.

My mind was clamoring for me to go into a full panic mode. I fought off the overwhelming temptation and thought.

"Betsy, give me a random jump, say about a light-year. We've got to study the area from afar."

Bang, we were a light year-out.

Nothing.

Instrumentation showed Roanoke and the star were gone, yet the light from the sun was still pulsing through space.

Roanoke was an only planet around a lonely star. We keep to ourselves and don't use the Plex Net much. We've no real commercial products to interest the rest of the galaxy, just manufacture what's necessary to subsist on a rugged planet. Glaciers had scarred the entire world for so long that it looked like all angles and chopped places, not your basic smooth, rounded-off world.

My father's father had *discovered* Roanoke. Both had been spacers, and as they were, so was I. While I loved space and wouldn't think of being a permanent groundhog, I still needed Roanoke to return to.

"Look, are we even in the right place? Give me a few referents."

"Right, Rusty. Highlighting local reference points on the screen."

Screen light pulsed and I saw the few local stars in the right positions and formations.

I still couldn't believe it. I pushed a wayward palm frond out of the way. There were many plants on Betsy's bridge.

"Hop back to where Roanoke should be," I directed. Maybe we'd just missed it the first time.

Bang.

Nothing.

The same nothing.

"Another random jump, say point one."

Bang.

Different perspective.

But nothing where Roanoke and Zira should be.

A different display on the screen confirmed that we were in the right starfield.

In and out of transpace we moved, finally seeing Roanoke's sun 0.16 light-years away, meaning Roanoke had disappeared about eight weeks ago, standard—long after I'd departed on this current trip.

"Betsy," I said slowly, dreading what I was afraid of, "put us as close to the black hole as possible."

"Done," she said.

Bang.

The simulated images on the screen were menacing. Instruments bleeped and alarms pinged and lights throbbed and klaxons klaxed.

"Betsy, override all that crap."

"Yessir." Her mechanical voice seemed a bit apprehensive to me.

"Shoot a probe into the area and feel around with instrumentation."

"Right, Rusty."

Our "neighborhood" black hole was your average-to-small discontinuity, light-years away from everything, just doing its job of sucking up space junk and warping light and any other kind of signals on all bands of the spectrum happening by. Off in the distance was a star which had been going nova. The instruments told me it had expended much of its energy and was now dying back.

"No discernable debris," Betsy said.

Even had Roanoke exploded, there was no reason for the remnants to float all the way over here and voluntarily head for the yawning maw.

Nevertheless, I had to make certain. It was the only thing I could think of.

"Do you see anything?" I asked.

"No, Rusty." Betsy's voice told me that if light cannot escape from the damn thing, how the hell could she see anything? Or how could her instrumentation sense anything?

"I know that," I said unnecessarily, "but I don't have anything else to suggest."

"Yes, Rusty." Reassuring mode.

It was *not* reassuring. My mother and brothers and sisters were on that missing planet. Not to mention Virginia Bavarro, slated to be Mrs. Rusty Wallace.

An atavistic fear crawled over my body like slimy snakes.

"Recompute the whole thing," I said. "Start with clean data from the data base, not figures you've used before."

"Complying." A moment filled with no hope at all passed. "The results are the same."

"Can you find any similar situations in your historical data file?"

"None. There are a few instances of planets being

destroyed during wars, but the immediate area was lousy with evidence, along with residual radiation and gravitational impact on nearby celestial objects."

"Any astronomical warnings?"

"None."

"Any indication of oddball space clouds, magic, trickery, anything?"

"None."

I sank back into the pilot's chair. My mind was blank. "Can you account for the disappearance?"

"Not logically, Rusty. Even using some of the ideas you just mentioned, I can extrapolate no possible sequence of events which would account for the complete disappearances of a planet and a sun, either simultaneously or individually."

"Me, neither. Any response from your probe yet?"

"There hasn't been enough time."

"Right." Massaging my jaw, I tried to think of what to do next. I didn't even know enough to ask the right questions. "Take us back to the vicinity where Roanoke is supposed to be."

"Done."

Bang. We were there and Roanoke was still missing.

Invisibility shields were too much to ask for. That's one the scientists haven't been able to come up with.

"See if you can locate the Plex beacon."

"Checking."

To translate people and things from one world to another, the Plexus has to install one of its wondrous beacons in space nearby. The beacon's computer senses changes in the local gravity field and whatever else the tech guys need in a constantly moving universe for their machinery to operate accurately. You can't very well translate somebody from the sector capital to a planet without the proper data. Your planet's beacon is linked with the Plex Net throughout the galaxy, and while the tech and math guys would spit out a freighter's ton of mumbo jumbo, you could zap between planets or anywhere on your own planet—as long as the equipment and machinery were there and operational.

Colonization of Roanoke hadn't proceded far enough for too many Plex stations to have been established. There was the main off-planet facility near the Wallace home and a couple of feeder stations mining companies had set up for their own use.

"Back to the black hole and check on the probe." My voice was as leaden as my mind.

"Right."

Bang.

A moment. Then Betsy said, "The continuous data link I instituted did not change; therefore there was no new information. The comm from the probe became garbled, then became nonexistent."

"You mean the black hole swallowed the probe and we ain't going to get anything further?" Something she'd said tickled my mind.

"Exactly."

I had to shut her off sometimes. For instance, this time she would have been full of technical details such as event horizons and all kind of other stuff I wasn't interested in. I just needed to know what, not why or how.

What had happened to Roanoke? If at all possible, someone would have gotten word out somehow. Both Dad and Granddad were schemers like me; maybe that's where my penchant for scheming came from. Which all made me think: what would I have done? Unconsciously, I chewed on the scar on my lip.

"Got it," I said. Betsy had said the word: commed.

"What do you have?" she asked.

"If the Roanoke beacon buoy is gone, then no one could have commed out." The Plex Net provided the FTL communications network, I was reasoning, so no beacon, no comm link. Nobody uses regular comm channels any longer—except us spacers, and then infrequently. "Betsy, right where Roanoke vanished, 0.16 light-years, see if you can find any *broadcast* transmissions."

"Done," she said. "That is something I should have considered."

"Nah," I said, "you ain't the schemer I am."

"I hope not, everything *I* do is supposed to be legal."

"What are you saying—?"

"I have something, Rusty."

"Display it."

"Done."

The screen lighted. Dad appeared, sitting at his console. He faced the camera pickup and ran his fingers through his red hair. Everybody calls him "Red."

His face was worried. "Hurry. We might not have much time." He was talking to someone off-screen, probably Roanoke Control.

Then he nodded and cleared his throat. "This is a Mayday. I say again, Mayday. I am transmitting from the planet Roanoke in the Zira star system. I say again, Mayday. We've destroyed our Plex beacon before we understood the nature of the threat; therefore, we cannot comm through normal Plex facilities."

Dad would know this would be a long shot, hoping I—or another Roanoke spacer would return and think to check non-Plex comm possibilities.

Dad's face looked perplexed. "Whoever receives this transmission, please copy and forward it to any Roanoke spacer—or the Sector News Service, for that matter." He took a deep breath. He wasn't reading a script. He was composing as he went. "The way I understand it, we have only one hundred days—"

"Betsy, what's wrong? He would have put the message on a continuous loop."

"It appears we have just witnessed the exact moment Roanoke vanished. Therefore, the transmission was interrupted at that point in time."

"You're telling me he didn't get to finish his message and we don't know what he's saying or going to say."

"I wouldn't say it like that, but, yes."

"Are you making fun of me?" I demanded.

"Not at a time like this," she said.

I sat there on my command lounge. The jungle of plants usually calmed me, but not this time. Was Roanoke's disappearance final? Or did Dad's one hundred day statement refer to something yet to occur? I had to believe the latter; if not, the planet was gone forever and the people dead or might as well be.

It had been slightly over eight weeks since Roanoke vanished. Which gave me approximately forty days, standard, in which to unravel this mystery.

The nearest planet to Roanoke was Harrygant, named after some guy in antiquity. I wondered aloud. "I wonder if Harrygant is still there? I wonder if I can use their Plex facility to translate to Roanoke?"

"Good thinking, Rusty."

"Get us there. Now."

"Done."

Bang.

Longer in transpace this time. Enough time for me to lose my lunch in the head and gargle away the aftertaste.

Would Harrygant be there?

Why not?

The universe was going out of kilter for me. I needed something solid, something hard and present to reassure me.

Harrygant was there. I parked near the Plex beacon and was able to translate down to the main facility.

Betsy's words still rang in my ears. "Rusty? It occurs to me that if you go into a Plex station and translate to Roanoke which is no longer there that you might translate into infinity."

With no end Plex facility to capture you, it was possible. I'd heard of it happening in the old days, before they ironed out all the kinks in the system. It was one main reason for the beacons and their supercomputers monitoring local fields.

I didn't know if I had the guts to attempt to translate to Roanoke or not. But that wasn't the question. Not yet.

Unless translating through the Plexus Net were the only way to find Roanoke.

Would I be able to stand on the target plate of a Plex station and zap myself to a destination which no longer existed?

2: HARRYGANT

Harrygant was a pleasant little planet if you didn't have pressing business. I had pressing business. The world was a soft, high tech place which shipped electronics components everywhere in Sector VIII. The people were well off and an easygoing bunch—though it always irritates the hell out of me when people generalize about planets and their citizens.

Harrygant had maybe a hundred times more people than Roanoke, perhaps five million citizens.

From orbit near the Plex beacon I saw a pretty world, your basic green and blue. But I paid no attention to any of this. Betsy extended an airlock tunnel to the buoy and I hurried down it, stepped into the beacon's Plex station and, zap, I was on the surface.

Once translated down to the main Plex station, I moved out quickly and with a purpose.

If you've seen one Plex facility—aka Plex fax—you've about seen 'em all. Typical government thinking—standardization and uniformity.

The major Plex fax on a world contains a great main hall with info and data stations and even people behind desks. One side of the main corridor is usually the freight section, which is always busier. There are translation stations of all sizes to fit anything you can name. Just pay more and you can send a hundred ton machine—or pay less and send a person—down the block, across the world or the galaxy to another system. You're paying for distance traveled. The freight section had its own external access on the far side away from the passenger (passengers are also known as pax) section.

Depending on the traffic, the pax section is designed to meet your planet's needs. With the pax and freight handling capabilities, it's no surprise that the plex facility usually becomes the hub of the planet's activities and, most of the time, that city evolves into the capital of the planet.

The Plexus administrators frown on opening a Plex facility on a planet with more than one government or political entity. Of course, like everything else, exceptions are made.

Just before stepping out of the station I'd translated down to, I thought of something.

"Station, can you translate me to Roanoke?"

"Sir, we have many substations on Harrygant and none are named Roanoke."

"Roanoke is a planet."

"Sir, you will have to obtain the official Plexus destination designation code."

"Skip it."

I never was very trusting of the Plex Net. Give me a starship any time. Of course, that put me in a shrinking miniscule minority. One of these days, there won't be anybody left to take their damn beacons out and plant 'em in space.

Coming out of that station, I joined a softly lighted corridor and let it do the walking for me to the main concourse. My knees were a shade weak. Technically speaking, the people around me were collectively and often awkwardly known as Plex fax pax.

The Plex on Harrygant hadn't automatically known about the nearest planet.

Although, upon review, distance doesn't mean a whole lot to a machine which can translate you fifty miles or a thousand light-years in an instant or two.

In the main concourse, I headed for an INFOR-MATION booth.

Stepping under the hood, I enunciated slowly—these

machines must deal with many dialects and quite a few languages. However, the very existence of the Plexus Net has sort of fostered standardlingo. And since I spoke standard, being from a new colony and all, that suited me just fine. I had more important things to do with my time than learn languages all over the place. On the other hand, a spacer does in fact need languages, and while I didn't like it, I'd learned a few.

"Please give me the Plexus destination designation of the planet Roanoke in the star system Zira."

"Working."

I stood unhappily staring out at people moving through the concourse. Family travelers, businessmen and women, some personal package express. Harrygant wasn't as busy as some I'd seen. The pax section seemed to disgorge people every couple of minutes and occasionally ate one or two down its muted corridors. A small boy chased a rubber ball, a bald man with decorative leeches clinging to his temples hurried past, a woman with the infinity tattoo on her forehead glared at me as she rode by, and two attendants disappeared into a door marked AUTHORIZED PERSONNEL ONLY. One day I'd like to be authorized only.

Anything to divert my mind.

It shouldn't have taken the computer any time at all to respond to me. The delay was ominous.

"Sir," the booth finally said, "that terminal is unavailable."

"What does that mean?"

"I have a flag in my system which informs me to request that you inquire of a Plexus official."

"You could be a bureaucrat."

"Thank you, sir."

"It wasn't a compliment." I had a thought. "Give me the destination designation of a planet called Earburtholontomisque Four."

"Standby." A few seconds. "That terminal is unavailable."

"Thanks." I stepped from the booth. That confirmed my suspicions. I'd just invented a fictitious planet and the computer had responded as it had when I asked for the designation of Roanoke. I concluded that if you ask about a destination it knows nothing about, then the computer was programmed to respond with "that terminal is unavailable."

All of which did not bode well for Roanoke.

I found a pleasant young lady behind a counter. "Personal Service" said a day-glow tag on her lapel. She smiled institutionally when I arrived.

"Listen," I said hesitantly. How do you ask the question without them thinking you're nuts? "I can't seem to determine the destination designation of Roanoke."

"Did you try the info booth?"

"Yes, ma'am."

"Let me check for you." Her perfunctory smile told me she dealt with dipsticks all the time, but she'd see it through anyway. She frowned. "My screen shows that terminal is unavailable."

Behind her, scenes from strikingly beautiful places appeared and disappeared. Whatever vacation spots they were pushing these days.

"What does that mean?"

"Why, sir, it means that the terminal is unavailable."

"I know. But why?"

"Oh, perhaps maintenance. Relocation of the beacon buoy. I've even heard of worlds turning off their Plexus facilities and beacons."

I must have looked curious.

"They want to withdraw. Sometimes religion or politics interfere and they no longer wish to be part of the Galacticon." She grimaced sincerely. "Crazy fanatics. It might be a trade war. Galacticon authorities could be isolating a world—"

Not if that world had physically disappeared, I reminded myself.

"Would you check with the system and see if it's

maintenance? Its sun is called Zira. Perhaps they'll show an estimated time in commission."

She frowned at this over-and-above the call of duty request. "I guess so." Then she frowned at her screen. She was doing a lot of frowning. "I get the same answer." She looked up at me under dark brows. "Are you sure of the name? The 'terminal available' response is also an answer if there is *no* such destination, and there never has been any such."

"I'm sure. You've never heard of it?"

She shrugged. "With millions of planets in the Galacticon, what do you think?"

I shrugged back. What she said was likely true. Roanoke wasn't a high-frequency destination and probably nobody had ever brought it to her attention.

"Is there anything else I can help you with?" She gave me her minor-official-but-better-than-you frown.

"Look, ma'am, Roanoke is, was, um, make that is, a place—I mean a planet, a world. I've been there, I was brought up there—"

"I believe you, sir." She looked at me askance.

"Sure. You got a supervisor?"

She nodded and eyed me. I hadn't quite got around to shaving in the last cycle or two, a benefit of the job, and my jumpsuit was designed for utility, not fancy Plexus traveling.

She must have pushed a hidden something or other, for in a moment a tall lady came out of the AUTHORIZED PERSONNEL ONLY door. "May I help you?"

She'd been trained, I could tell. Her manner was smoothness personified. Quickly the first girl explained.

The supervisor stepped behind the counter and did things to the console. "What's the problem?"

I really didn't want to tell them I'd been to where Roanoke was supposed to be and it hadn't been there. "I want to get home," I said lamely.

"The system is indicating you cannot, or that the destination is not available."

"I've been there."

"And this Roanoke has a Plex facility?"

"A small one, yes."

"Perhaps it was only temporary," the older woman said, "and subsequently discontinued."

"No, it was legitimate."

"You've traveled the Net to this Roanoke?"

"I have."

"And you state that you are a resident of that planet?" She looked at passersby.

"I am."

"Well, then your credit card should reflect a balance and source of origin of funding."

That's right! I—Oops. "Ma'am? I am a spacer, a courier, a freighter, and explorer. Which is a dwindling profession. Hell, I'm not even sure the guild is still active."

Their faces reflected what I was becoming used to. Distaste. Social prejudice. People don't like space; therefore, they don't like spacers. Right then, I lost a lot of points on their social register. Sort of like I was a sniveling rodent.

I got to the point. "I maintain my banking at the sector capital out of necessity. Thus it's guaranteed by the Galacticon banking system." Even my ship's registry was Galacticon out of D'Earnhardt, the Sector VIII capital, not local. It then occurred to me that I had no documents proving the existence of Roanoke. My ID would list Roanoke as my current residence, but that could be easily faked and was thus no proof of Roanoke's existence.

"Would you have a birth certificate?"

Sadly, I shook my head. "I was born on a starship."

Four eyes stared at me disapprovingly. Now I was a disease-ridden, contagious sniveling rodent.

I spread my hands wide. "Please believe me. I have no reason to try to fool you."

The older lady looked at the younger lady and touched the console. Almost immediately, a man stepped from the AUTHORIZED PERSONNEL ONLY door. The older lady went over to him and began whispering. After a few moments, and many sideways glances at me, the man came to my side. He held out his hand. "My name is Ferguson. I believe there is a problem. Would you follow me?"

Right into AUTHORIZED PERSONNEL ONLY. Was I now authorized? It was a disappointment. I found myself following the man in a well-lighted corridor of standard blue. He let me into his office and said, "I'll be right with you." He closed the door behind me and I was on my own.

I should have known it was a setup.

The office was standard. Moving scenes on the walls. Onyxlike material for the desk when most people prefer pseudo-jade.

I scarcely wasted time looking once I spotted the executive console. The scheme leapt fully formed into my mind. Three long strides and I was around his desk.

Immediately, I hit the NO VOICE keypad, then DATA RECALL.

The screen glowed, SUBJECT?

ROANOKE. ZIRA SYSTEM.

It should have begun the search, but it didn't. I hit EXECUTE and nothing happened. ROANOKE remained on the screen.

"Uh-oh." I realized I'd been had.

Ferguson opened the door and two gray-clad security types came in ahead of him.

Shortly, I was being marched down the hall farther and deeper into the Plexus facility. Soon, I was sitting in a sculpted chair in front of a security officer. The two goons stood behind my chair.

Patiently I explained to the security officer that I merely wanted to translate from Harrygant to Roanoke and nobody could tell me the destination designation code.

Something blinked at the corner of the screen on his executive console.

His voice was dead level. "The sensors in the chair indicate you are lying."

He could have asked a dozen questions or told me a hundred things. He did none of these. He merely looked at me.

Sensing it was time for me to stop being the yokel in the big city, I folded my arms across my chest and sat back.

He waited, too. I wondered why he hadn't introduced himself. I wondered why these public servants didn't have name tags on their desks. His eyes were standard gray to match his standard security garb and his hair was turning gray also. He eyed my curly red hair jealously.

Finally, he glanced at his console. "The sensors indicated a high emotional state."

I said nothing.

"I can generate a few charges against you." His voice was tentative.

"None will stand up," I said. I had nothing to hide and had established myself to him. So briefly, I told him about Roanoke. I finished, "Thus you can see how people would consider me nuts. Planets don't just disappear. At least not without a lot of wreckage and pieces floating around, making rings and belts around suns. So, I thought about the Plex Net and came here. And you know the rest."

He turned and studied his console for a long moment. "The sensors indicate you *believe* you're telling the truth."

I groaned and leaned back.

Not only was defeat staring me in the face, not only had I lost Ginny and my family and friends and home planet, but now I was losing my sanity?

What he was suggesting hadn't occurred to me. Had I been drugged? Was I operating under some schizophrenic condition? Maybe I *was* crazy and making all this up.

I glanced at my hands, now trembling slightly. The tips of my left fingers were scarred from an earthquake tragedy I'd been involved in when I was about ten. On Roanoke. And that same hand had held the warm body of Ginny Bavarro. A phantom itch in my palm verified that.

"Spacers," I told the security man, "as a prerequisite, have to maintain mental discipline." It struck me Betsy would have been affected, too. I said nothing about her—or Dad's message.

He nodded. "I've heard that. I've also heard that spacers frequently lose their sanity." He surveyed his two men and spoke over my head. "Why do you think spacers are a dying breed?"

He was right. Traveling by Plex net was much more appealing.

"Look, I've nothing to lose. Bring on your house shrink." I paused dramatically. "I've no doubt you've got one monitoring this conversation."

His surprise glance at his console confirmed my suspicions.

In an hour, I was stripped and standing in front of a mirrored booth answering questions and being recorded by sensors attached to my head and body.

The shrink eyed several of my scars but said nothing. The ridged flesh on both my legs from where I'd lain in a crushed aircar for three days were of particular note. He went through the basic questions about my mother and teachers and Ginny and everything you'd expect.

When he got to asking questions about my loyalty to Galacticon, I peeled off the sensors. "You've got what you want, doc. I never was required to swear allegiance or loyalty to Galacticon. It's not required; and as a citizen, I don't have to. Skip it."

That he asked those questions should have told me something. They took a blood sample and ran it through an electronic scanner.

The shrink read the results. "You're perfectly healthy, Captain Wallace. You've no foreign presence in your body—"

I hoped he was talking about some mysterious virus or drugs, not some alien in my head.

"—and you show a steady and even mental keel."

I wasn't happy about the way they were treating me, but I did begin to like the psychologist because he wasn't pushing the fancy terminology.

Ferguson talked to me after the shrink. "Good-bye. I am sorry we cannot help you."

"I'm not satisfied."

"We have other concerns," he said. "What would you have us do?"

"Find Roanoke."

"Good-bye," he said, rising.

I stood. "I'm heading for the press. The Plex Net officials don't care." I was winging it. "Already there isn't a great deal of public confidence in your system— the small amount of traffic out there proves it." I jerked my thumb toward the Plex fax. "People will pay attention; after all, this isn't D'Earnhardt."

He sat back down and keyed his console.

He was called "Splash" and he was the highest Plexus official on Harrygant.

His office was a swimming pool with red water, doubtless reminiscent of some planet. He was taller than me, maybe six four. But you wouldn't know it because most of the time he floated on his back in the water.

I sat in a special power chair which kept me dry, one that I could control and follow him around as he piddled about the pool.

While he was taller, he was also heavier, much much heavier. He had to be pushing four hundred pounds. Maybe that's why he spent so much time in the pool. Why his skin wasn't all wrinkled, I don't know; maybe the answer could be found in the red water.

I had been told to call him "Splash," and now I knew why.

"Mr. Splash—" I began.

"Just Splash. The mister is not necessary." He flipped over and tread water in front of me.

"Right. Splash. Surely your people have briefed you why I'm here."

"They have, they have. You've, er, misplaced your home planet?"

"*I* haven't misplaced anything, Mr. Spla—I mean, Splash. I can't *find* it."

He spit a mouthful of water like a fountain in front of a university. "It appears that we cannot find it either."

I sank back. I'd been prepared for more administrative gobbledegook. "You believe me?"

"I don't know. The psych office passed you with high marks, though you might well consider reviewing your attitudes on interpersonal cooperation as it seems your individuality quotient is quite high to the detriment of your potential for contributing to the common good and therefore, translating to your distaste of Galacticon and much of what it stands for, not to mention—"

I think I understood what he was saying. While I tuned him out, I admitted he was probably correct—for I'd heard it all before. It was one of the major reasons I was a spacer. I'd been branded a maverick before and would be again. The trait ran through the Wallace family. It was why my grandfather was a spacer and ended up discovering Roanoke and founding the colony. It was why Galacticon ignored our planet; we didn't generally support much of anything Galacticon wanted to do. My dad was in fact currently the Managing Director of Roanoke—or should still be, if the world was still in existence.

Waiting until Splash wound down in his amateur psychoanalysis, I fought the inner battle again. Dad had said one hundred days until??? Now there were less than forty. Since Roanoke days were longer than standard, I was using standard—which, in an off-planet message, Dad would have used also. My brain and my guts were churning. What had happened to Roanoke?

"It's reassuring," I interrupted, "that at least you've heard of Roanoke."

He stood up in the water. "Son, do not let your preconceptions and impressions fool you. Yes, I've heard of Roanoke. I've never seen it or had anything to do with it, but astronomically speaking, Harrygant is the closest planet—while, on the other hand, there are many planets closer to us than Roanoke.''

"Good. Now I—''

"I wasn't finished. All I know is that Roanoke is found in black and white in an old printed catalog my staff dug up. The Plex doesn't keep records for very long, just financial transactions. If we did so, we wouldn't have memory space. For these reasons and the fact the system says the terminal in Roanoke is unavailable, I'm not necessarily convinced we've ever had a commercial Plexus facility on Roanoke.''

"But—''

"I'm still not finished.'' His hands were on his waist above the bloomerlike swimsuit he wore. "Into our orderly life you come, insisting this alleged Roanoke has been blown to pieces—''

"No.'' I sat up straight, awkward in that chair, but no water got on me. "I never said anything about an explosion. I merely said it wasn't there any longer.''

He shrugged. "Either way, it's the same.''

"I hope not.'' My initial enthusiasm for Splash was evaporating. "However, I say again, the planet is not there.''

"How do I know what you say is true?''

"Take a trip and see.''

He made a sour face. "You mean in *space?*''

I nodded uncomfortably.

"Me?''

"Sure. Or send somebody.''

He sank to his knees, the water coming up to his chins, "In a *spaceship?*''

"Look, Splash, I don't care if you send 'em in a cup of coffee.''

He sighed and closed his eyes. "I'm told you came here aboard a starship.''

"Right.''

"You parked near the Plex beacon?''

"I did.''

"How many other ships were parked there?"

"None." My answer was immediate and I saw his point.

"Exactly."

I sank back and the chair adapted. "Sometimes the answers don't come easily."

"Not at all," he agreed.

"You've got to believe me," I said, with nothing else to say.

He stood to his full height, some unseen platform raising him a bit. He was quite impressive. "I'd much rather believe you were in error than believe an entire planet has disappeared—even if that planet is Roanoke."

Ignoring the slight, I tried to think of what else I could do. "Perhaps you could have Plex Maintenance look into it."

"Here? On Harrygant? I've already done so. The computer responds the same, 'No terminal available.' What else can I do?"

"Send a maintenance team to Roanoke."

He grinned and, surprisingly, it was infectious. "I'll do that, Captain Wallace. You simply tell me what destination code to give them."

"I see your point. How about Plexus Central?"

"I don't know much about Plexus Central. It's co-located with Galacticon Central and is more administrative than technical."

"Oh." I'd thought that there had to be a central controlling location. "Why isn't Plex Central more technical? I always heard it was the center of operations."

"That's a myth we don't disabuse. If people thought there was no central system operational control, we'd suffer a crisis of confidence. While Plexus Net headquarters is on Galacticon Central, it's mostly an administrative function, not operational. The system is set up, linked throughout the galaxy, and the entire system net comprises the functions of a central control."

All the parts added up to greater than their sum. Some computer systems are like that. That's one reason why mankind was doing so well while simultaneously retreating into its shell.

He must have seen my mind working, so to change the subject from the Plex inner workings, he said, "Of course, I will forward a report."

"Great." I dipped my left hand into the water. It was surprisingly soft—almost compelling. I jerked my hand back out. I didn't need whatever narcotic effect it offered. I needed my wits about me.

"It's all I can do."

"The bureaucracy will eat it up, Splash. And nothing will ever come of it. You know the reputation of the Galacticon bureaucracy."

He shrugged. "I'll send it through Plexus channels."

"And if they're covering up something?" My voice was soft, but his eyes told me he read the danger in my tone.

Then his eyes glazed over. "*I* don't know. I've never had to report a planet missing before. I'll have to find a procedure for that."

"Maybe the maintenance department which places the beacons would be appropriate," I suggested hopefully.

"I don't know who that is, but headquarters will have to make that determination. My chain of command is administrational, not operational or maintainal."

I groaned, not entirely to myself. "What would you suggest I do?"

"Go on about your job."

"Right now my job is finding Roanoke."

"Then make your own report."

I shook my head. "I face the same problem you do. To whom do you report a vanished planet?" I wasn't going to tell anyone about Dad's comm.

He squeezed both hands at the same time and water squirted from them. "I don't know. Galacticon?"

"Who in Galacticon?"

"The executive?" he said, eyes brightening.

"That's just a big bureaucracy. Look how much trouble I had getting to you."

"And you were very effective doing so," he admitted. "You have a tenacity which is becoming apparent even in our current conversation."

"Any other ideas?" This was discouraging.

"Perhaps the Navy?"

I thought about that. It wasn't a bad idea. "I haven't seen any Navy hereabouts lately, have you?"

He shook his head. "I heard they're mostly using the Plex Net nowadays." He looked conspiratorial. "I also heard that we've only three Naval ships in Sector VIII and no one has seen them in months." I detected a note of organizational pride there. After all, he was in charge of the Plex fax here, and the Plex Net had made space travel obsolete.

"It figgers."

He snapped a finger and splattered me with red water. "The Diplomatic Corps."

"It's possible."

"Or the Interior Department?" he added.

"All of them are possibilities," I said, backing the chair a bit away from him. "Galacticon is a long way from here."

The bright light in his eyes returned. "It isn't if you take the Plex."

Wondering why his skin wasn't red from the water, I said, "I've a feeling I'll need my ship nearby." Though Betsy would be nearby anywhere I left her, the Plex providing near instantaneous travel. But I remembered stories of criminals nailed and apprehended while in transit on the Plex, people barred from using the system for many reasons. And I was going to raise hell, one way or the other, so I might be *persona non gratis* right quick. It also occurred to me that I might well need Betsy and her resources.

"Well, you might start at D'Earnhardt." He was talking about the sector capital.

Taking Betsy and going transpace wasn't near as fast as traveling the same distance by Plex, but space was more comforting. I never know what goes on while I'm in the net being translated. I don't know how long it takes because clocks and time work different when superlight speeds and distances are involved. Not to mention my childhood dream where they dissect my mind while I'm in the translation process.

"I'm certain you will find your Roanoke," he said and pushed off, red water lapping over his belly.

Propelling the chair to the upramp, I hoped so. I'd try the sector capital government on D'Earnhardt. Being the local sector and controlling only a few million worlds, the sector government should be more concerned with local affairs than Galacticon Central. But should that prove unproductive, other options were beginning to occur to me.

Like the press. Or the Galactic Geographic Society.

These thoughts brought me to one worrisome question: Why hadn't any of these organizations raised hell already? A missing planet isn't some everyday routine occurrence.

Although, how could these organizations instigate a search for a vanished sun and world if those same organizations didn't know the sun and world existed?

I was going to have to be the one to inform them.

In thirty-eight days I had to have answers.

3: THE GALACTIC GEOGRAPHICAL SOCIETY

The instant I spent translating up worried me, but I arrived with nothing wrong. No sinister presence snatched my body while I was translating.

Betsy got us in gear and we made it to D'Earnhardt. The Plex would have sent us there PDQ, but Betsy took a day longer. However, I felt a lot safer. Down to thirty-seven.

Shaved, cleansed, and in groundhog garb of the tight slacks they were wearing there at the time with an airy barong Tagalog top, I translated down to the surface of the sector capital.

I didn't miss the fact that Betsy was one of two ships parked in orbit—and that's around the sector capital, the economic and political center of this part of the galaxy. The admin hub for a few million planets and only one other ship out there? I hoped that wasn't a measure of the degradation of our society—but I was afraid nonetheless.

The Plex fax was *mammoth*, which only made sense. There were even intermediate Plex stations within the facility if you didn't want to take the time walking or riding the autosystems. I stood in one of the twenty or so main concourses feeling like a country boy in the big city—which in fact I was.

Noise rolled over me as more people than actually live on Roanoke clogged the facility. Some even *jostled* me! "Pardon *me*," sarcastically said didn't even get a rise out of the jostlers. Perhaps it was indicative of a communal psyche on a planet a few hundred thousand miles in circumference and chock full of people.

I wanted to find a suggestion box and recommend they make all translation stations one way out of this place.

Instead I found an info booth and began requesting destination codes and locations. The government was so layered that I changed my mind right away. I selected one location and it didn't even have a Plex station nearby—which in turn eased my mind.

The aircar park atop the Plex facility was buzzier than insects on carrion and seemingly just as organized.

While I was by no means wealthy, I took an aircar, giving the grid designation. As an explorer, scout, whatever it takes to stay in space, I hadn't struck the mother lode yet. I'd carried some important medicine on occasion as a courier, and discovered a few nonhabitable planets. My big score had been a mineral rich asteroid that I was able to claim. The mining combine which bought it from me also hired me to take the mining Plex beacon to the asteroid. Robots gobble up the whole thing and feed it through the specially designed beacon station which translates the asteroid piecemeal to the right worlds for processing. It's a neat system, you don't have to hire real miners or even spacers except for arranging the initial delivery of the robots and beacons.

However, I spent the credits on the aircar, Roanoke being more important than current financial frugality.

In an underground city a couple of hundred miles from the main Plex fax, I found the local branch office of the Galactic Geographical Society.

There was no receptionist.

"Hello," I called; a mechanical voice from a hidden speaker said, "Someone will be with you in a moment."

I stood and stared at the walls. It showed rolling pix

of what I guessed was Earth at some unspecified time in the far past. It was hard to believe we'd all come from there. In fact, nowadays, we had more planets than they had people on Earth for much of its history. Hell, we were even crowding the galaxy. That's an exaggeration I always make, and it's not really true. It just seems so, what with people not trucking around in space so much anymore. I thought a broad study would show the creeping galactic-wide ennui was matched directly by a lack of population increase.

"Hi, there."

I knew it. An old man who matched the stereotype of a fuddy-duddy professor peered through the wall screen.

"Hi, yourself," I responded.

"Are you looking for someone?"

"About fifty thousand of them."

He frowned. "A joke? Did I miss it?"

"No, sir. I'm looking for some information." It was hard to spill my guts to his image on a wall.

"Well, come on back if you must."

The screen dissolved and showed a schematic. The red line traced my route. Why they go to all that trouble, I'll never know. I didn't need a computer to tell me down the hall and second door on the right.

The second door on the right swished open and I strode in.

The old gent was standing in front of a chest-high desk staring at pages of actual paper as an automatic flipper went through them.

I cleared my throat.

"Stand by, young man. I know you are there."

"Yes, sir." I don't know why, but I liked the crusty old geezer right off.

Shortly, he turned to me. "Fifty thousand. Was that a joke?"

"Let me start at the beginning." I began pacing a little, and tried to put my hands in my pockets, but those form-fitting slacks they wear here didn't have any pockets. I noticed the old guy had a comfortable one-piece suit on. "I'm from—"

"Tell me your name, young man."

"Rusty Wallace."

"Very good to start. I am, of course, Egbert Owens Girrard Simpson, doctor of geography and history, and director of this office. I am also its only employee. I am also far behind on my cataloguing, though not nearly as much information comes in as used to."

"That's probably from the wave of human entropy sweeping the galaxy," I said.

"It is a terrible thing, no?" He stepped near me. "Perhaps you could be more concise than I am? I'm far behind and have no other help. Would you like a job?"

"No, thanks, doc. Listen, have you ever heard of Roanoke?"

He nodded. "It was one of the original colonies in the new world on Earth."

"Yes, but I'm talking about the planet."

"No, I've never heard of it."

Which made my job more difficult. "It's my home planet, and it's gone."

"Gone?"

"Right. Gone. Disappeared. I rode my starship home and Roanoke wasn't there any longer."

"Gads," said Simpson. He looked at me under bushy brows. "And you don't find that strange?"

"Well, yes. That's why I'm here. Do you have any information on what happened to it?"

"If I've never heard of the place, how would I know if I had any information on it?"

"I thought maybe you could check," I said lamely.

He paused and walked back and forth in front of me for a moment. His left leg seemed to hitch when he turned. "It's obvious you do not know to what I was referring."

"The strange part?" I thought he'd been agreeing with me.

"Roanoke," said Egbert Simpson. "One of the

original colonies in the new world. It disappeared, sort of, too."

I shook my head. "No. I don't believe it. Surely it's a coincidence."

He nodded. "I'll guess. Your planet Roanoke is a relatively newly founded colony."

"It is."

"I have encountered several Roanokes." He glanced at a stack of old books. "Spacers are sometimes history buffs and name newly discovered planets after historical precedents. Much of the time, when the planet is tamed and they build up governments and so on, they change the name."

That made sense to me because the Plex Net wouldn't allow more than one planet of the same name in a sector.

I nodded. One of spacers' biggest all time gripes revolved around groundhogs renaming their discoveries. I suspected writers feel the same about their titles and mothers about their kids who change their own names. Though if I had Egbert's names, I'd be sorely tempted to beeline for the nearest admin center and register a new and more assertive name.

"What do you mean 'sort of' disappeared?" I asked.

"Roanoke was an island off someplace named Carolina or something similar. It was the site of the first English colony, if I recall correctly. A ship a year or two later came to check on them and all the people were gone. Then they established a fort and some of the soldiers or naval personnel disappeared also, on exploration trips or some darn thing. The difference is that you claim the land is missing, too. Want a doughnut?"

He touched a wall access and the door flipped open and there was a plate of doughnuts.

"My vice," he said and held out the plate to me.

"No, thanks." I took one anyway and bit down. It was sweet and crumbly and tasted good but I didn't know that then. I wished I had some peanut butter sprinkle to top it with. I was still trying to reconcile the seeming repeat of history. "Um, did they ever find those people? At the original Roanoke?"

"Nope," Egbert said around half a doughnut. "It was speculated that Indians got them. Or, much later, aliens in something called 'flying saucers,' which appears to have been a mode of transportation."

"I've heard of different lifeforms, but we've encountered no intelligent beings yet," I said. "No aliens."

Crumbs cascading, he ate another doughnut. "It would have been fortunate. It was part of my doctoral dissertation that had we encountered aliens, then we as a race might well have been challenged more and wouldn't right now be so planet-bound." He looked up sharply. "You! You intimated that you are a spacer?"

"I didn't intimate anything, doc. I said so and I am." I returned to the subject. "Anyway, *my* Roanoke has vanished along with the people. The difference is significant."

"Did I not say something similar?" he asked. "Oh, well. Fascinating, fascinating. Rusty Wallace, is it?"

"Right, doc."

"Good, good. I'd like to talk to you in depth. Do you know that you're the first spacer I've ever met?"

I shrugged uncomfortably. "Er, doc, listen. I got a problem. My planet's missing and I don't know what to do about it."

"And that's why you came to me?"

"Well, I kind of thought that the Galactic Geographical Society kept track of geographical kind of stuff. I hoped you'd know what happened to it." I looked around the musty room and wondered why I'd thought that.

"Conceptually, at one time you might have been correct in your assumptions. However, we've become merely a documenting, or historical recording organization. All I do is catalog and organize the data I have. We're no longer an active exploration society as we once were. Just an historical society now. Sorry. At one time we even had scientific and exploration ships. We—they at the time—went to where interesting discoveries were. Now we don't. Nowadays, there aren't even any more interesting discoveries, what with so few spacers remaining willing to explore and expand the human sphere—"

"You can't help me." My voice must have shown the disappointment I felt.

"Not really. I've seen no information on any missing planets." He scratched his armpit. "In fact, I'm not certain I've ever actually encountered a *report* on a missing planet, much less heard of a confirmed missing world. Now that I think of it, that's right strange; no, not strange. Unusual, out of the ordinary, nonroutine."

I dusted my hands and jealously eyed the doughnuts, surprised at how hungry I was.

"There are plenty more where those came from," Professor Simpson said. "Now, I'd like to talk to you about space and traveling therein."

Eating doughnuts, I answered his questions. I was chafing to get on my way, but hunger overcame me and I allowed him to buy me off.

"Most people do not wish to have anything to do with spacers," he told me.

"I know that," I said unnecessarily.

"The malaise which is creeping over us contributes significantly toward those attitudinal changes."

"Huh? I think I understand what you just said." I licked my lips. "I keep seeing more and more of these groundhoggish freaks—" I hesitated as he looked under his brows at me. "Um, I mean, people with the infinity tattoo on their foreheads."

He nodded. "Those are merely the ones who advertise their provinciality and distaste for space, stars and other—"

Stars!

I interrupted. "Look, doc. Maybe you've got a star

chart with Zira listed. That's Roanoke's sun. It vanished also.''

"A star?" His voice was incredulous. "A big star?"

"Well, not very big, but big enough."

He shook his head. "What a strange, unusual, unique story." He sighed. "I'll look."

He tapped into a monitor.

I waited expectantly.

"I find nothing," he said. "Earlier we spoke of Roanoke being a newly founded colony?"

"We did. It was discovered perhaps seventy standard years ago by—"

He shook his head again. "I don't think I'm that recent with my filing systems."

Surveying the mess in the office, I knew whether he had the info or not, it wouldn't matter. The Galactic Geographical Society was no longer an action agency.

Full of doughnuts and sugar, I took my leave. Egbert was a nice old guy.

Exiting, I stood aside for this rangy looking woman. She strode into the Galactic Geographical Society Office like she owned the world, or at least had an option on it. Like a spacer. She was a bit gangly, a word until now I'd not understood the definition of. Her features were sharp, especially where they should be. Her face was a bit too angular and her hair sort of dirty blonde—not soiled, but sandy—like my hair wasn't flame red, but rusty. Her eyes were hard and intelligent.

While she didn't appear to notice me, I could tell her eyes had inventoried me and everything else within sight.

Had I not been chased by devils, I might well have stayed and tried to explore some inner space. I slapped my mental hand. Ginny wasn't as hard—or as tall—as this woman, and she was certainly more attractive than this woman. I felt like I wasn't being faithful to Ginny.

At least I hoped she was alive to be faithful or unfaithful to.

4: SUNDAYS

It all went downhill from there.

I tried the Executive branch first. Surprisingly, I got past two or three levels of bureaucracy to talk to real officials who had private offices.

Nothing.

Nothing except a promise of an appointment at a later date. Sure.

The Department of the Interior. An assistant to the associate deputy director for internal matters saw me.

"Certainly," she said, fingering her scalp, "Roanoke is right here in the computer."

"I surely hope so," I said, getting angrier, "for that's the *only* place it can be found."

She ignored my anger. "Now you say the world is gone?"

"Disappeared, yes."

"If that's the case, how do you know?"

"I went home and Roanoke wasn't there any longer; it wasn't where it is supposed to be."

She scrunched up her eyes making wrinkles between them. "If it wasn't there, how'd you get there? There's supposed to be a beacon for every Plex fax and—"

"I don't do much translating. I flew there in my spacecraft."

"Oh." Pause. "*Oh*. You went through *space?*"

I stood. "Who else do you recommend I might could see about this?" I tried to keep the pique out of my voice. I'm not fond of being a second-class citizen because I travel in space.

"You could try the diplomatic corps."

I did. It seems that since all of the planets were members of Galacticon, the diplomatic corps was non-existent—except on sector capitals and Galacticon Central. They did maintain an administrative section about one cubic mile in size right near the main Plex fax.

At the third tier, I asked. "Why is there an administrative section if there is no longer a diplomatic corps?"

"I'm sure I can't tell you. I just do my job." The infinity tattoo on his forehead told me more than he did.

Two levels higher I found someone with a few answers.

"We're in business to go out of business," she told me.

"What?"

"We're under Galacticon rules and regulations and must phase out in accordance with appropriate procedures. We can't just close down overnight, can we?"

They sent me to the Department of Transportation.

The DOT people were cooperative but their function was purely "administrative."

"We liaise with the Plexus Net folks," an officer told me.

Liaise?

I waved my arm around. "This warren of offices and people are just for liaison?"

He nodded. "Of course, we must have our admin control function to support the liaisers. And an Inspector General to insure everyone is doing their job in accordance with regulations and established procedures. Then we've a transportation section to insure we all get to where we need to be, and a logistics section to supply the other sections—and itself—with administrative supplies and furniture and stuff, and we have a facilities section to insure we have the facilities necessary to house and support the other sections, and then there's the appointment section and the house-keeping section and the public affairs section and, oh, do you want me to list them all?''

Shivering, I said no.

The Plexus Net offices were many, quite a bit more than on Harrygant. Automation ran the operational end of translating people and freight almost instantly about the galaxy. Because of the loose federated type of system Galacticon ran, nobody cared much so they didn't keep many records.

After bouncing off and through many offices, I found that they were like the rest of this planet: administrative functions supporting administrative functions. Bureaucrats feeding off of bureaucrats.

To climb into the hallowed halls, I had to threaten to call the Inspector General. While the real government seemed to be overburdened with overburdening itself, at least the Plex Net had an actual job.

Since they were actually performing real work, it was more difficult to make my way up the ladder.

Then it became impossible. Nobody cared about a missing planet; and if they did, it wasn't their job.

But they hadn't reckoned with the scheming Rusty Wallace. I got in to see a couple of officials by demanding to see them. ''What reason?'' their underlings asked. I gave them the old ''It's about my wife!'' line indignantly. That didn't work too well with women officials, so I became a console maintenance man, a building inspector, a radiation checker, and a tally counter. Someone actually asked me what a tally was. Then I had to change to a process server. I was becoming a familiar face around the Plex admin; but a cubic mile is huge.

Surprisingly, on the third day, I got in to see the Plex Fax Mgr. That was his title but, an aide told me, he was also in charge of the Sector VIII Plex Net.

''He'll see you, but you must promise to stop bothering us after that.''

I'd made a dent in the bureaucracy.

His name was Sunday B. Sunday and his office was somewhere far below the Plex fax. He had his own Plex station and could translate to anywhere on the planet, or be transferred through the main Plex fax to anywhere in the galaxy there were stations.

His suite was spartan.

When the secretary ushered me in, Sunday B. Sunday was running on a treadmill. He seemed oddly familiar.

He stopped and shook my hand. "Thank you for coming in," he said. Strange guy. His treadmill transformed itself into stairs and he began climbing, but staying in place. His face was nondescript.

"Thanks for seeing me," I said, returning the courtesy.

"You've lost a planet, I understand?"

"I keep trying to tell everybody, I haven't *lost* anything. Roanoke is gone. Disappeared."

He touched a control on the console alongside of him, but kept right on climbing stairs.

"The only thing the computer shows is that the terminal is unavailable."

"I've seen that before. I've heard that before." An edge had crept into my voice.

"According to this report, you went there—in a ship?" He glanced at me.

"I did."

He nodded. "Splash speaks well of you."

Old Splash had actually made a report and sent it out. Not only that, but the head Plex Net guy in the sector had received and read it. I kind of shrugged.

"You are making waves."

Good. "I just want to find Roanoke."

Sunday stopped climbing. "What is it you expect of us?"

"To tell me where Roanoke is."

"Captain Wallace, I have read and reread the Galacticon Plex Net charter and nowhere therein can I find where we are supposed to take a roll call of planets.'' He began climbing stairs again, this time at an advanced rate.

"You're telling me that a planet has disappeared and you don't care?''

He shook his head. "No, sir. I care. It just isn't my job to locate missing things—worlds included.''

I leaned against the railing of his exercise machine. "Shouldn't you be concerned with the loss of a Plex fax, a beacon, and the income from their use?''

He shook his head again. "Did you translate to our offices here?''

"Yes. From the DOT, who told me they were your liaison.''

He shrugged. "That might well be true, I'll have to check on it. However, my point is that you translated from their station to here.'' He touched his console. "And while we don't keep many records, survey data shows that station receives more use and thus more credits than the facility on Roanoke, considering both commercial and personnel transport.''

I saw his point. They didn't care if the facility on Roanoke existed or not.

"I have a recommendation,'' Sunday said.

"I'm about out of options,'' I said.

"Each Plex fax has a maintenance staff. Since the Plex facility on Roanoke is inoperational at this time, why not simply wait until they fix the equipment from their side and reenter the system?''

"Wouldn't they have done so by now if they could?''

"I don't know.'' His tone told me "Yes'', though.

"Suppose what's happened is a disaster?'' I asked. Nobody was going to know about Dad's message. It shouldn't matter, anyway. "Suppose they're waiting for help from *us?*'' Suppose they're all dead, I thought, but did not say the words.

"Suppose it is so. You tell me what to do about it and where to go to find them. And insure I can send people by Plex Net, not some archaic form of propulsion system.''

The trouble was that Sunday was making *too* much sense.

I sagged back. "I have no answers. I'm looking for them."

Once again he stopped climbing stairs. "I sympathize with you, young man. But I can do no more."

"You could make a report," I said, sarcasm dripping from my voice.

"While that was uncalled for," he said, "you're right. Perhaps I should contact Plex Net Central at Galacticon Central."

"Uh, Mr. Sunday? What can they do you can't?"

He waved a hand unconcernedly. "There's always a home office, a higher authority. They have admin and operational functions, too, for the whole galaxy, all sectors. Perhaps they know something we don't."

"Yeah, sure." Disappointment must have shown on my face or in my voice.

He flipped off the machine. "Oh, all right. Just a minute." He swung a privacy hood over and I couldn't tell what was going on.

What was left to do? I could only think of the press.

Sunday B. Sunday pushed away the privacy hood. "I've pulled some strings and gotten you ten minutes with the Administrator of the Sector."

I did a double take. "You mean the guy in charge of D'Earnhardt and a few million other plancts?"

He nodded. "Do not *ever,* Captain Wallace, say that the Plex Net does not care." His nose was much higher than it had been. He pointed. "The destination code has been input into that station. It will deliver you to him."

"Now?"

"Now. Why not?"

"Why not?" I was astounded. "I've been batting my head against D'Earnhardt bureaucracy for days."

"You're using up your ten minutes."

"Thanks," I said and was in the station. "Send me off," I told the station. "Execute."

Zap, and I stepped out and off the target plate and a security team met me.

Their equipment immediately located my two weapons. My knife and a small energy package I could use as a weapon—if I readjusted it correctly.

The security detail looked at me.

I shrugged. "Look, I'm a spacer. We're supposed to be weird, right?"

That seemed to satisfy them.

An adjoining door swished and a woman came out. "I'll take you to him."

She led me into an inner office. "Mr. Sunday has an update briefing in seven minutes. You must leave before then."

"Mr. Sunday?" What was going on here?

She stepped aside, turned, and went out.

In front of me—make that almost all the way around me—was an enormous fish tank. It was like this office was in a bubble in the middle of the ocean with only the spoke of the hallway leading into the office to connect it with dry land. Perhaps that was actually true.

Sunday B. Sunday sat in a lounge chair looking at some strange many-legged squishy thing creep across the outer bubble surface.

"Mr. Sunday. I don't understand." I stepped toward him. Now I knew why his brother sounded and looked familiar.

He looked at me for the first time and grinned his bland smile. "It seems my brother has played a small trick on you. I am the senior of quintuplets, Sunday A. Sunday. There are two more brothers and a sister."

I relaxed. In this crazy world of D'Earnhardt, a little nepotism couldn't make things any worse. "Well, that explains a lot. Listen, thanks for seeing me. I come from Roanoke, which isn't there now and—"

"How many people are there on Roanoke?"

"Fifty thousand, give or take. Or that's how many there were," I amended.

"About a thousand light years from anywhere, there is a planetary system called Laquinto. Within that system lie forty, I forget, forty-two perhaps, inhabited planets. The last figures I saw indicated an approximate number of one point one trillion people. The Laquinto system is so far away that we have to use relay beacons for the Plex Net. One of the relay beacons has become inop. At present there is no commerce, no travel, and no communication with one point one trillion people. Now you come in here all concerned with a mere fifty thousand? You're wasting my time.''

''Then why did you agree to see me?''

He stood and I read something in his eyes he quickly hid. ''Economically, one point one trillion people and their industrial and commercial bases are definitely impactful upon this sector. It has not escaped anyone's notice that you possess a starship. A starship which could deliver a replacement relay beacon where the old one failed.''

I held up a hand. His brother must have realized they'd found an answer to their prayer. ''Why me? Can't the Plex maintenance personnel deliver their own relay beacons?''

''They don't malfunction very often. In fact, this is only the second instance in recorded history.''

He still wasn't answering my question.

The door swished open and another Sunday walked in. The sheen of sweat told me it was Sunday B. Sunday, the Plex Fax Mgr. ''Not at all,'' said B. ''The system is highly reliable. And since we've not opened any new Plex facilities in the last twenty or so standard years, we've haven't maintained the delivery capability.''

That would make Roanoke one of the last discovered planets. No new discoveries probably could be attributed more to the fact that people no longer went into space looking for them than a lack of unexplored solar systems.

''The Navy?'' I asked.

''The Navy,'' Sunday A. Sunday, the Administrator, said, ''has a Galacticon charter nowadays to deliver relay beacons and new beacons to new planets. However, we haven't had that necessity arise in too long. And the local Navy isn't here.''

"Where are they?" I asked.

"Beats me," the Administrator said. "I'm of a mind to send in a report that the Navy is being revisional and nonfulfilling of their obligatorial role.''

"You do not really need a lot of Navy when everybody is traveling by the Plex Net," said B. Sunday in a proprietary manner.

"Let me get this straight," I said. "You don't really care about Roanoke and its fifty thousand people. What you really want is for me to deliver a beacon in my ship out to Laquinto?"

"Exactly," said A. "Except we want you to drop it between Laquinto and here. It will take some navigating to place the buoy properly."

"How long?"

The Administrator shrugged. "You'll have to locate the beacons just before that location and after that location, to locate the center location. A mere matter of stellar surveyance.''

"No," I said.

"No?" The two officials' voices spoke almost together like a quick echo.

"No. I don't have the time."

A. said, "It would be financially to your benefit."

"A lot of money," agreed B.

"No," I repeated. I had no time, even if I wanted to.

A. turned to B. "I believe Captain Wallace is being oppositional.''

I watched the bubble as a creature larger than the bubble drifted by. It was brown and had a lot of flaps. I'd missed its face. I could understand the bureaucracy on D'Earnhardt. If Sunday A. Sunday were a reflection of his constituency, then he was a bureaucrat's bureaucrat.

"You will not help me find Roanoke?" I said and

the two stepped back at the danger seeping from my voice.

A. shook his head. "Obviously, I've already checked. Nobody knows anything, nor has the system registered any reports regarding same. I could ask the Navy to look for it, but where shall I tell them to look? I can't even get them to drop a beacon enroute to Laquinto. The Navy's not available."

"But—"

"No, Captain Wallace. You have no more idea of what to do than I. I have other problems. I've one point one trillion people incommunicado, and most likely quite riled." His voice turned hard. "I've another two systems through which a lethal virus is sweeping. The death toll is now over ten million people. Human beings, Captain Wallace. Ten million of them dead."

"I sympathize and empathize, Mr. Administrator. However, my problem remains and I shall pursue it. Fifty thousand people might not even be a grain of sand on the beach to you, but it is to me and to those fifty thousand. I've no choice but to go to the press."

He held his hand toward the door. "Do that." His dismissal was obvious.

As I walked out, I wondered. If it had been me, I'd have commandeered old Betsy and delivered the beacon. Over one trillion people and their economic "impactful" impact were major worries. Could it be that they had no one whom they could con or coerce into going into space? Or was something else going on?

As I walked through the outer office, there she was, standing and waiting with the secretary who'd shown me into the Administrator's office.

The rangy woman I'd seen go into the Galactic Geographic Society as I was leaving. This time I noticed some soft places on her.

But I covered my surprise, knowing she'd seen me, and she knew that I'd seen her recognize me.

Was she some kind of agent following me? It certainly would have been easy. One of two starships parked up there, just follow me and report to one Sunday or another.

I was so busy trying to ignore her that I made a mistake. By the time I'd gotten over my macho reaction and decided to confront her, it was too late. Why not just ask her what she was doing?

I started to, but she was already into Sunday's office and security was hustling me into the Plex station.

"Hey. My things." I held out my hand and they gave me my knife and energy thingamajig.

One of them touched a control and I had a glance into the Administrator's office as the secretary came out. The woman with the sandy hair had partially turned and was looking out and watching me.

Zap.

5: DAY-GLOW WORMS

"That's why we're not fond of government on Roanoke," I explained to the young lady.

She was assistant editor of the Sector News Service. Actually, this sector was officially titled something like "Sector VIII", aka Eight, aka D'Earnhardt Sector of the Galacticon. That didn't fit well on names and electronic mastheads it was so awkward, so if you said "sector" everyone knew what you were talking about anyway. The Sector News Service was actually named something like D'Earnhardt News Simulcasting Press, subtitled "ALL THE NEWS THAT'S FIT."

Marion Zernickc, the assistant day editor, wore one of those day-glow green worms around her throat. They're supposed to be a calming influence, akin to a mild drug high. But I'd be dipped in somebody else's spit before I wore a live worm around my neck, never mind the benefits. Groundhogs'll do anything.

"I see." She glanced at her screen.

I'd just told her my tale of encountering bureaucracy.

"You can confirm the planet is missing," I said from my old-fashioned chair at the side of her old-fashioned desk. It made me feel comfortable with Marion.

She shook her head. "I can confirm that the alleged planet Roanoke is currently unreachable via Plex Net travel and comm link." She looked at me pointedly and I thought she was cute. "You are the only person who claims the planet is allegedly 'missing,' Rusty."

We'd hit it off right away and were on a first name basis already. An awareness was growing between us.

"First," I said slowly, "let us deal with this 'alleged' business. I ain't alleging nothing. Roanoke really exists—or did exist." I didn't even pause to worry. "Check it out. Look it up."

She hit a command keypad on her console. "Do we have any data on a planet named Roanoke in the morgue?"

A light pulsed. "Yes, ma'am." The voice was male, but obviously a computer. "We have four such planets in many references, including political, lifestyle, historical, and sports."

Marion looked expectantly at me.

"It's in this sector," I said, "and the closest planet to it is a world called Harrygant. The star is named Zira. Roanoke is still classified as a colony world and it was initially discovered about seventy standard years ago by a spacer named Rebel Wallace." Granddad.

"Searching," said the computer. "Confirmed, Marion. I have a passing reference to a Rebel Wallace reporting a new solar system, the thrust of the story was that the star had only one satellite, now called the planet Roanoke, and that it's location is isolated with no immediate stellar neighbors."

Marion sat back and her chair creaked. I thought about asking her to dinner if she wasn't hitched or intended, but I decided I wasn't going to be anywhere near D'Earnhardt in the very near future. Which ruled out dinner. But lunch was a thought.

"This is interesting," she said finally.

I perked up. It was the first time anyone had expressed specific interest.

She turned to the console's receptors. "Get me Public Affairs over at the Plex Net offices."

"Yes, ma'am." I guess some people need their machines to kowtow to them. Maybe it reminds them of their humanity. "On the line, Marion."

The face on the screen was female with that infinity tattoo on her forehead. It meant she wasn't having any children and would wait for the universe to end. This wave of human entropy was beginning to manifest itself in weird ways—but don't get me started.

"Zernicke of the SNS. Do you remember me?"

"Oh, I do."

"I'm following up a story. Could you double-check something for me? Tell me what your system says about a planet named Roanoke."

The tattoo turned swiftly for a moment, and then came back. "That terminal is unavailable."

"Another thing," Marion said, nodding to me, "Please check Sunday B. Sunday's schedule yesterday and tell me if he had an appointment with a Mr. Rusty Wallace?"

"Captain," I corrected, my vanity showing a little.

Tattoo ducked. "It's not on the prepublished agenda." Her head whipped back up. I would get disoriented if I moved my head so quickly and so often.

I leaned forward again. "Comm his office. The appointment was not scheduled."

Tattoo looked at me. "Who the hell are you?"

"It's okay," Marion chimed in, "I'll call myself."

"No, no, just a second." Tattoo whipped her head around again and talked into a different speaker. In a second, she whipped back, her short hair not having time to fly aside. "It's true, Ms. Zernicke. The official minutes of the meeting are classified, but it's public-releasable that there was a meeting in Mr. Sunday's office with a nonlocal man named Wallace."

"Thank you very much," Marion said and the computer cut the connection.

Now we're getting somewhere, I thought.

She looked at me. "Here comes the big question, Rusty." She paused. "So what?"

My face must have retreated to its look of incredulity. I'd been doing that so much recently that I was getting quite practiced at it. "So what?" My voice came out as if strangled.

"So what?"

"Fifty thousand people is what. An entire world

disappeared. Toss in a star. One of those big shiny things in the sky.''

She shook her head. "Fifty thousand people, okay. I don't know if the place has disappeared or not. All you've told me is that you couldn't find it."

"Send somebody to look."

Now it was her turn to give me her version of incredulity. "They'd have to go in space." She frowned. "You'd have me dispatch a reporter in a spaceship?"

"Yep." I decided I wouldn't ask her to lunch.

"And if I found a reporter stupid enough—make that foolish," she said seeing the new look on my face, "to go, any spacer would fake him/her out. Reporters don't know navigation. You could pop into empty space and say, 'Look there, no Roanoke,' and the reporter wouldn't have the mathematical and navigational background to be able to confirm or disprove your story."

She had a point.

"Another thing, Rusty," her face softened. If she hadn't been so afraid of space, I would have asked her to lunch. She didn't continue right away.

"The other thing?" I prompted.

She turned and touched a keypad or two and the wall lighted up. "Here're the news headlines."

Words scrolled across the big screen.

1.1 TRILLION DISENFRANCHISED BY MECHANICAL FAILURE. NO COMM NO PLEX NO LAQUINTO.

TEN MILLION DEAD IN VIRAL ATTACK

I quit watching. "I see exactly your point. Fifty thousand, so what?" It was downright discouraging.

"I'm sorry, Rusty."

"What can I do?"

Her eyes grew big and were quite attractive. "I will interview you. A spacer. There aren't many left. That way we can get your story to the public."

I shook my head. Now I had some leverage. "Run the story and I'll do the interview."

She studied me for a moment. "Okay." She hit a

keypad. "Gimme two paragraphs, thrust being that the Roanoke terminal is unavailable. Eyewitness states that Roanoke is not just unavailable, but that it has disappeared. Highlight a reference to the interview sidebar and vice versa. Interview to be broadcast real time and available on the news selection menu."

"Yes, ma'am."

I did the interview and took Marion to dinner. I decided to stay on D'Earnhardt one more day to see if there would be any response to the story or the interview. I kind of hoped some spacer would call in and say he or she'd seen something, some anomaly that would explain Roanoke's disappearance. Or maybe some scientist with the answer.

Later, I stopped at a public booth and keyed up the news. One of the interesting things was that you never see UPRISING ON, fill in the blank, or REVOLT IN SO AND SO SYSTEM, anymore, and it's been that way for a century or so, or so my dad and grandfather have told me. Another manifestation of the creeping heebie jeebies.

Finally, they got to the Roanoke story.

It was way back. Waaaayyyy back in the news. Only news junkies would see it in the myriad of items from which to choose. Or people with their computer system alerted to search for mention of certain items.

In the headlines it came right after VIRULENT FISH DISEASE PLAGUES D'EARNHARDT.

DISTANT ROANOKE UNAVAILABLE THRU PLEX, ROANOKE CITIZEN CLAIMS THE WORLD IS UNLOCATEABLE. (See also Interview with Spacer.)

Needles to say, I was underwhelmed.

I went into the Sector News Service the next morning.

Marion was not a bit contrite about the play the story had gotten. "I had to fight to get that much in," she said, "and the fact I had an exclusive interview with you gave me the fulcrum I needed to get the story some airtime." She shot me a grin. "Gimme a sports or lifestyle angle, and I'll get plenty of space and air-time.''

''Any response?'' I asked, hoping against hope.

She shook her head. ''Not the kind you wanted, Rusty. Mr. Sunday's Plex Net office commed and wants equal time.'' She hesitated and looked strangely at me. ''A woman commed and wouldn't give me her name. She wanted additional info. I didn't have any.'' Marion shrugged.

''Did she have sandy hair?'' I asked.

''She did.'' Marion looked a query.

I didn't respond.

She turned to the console, touched, and said, ''Excerpt the comm response to the Wallace interview and the Roanoke story.''

''Working, Marion,'' came a different male voice. I was beginning to understand the inner workings of Marion Zernicke's psyche. At least this morning she wasn't wearing that god-awful day-glow green worm. Nor had she on our date last night.

''Audio only,'' Marion directed.

''Yes, ma'am. Here it is.''

A montage of voices.

Female: ''Why is that terrible man on the news? Everybody knows spacers are dangerous.''

Female: ''You don't believe that bunk you publish, do you? Your source is a *spacer?*''

Male: ''That Walters space guy must be insane for going out there unprotected.''

Female: ''Your spaceman is very good-looking in a rough sort of way. If he is interested, have him contact our group.''

''Weirdo,'' Marion said and looked self-conscious.

''You don't have to tell anybody you went out with a spacer.''

She glared at me. ''I don't care. You're *not* weird like they say.'' She continued to look uncomfortable. ''You, um, care about a lot of the right things. You are not some mutated monster, burned by radiation and ready to eat little babies—no matter what you do for a living.''

Most people are like that, their mind-set locked against space and figger everybody else is, too.

Even my Ginny isn't too crazy about my being in space all the time. Of course, she's very young, eight Roanoke years younger than I am. But Ginny is Roanoke born and bred and is tougher than the average woman. And she's been through danger and calamities, too.

Ignoring Marion's slight, I rose and the old chair creaked as she stood, too.

''What are you going to do next?'' she asked, concern on her face.

''Galacticon Central,'' I told her.

She put a hand to her throat and tried to look hurt. ''Couldn't you stay perhaps one more day?''

I looked her in the eye. ''No. It's a long space flight—''

''It doesn't take much real time on the Plex Net,'' she interrupted.

''Well, I need old Betsy, and I ain't leaving her so far from me—''

''It's not far by Plex.''

''It is for me. Listen, Marion. I've enjoyed it and thank you very much for believing me about Roanoke and all, but I've got to get going. It will take several days, real time, and my sixth sense is telling me I'd best hurry.'' My normal apprehension about Plex travel was rising. I was thinking the longer I took, the worse off Roanoke would be when I finally found it. I don't know why I thought that, but I did. At least it meant I was convinced Roanoke still existed.

Her look was sad, and I think I believed her when she said she believed me. Sometimes you have to take people at their word.

She straightened and tried to smile. ''Well, from what you told me about your visit here, all I can say is that Galacticon Central had better brace itself for your arrival, Rusty Wallace.'' She hesitated. ''If you butt your head too hard there, call the Obfuscator. His name is Hyman L. L. Bookbinder. Tell him I sent you. Good-bye, Rusty.'' She reached up and touched my cheek.

Before I got maudlin, too, I turned and left. As her door swished closed, I caught a glimpse of her still watching me.

Warily, I looked around the downstairs entrance to the Sector News Service building. People going and coming, all with obvious purpose.

No rangy woman with angular features and dirty blonde hair. But she *had* commed.

My curiosity was piqued, and at any other time, I'd follow through and find the woman. But not now. Roanoke was still missing.

And what the devil was an Obfuscator?

It was snowing, which added to my depression. I took the ''UP'' autosystem to the aircar landing at which I'd arrived earlier. Because of the snow, the landing was deserted. The Plex Net or the autosystem was easier anyway.

I headed for a row of empty aircars nestled against each other, holding my arm in front of my face and wishing for a grilled peanut butter fritter.

An out-of-place noise from behind caused me to turn. Three men hurried toward me, indistinct because of the driving snow.

My spacer's instinct registered danger immediately.

They spread out, coming around one side and herding me toward the edge of the landing. Clearly, their intentions were to force me over the side. If all three grabbed me and tossed me, I'd miss the safety barrier below and die after a long, long fall.

So I turned as if to run, continued the turn building momentum, and nailed the short one on the far side with a slicing kick to his right knee. It buckled and he went down. I began to lash out at number two, the one in the middle, when he produced a stunner and I hit the landing on my shoulder to avoid the beam, rolled in the snow, and came up running. My breath exploded into puffs of steam.

Off to the side in the snow and gloom, I glimpsed a dark presence. I got close enough to see the surprise on his face. His hair covered his forehead. I had time to see him drawing a weapon, too. His compact, muscled frame was already in motion. This fourth man had the air of command about him.

I feinted past him and ran for an aircar.

An energy beam sizzled the snow behind me.

Now I was under the overhang and protected from the snow. I dove into an aircar, slapping the "MANUAL LAUNCH" button. "Main Plex fax," I told the car.

I scrambled up on the seat and looked out the bubble. Shrouded by snow, the man with the dark presence stood and watched me.

I'd gotten somebody's attention.

6: THE OBFUSCATOR

"**W**hy do they call you the obfuscator?" I asked. "It would seem contradictory as your profession is the opposite of the meaning. I'd think something like the *de*obfuscator would be more appropriate."

It had taken me several days real time to arrive at Galacticon Central, most of them wondering who wanted me out of the way. I'd decided I hadn't the time to waste by reporting the attack.

Galacticon Central is its name and it is not a giant place like D'Earnhardt.

It's a swirling ring of asteroids, or planettes, as they're sometimes termed, most terraformed and maintaining artificial atmospheres, with the accompanying minimal or adjustable gravity, and all linked by Plex faxes and stations.

I'd spent a few days bouncing off the bureaucracy, with fewer results and more frustration than on D'Earnhardt. After running out of patience and almost ending up with an assault rap on one bureacrat, I recalled Marion's recommendation to look up Hyman Bookbinder.

His name cross-referenced in the commercial section to one of several under the listing of "Obfuscators."

Hyman L. L. Bookbinder was a man of medium height whose bland appearance would make him be the first one in a crowd you'd forget. His voice was moderate and neutral, no trace of an accent.

"Captain Wallace— May I call you Rusty?" At my nod he continued. "In olden times, when Galacticon was merely beginning, the profession was, in fact, more of a lobby for government contracts and favors for its clients. In order to do so, the early purveyors of obfuscation were necessarily technically articulate in governmentese; thus they were actually word merchants giving the government agency they were addressing the regulatory language to protect and/or benefit their clients. Now the governmental employees have taken the specific language to the far extent with which they currently deal, and the obfuscation profession has evolved into one which is retained to interpret and deal with the specific governmental agencies."

"Go-betweens," I said.

He nodded. "At times, we even have to translate what the particular agency is saying to a client."

"I hate bureaucratic jargon," I said, getting off the subject.

"It has its uses," Hyman replied. "I suspect that far back in time, an attorney started the whole thing. However, we should address your purpose here today."

Bookbinder's place of business was a comfortable lounging room with a—gasp—view of the stars. A weak sun in the middle of the atoll-like ring of planettes did not obscure all the stars. He was located on a large asteroid, mostly private, not government, say about a thousand miles in circumference.

His lounge was designed to meet and entertain clients, so the overhead views were probably preselected to make those clients feel at ease. Since he glanced up occasionally and didn't show a total abhorrence, I figured he was both courteous and not one of the majority these days who held space and those who earned their living out there in contempt. Or fear.

I outlined about Roanoke being missing and what I'd done so far.

"That's quite impressive, Rusty. You've promise and might well make a decent living as an obfuscator."

"No, thanks."

"I understand. You say you've an official psych evaluation that will help corroborate your testimony?"

"I do."

He sat back and rubbed his jaw. I noticed that the room, while comfortable, was quite neutral, possibly designed to offend no one. And it held no hint of Hyman's personality. I'd never had to anthropomorphize a room, but most of them reflected somebody. This one reflected nobody.

I wanted to ask him if he'd take me on as a client, but I held my tongue.

Finally, he spoke. "For Marion Zernicke to refer you to my office speaks a great deal. She must think highly of you." His gaze was a question.

Not knowing how to respond, I said, "That's not something that comes up for discussion between acquaintances."

He crossed his legs. "This is not my normal fare; however, I believe the case is of sufficient uniqueness for me to take it on."

Sufficient uniqueness?

"Hyman? I'm not really wealthy." He had his own Plex station, speaking volumes about his fees and his usual clientele.

I could hock Betsy, but I doubted if any groundhogs would make me a loan on her. And I further doubted if I did try to sell her, anybody would want to buy her. I wouldn't do that anyway.

He waved a dismissing hand. "One, you're a friend of Marion's so I will apply my lowest rate structure and, two, if necessary I can put a lien against any financial accounts with an origin code of Roanoke. The latter would pay off if Roanoke is never rediscovered and, furthermore, would provide a flag should someone object."

He had a good idea. Tie up bank accounts and if anyone raised cain, we'd have a concrete lead.

"I've some limited funds," I said. "Or, I could act as an agent for all those on Roanoke and sign a promissory note." I well could be the last citizen of Roanoke alive, which would make me the heir of most of the fifty thousand or so people. If nothing else, we could tie up funds by saying so anyway.

"It is of no matter," he replied. "While Galacticon Central is not so centrally located, I will start immediately threading my way through the red tape and see where the trail leads."

"You don't know a sandy-headed woman," I asked, "about my age, angular features?" Next time, if there was one, I was going to confront her; failing that, I intended to take her picture.

"I know many people, some of whom vaguely fit your description. What is her name?"

I shrugged and told him about the woman I'd dubbed "Sandy." I said nothing about Dad's message or the attempt to throw me off the landing on D'Earnhardt.

"Then I cannot help you there. She does not sound familiar." He rose. "I will contact you."

"What can I do?"

"Wait."

I did. Twenty-seven days left. I spit-shined old Betsy and replaced a few electronic parts which had gone bad, redundancy circuits taking care of the problems temporarily. In a universe where people hated space, you had to learn to be your own repair technician, too. I always had nimble fingers, mostly because of a naughty little trick I'd picked up while grounded on a sleazy planet whose name I've forgotten. Actually, it was pickpocketing, and I haven't forgotten the name. LVD. You know a place is bad when they name it with initials only and nobody knows what the initials stand for. I'd fallen in with some thieves—mainly because they were preferable to the gentry who ran LVD. But all that's neither here nor there and none of it's applicable to my missing planet.

I fine-tuned a few programs, worried about my cash flow, grew an ulcer fretting over the whereabouts of

Roanoke, and worked my natural curiosity overtime wondering about Sandy. One thing I did do was correlate Betsy's navaids with the data in the Galacticon Approach Control. I wanted to be absolutely certain about the figures I'd used back where Roanoke was supposed to be.

All data correlated properly, and the navaids were calibrated exactly, meaning that Betsy and I hadn't been wrong and dropped a decimal or something.

Roanoke was indeed missing.

"Rusty?" Betsy said during lunch.

I put down my peanut butter deviled egg. Her voice was pure professional. "What?"

"I monitored a translation to the beacon buoy." Which was a little safeguard program I'd initiated here since they tried to toss me off the aircar landing.

"And?"

"Whoever it was translated back out again."

"Good girl." No one had any reason to come to this buoy except for business with me. Could it have been Sandy?

Being a schemer, I wasn't very trusting. "Ease over there, connect the airlock tunnel, and tell me if anybody or anything heads this way."

Nothing happened.

I ran a remote control robot down the tunnel. I should have installed a tiny camera and saved myself this trouble.

"I see a proximity-explosive next to the comm box," Betsy said. "Human body heat would activate it."

Using the robo unit, I removed the tiny device. Betsy pulled the tunnel back and I manipulated the robo unit to drop the explosive into space where Betsy zapped it with an energy beam.

"I'm still making waves," I said. I thought about the man with the dark presence.

Two long days later, Hyman called. Though how you tell two days when your planette is twirling like a corkscrew through space, I'll never know. Maybe it's a good thing the sun at the core of Galacticon Central was so weak as to not affect their personal biological clocks.

We translated from Bookbinder's suites to an underground office in a planette a few degrees around the ring.

Hyman had gotten farther than I expected, for the Plex station at which we arrived was an executive model whose destination code was unlisted.

Cameras. Security gates. Weapons' sniffers. Very limited access. Guards.

I felt close scrutiny, too close. Spacers should be used to confined areas, but not like this.

This place was virtually impregnable.

7: SANDY

"The entire office is a secure vault," Hyman told me. We stepped from the Plex station and a security officer glared at us.

Hyman gave our names and another security guy checked his monitor. "You're okay."

The Obfuscator had warned me obliquely when he'd commed about the appointment: no weapons. I could hear them all now, "You just can't trust spacers; you know how it is." The Plex station obviously contained a weapons' sniffer to check arriving people. To be certain, they'd have an additional monitor at the gate guards' post.

If the whole suite was a secure vault, that meant that it contained many sensitive or classified documents—or equipment. I'd bet on documents, this being a government office and all. And it was easier to lock the whole place up than account for all the security rated documents at the end of each workday. All of which further impressed me with Hyman Bookbinder, the Obfuscator.

The office was called ROAR, for Reports' Office of Approval and Review. ROAR just didn't evoke bureaucracy in my mind.

It was a standard government office, gray being the operative color—gray desks, gray walls, gray furniture, and even a couple of clerks who looked gray.

Undersecretary Plinktone was in charge. I was going to joke about that making him UPROAR, but doubtless he'd heard it before. And his dour appearance told me he didn't have much sense of humor anyway.

"Wow," I said as we entered his office.

Actual paper—real, organically derived paper. From my recent experience with government offices, I knew that they all dealt with computers and memories and networks. I did some fast thinking. Paper. Paper, or plastic derivative, meant words written. You could limit eyeball access to accidental or authorized. That is to say you could control who reads the report. A report buried in electronic memory somewhere can be dug out, no matter how expert the safeguards.

So this office contained classified documents. Reports of such a sensitive nature they couldn't be trusted to computer systems.

Hyman Bookbinder nudged me.

We stood in front of Undersecretary Plinktone's desk. He could have asked us to sit down.

Hyman was quite polite. "As you know from my preliminary contact, we've been referred to your good offices," he finished.

"I understand," Plinktone said. His voice even sounded sour—a trait I'd never before even thought possible. He wore a standard gray jumpsuit.

"Have you been able to come up with anything?" Hyman asked, his neutral tone offsetting Plinktone's dour notes.

The undersecretary pushed aside a red folder he'd been reading when we entered. It occurred to me that red usually means that thing is classified "top secret" or "ridiculous."

Yep, "TOP SECRET, EYES ONLY" was stamped right across the page on top. Plinktone glanced at it. Maybe he was following my gaze. Maybe not.

"Ah, here it is." Plinktone pulled a manilla folder out from under a stack. He opened it and scanned several pages. "I've a report, let me see. It is an original report endorsed by successive offices."

He paused and read some more. Information, right

there in front of me, within reach. Suddenly it occurred to me that this moment ought to be more dramatic than the standard gray surroundings were allowing. I'd always thought that *somebody* else had known about Roanoke's disappearance.

"I see it is classified 'confidential' " said Plinktone.

"You could consider me the acting de facto chief of state of Roanoke," I said hopefully. "Maybe that'll clear me. I was—am—a member of the Board of Directors."

He looked at me dourly. "It is not necessary."

My heart sinking, I didn't think I had to ask why.

Plinktone told us anyway. "It contains information on you of which you are obviously aware. A psych profile, security tests, and a background check; all these comprise the appendices. Hmmm, let me see. The original report was filed by a lowly Plex Net official named Splash—hmm, it seems they left off his full name. It's amazing we'd have a Plex Net report, but I have seen it happen before when they did not know what to do with a report. Hmm, and additional addenda reportage to, well, can you believe this? Sector Eight ranking personnel endorsed the report and forwarded it. Plexus Net chief and the Administrator of Sector Eight."

The Sundays.

He continued to read. "That is all there is." He glanced up at me. "Not many people can say they've even see a sector administrator. Sector administrators do not have the time to visit all the worlds in their sector, not to mention meeting with itinerant spacers."

Ignoring the slur, I thought it meant that I had at least generated a bit of interest in the disappearance of Roanoke.

But that was all I'd got. A passing interest reflected in a confidential report.

"There is also a copy of a news story," Plinktone continued. "This isn't news. Ah, I see. You must have high political connections, Wallace, to get interviewed and coerce a headline. Hmmm.''

I closed my eyes. It had all come to this. I opened my eyes, discouragement coursing through me.

Plinktone was looking at me. "Is there anything else I can do for you?"

"Is it possible that a nonclassified or electronic report has been made?" I asked.

Hyman spoke. "It is barely conceivable, but I have investigated that possibility and could find nothing."

Damn.

I enunciated each word. "It stands to reason that somebody in this galactic government knows something about a missing planet. I just need to discover who that person is." Especially since Dad had tried to tell me something in his message—and the attempt on my life.

Plinktone closed the folder. "It may well stand to reason," his tone was reproving, "but it is not necessarily true." He looked down. "I will tell you something I should not: that is, when a classified report comes in, the ROAR administrative staff inputs subject and important names into the normal computer system, initiating a search to reveal connections, duplications, and flagged subjects. In this case, your name would have gone in, as would Roanoke, planetary leaders, and so on. Any other reference in any data base would have been listed."

Nothing.

"I infer," Hyman said, "that under those procedures, it is a certainty that no one at Galacticon Central knows anything more about Roanoke than is in that report?"

"You infer correctly." Undersecretary Plinktone turned his head from Hyman to me and followed my line of sight down to the open red folder.

I could read slowly upside down. I'd seen a few words: SUBJECT: NEGATIVE IMPACT OF MISS-ING—

Plinktone slammed the cover over and I couldn't read anything else.

What did that report contain?

Was Plinktone covering up? He'd been reading the red folder when we came in. Had he been preparing himself for the meeting with us by reading *another* and different report?

"What's that one about?" I asked, anger rising in my voice.

"You are not cleared to know," said Plinktone.

"What are you hiding from me?" I demanded.

He must have panicked because his hand touched a red keypad on his console. I figured what he was doing, so I reached for the folder. He spun out of the way holding the red folder. I started around the desk and the door swished open and security guys flooded in.

Me hollering and Hyman protesting, they dragged us out.

Plinktone frowned as we left.

I'd really blown it this time.

Security released us outside the swishing doors. However, they escorted us from behind toward the Plex station.

"You realize, Rusty, what you've done?" Hyman asked.

"I'd like to get my hands on that report—or him." I started thinking. "What do you mean?"

"The undersecretary could very well take umbrage at your ah, indiscretion. Furthermore, he could well follow up his umbrage with a post-note in the database they all check when agreeing to appointments with strangers."

"You're telling me they might blackball me?"

"Yes, sir. And me, too."

"Oh, no." I stopped abruptly. We had been walking down a hall toward the entrance where the Plex station was located. The four-man security detail bumped into each other. "I could have ruined your access?"

He shrugged. "In a few hours we shall be able to answer that."

Suddenly, the air was full of blaring electronically produced *"WHOOPS."*

The security detail bolted past Hyman and me and disappeared around the corner ahead.

"What the dickens?" Hyman asked. That was probably the strongest language in his inventory.

I hurried forward, anxious to see. "Security alert, surely at the Plex station around the corner."

Not losing much of his dignity, he caught up with me.

What kind of security problem would a bunch of namby-pamby paper-shufflers generate? Somebody wanting a peek at those same papers, obviously. But during duty hours? It didn't make sense.

We rounded the bend in the corridor and the entrance was right in front of us.

Six security men in regulation gray were fighting, *fighting* a struggling woman.

A rangy, sandy-haired struggling woman.

Six to one offends me.

Without thinking, I jumped into the fray.

Maybe one of the factors which had swayed me unconsciously was the fact these same security men had just got done manhandling me. Spacers in general, and me in particular, don't like it a lot when groundhogs grab you with malice aforethought—or even without a forethought.

Sandy was punching and kicking, but the two gateguards had her cornered and the four men in our detail were forcing their way in the circle more hindering everyone than helping.

I snatched the outermost one, a little guy, from the fray and tossed him aside. The second guy, one who'd handled me with unnecessary force earlier, I took out with a carotid thump and stepped on his face as I passed him.

Now I had their attention. A swiveling kick to a knee put down a third. He yelped and grabbed his leg.

By then Sandy had the upper hand with the original two.

We found ourselves back to back, like spacers, with the enemy now at a terrible disadvantage. I mean, jeez, two spacers against three groundhogs? Especially government employed groundhogs?

Sandy launched herself at the largest, leaving herself vulnerable. My job was to protect her flank. One of the remaining two made a move toward her flying body and I intercepted him, flipping him against the wall, and channeled my momentum toward the last one. He was so surprised at my swiftness that he forgot to resist. I chopped him down with a closed-hand jab and was continuing my whirl toward Sandy and her opponent when I realized she'd already taken him out.

Again, without thinking, I twirled, not a dancing pirouette, but pretty enough in martial arts circles, ending up with my back against her warm back again, searching for the next wave of security who'd definitely be here.

Hyman Bookbinder was standing there with his hand at his mouth, awe written all over his face.

Behind him stood a security officer with pips or whatever you call those little tab marks on their shoulder straps.

He was a captain and he had a power gun out and pointed at us. "Hold!" His voice spoke with authority, backed up a lot by his weapon. His sudden appearance was a surprise.

I felt motion at my back and twisted and grabbed Sandy's arm. She was in the middle of drawing her weapon, a nasty little ice-needle gun.

She snarled at me.

I held her wrist. "The captain's got the drop on us. It'd be suicide."

She growled again but her arm relaxed and the ice-needle gun disappeared. Although, upon much closer inspection, there didn't seem to be room in her form-fitting jumpsuit for the weapon to disappear into.

"What is the meaning of this?" the captain demanded. His mustache marred an otherwise rugged face.

One of the gate-guards was standing now, rubbing his neck. "Unauthorized entry in a secure area, carrying a weapon, sir."

"It was an accident," Sandy said in a reasonable tone.

"The woman?" asked the captain.

"Yes, sir."

A couple of the other security detail were getting to their feet.

The captain addressed me. "What's your part in this?"

"It seemed like the right thing to do."

"He was just leaving," said one of the detail, the one I really didn't like, "after creating an incident in the undersecretary's office."

"He's the one?"

"Right, sir."

Maybe that explained the captain's sudden appearance.

"Look," Sandy said. "Just let me get out of here. I must have given the wrong destination code. I do that sometimes, accidentally switching numbers and the like."

Sure she did.

"Carrying a weapon in Galacticon facilities is illegal," said the captain. "Relieve her of her weapon, please." He directed his orders at the security team.

They all were on their feet now and looking anxiously at one another.

"You." The captain indicated the largest one.

He stepped forward and Sandy shrugged. "I know when I'm finished. I'll take it out slowly." Which she did and handed it to the big guy.

"She just came out fighting," said a gate guard. "The station indicated 'incoming' and there was nothing on our schedule and the screen didn't show the ID of someone working here and then the weapon detector went off and everything went crazy, then—''

"Crazy?" Sandy's voice was insulting. "It was crazy to touch me. Nobody touches me."

"We were apprehending—''

"Apprehending, nothing. You were throwing your weight around, jack. I say again, *nobody* touches me." She stepped toward the captain and I could tell she was still tensed for action. I couldn't tell if the captain was aware of the danger which was stalking him. She sure talked and acted like a spacer.

The captain stepped back and waved his little power gun.

Sandy stopped.

"It is sometimes necessary," the captain said, his mustache moving in exaggerated parallel to his mouth, "to take action, even when invading a person's rightful privacy, for the good of all and the protection of secure areas." He glanced at me, then back to Sandy. "Possession of weapons here is against the law. You broke the law."

"I've had enough of this whining, civil-service crap," Sandy said. She reached into a side pocket on her form-fitting light-blue jumpsuit. She produced a coded ID and offered it to the captain. "Run that through your machine."

The captain looked at it uncomfortably. Sandy's voice contained a new ring of authority. The officer nodded to one of the gate-guards who took the ID and slipped it into a scanner at the entry point.

The travelway had disgorged a few people who were all waiting to get in. Their regulation gray said they must work here. What a great thing to look forward to each morning.

The monitor pinged and all eyes went to the gate-guard. Monitors don't usually ping for peons.

He gulped. He removed the ID and brought it back to Sandy. "Her name is O'Clock and she's got a nine beta access authorization." There was sweat on his upper lip. "I've never seen a nine beta."

"Let me see," said the captain. He surveyed us and decided the situation was under control and replaced his weapon. He took the ID and ran it through the scanner himself.

I edged over to watch the screen myself.

All the encoded stuff on the ID and the monitor simply showed O'CLOCK 9B.

The captain removed the card. "Our commander does not even rate a Nine B."

The woman retrieved her own ID.

Hyman finally dropped his hand from his mouth. "Nine B is high executive level."

"Sandy, you've got 'em flimflammed," I spoke into her ear. "We better get out of here before they change their minds."

"My weapon." She held out her hand imperiously.

Against his will, the captain nodded and the security guy returned her ice-needle gun.

The captain was taken aback. "Why didn't you say something? You could have pulled rank."

She shook her head, rustling fine, sandy hair and I noticed again how form-fitting her jumpsuit was. "I came out of the Plex station and they jumped me. *Nobody* touches me."

"Yes, ma'am."

She turned to me and lowered her voice. "You've got a point, Rusty. Let's go!"

I waved Hyman over and all three of us stepped into the station. Hyman gave his destination code and zap we were translated.

Rusty?

8: SECRET AGENT?

"**R**usty," she had called me.

We came out of Hyman Bookbinder's Plex station and into his visitor's lounge.

Hyman went immediately to the wall console and addressed the speaker. Soon soft string music came on and lights changed to a muted blue hue and a calm ocean scene played on a wall.

Hyman turned to us. "I require this to restore my nerves."

We must have looked curious.

"I am reacting to the violence," he explained. "I have never witnessed, nor been a party to, any violent act." His voice was no longer neutral, it was trembling. He was the same as most of the groundhogs.

A manservant appeared. "Sir?" The man was bald and elderly.

"Vodka, straight," Hyman said. "And you?" He looked at us.

"A vegetable juice mix," Sandy O'Clock said.

"Peanut butter iced tea, if you have it," I said.

Sandy made a face.

The manservant faded away.

I had learned more about Hyman Bookbinder in the last hour than I'd learned in our previous acquaintance.

Sandy ran her hand through her hair, probably trying to fix damage she thought might have occurred during the altercation.

However, it was still pretty much in place, and rather attractive, too.

"You know my name, and this is Hyman L. L. Bookbinder," I said. "What is your real first name, Ms. O'Clock?"

"Sandy suits me fine."

"I can't have coincidentally guessed it."

She shook her head. "No." Then she shrugged. "I guess I'll have to 'fess up. It's Gusselwaithe." She sort of cringed. I didn't blame her.

"That's all right," I lied diplomatically. "Since you don't like that, there must be another name everybody calls you informally? A nickname?"

She frowned and looked away to the ocean scene. "Gussie or Gus."

"Sandy it is, then," I said, deciding quickly because I could tell she had this little streak of vanity.

The manservant reappeared and we had our drinks. The servant left through a recessed hallway.

Hyman sat down on an air-lounge and stretched out his legs, sighing. "Join me."

I took a comfortable sofa chair and Sandy sat in a straight back thing that looked like it was designed for orthopedic rehabilitation.

Hyman was in a world of his own, so I simply stared at Sandy.

She sipped her veggie cocktail and returned my gaze a bit, it seemed to me, uncomfortably.

"I don't suppose you're going to volunteer a long, detailed statement that will answer all my questions," I said.

"I don't suppose I am." She folded both hands around her mug.

My iced tea had the flavor of peanuts and needed more sourfruit juice. But I drank it anyway. I was watching Sandy's eyes and saw the same look in them I probably had when I was planning to be evasive.

"I've seen you not too coincidentally three times now." My fingers went one, two, three. "You know my name. I've a thousand questions, but I'll cut to the big one.''

She looked expectant and Hyman turned his head and propped one eye open, interest flaring therein.

"Do you know what happened to Roanoke?"

"No."

"Do you know where Roanoke is now?"

"No."

"Do you know where Roanoke is supposed to be?"

"Yes."

"Do you know that Roanoke is no longer there?"

"Yes." She paused. "That was more than one question."

We'd established more than I'd gotten accomplished in all my travels until now.

"Are you really a high Galacticon executive or was your ID fake?"

Hyman was sitting up straight, now.

Sandy looked around uncomfortably, but didn't respond.

I was becoming exasperated. "Listen, woman. You must damn well know what's going on. I can tell you are a spacer or have spent much time in space."

She nodded.

"Roanoke vanished along with fifty thousand of its citizens, many of whom are my family and friends. Perhaps you can tell from my ever-increasing angry voice that it is my highest concern, and I ain't interested in playing games here." I paused to control my breathing.

She looked at me, eyes and features unreadable.

"Since you're familiar with the spacer breed, you know that I'm going to get to the bottom of this or die trying."

She nodded. "It's in your personality profile anyway, whether you're a spacer or not."

"Right. Now it occurs to me that, while I've done nothing criminal, that if there is some kind of conspiracy to cover up the disappearance of Roanoke, that cover-up would require my silence.'' Which might well have been the case in the D'Earnhardt snow.

She was following my train of thought.

"From what I know of you," I continued, "and the circumstances in which I've seen you, your being a part of some alleged conspiracy doesn't fit, not at all."

"Right."

Hyman was watching with interest. I'd taken charge with more than a little bit of command.

"Therefore, it occurs to me that our interests might in some degree, lesser or greater, coincide."

"Right."

"Or," I said, "if you are in fact a Galacticon government flack, you'd want my silence, obviously, and to get my silence, you'd have to kill me or help me in some small or large way."

"Right." She was infuriating me, but I held my temper.

"If you wanted me dead, I'd already be dead or vice versa," I said and her eyes told me that would be an interesting test of talents and skills; and that look on her face told me what I wanted to know: that she was indeed capable of more violence than at the ROAR offices and that she actually *thought* she could take me out if necessary. All of which changed our nebulous relationship.

This logic chain told me that I'd best keep my cool and my own counsel. Mostly because if she were willing to tell me the whole truth and nothing but, she would have already done so. Right now she was scheming. I could tell because I was a schemer, too.

Which meant I had to add a little pressure. "Come on, Gussie, tell us what's going on."

Her cross look told me, "Hey, no fair." But she smiled faintly and said aloud, "If you want it that way, Rollingham."

"Hey, *no fair.*" She knew my real name. I'd probably never forgive my father. But surely like she had with Gus, I'd long since learned to live with it.

"Now that we're even," she said, "perhaps we can finish with all this jockeying for position?"

"Agreed," I said.

Hyman rose and went to his console. His voice was a murmur. He returned and sat upright in his lounge. "Undersecretary Plinktone has not filed a complaint against us for the incident in his office."

"What happened?" Sandy asked.

Briefly, I outlined my loss of temper.

"He won't make an official note of it, not now," she said.

"Not if he's lower than 9B," I said.

"He's a seven, special access."

She knew a lot. "Do you work for the government?"

"I do," she said.

I knew it. All along I'd felt that somebody in the government knew about Roanoke's disappearance.

"I don't suppose you were lying when you said you didn't know what happened to my world?" I asked.

She crossed her legs. "You're no fool. You can pretty well guess what's going on from our conversation so far. You might not be able to put official labels on it all, but you can and are right now deducing what's what."

I was. "You are an agent, likely from some operational branch of Galacticon Central."

"I am. We took notice, immediate notice, when you started raising hell."

"Until then, you didn't know Roanoke was gone?"

She shook her hair, shoulder-length sandy strands bouncing right and left. "You might just say that my, er, agency, pays attention to anomalous situations, out of the ordinary occurrences."

I could understand that. With I don't know how many millions of worlds and jillions of people in and about the Galacticon, there had to be a lot of strange, weird, and unusual things going on.

"So a planet disappeared and they sent you to check it out?" I said.

"That's what happened."

"Only you?" Hyman asked. "They dispatched only *one* investigator?"

I knew the answer before she said it; it was an old joke.

With a gleam in her eye, she said, "There's only *one* planet missing."

Hyman looked at her for a moment, then he smiled. There was a bit of character in him after all.

I could see that this enigma who called herself Gus O'Clock was preparing to spin her tale. "You were trying, just as I was, to find out what happened to Roanoke. Our thinking paralleled and that's why I ran into you on D'Earnhardt."

"Exactly. Part of it *was* coincidence, another part was I didn't know anything about you, so I had to monitor you and what you were doing; the best way to accomplish that was to follow you—"

"You can track people through the Plex Net?"

She looked very uncomfortable. "I can do a lot of things with the Plex Net." She gave the appearance she was offended. "I would have been here sooner, tracked you down earlier, and perhaps we could have gotten together, but I was drafted to carry a Plex beacon buoy to replace another relay to a faraway system called Laquinto."

"The other ship in orbit over D'Earnhardt."

"That was mine."

Of course she had to have a ship to fly out to Roanoke's location. "As a government agent, you had to perform the delivery chore."

"I didn't have much choice," she said.

I explained some of this to Hyman, why I don't know. I suspected his usefulness was at an end.

Turning back to Sandy, I said, "So you were following me, then got stuck with Administrator Sunday's and Plex Fax Manager Sunday's problem. Had you made any other progress toward finding out what happened to Roanoke?"

She shook her head sadly. "No." I believed her. "I

was able to comm through the Plex Net to the astronomical observatories in that sector, but none observed anything anomalous, and I didn't tell them what to look for. Not yet. Not until I find out more.''

"You checked public, private, university, institutional observatories?" I asked.

"All of them." She gave me that look again. "The single planet and star system of Roanoke is—make that was—way out away from other systems. Most observatories aren't interested in that direction. After your story broke on D'Earnhardt, I asked two observatories confidentially to confirm, and they did by sending unmanned probes through transpace." Sandy tucked her leg under her rump. Her movements were fluid. "That newswoman certainly was accommodating."

Marion. "She was," I said with a grin.

Sandy favored me with a disdaining look which said, "A groundhog?"

"Do you own any soporific worms?" I asked.

Sandy looked at me as if I were roadkill. "Why do you ask?"

Good. To irk her, I didn't answer her question.

Checking with astronomical observatories had been on my list to do, but the mechanics and logistics of doing so put it at the very tail end of the list. Especially since light from Zira was still trucking along out there. Government had handled the chore easily. It was one of their advantages.

Impulsively, I reached out and touched her knee. "Thanks for leveling with us."

She glared at me and my hand. My intention was not sexual or to add or detract from the battle of the sexes. It was a simple personal move. I could just hear her thinking, "Nobody touches me." I withdrew my hand but didn't apologize.

She rose and asked Hyman where his facilities were. He directed her.

While she was in the bathroom, he whispered. "I had my computer check as well as it could. The only thing it came up with was a confirmation that an agent named O'Clock had more clearance than my system could inquire about.''

Hyman surprised me again. It was a good move on his part, though it did not tell us anything one way or the other.

When she came back, she said, "It is a minor possibility that somebody somewhere in the government knows something about this and isn't telling or isn't telling the right people. A case of the right hand not knowing what the left hand is doing. It's unfortunate, but it happens. How many offices and people work directly for Galacticon, Hyman?''

He scrunched up his face. "I do not know exactly, a few billion? I doubt anybody knows.''

A sad commentary on our system. And damn near all of them groundhogs. A twinge of despair washed over me. I had not approached fifty people yet in my quest and there were billions left? How was I going to crack that nut?

Sandy must have read my face. "Listen, Rusty. We're not all ogres. Just because you haven't been able to interest anybody in Roanoke's plight, doesn't mean we're all cold and callous. Fifty thousand missing people is fifty thousand too many. Yes, we've noticed. Furthermore, we can't have planets disappearing on us.''

I saw what she meant. "I see. Your problem is that Roanoke might not be the last one.''

She curled her other leg under her rump on the chair. "Yep. While we have the utmost sympathy for you and Roanoke,'' which I didn't exactly believe, "suppose the anomaly of disappearing planets and their suns continues? It does bear immediate investigation.''

"What's your next step?'' I wanted to know.

She shrugged. "I was going to either follow you and see what you turned up or introduce myself and suggest we join forces.''

I almost believed some of what she was saying. "Do you have any other leads?''

"No. I was hoping you had some ideas.''

"I can think of nothing outside the government," I said, holding my ace in the hole for now, "and if we're talking billions of Galacticon employees, that's a tall order." I looked pointedly at Hyman.

"Ah," he said, "I will continue my efforts, though the ROAR office was our best bet. Additionally," he was regaining his stride, his voice back to professional, "since Ms. O'Clock has done a data search—as had Undersecretary Plinktone—I do not hold out much hope for a successful completion of this project."

I nodded. "I think you might bend your efforts in a different direction." I thought for a quick moment. "There are two possible reasons Roanoke could have disappeared. Natural or unnatural. If there are natural, scientific explanations, then somebody, some scientist will know them—or be able to figure them out. If there is another reason, a nonscientific explanation, then somebody knows it because it had to be human-initiated. And if that's the case, then that person or persons had to have something to gain."

"Motivation," said Sandy. "Our agency has a science team, but I doubt they can come up with anything. My ship has plenty of sensor capability and you need clues, somewhere to start."

I nodded. Betsy had found absolutely nothing, either. All this and Dad's ability to begin a message had led me into thinking *someone* was responsible. And while I had heard speculation about antimatter universes and interlocking bubble universes, I put little stock in these so-called theories—or, more appropriately, I put little stock in their ability to accidentally or on purpose zap a star and a planet without any traces or astronomical indications.

Hyman was nodding like a bird pecking at the ground. "I can do that. I will search for a person or organization who would profit from the disappearance of Zira and Roanoke. It will take a while, but it's the kind of thing I'm trained to do."

"Good, because I wouldn't know where to start,"

I said. I was thinking that if Galacticon really cared and wasn't covering up some great accident, then they had plenty of scientists on retainers whom they could put to work on the problem. "However, be advised that Roanoke is self-sufficient in agriculture and natural resources; I haven't heard of any large mineral deposits, for example, or anything else which would profit anyone off Roanoke. Believe me, I would know." Being on the Board of Directors, I was privy to all new information. "Finally, we haven't angered anyone—not very much—or any galactic-wide powers, government or private. What I'm saying is that I can't think of anyone who'd have a nefarious reason to steal the star and planet."

Nobody said anything for a minute.

"Rusty?" said Sandy. "What are you holding back on us?"

"Am I that easy to read?"

"Not really. I'm a trained investigator."

Turning to Hyman, I said, "Recall that red folder Plinktone was so upset over?"

"I do."

"I'm going to find out what's in it."

Sandy shook her head. "Red is top secret, 'eyes only' kind of stuff."

"Then why did a bureaucrat such as Plinktone get it and why was he reading it?" My tea was empty, but Hyman was watching Sandy and I didn't want to be impolite, even if I was a spacer and had to keep up our collective reputation.

"He's the undersecretary of ROAR, Reports' Office of Approval and Review. They handle classified material. A subfunction is that *somebody* must route the classified documents to the proper officials and organizational function—"

"You're beginning to sound like a bureaucrat yourself," I shot at her.

"I have been," she said with a depracatory sneer.

"That explains a lot," I said. Us spacers are quick on the uptake sometimes. "You fit like a stinkbomb in church and somebody at your so-far unnamed agency got hold of you because you didn't fit and would make a perfect clandestine agent—''

"Yes, and I knew the system."

Hyman's head was going back and forth between us. He drained his vodka and held the glass up and the servant scurried out with a new glass. The old man picked up my glass and Sandy's mug. I nodded and she shook her head. Soon I had some more tea. This tasted more like peanut butter than peanuts and I liked it better—being a peanut butter freak and all; extra chunky if you please.

At any rate, I explained to Sandy about the red folder and Plinktone's inordinate proprietary manner.

"It might not mean anything," she said.

"Then again, it might. And I've no other trails to follow right now." I eyed her speculatively. "Could you try to get a copy through your agency, whatever that is?" She'd successfully avoided naming it each time I'd gotten close.

She shook her head. "No. We don't have the power," which I don't know if I believed or not, "nor the authority. You said it was marked eyes only?"

"Yes."

"That clinches it. We're not in any kind of normal chain of command, and we don't even appear on the organizational chart. We wouldn't be on the eyes only list."

Even though this mysterious agency investigated anomalies?

"Call your boss," I suggested, "and have him pull some strings."

"Eyes only means eyes only. You'll note in your contact with all these bureaucracies that none of them solicited bribes?"

"Yes." I'd tried that surreptitiously. But honesty was the best policy. Not only were people afraid to go into space nowadays, they were afraid to lie and take a little graft. What was this galaxy coming to?

"Also there are too many offices and too many bureaucrats in between," she said. "We're geared for *ex*ternal investigations anyway."

She'd pretty well eliminated her agency as giving us any help for whatever that was worth.

"Guess I'll have to go after it myself," I said.

"How?" she said.

"Beats me right now. Breaking and entering. I'll think of a way."

Hyman stood and walked out. "I don't want to hear any of this." He left through the same recessed door the butler had used. Hyman probably wanted another vodka. Certainly everything we said was being recorded. But I couldn't see how that would cost me, one way or the other. Except as evidence one day. Hyman was just being bureaucratic himself and covering his own rear end by recording this conversation.

"Certainly there will be guards outside and alarms," she said, her eyes growing larger and demanding more of my attention.

Her enthusiasm caught me. "We spacers are not unresourceful."

"We are that." She leaned toward me and touched my knee. In her eagerness, I don't think she knew she was doing it. "The ROAR office is a vault with all the security *external.*"

I knew what was coming, but I said "And?" to prompt her anyway. Let her win one. It was obvious that she wanted to accompany me. If for no other reason, to keep track of me. So I'd let her solve the problem of entry.

"We don't go in from outside. We enter from *inside.*"

"You can manipulate the Plex Net, destination codes and all?"

"I can."

Unaddressed was the fact she had done so earlier and conned the security captain into believing her arrival was a technical glitch or a number flip flop.

"Suppose there is security inside during the night?" That is, however they worked nighttime here.

"We stun 'em."

If that became the case, I'd think there could only be two people in the entire galaxy who'd be on the immediate suspect list. Rusty Wallace and Gusselwaithe—Sandy—O'Clock. But I said nothing.

Finishing my peanut butter tea, I said, "It could be they have an around the clock operation there. Or at least another shift. They're paper pushers, don't forget. An intermediate destination between offices."

"Phooey. They're entrenched bureaucrats with union rules. Nothing happens at Galacticon with any alacrity. They don't have any reason to do anything except for the doing itself. It's been in place so long without change that it is petrified and will never change."

Hyman walked in, went to the console, spoke, and turned to us. "The ROAR office workday completes at 1630 hours."

"I told you," said Sandy.

"Just in case," Hyman said, "I would appreciate the point of origin of certain upcoming Plex travel differentiate from this station."

Trying to sound unhappy, I said, "I guess I don't have much of a choice. Your way offers the highest probability of success."

She smiled and it was genuine and I regretted that we were still probable antagonists. But I'd damn sure use her—just as she was using me. Roanoke and my family and Virginia Bavarro depended on me.

"Is your manipulation of the Plex Net legal or illegal?"

She didn't answer.

"I don't need to know, huh? You're hinting it's illegal. Which puts us in worse trouble. I've heard the Plexus Authority has more power and influence than Galacticon." Which was only natural. The Plex Net provided the one indispensable service to all of humanity. Not to mention Plexus was a semi-quasi governmental independent agency and corporation.

"When do you think would be a good time for our little trip?" Sandy asked, ignoring my point.

"The sooner the better. Plinktone might forward or file the report, so I recommend sooner, namely tonight. Any time not on the hour or half hour," I said. "Those times have higher probabilities of monitors scanning security camera pictures. Also, that would avoid shift changes when they pay closer attention. Did you notice any?"

"Cameras?" she said. "Two in the lobby there. I was in that room only, remember."

"Three," I corrected.

"Can you take care of that?" she asked.

"I can."

Hyman looked aghast.

"Well, it's now 1712, well after 1630," Sandy pointed out.

"I can tell time. I'd like to get a full meal first."

"Why?"

"I'm hungry," I said, "not to mention if something goes wrong, you want to have a full belly because you might not get a chance to eat again any time soon."

"You've done this kind of thing before," she said, voice accusing.

"I'm a spacer. I've been to a thousand and one planets on which sometimes the situation wasn't full of professional or legal etiquette." I eyed her suspiciously. "This won't be *your* first time in an illicit operation, will it?"

"Of course not," she said defensively.

"Good."

Hyman waved his vodka glass and instructed his manservant to prepare a meal. Quite a meal, too. While we ate, I planned. I wondered how I would ever pay Hyman. Maybe I wouldn't live through it and not have to worry about it. Maybe I'd be indentured to him forever.

But his background searches were going to be costly. I hoped they'd be fruitful, to hell with the cost. Perhaps I could get Sandy's agency, if that were in fact the case, to fund the search.

Hyman's job was worse than ours. And with a lot lower probability of success. And it would take inordinately longer. But I was beginning to learn about Hyman. I watched his face and eyes. Even as we ate, he was planning his attack.

As we did.

After the meal, we took our leave of Hyman.

Hyman's station zapped us to the beacon where Galacticon Approach Control had made me park Betsy. I called Betsy over and the beacon's tunnel mated with Betsy's and we went aboard. "Hold the contact," I told Betsy. "We won't be long."

"Yessir, Rusty." Her voice was the one she used when she wanted to know something. Usually, she wasn't very curious—I didn't want a machine too human. But she'd developed a personality, probably in counterpoint to mine, and certain things interested her.

I ignored her, then thought better of it. "Betsy, this is Secret Agent of some kind or other Sandy O'Clock."

"Thank you, Rusty. Hi, Sandra."

"Hi, yourself." Sandy didn't correct the ship.

I got the equipment I needed. "Just for the heck of it, Betsy, I want you to run a full systems check and be prepared for immediate departure."

"Aye, aye, Captain. Will this be a legal or illegal departure?"

"I don't know." As an afterthought, I warned her. "I could be transmitting a scrambled signal. I don't know how long it will be, but be ready."

"I always am."

"Smarty."

"Yes, Rusty."

Sandy was following our conversation with interest.

We went back down the coupled airlock tunnels and into the beacon.

We translated to the central Plex Net facility here. It was located on the same planette as the Plex Net Central Authority offices. Concourses and corridors and Plex stations and, surprisingly, fewer people than I would have guessed. I mentioned this to Sandy.

She shrugged. "People just don't travel if they really don't have to, I guess."

We got into a station different from the one in which we'd arrived, not wanting to connect us with Hyman's station or the beacon station out there in the parking orbit.

"You pay," I said. I handed her my stunner. She'd handle people, I'd take care of electronics.

Sandy slapped her card against the scanner and gave the exact destination code of the ROAR office.

Zap.

9: B & E

Z ap.
  We stepped out of the Plex station into ROAR's lobby.

I had my hand-dandy little power pack out. I frazzed the three cameras at once. They'd show a garbled picture, their transmission discombobulated.

Even as I was doing my job, I could tell Sandy was doing hers.

The stunner hummed.

Unfortunately, there was a security officer on duty in the lobby.

Sandy nailed him and I smelled ozone.

"This ain't all that auspicious a beginning," I pointed out.

She held a finger to her mouth. "Might be an audio recorder on," she whispered.

"It doesn't really matter," I said. "There will be only two suspects in this sector who have anything to gain by breaking in here." I pointed at the slumped security guard. "Unless you want to kill him? And even then, it'd be obvious."

"If you want him dead, you kill him yourself," she said, no longer whispering.

"He never did anything to me," I said, stepping over him, and heading for the hallway to Plinktone's office. I should have brought an infrared scanner to be able to tell if there were any more guards ahead. I zapped the camera in the hallway ceiling.

Then we were at the suite housing UPROAR and his staff. The outer door was easy; it just opened. I hosed the immediate area down with my gizmo because they had to have some sort of management surveillance device to insure the night shift security guys didn't stop to read classified material.

Plinktone's door was different.

I changed the gizmo and and pointed it toward the mechanism in the wall alongside the door jamb. They weren't stupid enough to put the locking and automatic activating device in the center of the swishing double doors.

I took a deep breath and put my hand in the slot for manual operation. It didn't move.

"Uh-oh," I said.

This office might well be a product of a frozen bureaucracy, but it was still a top secret facility and well protected.

Sandy waved her ice-needle gun and lifted her eyebrows.

I shrugged. "They already got us for B and E, and probably assault on the guard—though it's likely he was asleep when we got here and we simply reinforced his nap."

"Reinforced his nap?" Sandy said with a not-very-well suppressed smile. "You sound like one of these bureaucrats."

I made a horror face. "Go ahead with the ice-needle gun."

She backed off and pointed the weapon at the wall where I'd located the activating mechanism. She fired a one second burst.

"Brrrrrrpppppp," went the gun.

An ice-needle gun is a wonderful weapon. You simply fill the compartment with water and the power pack does the rest. When you trigger it, the power pack is able to freeze and fire a couple dozen or so super slender needles of ice per second. It's good for close-in work and doesn't leave a specific signature trace law enforcement likes so much. The ice needles melt and you've no hard evidence. The weapon is quick, rapid fire, preferably in no more than three second bursts to keep from overheating, small and easy to conceal, neat with no residual radiation, and a number of other benefits.

The air chilled as she fired a three second burst. "Brrrrrrpppppp."

I tried the door again and it still wouldn't move.

"One more time," I instructed.

Again, and this time three timed bursts.

The ice needles shattered on the wall and the impact melted them immediately. Water soaked papers on a desk adjacent to the wall.

The door still wouldn't budge.

"The device must be pretty well frozen by now," I said and moved toward the wall.

Whirling to build up momentum, I did a three sixty and kicked the hell out of the wall. The entire wall shuddered.

"Suppose there are sonic alarms inside?" Sandy asked.

"Then we'd best hurry." I grasped the door, pulled hard and the left side slid open easily. "Nothing to it when you know how."

She tried to beat me inside, but I was already moving and frazzing the cameras I'd automatically cataloged while standing in front of Plinktone pleading my case.

"How do these groundhogs work all day long with cameras maintaining constant surveillance?" I wondered aloud.

"Unappetizing," Sandy said, heading for the central desk, "perhaps they got trained in a casino."

And suddenly I knew a lot more about one Gusselwaithe O'Clock.

"Uh-oh," said Sandy.

"Me, too." Plinktone's desk top was clean; no longer was it overwhelmed and disheveled. I looked around at all the file cabinets. "We got troubles."

"Especially if we're working against a clock."

"I'd wager on that," I said. "I hope this file system is alphabetical."

I was already at the R's and dragging drawers open. "Nothing in R as in Roanoke," I said.

She was at the far end. "No Wallace."

I remembered the word "missing" on the report. I looked in the M's with no luck.

Sandy was going through more drawers, methodically and rapidly. "How much time do you reckon we've got left?" She was in the A's, why I didn't know, because I couldn't think of anything connected to this mess beginning with an A.

"Not much more than a couple of minutes," I said. "We should have pulled the circuit breaker on the Plex station."

She glanced at me. "My code included a freeze command."

I whistled. "Good thinking. It'll take 'em longer to hotfoot it up here."

"That's no reason to stop your search," she said accusingly.

I was standing back. "It occurs to me that if Plinktone was reading the documents, that meant that he had to digest and decide which office the report had to go to—though I'd think that whoever made up a top secret report would know what office he'd want to send that report to—"

"They file stuff here, too," Sandy said, going through the E's. "Remember this is a vault and normal offices don't have the security for this kind of documents, not written reports."

"I see." I moved toward Plinktone's desk. "The undersecretary reads and decides routing on new reports; if the report has already been someplace, he reads it and determines filing locations."

"That's what I said." She looked at me angrily as if to tell me to get a move on it. She was in the S's now.

"Plinktone wasn't the kind of guy to handcarry paperwork; that would be done by couriers who can't read or something equally foolish. Also, *he* certainly wouldn't do the physical work of filing, not if I read his personality right.'' I pulled on a desk drawer.

Of course it was locked, electronic and mechanical. I kicked the hell out of it and the drawer popped open.

''You've a talent there,'' Sandy said.

''Should have thought of this first,'' I said. The tab on the drawer said ''In.'' Another drawer said ''Out.'' I kicked that drawer, too, and it opened when I tugged on it.

Both contained neatly arranged stacks of folders.

Each held one red, top secret, eyes only, folder.

The Out drawer held the file with the word ''MISSING'' in the title. It had a file designation slip on it, with ''P for Pop'' checked. ''This is it.''

I scanned the report with my device, transmitting a copy to Betsy. We might get nailed for breaking and entering, but I sure didn't want to take a fall for espionage or stealing top secret data; or they could even charge us with an official secrets violation. But not if we didn't give them any evidence.

My efforts were rewarded. I didn't take time to read anything, for we were out of time. But I did recognize the report. ''Negative Impact'' jumping out at me.

''Bingo, and done,'' I said. ''Let's go.''

She looked disappointed. ''If we had time, I'd bet there is a gold mine in here.'' She was beside me going through the ''OUT'' drawer.

I nodded. ''Probably stuff we could use to blackmail high officials to get out of whatever charges they're going to lodge against us.''

''Maybe,'' she nodded and looked wistfully at the filing cabinets. ''Isn't that called extortion instead?''

''Beats me. Both are illegal.''

''So's breaking and entering a top secret vault.'' She moved over to the ''in'' drawer and dug through that. ''Ah,'' she said, flipping open the other red folder. ''Here, transmit this.''

''Why?''

"It might be important, too."

I glanced at the routing checklist and it was checked in red. "Executive Administrator Eyes Only." "Whew," I whistled. "Why?"

"Do it!" Her voice was commanding.

"Done." As quick as I could flip them, I clicked the device at the successive pages. Were my hopes paying off?

I tugged her out of there. But she wouldn't budge. She hit the orange button on Plinktone's console and shoved the report into a chute.

"Disintegrating." The computer voice made me jump.

Sandy had destroyed the file. Being in the "In" basket might mean Plinktone hadn't read it yet. Meaning Sandy didn't want him to read that specific report.

Curiouser and curiouser.

Now I was dragging her out. Fortunately, the lighting was permanent.

We were running by now.

When we burst into the lobby, the access doors were swinging open.

Sandy traversed the stunner left to right and three gray-suited security men tumbled in and lay unconscious where they fell.

A shout outside told me that there were more of them, but they weren't ready to come in yet. We had about ten seconds.

Sandy was already half in the Plex station and I jumped over the prone guard she'd stunned upon our arrival.

As I stumbled in, her card was already against the scanner and she was repeating the code for the beacon buoy station. As I always do, I tensed.

Nothing happened.

I could hear my heart and Sandy's harsh breathing.

I hit the control which gives you an opaque privacy shield to buy us more time. I imagined I heard them coming in the front door cautiously, then more confidently when they found they weren't targets any more.

"Hurry!" I put a lot of urging in my voice, but I maintained my normal decibel level to show her I had confidence in her. While I did have confidence in her, I had no confidence in her so-called agency to bail us out if we got into real trouble.

"A freeze. Their security alert program has an automatic Plex station freeze built into it."

"That makes sense," I said matter-of-factly. "But it doesn't help our immediate problem. I doubt we have five seconds left."

She wasted two of them burning me with a withering look.

She broke her focus on me and closed her eyes as if trying to remember. "Plexus, Plex Command Authority Override. Confirm my voice now—"

Our five seconds was up and more. Shadows were flitting through the lobby and several converging on our location.

"Confirmed." The Plex computer voice was oddly out of kilter in this panic charged atmosphere.

"I say again," Sandy repeated, "Plex Command Authority Override, 9beta875OClockMARK9, *now!*"

One of the shadows was about to reach us except in her haste she tripped over the unconscious security guard's body and gave us the extra second we needed.

I'd grabbed the stunner and was aiming it and beginning to trigger a beam when—

Zap.

We were in the buoy beacon station.

"Betsy," I hollered into the comm box while punching in the commands to connect us.

And she was there immediately.

"My ship?" asked Sandy.

"Is it near enough?"

She looked at me sourly. "We've been on the go, remember? I didn't have time to prep him like you did your Betsy."

I tsked a couple tsks. "The Seven P Principle."

"What's that?"

I was heading for the tunnel.

"Proper prior planning prevents piss poor performance."

I'd sort of hustled things along to put her at a disadvantage. I didn't know exactly the next steps, because they depended on the reports, but I did know that I'd feel a lot better if I had Sandy along with me and at least where I could reach her.

"You planned it this way." Not a question, a statement a prosecuting attorney would be proud of.

One up on her, I shot her a grin and said, "You want to read the reports, don't you?"

That seemed to ameliorate her and we hustled up the tunnel and were inside Betsy.

"Disconnect and return to the parking space," I directed.

"Done, Rusty," the ship said.

We settled into the cockpit. "Something to drink?" I asked Sandy.

She shook her head.

"Well, let's see what those reports say. Display the copied transmission," I told Betsy.

"Incoming comm," she replied.

"Put it on the screen."

"Done."

"This is the starship *Virginia*," I said.

"Who's Virginia?" Sandy asked.

All this was making me uncomfortable. "Somebody I know."

"Why do you call the ship Betsy?"

"You're getting under my skin. It's none of your damn business." Ships and women are different. I felt more comfortable with "Betsy" than "Virginia."

A pale female face appeared on the screen. Her hair was cut too short and she had some kind of live insect dangling on a chain from her earlobe. Ugh.

"Port Authority," the face said. "Captain Wallace?"

"Speaking."

"I have here a warrant from Galacticon Central Security. Galacticon Approach Control has been directed to disallow any ship movements by your ship and the starship *Alfredo*—"

"Who's Alfredo?" I asked snidely.

"None of your damn business."

"A croupier? A dealer?"

"Leeme alone." Sandy shot me a scathing look.

"—You are directed," the Port Authority woman said, "to dock, disembark, and report to the security squad awaiting you in the buoy."

"Me?"

The woman seemed distracted for a moment and then said, "And if a Ms. Gusselwaithe O'Clock is aboard, she is directed to follow the same instructions."

Sandy leaned over into the pickup. "That's pronounced like 'wait,' not with a damn lisp."

Gently, I pushed her aside. "Some secret agent you are."

She glared at me.

I turned to the screen. "We need some time."

The woman didn't change her expression. "Request denied. Please expedite your compliance."

"Bureaucrats everywhere," I said.

"They might well be bureaucrats and move like glaciers," Sandy said, "but they certainly caught up with us quickly enough."

"You've a point."

"Please comply with previous orders," said the Port Authority woman, voice now showing a little agitation.

"Bimbo," said Sandy.

"Port Authority," I said, "I don't understand your request. Is your warrant issued by a judge?"

She looked aside, as if at another screen. "Not yet, Captain Wallace. Security assures us that is forthcoming."

"Then I shall respectfully decline.'

"Understood, Captain. You are directed to follow Port Authority directions and do not move your ship."

"Not directly," I said.

She looked aside again. Then she turned back. "Security invokes the immediate pursuit rule and you are directed to comply with my previous instructions immediately."

"These guys have a redundancy problem," I said.

"Do something," Sandy urged.

To the screen I said, "*I* invoke my rights. You are talking to the last citizen of Roanoke. Since Roanoke is no longer there, then I declare Roanoke sovereign and independent from Galacticon and therefore the Galacticon laws are not applicable to me, a sovereign head of state."

Sandy was looking at me with amazement. "That's the biggest bunch of malarkey I've ever heard; however, it was brilliant."

"Thanks."

"Captain Wallace, the Port Authority and Galacticon Central recognize no sovereignty other than their own and insist that civil and criminal codes be adhered to. You are again directed to dock."

"Port Authority, as Captain of the, ah, *Virginia*, I invoke Galactic Space Law. Stand by while I contact my lawyer, my agent, and my banker."

"You could get a job as a bureaucrat," Sandy said.

"I haven't been banging my head against red tape and official officiousness and not learned something." I cleared the screen. "Betsy? Go translight, if you please?"

"Where?"

"Anywhere, just get us out of here."

"From right here in parking orbit under control of the Port Authority?"

"You can do it," I coaxed.

"You sweet-talked me again, Rusty. Done."

Bang, we were gone and enroute to somewhere.

I just needed time to think. Not to mention reading the contents of the red TOP SECRET EYES ONLY folders. While I really wanted to see the "MISSING" folder's contents, I couldn't help but wonder what Sandy was doing, what agenda of her own she was pursuing.

I was beginning to feel used.

10: IG

Side by side we sat. Betsy had extended the command chair into a lounge.

I had finished off the left-over peanut butter and garlic stuffed mushrooms. Sandy had suspiciously accepted a nuked peanut butter burrito with my special mustard sauce.

Betsy's bridge was larger than you'd expect, for she was also designed as a freighter, and required commensurately larger accommodations than a normal courier or explorer class vehicle. I'd stuck plants here and there to spruce up the ship and make it smell and look more like a home, not a metal bucket. Odd flowers and greenery added to Betsy's personality.

Sandy sank back. It wasn't often you could smell woman in this ship. I couldn't remember the last time. Virginia had visited once or twice, but didn't have the normal Roanokean taste for space, so I hadn't taken her anywhere, just gave her the cook's tour. But still, it beat the hell out of smelling metal, electronics, peanut butter, weird plants from different worlds, and spilled tea and coffee.

"I'm ready," Sandy said.

"Go ahead, Betsy," I said.

Betsy split the wraparound screen in front of us. The report I wanted to read was on the far left, and Sandy's report was the far right with a lot of neutral space in between so that the other display wouldn't distract us.

The screens lighted.

TOP SECRET EYES ONLY

TO: ROAR, UNDERSECRETARY PLINKTONE
SUBJECT: REPORT OF MISSING REPORT, NEG-
ATIVE IMPACT THEREOF
FROM: OFFICE OF POPULATION RESEARCH
[OPR]
DOCUMENT #: 88B49POPDOCCYC5588T4Q2
DATE: 103 OF CYCLE 5588
REF RPT DOC #: 88B49POPDOCCYC5588T1L1

Undersecretary Plinktone,
Pursuant to your request and in accordance with
GALACTICON ADMINISTRATIVE PROCEDURES, Vol
132, paragraph 65, subparagraph a, acknowledgment of lost report is formally made.
In accordance with referenced regulation, the below
summary of referenced missing report is provided for
administrative reference and filing purposes. This office understands the routing was complete and the
report was misplaced by ROAR, which your office implied, but failed to acknowledge, in your follow-up
memo requesting this report.
OPR provides the following summary. The summary is classified TOP SECRET EYES ONLY.
Attchmnts 1-8 are provided as background as required when filing background historical data.
Attchmnts 1-8 are copies of copies and, while still
sensitive, are replaceable if rerequested under appropriate guidelines.
SUMMARY OF REFERENCED DOCUMENT by
OPR:
Referenced document by Ofc Pop Rsrch addressed
population curve decline in most sectors of Galacticon. While production of people has declined, with as
many citizens as inhabit all the sectors and systems
of Galacticon, there are still sufficient minimal births
to preclude public notice of trendial data except on
very local levels. The refd rpt refd two previous Off
Pop Rsrch rpts identifying earlier portions of the de-
crease trend and recommended high executive level
attention. OPR acknowledges those earlier rpts con-

tained exec lvl initials on routing slips. Attchmnt data
reflects base data from which conclusions drawn.

Conclusion by OPR: Significant decline in births.
Population increase curve flattening. Neg pop growth
expected w/in 100 yrs standard, local variations expected. Recommend exec lvl action to involve social
science bureaus and departments for possible ad-
verse or beneficial effects on Galacticon political and
economical structure. Data reflects no new factors
such as disease, radiation, or religion impacting upon
data sufficiently to violate statistical veracity.

It was signed by somebody named Ralph E. Smith,
Director, OPR.

At the bottom was a scrawled note: "Plinky, one of
these days I'll get their attention. Could you have accidentally nuked the missing report in your disintegrator?" The signature read "Ralph."

Out of the periphery of my vision, I'd seen Sandy
speed reading her report and she was now leaning my
way, reading, as it were, over my shoulder. Her screen
was blank so I shifted the "missing report" report to
the center of the screen.

While I was curious about what the report she'd stolen was all about, I was close to being overwhelmed
by disappointment. I'd put a lot of stock and hope into
finding some answers and it turns out that I was mis-
taken. In there somewhere was a lesson about jumping
to conclusions, but I was in no frame of mind to think
about it.

Absently, I scrolled the "attchmnts," which were
tons of data, figures from different sectors of the galaxy, fancy graphs, statistics which would require a
synthesist to put together in a coherent fashion to make
any sense to me. The point was made in OPR's summary, if you could get through the governmentese language. Fewer people being born. Were they talking
about the end of human expansion?

"They could've asked me," I said bitterly. "Nobody goes into space anymore."

"Some of us do," Sandy said, patting my arm to reassure me. "I've noticed a decline in Plex Net travel."

For a spacer, she certainly used the Plex a lot—and knew more about its inner workings than she should. I'd remember that observation later.

I shrugged it off. Spacers could and did use the Plex Net all the time. Even me.

The attachments trailed off and I didn't bother to read them all.

Slumping back, I closed my eyes. The couch adjusted. I was no further, really, than when I'd started.

As if reading my mind, Sandy said, "Well, Rusty, at least you've eliminated a lot of possibilities and you know where at Galacticon Central not to look for the answers."

Opening my eyes, I said, "That may or may not be true, but I can't go back. I'm a fugitive—as are you."

She didn't seem very upset about it. But she reacted to the bitterness in my voice. "You've done as much, no, you've done more than any human can be expected. You've given it your best shot." Her words were soft and understanding.

"Not yet, I haven't."

She was holding my right hand now. "Nobody could blame you if you quit now. Perhaps we could get ROAR and Galacticon Central Security to drop the charges."

Angrily, I jerked my hand away, and regretted my haste. Like any stupid guy, I felt I had to hurt somebody to ease my pain. "You're just being nice to me to divert my attention. I saw you clear and destroy that file. So now I can't read it."

She turned her head. "I didn't think you should read it."

"Why not?"

She shrugged and turned back. "It has nothing to do with you. It is government business."

"So your sympathy was merely an act."

I saw the hurt in her eyes. "If you want to think so."

"I don't know what the hell to think. I *trusted* you, and you failed to reciprocate."

She shook her head. "No, I trust you. I was just doing my job."

"Which I ain't altogether certain I believe, either." I sat up angrily.

"I'm sorry."

"Yeah. Betsy? Why'd you let her wipe that file?"

"You didn't tell me not to, Rusty." I imagined the sniff at the end. "I thought you might have read it, anyway, Rusty. You were sitting there so long, I must have misunderstood."

"New rules. Nobody does nothing on this ship without my approval. You accept no orders without my okay. Understood?"

"Yes, Rusty."

I faced Sandy. "This is my ship, you will perform no operational or functional activities without checking with me first. Understand?"

"Take me somewhere and drop me off," she responded.

"Not until I find out what you're so anxious to hide."

While Betsy was just a machine, she was no dummy. She knew I was up to something. She wouldn't have erased the report without me telling her to. She might have said she would, but she'd keep a copy. Additionally, she knew I'd still have a copy in my little device. I pulled my electronic gizmo out, waved it in Sandy's face, punched the "xmit" code, and said, "Display that report on the center screen, please."

"Yes, Rusty."

Sandy sat up straighter. She was indeed an enigma, and a mystery. "You were only posturing." Her voice was chock full of accusation.

"Nope. I'm still angry at you for not trusting me. The possibility of course occurred to me that you might be concealing something involving Roanoke's disappearance for purposes of your own.''

Her shoulders slumped. ''No, not at all. It's just as I said: I was only doing my job.''

Her voice held something that made me believe her. Instead of reading the report, I studied her. She was now propped up on the lounge, right leg under her left thigh, her hair brushing her shoulders like a caress. I don't think it was the appealing, vulnerable picture she made which convinced me to believe her—though that might well have had a little to do with it. I think that somehow we'd connected on a more basic level and my gut just told me she was telling the truth.

I grinned. ''Well, hell, Gusselwaithe, let us see what you're trying to hide from me.'' I turned and read the report. This one was quite a lot less bureaucratic. Top secret, eyes only stuff.

It was from Sunday A. Sunday, Sector VIII Administrator, to the Galacticon Executive Administrator.

SUBJECT: ALIEN CONTACT

The subject grabbed my interest right away. ''Real aliens?''

Sandy said, ''Real. Or so it seems.''

Man has settled or visited much of the galaxy and has yet to encounter an intelligent species. Of course, most planets contain their own native life, but no species we'd found had yet evolved sufficiently to be considered anything more than animal level.

Hope leapt and died in one breath. ''I guess it would be too much to find that these aliens had come along and stolen Roanoke for some zoological purposes, merely leaving me with rescue duties.''

''I doubt it,'' she said, watching me. ''At first I thought there might be a connection because two anomalies occurred almost simultaneously in Sector VIII. Actually, they received proof of the aliens' existence before Roanoke disappeared.''

The meat of the correspondence:

Sir,

Acknowledgment is made of your directions to approve my recommendations to withhold disclosure of contact from nonhuman intelligent beings.

Be advised that since the moment the initial contact came through the Laquinto system we have been working the problem.

Fortunately, my ability to limit comm and Plex Net travel to and from the Laquinto system is enhanced by the fact that Sunday B. Sunday is the Sector VIII Plexus Net Manager. Per our agreement, I secured his cooperation and, via remote command, one of the relay beacons to the Laquinto system was decommissioned.

Publicly, I have attempted to locate a spacer to send to repair the decommissioned beacon buoy, failed once, and succeeded once. However, having control of the master Plex fax on D'Earnhardt allowed us to disallow travel and comm through the Plex Net after the beacon was replaced. The spacer departed and we decommissioned another buoy. That is to say, travel and communication with Laquinto is still embargoed.

Incidentally, the woman spacer who replaced the buoy claimed to be part of Galacticon Central's bureaucracy. Upon cross-checking, I can find no authentification for that claim. Her ostensible credentials are reviewed in attachment 1. This fact alone could show us that there are suspicions loose in Galacticon, and that wo might not bo ablc to maintain secrecy on this project.

Awaiting your further orders,
I remain,
Respectfully yours,
Sunday A. Sunday

That was it.
"Sunday A. and B. Sundays aren't as dense as they'd

have you think," I said for lack of anything else to say.

Sandy nodded agreement.

"And the contents of the letter gives us not much information on the aliens," I pointed out. While it was all fascinating, it didn't get me any closer to Roanoke.

"No." Sandy was very demure.

"It's also pretty evident to me that you are not a Galacticon secret agent. I doubt if there is such a thing."

"There isn't; but Galacticon is so big, nobody knows there isn't."

"Oh," I mused, "that makes about as much sense as anything has lately."

She looked like she had a lot of explaining to do.

Shortly, we were eating frozen chunky peanut butter, twirled with chocolate, and in which I'd added a bit of amaretto to provide that exotic touch of taste.

"These *are* good," said Sandy.

"Thanks. I made them myself."

"With my help," said Betsy.

We were in the galley and had eaten dinner. Action and tension make me hungry.

"We've a lot of unraveling to do," said Sandy.

"I could put it all in perspective much better were I to know who you are and what you're up to."

"Oh, that." She hung her head and batted her long eyelashes. She licked at her dessert on a stick. Her eyes darted, flashing green.

I waited.

She finished and put the stick down the chute. She leaned back in the chair. "It's really rather simple. In matter of speaking, I am an agent. But not exactly for Galacticon."

It had to be only one thing.

"I work for the Inspector General at Plex Net Central."

"You're an IG."

She nodded.

"That would explain a lot of things," I said, getting a peanut butter and mustard swirl cookie from the compartment alongside the table. "For instance, your knowledge of the Plex Net and its operations. Your high frequency of Net travel. The buoy you had to replace in the relay location en route to Laquinto—"

"The one they didn't want me to replace."

"It would also account for your ability to override a security freeze on the ROAR Plex station, and a few other passing items."

"It would," she said, eyeing my cookie. I gave her one and she nibbled it appreciatively.

Sticking my fingers in the automatic swisher to remove the crumbs and the stickiness from licking them, I said, "There remain several items to be addressed." She wasn't getting off that easily.

"Which are?"

"Namely, how is it you got involved in the first place? What stake does Plex have in this alien contact?"

"There are still some answers I don't know yet," she said, finishing her cookie and using the swisher. "I follow orders like any good soldier. The Inspector General himself sent me out. He's busy with an important investigation himself, so I got this one. He'd picked up a rumor, or perhaps something leaked from the Laquinto relay beacon business."

I didn't really see yet.

She rose and began pacing. I had the gravity at point nine norm. "The thing about the Plex Net is that it serves as the FTL comm link, too. Faster than a starship, just as translating through the system is, we provide the galactic communications."

It was beginning to fall in place. "If the human civilization were to receive transmitted signals or communication from some yet-undetermined aliens, it would be via Plex Net."

"Exactly. From my experience and from reading Sunday's report, I'd say that somewhere in the Laquinto system the Plex Net received the alien signals.''

"Laquinto is far and out of the way," I said.

"It is that. Which could be the explanation in itself.''

"Makes sense to me," I said.

"So the IG sent me off to Sector VIII," she continued. She stopped her pacing and eyed me. "At that time, it came to light someone, a spacer, was raising a ruckus about a missing planet. As I told you earlier, you don't get two such irregularities that close together in the same approximate time frame.''

"I can't argue the point." I stretched my legs. I was right tired. I'd been on the go for a long time now.

"So, I had to investigate both occurrences as if they were connected. The most facilitating manner in which—''

"Most facilitating?" I interrupted. "You've been reading too many reports.''

"The easiest way," she said, sticking her tongue out at me, "was to see if you'd found anything I could use or correlate with anything I knew.''

"And we were thinking alike, for instance going to the Galactic Geographic Society, and other places—'' I zapped the table into the bulkhead.

"Even if they were populated full of female groundhogs wearing groundhog worms,'' said Sandy.

"That's neither here nor there." I sounded defensive even to me.

"That's so," she looked at me funny. "Even if you did take her to dinner.''

"I've no secrets, do I?" Sandy had been thorough. "Just doing my job.''

"Did you spy on me in the bathroom, too?''

"Don't be ridiculous.''

My voice went up a few octaves. "Ridiculous? Look who is being ridiculous.''

"Listen, Wallace, do you want me to finish or not?

If not, I've got things to do, not to mention about twelve hours of sleep I owe my body.''

"Okay, okay. Truce. So you were merely doing your job when you took the relay beacon and dropped it off on the route to Laquinto.''

She sat down opposite me again, overemphasizing stepping across my outstretched legs. "Yes. I felt obligated. And then they knocked out another. They're covering up, and I'd like to know why.''

"Me, too, but there are some answers I can guess.''

"After reading both reports,'' she said.

"Right. Laquinto is out of the way and, if I recall, in a direction past which is nothing.''

"Say that again, only make sense this time?'' said Sandy.

"Betsy, gimme a star-chart on the screen with Laquinto centered.''

"Done, Rusty.''

The galley screen glowed to life.

"See, Laquinto is alone out there on the edge of the galaxy.'' I was pointing. "It's counter clockwise at the galaxy's edge from where Roanoke and its star used to be.''

"Nearly out in intergalactic space,'' said Sandy.

"It's this side of a star wall, called, lemme see, Duke's Cloud, a primeval murk full of pulsars, gas clouds, stars going nova, white dwarfs, and even a couple of black holes.'' Only Betsy's color-coding made sense of the mess.

"Rusty, the Plex Net can and does act as a giant signal receiver. It's designed to pick up transmissions—and those transmissions don't have to be from humans. . . .''

"But there's nothing out there,'' I said absently. "Void and more void until you run across another galaxy. Other galaxies *moving* away and at angles to ours. If it's aliens, where are they transmitting from to reach the Loquinto Plex Net?''

She shrugged. "Sunday's report didn't say what kind

of aliens, either. It simply said 'contact from' and not 'with.' ''

This speculation was getting us nowhere and not helping me find Roanoke. "About you erasing the report a while ago?"

"A judgment call," she said. "I had little time and a decision to make. I blew it. I decided to err on the side of caution." She clenched her mouth tightly in anger. "You see, don't you, that *nothing* happens on the Plexus Net, nothing major, without the Plex Central execs knowing about it?"

"You're right." I was thinking furiously. "That's where the rumors you mentioned came from."

"They did. Keep in mind The Inspector General himself dispatched me."

"Meaning he knew nothing."

She nodded. "Also meaning that this indicts the top level of Plex Central, all of the why's and wherefore's we don't know yet. So I tried to dump Betsy's file on it. My call was that of a natural protective reaction. I should have trusted you."

I waved a magnanimous hand. "You've apologized enough for that."

She glared at me. "Don't be so smugly patronizing."

"I'm still not happy about you spying on me."

"Jeez, Wallace, you get something on somebody and you use it to death."

"Call it residual chagrin."

She turned her head and faced the wall.

"Why'd you drop Plinktone's file in the disintegrator?"

"Another gut reaction," she said, speaking to the wall. "I thought if the report hadn't gone out through channels, maybe I could limit the damage. Don't forget, at the time I didn't know what was in it; I'd just glanced at the front sheet with all that stilted language. By that time I knew something was badly wrong in the rarified management air at the top of Plex Central.

Especially when I double-checked and found Laquinto still incommunicado.''

"And the all too coincidental meeting slash altercation in the ROAR office lobby?''

She turned her head from the wall. Again, she looked down and a blush crept up her attractive neck. "Pre-arranged with the security captain.''

Understanding flowed over me. "To get on my good side. We'd inadvertently run into each other too many times and another cute-meet wouldn't cut it.''

"That's not the way I'd describe it,'' she said, squirming a little. Her face was losing the red tinge. "I'd call it a tactical move which paid off handsomely.''

It had. I'd set her up a time or two, but she'd set me up to begin with. "And the break-in at ROAR? Was that set up in advance, too?''

"No, it wasn't.'' Her voice told me she was angry at me for accusing her.

"Duplicity doesn't engender trust,'' I said.

"La tee da,'' she said. "You forget the break-in was your idea. One which I merely took advantage of. I looked in the files where I thought I might find anything relating to the aliens, but found nothing except that folder in Plinktone's desk.''

"Betsy, display the routing slip on Sunday's report.''

The Laquinto section of Sector VIII faded and the routing slip from atop the red folder appeared.

"See.'' I pointed to the bottom. "File category: Contact.''

"Stupid bureaucrats,'' said Sandy. "Whyn't they put it under A for aliens?''

"Why do they do anything?'' I asked. "My report was to be filed under P, P for pop, as in -ulation. Who understands file clerks? And Plinktone is simply a glorified file clerk.''

"Plinktone used to be high up, but he burned out and they gave him that job because he knew almost everything anyway.''

"No wonder he was such a sour jerk," I said. "On top of the world one day and the next day in the outhouse."

"What's an outhouse?"

"A place in which you'd have spied on me if you knew what it was."

"You're beginning to sound redundant, not to mention catty."

She was right. "You're right. Hereafter I will no longer refer to those unfortunate incidents and invasions of my privacy."

She simply watched me.

"There is a small matter of several things we should address," I said.

"Sleep and what else?" She stretched in the chair and the material augmented.

"Two things. Namely, fugitive status for both of us. Two, what's next?"

"I've been worrying about that, too," she said, seriousness creeping onto her face. "I think we need to keep a low profile until we can clarify our status."

"You mean stay out of sight until we can get it straightened out?"

"That's what I said." She yawned.

"*If* we can get it straightened out," I amended. "We did a real bad thing, not to mention assault with a stunner on official security personnel doing their official security job." I was also aware that our situations were different. She was an agent acting on behalf of the plex IG, and the Plex was the single most powerful institution in Galacticon. I was just an ordinary citizen, but our different situations would all come out in the wash—I hoped.

She yawned again. "And maybe we could talk about what to do next after a little sleep?"

"We can. But it seems to me that your original approach wasn't all that far off base."

"The coincidence of two anomalous situations?"

"That's what I mean." Yawning is contagious so I did it, too. "Which gives us a lead."

"Somebody in Plex Central?"

"That's what I was thinking. Perhaps if we find something about your aliens, we might coincidentally find something about Roanoke." It was the only trail left for me. Somebody high up in Plex Central knew something to initiate the rumors the IG had picked up.

She yawned. "Which means we have to ask my boss."

"It is a trail to follow."

She fought a yawn and lost. "General Kalhen is a fine man; he'll level with me. His integrity and loyalty earned him his job." She thought for a moment. "He's been there a long time, which accounts for the sources he'd cultivated, and that's where he came up with the alien rumor. . . ."

"And you said he's working on something of a higher profile than this?" I asked, stifling a yawn.

"You bet. Remember he's Plex Net. What's the biggest money maker in the history of man?" she said.

I didn't hesitate. "The Plex Net."

"You win the vacation trip. Somebody's skimming off the top, has set up false billing for phantom contracts and the like. He's close to making a case . . . but that's not our problem. We just have to see what he knows about aliens and maybe Roanoke."

I stood. "You convinced me." I pointed. "Take your pick of staterooms. You'll find everything you need. There's a legit bed, or if you want, there's a retaining hammock. I usually sleep at a fraction of gravity."

"Less than ten percent?"

"Yep."

"That's fine with me."

"Thank you very much."

I was going to make a snide comment about her not having to lock the door but my throat got constricted and I said nothing.

There was enough to worry about. We were fugitives under the gun, thrown together by circumstances. Right now Galacticon and its security were hot on the trail after us. And we had to return to Galacticon Central, right back into the lion's den.

My quest had been made more difficult, compounded by events and people beyond my control. But I was a spacer and odds, while they should be factored in, were not the limiting factor.

I felt Sandy's eyes on me all the way to my stateroom.

But I was thinking. Twenty-four days and change left.

11: DUPLICITY

We stopped at the nearest metropolis, Ottolobe, from Galacticon Central.

I might be subject to apprehension and arrest and no longer able to bounce about the bureaucracy, but I wasn't going to quit. Time was running down.

We could tell the alert hadn't gone out for us, because when we parked above, nobody sent the cavalry after us. However, a check showed they'd taken Sandy's ship *Alfredo*.

We hit the beacon and translated down to the Plex fax. I wandered around the pax portion of the Plex facility for a while, pickpocketing, so that we'd have some different IDs to use in the Plex stations. We didn't want to take the chance of being caught. There was also the possibility that they'd flagged the system to freeze us in transit. They could also have changed instructions so that Sandy could no longer do any of her tricks like override security commands. Then we translated to Galacticon Central.

The route was torturous, but it was possible that security was monitoring the Plex stations at work or home which would give us access to Sandy's boss, the Plexus Net Inspector General.

"General Kalhen is a good man," Sandy told me again. She must respect him a great deal to repeat herself.

His home was on a large planette, one which had its own atmosphere and one small ocean.

We translated to the nearest city and took off on foot. About four miles out of town, we found the IG's home, a tall building of luxury apartments overlooking a bay.

We took the outside bubblevator to his floor, marched to his door, and pressed the announcer.

An elderly woman in a baggy bathrobe answered. Since this was early evening, local time, her dress was strange.

"Can I help you?"

Sandy said, "We're looking for General Kalhen."

"He isn't here."

"Is he still at work?"

The woman pushed an errant strand of gray hair aside and looked confused.

"Mrs. Kalhen?" said Sandy. At the woman's nod, Sandy went on. "My name is O'Clock, perhaps your husband has mentioned me?"

"Gusselwaithe? Certainly, my dear."

"We've got to find him and talk to him."

Mrs. Kalhen shook her head wistfully. "It wouldn't do any good. He isn't here. I mean, he's gone. He's at our home planet, Chalan Kanoa."

"When will he return?"

"He won't. Don't you know?"

"Know what?" Sandy glanced at me. Her concern flowed from her green eyes like green fire.

"He's there, finding us a place to live. He just retired."

Sandy looked incredulous. "I heard nothing about it."

Mrs. Kalhen flattened her lips together tightly. "Neither did I." She looked about. "While I've been after him to retire, he did not do it at my behest. He was asked to retire. There was an implication he would be removed formally if he did not cooperate."

"Oh."

The trail was leading up the Plexus Central corporate ladder.

"We're terribly sorry to bother you," said Sandy.

We took our leave. Riding down the bubblevator, Sandy was strangely silent.

"You're strangely silent," I said.

She looked me in the eye. "Whatever the intrigue about funds is, it cost him his job." She was visibly shaken.

We walked along a pleasant country path back toward the city. Aircars occasionally flew over our heads, but we didn't encounter anyone else walking. It was a nice little hike there, just Sandy and me. A time of quiet, a time to reflect, a time to enjoy. The walk helped calm her.

"You've probably already figured this out," said Sandy. "The IG reports to one person, and one person only. The CEO of Plexus Net."

"It's only logical. Who is this man?"

"This man's a woman. Helen Merritt-Browne."

"Our next step would seem to be rather obvious," I said, sitting down on a rock.

Sandy stopped with me and we were silent for a while, watching a brook trickle down a slope. The light was pretty well gone by now, but the night skies had that odd reflection of a couple of dozen planettes, and I could see well enough.

"It's kind of discouraging," Sandy said after a few minutes. "Every time we take a step forward, we go back two." She leaned against the rock alongside me.

I began kneading her shoulders and back. She tensed for a moment and then relaxed. Nor did she say anything about "Nobody touches me."

"What you say is true," I said, "but we are getting closer. I feel the heat."

"Me, too. Um, that feels good."

"My specialty. Listen, you don't happen to know where Helen what's her name lives, do you?"

"Helen Merritt-Browne. No, I don't. We're not going to be able to walk up to where she lives or even make it through the flunkies to her office."

"She'd have personal security, wouldn't she?" I dug my thumbs into Sandy's lower back, my other fingers holding onto her rib cage. She must have been ticklish, because she squirmed a little.

"She would." Sandy leaned forward.

"If we knew the layout and where she is," I said, "then we could make a plan, something on the order of diverting security, and so on. We don't even know where she is."

"Oh, I can find her office. It's right there in the Plex Central complex."

"I keep having this feeling that I don't have much time left." I was tattooing my hands across her entire back now.

Sandy sighed, rose, turned, and faced me. "I can pull a rabbit out of a hat, but it has a high probability of failure."

"What's a rabbit?"

"It's an old saying meaning a magic trick."

"The trick being?"

"The IG has access to any Plex fax, any station, and most operational data concerning Plex travel. If they haven't frozen up the system completely, I can find Merritt-Browne's home or work station destination code, and override security locks. Maybe."

"A plan they might have considered and taken measures to preclude." I thought. "If we come bursting out of a Plex station, we'd best be armed to the teeth."

She cocked her head. "You know something? You'd look like a pirate with a knife in your teeth."

I didn't know how to take that so I said, "If you're waiting on me, you're backing up. Let's eat and plan. Then let's do it."

We did.

Actually, what we did first was Sandy tried to comm Helen Merritt-Browne. The response was immediate. A high ranking security officer appeared on the screen and demanded she "come in" for urgent consultation.

"You can use me," I told her. "Tell them I forced you to help me break into ROAR. You'll be clear."

"Think what they did to General Kalhen. How do you think I'd fare?"

"Beats me. You're rather resourceful. You'd get by."

"We'll see." She looked like she was far away. Then she shook her head.

Whatever that meant.

She looked at me strangely. "We don't know enough. Roanoke gone and signals from intelligent aliens. It's not enough, Rusty. We've got to find out what's going on, who knows what."

I agreed. My concern was Roanoke. Her stake was the alien signals. However, since Kalhen was no longer the IG, her assignment might have changed. I mentioned that.

"It's a valid consideration," she said. "However, there is some high-level conspiracy." She took a long breath. "But we don't know that this alleged conspiracy is illegal, against criminal or moral codes—"

"Moral codes?"

"I was making a point. Change that to ethical behavior."

"It comes down to the fact that we need to talk to someone who knows what is going on, or as much as anyone can. And that's the head of the Plexus Net."

So we got to work on Plan B. How to use the Plex Net illegally and to our advantage.

What they had was a security lock. You couldn't translate to Merritt-Browne's office or home without first sending a comm and receiving approval. Sandy also found that the stations at the CEO's office and home were secure stations, meaning that you zapped in to a locked room or chamber and had to wait while someone eyeballed you through a window, and activated weapons detectors, explosives detectors, poison detectors, and, for all I knew, wart detectors.

When you translate in to a Plex station, you immediately move off the target plate. Sensitive or security stations have electronic or manned security posts. Once you're cleared, a door opens and you go in to wherever you just translated. The opening of the door automatically prevents any incoming translations until the door is closed and the area is again secure.

"You'll have to trust me," said Sandy.

I looked at her. "I trust you."

She had all the weapons.

I was the bait.

There's one absolute safeguard in the system. If someone is standing on the target plate, then the system *cannot* operate and translate anyone in. That way the same station can be used for incoming and outgoing travel.

Our plan hinged on Sandy's ability to translate in an instant after I stepped off the target plate.

I would remain on the plate until the security door opened so she could have the code input and execute order given already, and thus zap in once I stepped off the target plate. This was the critical point, the point of highest probability of failure. If for any reason, I stepped off the plate and the security door wasn't open, our plans were ruined. Not to mention we'd be captured and likely imprisoned.

We used a privacy curtain on this station so we could juggle weapons and equipment.

"Ready?" asked Sandy.

I nodded and touched her hand. "Good luck."

She looked at me in her funny way with her eyes slightly crossed. "Good luck? Me? *You're* the one who needs the luck." She stepped back and said, "Activate."

Zap.

I was standing in a station like any other station, but in a standard secured room. I fancied I could feel automatic detectors boring through me.

Lights glared and I felt like the escapee caught against the wall in the prison scene.

The natural thing for you to do is to step forward and thus off the target plate.

I didn't.

A voice through a speaker said, "Move out of the station."

I shaded my eyes with my left forearm and tried to look like a country boy in a big city. "Where in the *hell* am I?" Anything to divert their attention, to cause them one tiny bit of doubt. I didn't move forward, either. Sandy should be ready by now, should have already given instructions to the Plex. Her command-overriding must be working because I was here.

"Is this Billie-Joe's Barbecue Restaurant and Emporium?" I asked innocently. Keep 'em wondering.

"Come forward," the voice told me again.

"What *is* this? I get the wrong number?"

My forearm shading my eyes also kept them from having a real good look at my features, in case someone had enough foresight to paste my photo on the wall for recognition purposes.

"You have entered an unauthorized area." The voice was deep and held a note of exasperation.

I wished mightily that right now I was on a warm beach far, far away sipping on a peanut butter daiquiri in a tall, frosted glass, with Roanoke back in the right position in the sky and my bank account overflowing.

Time for offense. "I don't care what kind of area this is," I shouted, "get that light out of my eyes." The old angry citizen ploy.

Surprisingly, the light dimmed a bit and the door opened. I caught a glimpse of security uniforms entering and moved off the target plate.

Someone hollered. "Stay where you are."

"Says who?" My voice was belligerent.

I knew when I was out of the proximity of the translator because the air frazzed behind me.

Unfortunately, the door swished closed, locking two security men in here with us.

An odd hissing noise intruded.

I turned and there was Sandy, arm outstretched with stunner aimed.

At me.

She fired.

Tingling flashed over me. My innards were boiling

from being stunned at so close a range. Ordinarily, the setting is for farther away.

Immediately, my limbs disappeared from my repertoire of functional body parts.

I fell, struck sideways, bounced, and ended up on my shoulder and right chest looking toward the now-closed doorway.

"It looks like I got here just in time," Sandy said, dropping her stunner, not taking aim at the two gray-uniformed security guys.

The strange hissing continued.

The guards were wild-eyed and folded over, one at a time, surprise and anger showing on their faces.

A thunk beside me told me that Sandy had fallen to her knees.

Then she collapsed over me, face on my left shoulder, sandy hair splayed over my face so I couldn't see.

She smelled pleasant.

Which was the last nice fragrance I'd breathe for a while.

Being already on the floor, it took the gas longer to reach me.

As I faded from consciousness, I felt Sandy's soft breath stirring her hair, brushing my cheek.

Sort of receding quickly from the present, hard world, I plunged into darkness wondering at Sandy's duplicity.

12: ZAPPED

The woman was dressed in black. Black slacks, black toreador shirt, black band around a chock of her black hair. I suspect she wore red contacts, because her eyes shining red seemed more of a calculated effect than a natural occurrence.

She was middle-aged and her face was hard, augmented by her high forehead which, in turn, was emphasized because of her hair being swept up and tied.

Helen Merritt-Browne.

I sat in front of her in one of those executive restraining chairs that use a stun field so that the occupant is at the mercy of the person with the controls. They can let you move a little or a lot, by degrees. The thing is so fine-tuned, a good operator can allow you to restore movement in your legs or your arms and not the other.

Sandy was standing next to a guy in Plex Net security clothes. He looked like he had an air of command about him. Additionally, now that the cobwebs were receding and I was able to concentrate, I saw he was familiar. The dark presence on the aircar landing. Hair over his forehead down toward his brows, a compact, muscled man whose eyes darted constantly. It didn't take much to figure he was the one who'd planted the bomb.

Sandy was drinking something from a cup, likely a potion which helps counteract the residual effects of the stunner—or disabling gas.

"You did well, O'Clock," said dash Browne.

Sandy looked at me then away as if embarrassed. She sort of shrugged. "I had to play along until I found out all he knew." A statement which was quite out of order considering all we'd gone through together. It could well be that she'd seen her opportunity to double-cross me and taken her chance. This reasoning would allow her to get back into the good graces of the Plex Net management and explain why she'd waited so long to return to duty. It was beginning to make my choice not to tell her about Dad's message, et al, appear a wise move.

My head hurt. My mouth felt like it was full of decaying peanut shells, dry and icky. I tried to work up some saliva but was unsuccessful.

The shoulder and right side I'd struck when falling were beginning to ache. The restraining chair doesn't take as much out of you, and your innards fare a lot better because of it. My problem was that Sandy had frazzed me from such a short distance. Not to mention that being topped off by the disabling gas. We should have figured on secondary and tertiary security levels. When you're guarding one of the most important people in the galaxy, you're gonna have to have fail-safes even spacers can't overcome.

I guess I'd been suffering from a severe case of over-confidence. While it helps your humility quotient to be taken down a peg or two when you're a spacer and riding too high, this wasn't the time for me.

"He knows nothing," said Sandy with a sneer. She straightened. The potion was reinvigorating her. "Except he is aware of the communication from the aliens."

Browne was perched on the corner of a desk. This must be her office in her home. Sandy had been able to dig out Merritt-Browne's destination code from the database. Or so I thought. From what happened, it's possible that Sandy already knew the right code. We'd decided to make the attempt at the CEO's home where the security would probably be less than in the middle of Plex Central.

"And what do you know?" Browne asked Sandy.

"Not much, Madame. I disintegrated the Sunday report I told you about."

"That was good thinking, as was your effort to keep this, this spacer from meddling in our affairs."

"It's come to my attention," Sandy said slowly and with measured words, "that the position of the Inspector General is open."

Browne shot Sandy an appreciative glance. Apparently, the Plex boss could relate to Sandy's opportunism.

"I like the way you think, Agent O'Clock. I moved up the career ladder in much the same fashion. I have use for people of your talents—and quick thinking ability. I'm still amazed at your ability to make the Net do as you wish."

Sandy was avoiding looking at me.

"The priority problem is disposal," Merritt-Browne said. She looked at me distastefully. "I don't suppose it's worth our time to question him?"

"No, Madame," said Sandy.

"He knows too much to send him over to Galacticon authorities—and they just might let him go. Incompetent bureaucrats." She watched me with interest. "He's causing too much attention to the Plex Net; we cannot trust him about Roanoke and now the aliens." She hesitated. "We do not want any more undue attention." She surveyed me. "I'd like to stay and observe; unfortunately, it's beneath my station. Churnenski?" Dash Browne nodded at the man "You and O'Clock take care of him." Her eyes glinted. "And do it right this time."

"We will," Churnenski said, his voice low and soft, oddly augmenting his dark presence. He probably did not appreciate the irony of me delivering myself to him after he'd twice failed to knock me off.

Helen Merritt-Browne left and Churnenski grinned. He worked a handcontrol unit and the chair rose and moved out of the room into a short corridor. At the end was a Plex station, probably a private, outgoing unit only, one designed for quick travel to avoid the security team and the secure room.

The chair stopped in front of the station.

Out of the periphery of my vision, I saw Sandy trailing behind us.

Both of them stopped beside me.

Churnenski produced a power gun and handed it to Sandy. "Kill him."

"Kill him?" She looked like somebody just strangled her.

I moved my mouth, suddenly full of saliva. Staring death in the face does that to me.

Sandy gazed at the weapon.

"Go ahead," Churnenski said.

"No guts, no glory," I managed to spit out.

She looked from me to Churnenski. "*You* kill him." Disdain crossed his face. "Me?"

"I'm no killer, you kill him," Sandy repeated.

Even these fancy executives were victims of the galactic-wide ennui.

"I've rank on you, O'Clock," he said. "Give me the weapon."

Sandy studied the power gun and handed it back to him.

Churnenski took the weapon and held it loosely. Absently, he moved his hands together and something snapped. I couldn't be certain, but I'd bet that earlier he'd removed the power pack and the whole episode had been designed to test Sandy. If it was, she hadn't fallen for it; and she was making a point that she was her own woman.

"Not if I'm the IG you don't." She glanced at me speculatively. "Look. I've a solution. Let's just put him in the station and send him somewhere he'll be out of the way."

"Nowhere," said Churnenski with a relieved smile. "We'll translate him to Nowhere. That's where Helen wants him sent. Technically, we will be guilty of nothing.''

Uh-oh.

My long fear of the Net rose in me like gorge.

I tried to remember the rumor about Nowhere. There were a few destinations which the Plex Net system would accept, but which did not exist. No beacon, no station, no target plate, no nothing. Nowhere. It was said the Net translated you out to the stars and you continue because it isn't aimed and there are no receptors, so your translated molecules just keep going until the energy dissipates and so do you.

''Do you know the code?'' the Plex security chief asked.

''Yes,'' said Sandy.

She punched in the code manually on the external control panel.

Churnenski stood behind her, observing over her shoulder, the energy weapon in his hand and not returned to his pocket. The point being, I'd say, that she'd better toe the line or she'd join me.

She turned to me and touched the control panel on the chair. ''I've a recorder going. I need you to tell Betsy to cooperate with me.''

''Hurry up,'' Churnenski said. ''Who's Betsy?''

''A ship. The reports are still in the ship's memory. I just have to find her, that's all.''

Since the authorities had long since confiscated Sandy's ship *Alfredo*, she might need another, and Betsy would be available. Opportunistic thinking. Sandy obviously didn't want Churnenski to know she knew where Betsy was located.

I felt like a fruit on a vendor's stand as customers argued over the best way to eat it.

The stun bonds were gone, but my body needed time to repair itself, regain its equilibrium. Sandy must've terminated the chair's stun field when she activated the recorder control.

''The ship will never respond to me,'' Sandy said, ''without your telling her to.''

I said nothing.

"She'll sit wherever you left her, probably forever, circling some dead star." That wasn't true, but Sandy was trying to keep Betsy's real location secret. I didn't think she had anything to worry about since nobody outside of Roanoke and a few scattered spacers remaining in Galacticon wanted to go into space anymore. "You wouldn't leave her to float alone through eternity, would you?"

Churnenski was stepping from foot to foot, acting impatient.

I sighed. "Betsy," I croaked. "I remand you into the temporary control of Gusselwaithe O'Clock."

Sandy frowned.

"Good," said Churnenski. "Let's get him into the station." He pocketed his gun.

"He's too heavy for me," Sandy said.

She touched the controls and the chair slid to the edge of the station.

"You push," Churnenski said, and began tugging me forward and out of the chair.

Sandy pushed on my back.

I sort of slumped out of the chair, my muscles still not responding, but raising hell with my brain.

Churnenski guided my fall.

My stomach was flip-flopping like a fish out of water. I was finding it difficult to breathe.

As I plopped onto the target plate, I saw Sandy's hand snake to the external controls and touch a keypad. What was she up to now?

Churnenski turned and moved aside to pass behind the chair. His attention hadn't been diverted for a second. If Sandy's intention had been to change the destination code to send me someplace other than Nowhere, she hadn't had time enough.

Churnenski moved the chair.

I lay there in an awkward bundle, muscles tingling as they came back to life—or, more accurately, nerves sending pain signals throughout my body.

"Do it," Churnenski said. "Send him to No-where."

My entire life I'd been apprehensive about translating through the Plex Net. Now I knew why. No more chunky peanut butter.

Sandy stood back, a wistful look on her face. "I'm sorry I have to do this, Rusty."

"Double-crosser—" was all I had time to get out.

"Execute," Sandy said with a hitch in her voice.

The last thing I had time to think was that at least she was a little bit sorry—

Zap.

13: NOWHERE

Apparently I was still alive.

I was still in the same awkward position.

"Why me, Lord?" I groaned.

Struggling to sit up against uncooperative muscles, I began to notice where I was.

The Plex station was open onto a room, no, make that an enclosure.

Something stank terribly.

Something started to howl horribly.

The odor was so bad it seemed to attack me.

My head hurt worse.

The howling went up and down the scale.

"Boy, this just ain't my day," I said, not knowing why I was talking to myself.

Faint light poked its way into the enclosure. It was like a primitive shack, built of nonuniform timber, small rock slabs, and mud. The roof had holes in it. Actually, there was more hole than roof, the strawlike material shedding all over and lying about in clumps.

The howling continued. I tried to spot whatever it was, but it must be through the entrance—and I was being charitable when I used the term "entrance." Whoever had built the shack just hadn't bothered to finish the wall at that point.

I connected the howling animal with the stench. I was in its place of residence and it had run out upon my startling arrival. Rather, from the noise, make that "they" instead of it.

My bones complained when I stood up straight. I knew there'd be aches and pains for days. After all, I'd been hit by a stun gun at less than minimum range, breathed disabling gas, and been imprisoned by a stun field chair. No, this wasn't my day.

Trying to breathe through my mouth only, I looked around.

"Uh-oh."

The Plex station contained neither internal nor external controls.

Just as some stations are outgoing only, some are designed solely for incoming travel.

I'd heard this was how they treated prison planets, though with the dearth of crime along with the creeping malaise, I wasn't sure they needed prison planets any longer.

I'd been sent to where you can't translate back from. Uh-oh.

Something squished beneath my left foot and I smelled the stench worse and the animals howled louder and I felt like I'd been dropped from a mile up and my head wanted to explode.

However, it never occurred to me that I'd be better off dead.

I simply decided I'd have to show these groundhogs a thing or two about being a spacer. But a painkiller chased by a heaping bowl of peanut butter and okra soup would have put me on the road to recovery—and a bath would have been a godsend.

Limping over to the opening, I peered out.

Four fat, hairy brown things scurried away from the opening, squealing and howling. Watching my step, I made it over a low fence.

There was a chill in the air—but I will say that the air was fresh and untainted. Which I didn't like one bit; that is, it didn't auger well for high tech.

Leaning against the fence, I surveyed the surroundings.

This was a tiny plateau on the side of a mountain. Off to my left, a stream ran down the mountain onto this plateau, from which in turn it tumbled through a series of terraces below. Farther downhill from the terraces, a pioneer type village sat against a lake.

How I knew it was a pioneer village was that there wasn't any look of manufactured anything. Nor did any of the dwellings, buildings, appear standard. Doors and windows were open, telling me environmental control was nonexistent. I scanned the sky for signs of aircars. Nope.

On this plateau, over toward the stream, was a house. It was built of staunch local timber and what I'd call adobe on another planet. I didn't know what they called it here. I didn't think I wanted to know what they called it here. In fact, I could tell there were a whole lot of things here I didn't want to know anything about and I had this terrible feeling that I was going to have to learn anyway.

A woman was hurrying across the yard from the house. She was tall and wore a real dress. When she got closer, I could tell her face was weather-worn, but not unattractive. Her hands were strong and she patted back a strand of hair. She was the stereotype grandmother type the ad agencies like so much. There was a familiar look about her.

"Hello," she said, stopping in front of me. She surveyed me. "They don't send many here anymore. I've seen them come in hungover, and I've seen them come in physically beaten. You look like both." She scrunched her face and put her hand to her nose. "Pee-you. You got into tinit manure."

I tried to look hurt. A little sympathy always goes a long way. "I don't know what you call them, but yes, I got into it."

She smiled in sympathy and the world brightened. Some people have that empathetic ability. I recognized that smile; I'd seen it before and then it had been cruder, not yet tempered by years and years of hard life.

"What is it, young man? Why do you look at me that way?"

I shook my head to rid it of haunting devils. "It can't be."

She took my arm. "Are you all right? You seem a tad woozy."

I steadied myself. "Gusselwaithe sent me here."

She shrieked. An honest to God one hundred percent shriek.

My already bursting head reacted by exploding. I still wasn't controlling my limbs all that well and I slid down against the fence. Even though on the outside of the fence, I didn't want to think about what was on the ground.

"I am Edna O'Clock," the woman said, wrapping her hands in the large fold on the front of her dress. "I'm Gus' grandmother."

"The resemblance is there."

Through all the pain and discomfort, I wondered just exactly what in the hell was going on. Obviously Sandy had changed destination codes when Churnenski was dumping me so unceremoniously into the Plex station.

Edna said, "Now come on, we've got to get you taken care of."

She dragged me to the house—and past it to the stream. She pointed at a pool at the edge of the plateau from which the water poured over the lip and down the streambed to the farming terraces.

"Wash," she directed.

I stepped back. "Me? It's cold here."

"Aw, don't you be afraid of a little cold water." She ran her eyes up and down my frame. "A big fellow like you shouldn't be. Are you?"

Ulp. "No, ma'am." Hadda keep up my image. Being a spacer ain't easy all the time.

"And wash your jumpsuit. It looks like one of those quick-dry things."

"It is."

"Good. Wash and I'll bring you a towel."

Debating whether to get my boots wet, I saw a clay pipe leading out of the stream above the pool, meaning they got their drinking water above here. So I didn't have to worry whether the tinit manure would foul their water supply.

I gritted my teeth and walked into the water. It took all the composure I had remaining to keep from screaming. I took off my boots and scrubbed them with sand. I tossed my jumpsuit up on a rock to dry.

The icy cold water repaired my aching muscles by simply numbing them to where I could feel nothing.

Shortly, I was sitting at the rough-hewn table in homespun and a work shirt which was actually big enough to fit me.

Fortunately, Grandpa O'Clock was my size. His name was Major Linewood O'Clock.

We ate, a pleasant affair with a fireplace burning wood which gave off a savory aroma behind us.

The meal was simple: biscuits, a bowl of greens, and a meat called cham, one with a faint wild taste. I drank a warm fruit drink which tasted peppery.

Feeling had crept back into me, and the food and drink were helping me return to human status.

Keeping my own counsel, I answered all the obligatory questions about "Gus."

"She's fine and in good health, the last time I saw her." Stuff like that. I couched my answers in general terms, vague enough not to commit myself. Not until I found out what game Sandy was playing, and not until I discovered what I was doing on a no-tech world.

I was looking forward to making a quick exit and getting back into the thick of things. Roanoke was waiting for me to find it. I hoped.

Major O'Clock was weatherbeaten like you think of outdoorsmen. His short beard was sandy. Apparently he was a farmer up here on the side of the mountain.

"Bristlebrush, that's the name of this world," he told me. "A fine world, one sculpted by glaciers time and time again."

I took the opportunity. "Listen. How far is it to the nearest Plex fax?"

They looked at me strangely. I was getting a lot of that lately.

"Or just any Plex station," I said. "I'm good at walking. I can walk all day and into tomorrow." I waited expectantly.

"That could be the reason he was evasive about our granddaughter," the old man said.

Edna gave me a sympathetic pat on the hand. "We do not know what happened to you, but Gus should have told you. This is the end of the line. There is no escape from Bristlebrush."

"I don't think I want to hear any more," I said choking on a biscuit and thick, rich gravy.

Grandpa pointed toward the shack. "We live up here to watch the Plex station. Used to be people came through frequently, but no longer. It is an incoming station only. There is no other Plex station or facility on Bristlebrush."

I gulped and had to drink some of the fruit drink to clear my throat. "Ah, could there possibly be a space-port? Perhaps any type of space transport?"

Grandpa turned to Grandma. "They send the malcontents, but most of them have been averse to space—"

"Until now," Edna put in.

Major leaned back. "Not in my time." He glanced guiltily at his wife. "Not in our time, I should say, Grandma. Not for us anyway." He snapped his fingers. "Nothing frightened us. We were going to take the universe by the horns and—"

Edna rose and went to him. "Now, now, darlin', do not get started." She eyed me angrily. "See what you've done? You got him started."

"Why, I—" said Major.

"You-all remind me a lot of your granddaughter," I said. I thought, like interrupting all the time and going on about philosophy of life, and always having an opinion about everything—and offering it.

"Why, thank you," said Grandma.

"Um, maybe you could tell me why Bristlebrush has no other Plex station?"

"Don't you know?" Edna's eyebrows were lifted high.

"Know what? Ah, um, this, er, me coming here was kind of a last minute thing. I didn't have time for the in-depth research you seem to think I should have done."

Major slapped his leg. "I knew it! They knocked him out and shipped him here unconscious. He never knew what hit him."

Edna looked worried. "I don't know about that, Grandpa. Where does Gus fit in?"

That was something I'd like to know, too.

Continuing, Grandma said, "Hon, he told me Gus sent him here."

"She *wouldn't!*" The old man was aghast.

"She did," I said. I ate another slice of cham. I didn't think it was fowl or fish. At least it wasn't that smelly tinit animal.

"She wouldn't do such a thing to a friend," Grandpa said, eying me suspiciously.

"I can see I'm going to have to tell you the whole story," I said, trying to lessen the hostility in the room.

"Aye, that you are, young fellow." He was getting quite impersonal.

While it was possible they were lying to me about the lack of Plex faxes and stations hereabouts, I believed them. I'd never heard of an inhabited world without Plex Net facilities, except a newly discovered world that hadn't got a Plex beacon yet.

So here I was.

Stuck.

Abandoned.

Nowhere.

Bristlebrush with no escape.

And twenty-two days and a bit.

14: BRISTLEBRUSH

" And that's how I wound up here," I finished. The story had taken longer than I thought it would.

We were sitting in front of the fire, Granny in a rocking chair, Grandpa in a rocking chair, and me on the floor near the hearth. I was drinking pure mountain water from a clay cup and it was as good or better than any water I'd ever drunk.

"That shore is a strange story, son," Major Linewood O'Clock said.

Edna said nothing, she just rocked. But her intelligent eyes told me she was digesting what I'd told them.

"I wonder what happened to that planet Roanoke?" Grandpa said.

"I'd like to know that, too," I said.

"Obviously your priority is to get off Bristlebrush and back on your quest," said Grandma.

"Yes, ma'am."

"Wisht you could," said Grandpa.

"Damn," I said.

The old man cocked a warning eye at me.

"Sorry," I muttered.

We were silent for a minute.

"Why can't you leave Bristlebrush?" I asked. "I never heard of a place you can't leave if you want—if you can afford the passage."

The old man's eyes narrowed. "We're expatriates, expelled, banished, disenfranchised; we're exiles, outcasts—"

"Major—" Edna said in a tired voice. She'd heard it all before. "*I* will tell him." She turned to me. "The population of Bristlebrush is comprised of people banished from their home worlds—and those offspring born here."

"Those sons of—"

"I'm not finished yet, dear," said Edna in a firm voice. "As I was saying, we were cast out and away from the planet Tanapeg because we, uh—" She glanced at her husband.

"Rebelled," said Major, his voice strong and vibrant. "Those Casper Milquetoasts were afraid of their own shadows. The government was not a free one, not elected by the people, nor was it a representative government comprised of representatives selected by the people. I chose to speak out—"

"We," his wife corrected.

"Right. We spoke out and they didn't appreciate it and zapped us here to this planet of exiles."

"We didn't simply 'speak out' as he'd have you believe," Edna told me. "Uh, we sort of bombed the seat of government—"

"Nobody got kilt," said Major, sitting up straighter in his rocker. He was swishing back and forth much faster than he had right after dinner.

"It was just a small building—" Edna started.

The old man snorted. "It wasn't all that small. During the day it was full of bureaucrats."

"Unfortunately, they had concealed security cameras," Grandma continued, "and in the morning they came for us."

"No trial, no judge, no nothing," said Grandpa.

"That's the kind of government it was," she said.

"They zapped us to Galacticon Central and a holding room," Major continued.

"Then they zapped us here," said Grandma.

"Why haven't I ever heard of this?" I wanted to know.

"You're here, ain'tcha, son?"

I had to admit that was true.

"Apparently it's not a widely known thing," Edna said. "Just top government people on the planets seem to be aware of that use of the Plex Net."

"I'm on the board of directors of Roanoke," I said. "I ought to have heard about banishment to Bristlebrush."

"The boy's got a point," said Major.

I didn't want to say I wasn't a boy so I didn't, as much as it called for saying.

Edna was looking at me with nothing else but admiration. "Board of directors? You? You must be a very important person."

"Not on Roanoke. On Roanoke everybody's important."

"But still, you're a ruler."

I shook my head. "The board of directors simply approves or disapproves what the managing director does. He runs the planet. The rest of us go our own way. The whole set-up is based on maintaining as little government as possible. If and when there's a big issue, the managing director calls a plebiscite and whatever everybody decides is what happens." I smiled at a memory. "Dad is currently running Roanoke—or so I hope. He used to quote somebody named Lao-Tze. 'Govern as you would cook a small fish; do not overdo it.' That's what Dad says."

Edna nodded approvingly.

"How does someone your age get to be on the board of directors?" Grandpa had slowed his rocking.

I stood and sat on the hearth, my back starting to warm too much. I felt uncomfortable. "They needed an active spacer and I was nominated and voted in."

The old man nodded. "Political connections, I knew it."

"Not at all," I said. "While my father is managing director and my grandfather discovered and founded the colony, I earned my position by merit. My dad and grandfather both voted against me—"

"Why is that?" Edna asked, picking up on something in my voice.

"Because I don't always agree with them and they knew they'd have to do a lot more public explaining and get more 'no votes' from the board of directors."

"That figgers," said Major. "Nepotism, it always falls apart."

"It's not nepotism," I said. "And it's not falling apart, either."

"If you say so." He sat back smugly.

"Still, I never heard a whisper of the banishment code thing, destination Bristlebrush."

"They must have a couple of other planets they do the same with," said Grandpa, " 'cause remember I said not so many people come through here anymore. We put them stinkin' tinits at the station to warn us."

"You know," said Edna, "the reason you might never have heard of this is because you're eligible."

"For what?" I asked.

"To come here."

"Me?"

"You are here, I already pointed out," Major said.

"I am," I said, throat constricting.

"That's not what I mean," Grandma said. "You told us your Roanoke citizens dislike government, that Roanoke actually has very little government."

"That's correct." I shifted so my back wouldn't spontaneously ignite.

"The Galacticon authorities don't like rebels and misfits," she continued. "You can tell by the very existence of Bristlebrush. It sounds to me like you've an entire planet full of rebels."

She was right.

"Or," said the old man, "it could be that Roanoke wasn't big enough or in business as a viable member of Galacticon long enough to merit them telling you people about all their dirty secrets and tricks." He rocked some more and looked more smug than before.

"That's true, too," I said. It could be all of those reasons—or none.

As I was performing quantum leaps in logical de-

ductions and reasoning, I moved away from the fire
and leaned against a rough wall.

"I see he's thinking about it," observed Grandpa.

"It doesn't take him long at all," said Edna. "I'm
glad our Gus likes him."

I missed the comment the first time my mind thought
about it. "If Galacticon does stuff like that, it wouldn't
bother them to do away with an entire planet, then,
would it?"

"Nope," said Major, "not a bit. A mere fifty thousand people don't mean nothin' to them."

"But I don't *know* that."

"You got any better ideas?"

"I don't have *any* ideas." I shook my head. "What
do you mean Gus likes me?"

"You're here, aren't you?" said Major. That was
the third time he'd said it and was becoming his ubiq-
uitous answer to everything.

"Yes, I am." I thought back. "If Galacticon has
several top secret Plex codes, banishment destinations, then perhaps they're all alpha-numeric, or se-
quential or something with single digit differentiations.
Helen Merritt-Browne and security chief Churnenski
wanted to zap me to the next galaxy forever and
Sandy—Gus—changed one digit. And here I am."

"That's what I been saying," Grandpa said.

To keep from groaning, I paced.

"Why do you keep calling Gus 'Sandy?'" Edna
asked.

Suddenly, I was embarrassed. This couple's son or
daughter or in-law or somebody or other had given
Sandy the name Gusselwaithe. And my prejudice
against the name would be an insult.

"Um," I said intelligently and quickly, "ah, rather,
I," that's it, "I didn't know her name at first and the
situation wasn't such that I could ask so I simply called
her 'Sandy' after her striking looking hair. I can see
where she gets it—and her looks, too." I stopped in
front of Edna O'Clock and looked down at her.

Grandma blushed and I knew I'd won a round and

maybe more. "Aw, shucks. You didn't have to go and say that."

"Well, it's true." Strike while the iron is hot, I always say. Also, the opportunity might not come again.

I moved back. "So how is it that Gusselwaithe got her name? It certainly is unusual."

"Our son and his wife selected the name," Edna said.

"Ask them," said Major.

"Them?" said Edna. "You mean her."

The old man shook his head. "He's dead. Long gone. A fine son."

Edna wiped the corner of her eye with her apron. It occurred to me then I hadn't seen an apron in—now that I thought of it, I'd never seen anyone wear an apron.

They were silent, and the silence was awkward, so I didn't follow up the question. Instead I asked the question about the glaring inconsistency.

"If you were banished to Bristlebrush, and you cannot leave and there is no outgoing Plex station, why is it that, um, Gus, is out there in the galaxy and not marooned here?"

"Bright fellow." Major's voice regained its initial enthusiasm. "I been wonderin' when you'd put two and two together."

"And?" I prompted.

"See, we were the ones banished. Our son did nothing against Galacticon or our home world Tanapeg. He was born here on Bristlebrush. And married here to a woman who was born here of penal parents—"

"Exiled," his wife corrected.

"That's what I said, Edna. Am I telling this or are you?"

I didn't care *who* told it so long as it got told.

"Go ahead, dear," Edna said sweetly.

"If you aren't the one banished from Galacticon, you can leave Bristlebrush."

Many things occurred to me to ask right then and I almost choked getting the important two ready to fire.

Asking the easy one first, I said, "Why, then, if there are people born here who've moved into the galactic mainstream, hasn't the general public heard of these exile planets? They should no longer be secret."

"First off," Major said, "Most of 'em *don't* leave here, anyway. I don't actually know about the existence of other exile planets; I'm just speculating about them. Most people stay here. While they're offspring of rebellious type people, that don't mean they're adventurous themselves."

I nodded. "They share the growing angst about space travel and so on?"

"Exactly," he said. "Secondly, to get off Bristlebrush, they got to go to a staging planet and live and work there a long time. And thirdly, they got to sign a statement that they won't tell anybody." He grumped. "Even if they break their written promise, the galaxy is so big, there can't be but a couple of these refugees in each sector and then people gotta believe them. And these same people don't believe in space travel anymore, they ain't gonna believe or even worry about a planet of outcasts, exiles, expatriates—"

"Major—" interrupted Edna.

"Along with reduced Plex travel," I said. "The pattern repeats itself."

"Yep."

Remembering something, I told them about the story in the Sector News that Marion Zernicke ran and the zero response to date. I made a mental note to check back with her to see if she'd gotten anything new since I left. Perhaps contact from one of the few Roanokean spacers that had been out for a short time. There could only be a couple of them in my situation—if that. There were a few more out for longer terms, on contracts and so on, that I could think of. I think I knew the answer beforehand: Nope, it's a big galaxy.

It also occurred to me that the more spacers who were on Roanoke, the more people who'd disappeared, too. I wrenched my thoughts back to the present.

"Your butt's gonna burn," Major said, pointing.

I jumped. It was hot as the hinges on the gates of hell.

"It wouldn't have bothered me if you wasn't wearing my pants," he said.

"Right. Listen. How, exactly, does one get off Bristlebrush if one isn't an exile—" I moved farther away.

"Or an expatriate, an outcast, a banee, a cashiered—"

"Major," warned Edna.

"Yes, dear, but he got me started."

"Rusty," Edna addressed me formally, as if trying out my name to see if she liked it. "They come by sometimes on an aperiodic basis—"

"Means irregular, son," said Major snidely as if to get even with her.

"And they take you to the staging planet."

"Which is?"

"T-hoe."

"Tee-ho?"

"No, T-hoe, just like it sounds."

"Yes, ma'am." I stepped back to the cooler, darkened room behind me. "They make the people who leave from here stay on T-hoe, that's what you said?"

"I did." She rocked away contentedly.

"I thought *I* said that," Major said.

"Did you?" She hmmmmmed for a minute. "Maybe you did at that."

"That's what I said."

"Well, I'm sorry, dear. Go ahead."

He looked at her, then at me, then back to her. "Go ahead with what?"

"Telling him what he wanted to know."

"Oh." He glanced at me. "What was that?"

Trying to keep myself calm, I took a deep breath. "Ah, you were beginning to address the manner in which people can depart Bristlebrush for T-hoe."

"Oh, that. We get enough people to support the trip, we comm for an old Navy ship."

"Comm?"

"Sure. We've a radio. Above us in a geosynchronous orbit, there's a Plex beacon. It relays our radio signal to the Navy. The one old ship which comes to this system sometime—''

"In case of medical emergencies like back in cycle dash sixty two," said Edna.

"That's what I was saying," said Major. "As I was saying, they come along, send a shuttle down, take those non-exilees who want to the beacon buoy and zap 'em off to T-hoe."

It was all beginning to make sense to me. "Another roadblock. You have to go into *space* and translate through a Plex station both to get out of here."

"Exactly," he said. "It surely cuts down on the number of applicants."

"I don't suppose the life and obligatory work on T-hoe is very pleasant, either."

"Nope, not a bit from what I hear." He pulled out a knife and a stick and began whittling.

"Major!" demanded Edna.

"What?"

"Do you want to sweep and clean the house your own self, you just keep right on whittling."

"Oh, ah, sorry. I got carried away answering all these infernal questions." He eyed me suspiciously. "You ain't thinking of leaving, are you?"

"Me?"

I was thinking in terms that if I got near a Plex station, I was a goner. Anywhere in the galaxy.

Though I had no money or ID—they'd removed all that when searching me. I guess the few IDs I had on my person at the time, lifted from pax at the Plex fax, had sort of preconvicted me. But a resourceful person like me shouldn't have much trouble ah, liberating some funds somewhere.

"You can't get there from here," Major pointed out. "Not to mention the fact that you're now a banishee, an exile, an outcast—"

"Major—" said his wife automatically.

"Yes, Edna. That is to say, your name is in their files and in the Plex data banks. The Plex Net won't take you anywhere."

"I was thinking of borrowing the radio," I said, thinking I could raise spacer help.

The old man shook his head. "It is a special channel. The computer in the beacon up there processes it and comms it through the Plex link to the one Navy ship. That's it. No other comm destinations are allowed."

And radio waves would take forever plus to get anywhere to help me. With Roanoke gone, I wasn't sure who'd help me anyway. My bank on D'Earnhardt maybe. Marion Zernicke for the news story maybe. Hyman Bookbinder would help.

But not one of those people would dare buck Galacticon in the open, and doubtfully under the table. And not one of those people would dare put one foot in space to come and rescue me.

I didn't think Betsy was smart enough to do so, even if I knew the coordinates of Bristlebrush to give her, which I didn't. Also, I'd have to kind of word around my instructions to Betsy on the comm link.

I could think of only one spacer who had the guts and the wherewithall to rescue me.

But did "Gus" have the desire? She'd saved my life, sure. However, she was now running with elite company. She'd wanted the IG job, hadn't she?

It didn't matter anyway; I couldn't get word to her— or to anybody, for that matter.

No Plex station, no spaceship.

This was a dead end all right.

Marooned.

"—now, Major," Edna was saying and he shut up and glared at her.

Marooned with them for the rest of my life.

Why me, Lord?

15: DRUPPLINGBROO

Turning the ballcock, I drew another cup of what I'd decided was the best water I'd ever run across. The plumbing affair was crude, but it worked.

Next I found the outhouse and, as I was returning to the O'Clock's warm home, I recalled Sandy saying she didn't know what an outhouse was. Had she been jesting, having a joke at my expense? The O'Clocks called it a "privy." Maybe the word outhouse wasn't used here. The contradictions made me wonder about a few more.

"It's time for bed, Grandma," Major said when I came back in.

"Excuse me, may I ask a couple of more questions?"

They looked at each other and Edna said, "I guess so."

"I got to get up early and slop the tinits," Major said. "Make it snappy. Say, if you help me, we could clean out the pen, too." He looked expectant.

I've learned you have to take a few hits in life to get along. So, much against my will and my already rebelling nose, I said, "Yessir."

"Good." He sank back into his rocker and stroked his beard.

"Has Gus ever visited you?"

Grandpa snorted. "Not likely."

"Why is that?"

"It's a one-way Plex station."

"She's a spacer, she could have traveled here on a starship."

"Not if she don't know the coordinates."

"Right," I said. "It is a big galaxy. And I suppose that the Galacticon government doesn't give out that data, or allow it to be known."

"I heard you can't even retrace your route when you go from here to T-hoe," Grandpa said.

So much for that avenue.

"Gus used to send us stuff through the Plex station," Edna put in. "Books and things. Then she sent a mini-power plant and some lights and an environmental control apparatus."

I looked around the primitive cabin.

"We don't have it anymore," Grandma said. "We gave it all to the hospital."

"Then it stopped," Major said. "The shipments."

When no one continued, I asked, "Why?"

"One fellow carried a letter with him some time later," Major said. "It was from Gus and she explained that she'd been caught sending stuff. She also went on to tell us that they'd adjusted the Plex destination code for Bristlebrush—and presumably other exile planets—which disallowed the translating of any inanimate objects by themselves, that is without people being translated here, too. And a branch of security checks each person coming here to insure he or she don't bring nothing proscribed."

Both Grandma and Grandpa O'Clock were probably crazy, and they used discordant words in country-fied convoluted sentences; and not least, they were driving *me* crazy. Nonetheless, I liked them a lot. I felt a trust between us.

"It wouldn't have taken her long to think it through," I said, thinking it through myself. "She could have sent a nav-aids computer to you, and you could have shown it the night sky, and it would have identified the location of Bristlebrush, spelling out the coordinates. Then all you had to do was to just send the info out with the next people heading for T-hoe,

to in turn send with the next Bristlebushers to be freed
into the galaxy.''

"Bristle*brushians*,'' Major corrected. "And that's
what I always said. But Galacticon was one jump ahead
of us. They stopped it in time.''

"She'd send us food and things to read,'' said Edna
wistfully. "It took her years to reach a position where
she learned our Plex station's code.''

Remembering something, I asked, "Who's Alfredo?''

"Beats me,'' said Grandma.

"Is that a first name or a last name or what,
Sonny?'' said Major.

"I don't know.''

"Why'd you want to know?'' he asked.

Uncomfortable, I shrugged. "It's just somebody Gus
mentioned once. I thought I'd ask.''

"Dunno about that,'' said Grandpa, "sounds like
one of them furreners with one of them turbans on his
head. It's a weird name.''

This from people with names like theirs? And Gusselwaithe?

I slept on a pallet in the attic where, Grandma told
me, "little Gus'' used to sleep when she was a very
young girl and just before she and her parents made
the one-way trip to T-hoe. While the gravity wasn't
the way I like it for sleep, still I was a spacer and
could sleep anytime, anywhere. That was about as
comfortable a sleep as I'd had in years. Perhaps it was
due to all I'd gone through and my body needed it to
catch up and restore itself. Nonetheless, I slept comfortably and well.

In the morning, I helped Major slop the tinits and
clean out the pen. Then we did some more bucolic-
type chores which, while menial, were not all that dis-
tasteful. Power, electronics, mechanization would have
increased the output of the farm and greatly decreased
the input of human labor.

Of course, when we were done, Edna wouldn't let

us in for breakfast without first we took a bath in the pool. Also of course, the pool had cooled considerably from the overnight cold air and lack of solar heating. Finally, of course, I stuck my head under the water and screamed until I ran out of air.

Breakfast was traditionally large.

I spent all afternoon clearing bristlebrush and planning. Twenty-one days and a fraction left. Bristlebrush is like the old-timey tumbleweeds, but grows high and tall and never stops. It grows anywhere anytime with little or no water and nutrition. It also grows from root division, so there's a lot of it. It was the dominant native vegetation—hell, it was the dominant life-form, if you want to call it that, on the planet. I could see no reason for the plant whatsoever. It did no good, it provided nothing, except more of itself. It was weather resistant and had no natural enemies. It made about as much sense as poetry.

However, Bristlebushers, make that Bristlebrushians, spent much of their time keeping bristlebrush away from their crops and property.

Could this be the true penance the Galacticon authorities were extracting?

There were a couple of million exiles eking out a living from the land of Bristlebrush. This fact made me more optimistic. That many people ought to produce *some* kids who wanted to get off Bristlebrush, even for T-hoe.

The next night I couldn't sleep. I tossed and turned until I found the cause: in the pallet stuffing, I must have dislodged some stones cached in a corner, and they'd made their way to beneath my body. After removing them, I slept well.

In the morning I pocketed them. After my ablutions, I went inside to see if Major was ready.

He was already gone, but Edna was stoking the stove and saw me.

I was looking at the stones, three of them, highly polished by some river, I supposed. They had odd facets and reflected light well. Their natural color was from milky to clear. They weren't gemstones exactly, but could have been on some other world at some other time.

Edna walked by and saw them. "I haven't seen those for years." She sighed. "Gus found them in the bay, and she always carried them around." Edna sighed again. "She used to say they reminded her of the stars at night. I'd tell her tales of the galaxy and all the myriad peoples and worlds and she'd get that far-off look and take out her stones and rub them together and just stare at them." Grandma shook her head. "Little girls are too wonderful a commodity to grow up." She walked off shaking her head.

I looked thoughtfully at the stones, put them in my pocket and went to find Major and what new torturous chores he'd devised for me.

We spent days and evenings visiting likely candidates for T-hoe, me doing my best to persuade them to sign up to leave Bristlebrush. Time was speeding faster than I liked. The one hundred days were dwindling to a precious few, namely fifteen, when the Galacticon Navy arrived.

Commander Drupplingbroo was a little squatty guy with a pot belly. Only the high tech fiber on his uniform saved it from appearing to have seen better days. Drupplingbroo had a red face and appeared to be of retirement age.

He was the "local" Galacticon Space Navy Officer, or GSNO, or, as he liked to call himself, GALSPANAVOFF.

I was the last one of the group of Bristlebushers— Bristlebrushians—to be processed.

Major O'Clock had found a man, offspring of exiles, who was eligible to leave Bristlebrush but had no interest in doing so. A little neighborly pressure and bang, I got to fill his bill. I dressed in a set of his homespun clothes, cut my hair as he had, and memorized his family history and details. Bristlebrush wasn't much for paperwork, so that wasn't a problem.

Commander Drupplingbroo stood at the access to the shuttle he'd brought from his ship to ferry the emigrants to the Plex beacon above.

I outlined who I was supposed to be, gave him a family history, told him I was single and wanted to make my way into the galaxy.

"Why?" he asked unexpectedly.

I ran my finger under the rough collar of my workshirt and stared at him. "Because it's there."

"That doesn't answer the question." His voice was high, squeaky, and irritating.

"Well, I just decided a man's gotta do what a man's gotta do." My beard was more than stubble now and I couldn't stand the thing. It was all itchy underneath and made my neck feel like real bristlebrush was growing on it.

"What's a man gotta do?" he wanted to know.

I decided I was past the cliché stage and better come up with something more concrete. "This here Bristlebrush doesn't expand my horizons. And I've always dreamed of going in space."

He looked at me askance. "There's lots of dreamers, not many doers." He propped an eye open higher. "You're not wet behind the ears. You look like you've been around. How come is it that you want to depart now?"

I hadn't planned on all this questioning, but a spacer is never without answers, even if you have to lie to make them up. "Um, it's my girl. Or she was my girl, dammit. She didn't want anythin' to do with this, now she's up and run off with that Ollivant fellow from the village Glascow. I just packed my backpack and come here."

Drupplingbroo shook his head. "They'll do it to you every time. Go ahead, young fellow. Right there, ah, hold it in front of the screen. That's called a Body Matcher, or BM for short. Look into the screen, yeah, that's the way. It's got to match cornea details. Spit into the cup, go ahead, it won't bite your tongue. That'll be the DNA analyzer, aka Danny. Ooops. While the BM and Danny are processing, I couldn't help but notice that big knife. It stands right out on the scope."

My mind was racing. BM? DNA analyzer? You didn't have to be a professor of astrophysics to realize I was in deep trouble.

"That little old thing? That's my hunting knife. I don't go anywhere without it."

The commander was staring at a readout screen. "That's a fact, son, because these readouts say you aren't who you say you are and you aren't going anywhere, not with me."

"Ah," I gurgled. "There must be some mistake?"

"Hot nardly," he said spooneristically. "The BM sometimes stinks it works so bad, but Danny Boy never makes a mistake."

"Well, er, ah, I've got to leave Bristlebrush." My mind was working at translight speed.

"I knew there was some other reason."

"My girl's pa? He wants real bad I should marry up with her and that isn't at the top of my list."

"On the run, eh?"

"Yes, sir, Commander."

"Well, I can't help you, fellow. Regulations. You understand." He nodded patronizingly. He killed the electronics for the BM and Danny.

"Please?"

He stood aside and pointed down the ramp. "Soon's you clear, I close up and we're goners. Get off my ship."

I sighed and produced the knife.

With the glistening edge, I caressed Drupplingbroo's throat. "It makes me terribly angry I wasted time growing this damn beard and putting up with the damn thing. Maybe you can tell I'm mad?"

"I can that, fellow. Hah, hah. Take it easy, okay? Ho nard feelings."

"Just close up and get this barge into space."

He did so. I sat next to him in the copilot's chair, holding onto my hunting knife.

Through the window I waved at Edna and Major O'Clock who stood watching on a hill above. I believe they saw me wave, because they returned the gesture. I'd offered to hijack the shuttle and take them, but they said they were happy with their life now and didn't want to go back to the Galacticon which had exiled, outcast, abolished, banished, etc. them. Now I was hijacking it anyway.

Drupplingbroo rocketed into space with a faster than necessary take off. I could tell he was angry. Doubtless, he had never encountered nor ever thought of any kind of resistance to his formal position, especially from the docile animals humans were fast becoming.

On the other hand, I thought that he had acquiesced to my demands rather easily.

His starship was anchored near the beacon, I could see it hanging there in space.

As we approached the beacon, space crowded in on me and I felt a wave of relief. It had been a while. I was feeling more and more comfortable.

The shuttle docked itself and the tunnel snaked out and locked on. Drupplingbroo hit a couple of command keypads and the shuttle stabilized. "I've got to get these people into the beacon and zap them off to T-hoe," he said.

"Good," I replied. "Me, first."

He shrugged.

"You know, Commander, that if you alert someone at T-hoe or your superiors, that I've made it through, that very fact would be an admission of your incompetence."

He looked at me and scratched his pot belly. "So what? I'm the only GALSPANAVOFF they got around here. Who they gonna get to do my job?"

He had an excellent point. "But your reputation would suffer, especially if you are the only GALSPANAVOFF out here." I tried not to choke on the unfamiliar word.

His face appeared thoughtful.

"The ah, breach of etiquette, shall we call it," I said, "might make them so angry they'd ground you anyway."

"You think so?"

"Beats me," I said. "That's what I'd do. It's the worst thing you can do to a spacer, is it not?"

"Dang sure is, fella." He thought some more. I'd given him plenty to chew on. Maybe he'd take my advice.

"I'm not a mass-murderer or anything like that. No one will face any danger because of me." I tried to be reassuring. "It's no skin off your nose whatever I do."

"You a spacer?"

"I am."

"I can tell now; you ain't sick like them groundhogs in back." That seemed to sit well with him.

We went back into the cabin. Most of the pax knew what was going on and hadn't said anything, not even when I'd marched Drupplingbroo through there with a large knife at his throat.

These were sons and daughters of rebels and malcontents, so they were a tough breed. They understood for me. A further evidence of their toughness was that only a few were spacesick, though the shuttle had maintained a minimum gravity.

Of course, the beacon buoy wasn't a large one designed for much traffic. Internally, it was about the size of the O'Clock's house on the plateau (on which pond I didn't miss a bit). The Plex station was simple, just a pax fax, no freight or large items expected, only passengers one or two at a time.

The bad news was that there were no controls, only execute. The good news was, because of the same circumstances requiring the bad news, you didn't need an ID or fancy codes or anything. The other part of the good news was that because of all of this, I didn't have to provide anything which would preclude me from being translated—like tissue samples, whatever, to ID one each Rollingham Wallace. Though it was possible that once the Plex Net had zapped me off to exile on Bristlebrush, it had wiped the databanks of me, not expecting to ever have to deal with me again.

Before we'd entered the Plex beacon, I'd briefed Drupplingbroo. "Just activate the station and zap me to T-hoe," I'd told him. "Use only the right words. Anything that sounds like an emergency code, I'll take exception to."

He didn't answer.

My problem was that once I translated to T-hoe, Drupplingbroo could comm through the beacon to T-hoe authorities and I'd be instant security-fodder. Well, I'd have to face that when I got to it.

I concealed the knife under my workshirt and nodded to him. I'd be ready one way or the other. "Do it." With all my heart, I hoped I'd not wind up in tinit manure again.

Or something worse.

T-hoe here I come.

"Execute," said Commander Drupplingbroo, the GALSPANAVOFF.

Zap, I was gone.

16: T-HOE

"**Y**ou! Over here."
     The speaker was big and burly, but I thought I could take him. However, he had three friends similarly dressed in Galacticon security gray, a real creative color, and they carried power weapons.

Casually, I removed my hand from the hilt of my knife. An instant assessment of the situation told me there was no immediate danger.

Exiting the station, I saw the room was long. The way narrowed immediately, and I had to stop in front of the security guys.

The fact that Drupplingbroo might be comming these guys didn't escape my attention; but I didn't hurry. I remembered to act the country boy, wide-eyed, first time off planet and just finished with my first space trip and my first translation.

"Gollly," I said, drawing out the word. "Is that all there is to it?" A little disappointment would be in character.

"That's it, buddy," said the burly sentry. "Hold still." He grasped my right arm and slapped a device up against it. I had to steel myself from reacting. Spacers don't take kindly to handling by anybody, especially groundhog government employed lackies. But, as I said, this wasn't a threatening situation, so I endured.

A sting.

"There," he said, grinning. "Didn't hurt, did it? Big boy like you?"

"Nosir."

"Move along, then."

"What was it?"

"I didn't tell you?"

"Nosir."

"I'm required by Galacticon procedural regulations to brief you that you have just received a coded implant. If you attempt to translate off-planet from T-hoe before ten years standard expires, the Plex Net will detect the implant and disallow the translation." He grinned again.

Ten years?

This is how they kept descendants of exiles on T-hoe so long. They probably hoped that these emigrants would assimilate into the fabric of T-hoe life and fail to continue on out into the galaxy.

"Thank you very much." I wanted to cold-cock the arrogant jerk. Holding my temper, I moved ahead. Other pax from the one-way Bristlebrush station would be showing soon; and while I didn't think they'd rat on me, Drupplingbroo might have worked out a way of exposing me.

The passage widened and along the corridor walls sat dozens of men and women behind temporary tables.

"Sir!" shouted a woman on the left.

Turning my head, I stopped and looked at her. There had to be some sort of established procedure for new arrivals, didn't there?

As it turned out, nope.

"Earn great money," she was intoning. "The Silver Bell Casino. We'll train you and—"

"Mister, you don't want to work there," interrupted the man on the right. "The mines, that's where the money is." He looked furtively to see if anybody was watching and listening and continued though everybody along the corridor was watching and listening.

"I can guarantee double pay if you sign a five-year contract, triple for ten years. How about it?"

"I saw him first," said the woman.

"Uh, I'll think about it," I said. I wandered down the aisle, allowing these people to glad-hand me, giving them all the opportunity to make their pitch. I paid special attention to the really obnoxious ones. By the time I got through the rows of vultures, I had a half dozen wallets and again as many individual IDs.

The whole thing struck me as something designed to find quick, unskilled labor, taking advantage of people from low-tech worlds (however many exile planets there were and from the evidence, Bristlebrush wasn't alone). At first I thought it meant that T-hoe had a labor shortage. At least, that's what I thought all these hustlers were telling me.

Except the last guy in line. He was *big*. I mean, he moved into the aisle and the aisle was no longer extant. His voice rumbled. "Ay. You can't find a job, you come see me. I be here. I get you table space and you give me cut of what you get from the hicks, no?"

"If you say so," I said mildly.

"I am Mean Mike." Charitably speaking, Mike wasn't anything near pretty.

"Right, Mike. Thanks. I, um, am, uh, Rusty Wallace."

"You got weird name. Mike be your friend. Remember?"

"Right. I be gone."

Mike moved aside, his eyes narrowing, trying to figure out if I'd insulted him or not. I thought it over and kind of thought I had. My reaction had been a natural one, but it was a shade patronizing. Like I said, I hate intellectual arrogance worse than anything except plagarism and smooth peanut butter. So I turned and smiled and waved at him.

And saw the security team begin scrambling away from their bottleneck position and come this way.

I'll never know if an ex-Bristlebusher told on me or Drupplingbroo commed or signaled in some fashion.

I waved at Mike and began running down the corridor. Mike waved back and smiled appreciatively at my camaraderie and, most likely, my criminality.

The last I saw, Mike had moved back into the center of the aisle and was standing there with his hands on his hips looking meaner than ever. I'll never know how long it took security to get past him—if they did.

Cutting through an intersecting corridor, I soon found myself in the lobby area of a regular Plex facility. I slowed down and walked casually. My clothes made me stand out.

I headed for the nearest entrance and saw a clothier booth. I stepped inside and punched for a standard jumpsuit, maroon so it would glare and people might not remember my red hair. To pay for it, I inserted one of the IDs I'd liberated. I doubted anyone had yet discovered his or her loss. I don't like to be grabbed and pushed and treated as an inferior. Mean Mike was the nicest of the bunch.

As I pulled on the jumpsuit, I decided what it all meant. Mean Mike had been the tip. The market wasn't a worker's market, it was an *employer's* market. There was too much labor here. Which meant you'd have to work long and hard just to survive. And perhaps find yourself indentured to the company store. That's why the guy pushing mining was offering those long contracts.

Dumping the Bristlebrush homespun trousers and workshirt in the discard chute, I decided I didn't like T-hoe very much already.

Exiting, I had another thought. I went into a men's room, stuck a man's ID in the slot and put my head into the now-raised cubicle alongside. Two sponges moved against my face and neck and when I withdrew my head, I was clean-shaven, no more itchy beard.

Outside, the way still appeared clear and I mingled with a group leaving the fax.

I had an attack of the guilts, so I stuffed all the IDs into a sealed bag I liberated from a mail stop. Then

I found a hanger-on. "You know Mean Mike?" I asked.

He nodded. "Up at the special station."

"Deliver this to him, will you?" I gave the guy a banknote and he nodded enthusiastically. "Tell him Rusty sent it."

The loiterer took off in the right direction. Mike could return the IDs and wallets and enhance his position. He'd understand I was sending them to him in thanks. I was happy to reciprocate his assistance.

After all, those crowding me at the incoming station, while vulturelike, were working folks trying to make a buck, perhaps some of 'em supporting families.

The one most obnoxious guy, I kept his wallet. He actually had cash, not a common thing, but not uncommon either, now that I considered it, on a gambling planet.

The skies of T-hoe were dreary. Fog shifted about and water precipitated from right in front of your eyes.

A few minutes later, it rained.

None of that bothered me. I was free and nothing, I say again, nothing, is better than being free.

The cash afforded me an aircar to an arbitrary destination. I found the major business district and went to the aircar dock.

Since there was no comm into or out of Bristlebrush, the O'Clocks hadn't known what happened to their son, his wife, and their daughter one each Gusselwaithe.

Except in one of the few letters she'd sent before Galacticon caught on, she'd told her grandparents about her mother and father.

Her father was dead and her mother had remarried. Sandy's mother's name had been Rexann O'Clock, and years after her husband Major, Jr., had died, Rexann married a man named Elrod McSpanish. So I merely inquired of a public directory for the addresses of Rexann O'Clock McSpanish and Elrod McSpanish. Fortunately, they were the same. Grandma and Grandpa hadn't known whether things had changed in the intervening years.

It was my intention to say hi and immediately find my way off planet and back into the hunt for Roanoke.

However, I hadn't reckoned on not being able to use the Plex fax here. Maybe I could find a starship and make my way. But the dread was climbing within me. You generally get *access* to a starship via Plex station which translates you up to the beacon buoy.

Well, whatever, I wasn't going to give up.

The aircar dropped me at a dock on the top of a tall building. The roof upon which I stood poked high above the clouds and fog. A weak sun begrudgingly filtered down upon this world.

In the distance, giant flashing arrows indicated casinos. In fact, there was one way above me pointing, seemingly, directly down at me.

"Casino Casino," it was called.

This was the address I had for the McSpanish family.

I checked the outside YOU ARE HERE locater diagrams and figured my way around. The apartment number was high in the building. I doubted if menial labor were allowed to maintain their quarters in the casino building itself. Maybe far beneath it underground, but I didn't know.

The bubblevator took me to the ground floor. I wanted to check out the place first. It was a higher class clientele casino, not the shirtsleeves type I was expecting. Well, with as many gambling joints as I'd seen in the distance, there must be something for everybody on this planet.

The first thing I noticed from looking into the lobby, the restaurants, the gambling floors, the admin offices, and observing the maintenance and cleaning crews was that they used actual peoplepower, manual labor. No fancy machines and gizmos controlled by smart computers. Another sign of cheap labor.

Somebody somewhere was making a ton of money off this planet.

I wasn't dressed too far out of style; I could have been dressier for the place, though. People must be here from everywhere. Gamblers, I guess, by nature aren't afraid to travel the Plex Net. Maybe they figured life was a gamble anyway.

The trembling began deep within me and I detoured to the "PRSNL SVC RESTAURANT—OFFWRLD FDS."

The lady at the counter looked at me twice and shrugged. "The customer's always right," she said. "Pay first, though."

I paid.

It took them a while and I suspect they used a synthesizer because the peanut butter wasn't very good. I had an order of peanut butter and banana cream soup followed by macaroni and peanut butter, hold the cheese.

The water on T-hoe didn't hold a candle to that on Bristlebrush. Which told me I'd kind of enjoyed my stay on the planet of exiles. Physical labor during the day and talking and visiting at night. No artificial entertainment. I'd read many of the books Sandy had sent her grandparents.

It all made me kind of nostalgic for Roanoke. Like Bristlebrush, Roanoke was a planet carved and sculpted by glaciers, a rugged world, one with open spaces and mountains and valleys and oceans and forests. A place in which to be free.

Before I got maudlin, I decided to go find Rexann. Besides, the waitress had been shooting me furtive glances throughout the meal like I was some kind of zoo creature. Maybe she could tell I was a spacer.

I took the bubblevator to the three hundred and forty-third floor, bribed the floor captain, and was soon on my way.

This floor, 343, was quite plush. You can usually tell when the carpet feels thick and plush but doesn't look thick and plush. And the color scheme of the walls, ceilings, and carpets were not reminiscent of institutions or large businesses which are generally designed more for the staff and maintenance than for the customer.

The more I thought about it, the more I anticipated this meeting. Sandy's mom, the one who could tell me where she got the name Gusselwaithe. It also hadn't passed my attention that Rexann McSpanish might well assist me in escaping the trap of T-hoe.

I should have known. You just can't bribe anybody anymore. What's the galaxy coming to?

Before I reached the McSpanish apartment, a pair of security guys intercepted me.

They were local hire, but knew their job. I didn't suspect anything until it was too late, for they were dressed in civvies. I guess I was kind of difficult to miss, being the only spacer wandering around on 343 in a bright maroon jumpsuit.

See, I should have commed ahead. But no, I had to maintain a low profile, be secretive, not want to show my presence anywhere in case they were still looking for me.

These two goons wore green two-piecers with that icky fringe which, when charged, stands out in different directions. Groundhogs can take tacky to extremes.

"I just wanted to visit with Rexann McSpanish," I pleaded.

"If it'd of been me," the little guy said, "I'd of commed first. It's sort of an accepted little courtesy we observe in Casino Casino."

"Let me talk to her for a minute, I can straighten things out."

"Don't matter," said the other one around a vibrating toothpick. "She ain't home anyway."

"Ah," said Shorty, holding up my genuine Bristlebrushian hunting knife. He was as good as me at light-fingering—I hadn't felt a thing.

"If you get my cash, too, I'll press charges," I said for something intelligent to say.

He just grinned at me.

"Let's get him downstairs," said Toothpick, nudging me with a stunner.

It seemed the harder I tried, the more backward I went.

17: REXANN

They had bright lights on me and I was sweating and getting angrier by the minute.

"What's your name?"

"I want to see Rexann McSpanish."

"What's your game?"

"I want to see Rexann McSpanish."

"Why are you here?"

"To see Rexann McSpanish."

For the forty-leventh time.

When in walks this sexy-looking woman in a flowing dress. The thing was formal and glittered with those little sparkly things that imbed in the material. It offset her green eyes well. Her dark hair was swept back and bound up. A one hundred percent class act.

Upon reflection, there are certain good things you could say about groundhogs and groundhogism.

"It was the knife they showed me," she said, her voice like a bell on a chill and clear Bristlebrush morning.

Shorty and Toothpick moved back and stood straight.

I would have stood, too, had not the stun field chair been following its designed job description with gusto.

"Bristlebrushian hunting knives are distinctive." She stopped in front of me. "He does look dangerous, doesn't he?"

"It's anger," I said. "I'm tired of being restrained

and questioned. I didn't do anything except try to see you."

She hefted the knife and tested the edge. "My father-in-law used to hone a knife like no other."

"Major and Edna send their love."

"Unrestrain him," Rexann said.

Shorty and Toothpick bumped each other to reach the controls first.

"I'm Casino Casino's dbt adj," she told me.

"Deppedaj?" I repeated.

"No, as in 'debit adjustor,' " Rexann said. "Dbt adj for short."

"What's a deppedaj do?"

"Dbt adj, not deppedaj. I adjust negative credit flow."

"Oh." Now I knew. "A bean-counter."

"Accountant," she said.

"Right."

"Bean-counter is derived from old French. A slang term *biens* they used referred to valuable property. The term has stuck through the centuries."

"Right."

We were up in 343-1, everything well again. Rexann McSpanish was tall and beautiful, much more so than her daughter in the classical sense. Her formal attire settled around her comfortably as she sat across from me.

The room was darkened and we were in the corner looking out windows on the two front sides. The air had cleared over this part of T-hoe and lights were everywhere. I saw no moons and this part of the night sky had few stars; if there were more, the gambling resorts' lights overpowered them.

"When my husband, Major, Junior, passed away," I saw a flash of hurt dart through her green eyes and across her face, "I had to support myself and my daughter. I cleaned hallways right here in Casino Casino and took night courses in accounting—I was always a quick study. I got some degrees, and by the time Gus went out on her own into the galaxy, I was moving up the corporate ladder. As a debit adjustor, I'm the second executive vice president of Casino Casino."

I translated this to mean that she was third in command.

"You were doing so well that you didn't want to leave T-hoe when your mandatory ten years ran out."

"That's right," she said, patting the bound part of her hair in back to insure everything was in place. "I'd married Elrod and my career was progressing nicely." She sighed. "If Major, Junior, had lived, I might have—well, I don't know. You can't go back, can you?"

I shook my head.

"And can you believe," she brightened, "the O'Clock family penchant for oddball names?"

An instant bond formed between us. "Rusty Wallace sounds so bland next to them," I said with a conspirational smile.

"Not at all," said Rexann. "I like it. I kept the O'Clock name as my middle when I married Elrod."

"Where did Gusselwaithe come from?" I asked, no longer able to hold it in.

"That was from my side of the family," she said, voice containing the merest hint of warning. "*I* gave Gus her names."

Diplomacy and courtesy overcame me and I didn't follow up.

"She's a little touchy about it if someone mispronounces it," I said.

"She always was," said Rexann. "I always wondered if we'd have had a third Major, Major, III, had Major, Junior, lived."

"I'm sorry," I murmured, not wanting to open old wounds.

Rexann speared me with her eyes, even in the semidark I saw them. She held up her left-hand ring finger. "See this ring?" Her voice was flat and quiet.

"I do."

"It contains one shot of poison which kills upon skin contact. You have thirty seconds to fully explain why you know my parents-in-law *and* my daughter. Bristlebrush and the rest of Galacticon should be mutually exclusive. And toss in why you've as much self-confidence as a spacer."

"Ulp." She'd figured that if I'd gotten off Bristlebrush, then I must be a generation or two removed to be able to leave the planet. So this being my first step, I shouldn't have known anything much about the rest of the galaxy including her daughter—also including how sensitive Sandy was about the name Gusselwaithe.

"Twenty-five and counting."

For another couple of seconds, I pondered.

"Twenty."

"My home planet is Roanoke. Roanoke disappeared, it's not there any more. In my quest to find it, I ran across your daughter, Gus, who was sort of looking for Roanoke, too. Among other things."

"Ten."

"I got in trouble and your daughter was supposed to zap me off into intergalactic space, but instead she changed the destination code and dumped me into a pen full of little beasts called 'tinits' much to my displeasure." I sniffed for effect.

"Tinits? She did you no favors. That's a very intriguing story, Rusty." She dropped her hand and the ring no longer pointed at me. I wondered if what she said about the poison were true. I didn't think I wanted to find out in the worst way.

"It's all true," I said.

"It's so wild, it can't be a lie. Fill in the blank spaces for me. Can I get you anything? Food, drink?"

"No thanks, I had some peanut butter and soup down below a little while ago."

"*You're* the one! Everybody's talking about it already. Some of our customers are even trying it. I believe you've started a fad. I hope you don't want royalties?"

"What I want is to get off T-hoe and find Roanoke."

"Tell me," she said, her voice compelling.

I did. At the end, we were both eating peanut butter sandwiches with mustard and mayonnaise, and layered with something called Philadelphia cream cheese. One of these days I vowed to find out just exactly where Philadelphia was and send 'em a thank you note.

"The Casino Casino bread isn't as good as Edna's fresh-made," I said, "but it sure hits the spot."

"Grandma could cook," Rexann admitted. "That story is unbelievable. I've never heard anything like it. You seemed to pull your punches when you went over the last scene where Gus zapped you to Bristle-brush."

My eyes dropped. I'd been charitable. Sandy's duplicity seemed logical, right there on the surface. She'd stunned me when we translated to see the CEO of the Plex Net, Helen Merritt-Browne. From there I'd been zapped and stranded and dipped in tinit droppings. Well, they're not exactly droppings, they're too moist—but I digress.

I remembered the conversation between Sandy and me. We'd both used the word 'trust' freely.

"I was stunned and drugged, and had been slapped in a stun field chair so that I could only move my head and talk."

Rexann seemed to accept that. "I'm sure Gus had to do what she had to do. Loyalty is her strong suit—well, sort of."

"What do you mean, sort of?" My head had snapped up like there was a spring in my neck.

"There is a small matter of her fiancé," Rexann said.

"Fiancé?"

"Alfredo. Didn't she tell you about him?"

"Um, er, she kind of mentioned him in passing."

"Well." Rexann just sat there and stared out the window.

"Well what?"

She sighed. She sighed very well. "Alfredo—he's a single name person—and Gus were engaged when Gus reached her ten year point. Gus had always wanted to see what was beyond the next star, so she up and went. Alfredo is one who will have nothing to do with space or the Plex Net. He wouldn't go. She went. He waits patiently. Well, sort of patiently."

"Sort of patiently?" I was still stunned at learning Sandy was engaged. My senses weren't quite right.

"Just a minute." Rexann rose and went into another room. She returned and handed me a scarf. It was deep blue and seemed three dimensional. A swath of stars undulated as I moved the scarf.

"It's a simulacrum of a real star field," Rexann told me. "Gus had many of them." Rexann shook her head. "I cued up some pix. Here, look."

She touched a control.

The wall lighted. An average size guy stood there, then shuffled a deck of cards and riffled them over his knuckles.

"Alfredo. Quite a handsome young man, don't you think?"

I grunted.

"He used to deal 21," Rexann continued. "Now look at him."

The first shot froze and another appeared. Alfredo it was, but there the resemblance ended. Naked except for a loincloth kind of wrap. Every inch of his body was corded muscle. Even his cheeks stood out with knots.

"Gosh," I said lacking anything else to say that would keep me out of trouble.

"Is that body-building, or what?" she asked.

He looked like he could take me and snap me in half using two fingers only.

"He retreated into this professionally, I think," Rexann said, "to compensate for his loss." She shook her head sadly. "He works here at Casino Casino managing the exercise and training facility."

"Loss?"

"Gus never came back."

"She's been busy," I said, "I'm sure . . ."

Maybe Sandy was too nice or too soft to break it to Alfredo. Or maybe she'd seen a recent photo.

"She can't have been gone all that long," I pointed out.

"That's true."

"And she's probably just like her mother, pursuing a career, and that takes up most of your time. Not to mention learning to pilot a starship and all that technical stuff she knows about the Plex Net."

"You really thought she was a secret agent?"

"I did. Sandy, rather, Gus, is quite accomplished; additionally, she has a cool composure about her which is pure professionalism. Also, she is quick and alert, always in control and knowing exactly what she's doing—" I glanced up guiltily.

"You're very complimentary." Rexann studied me with renewed interest.

"Well," I hemmed and hawed—and I always wondered just exactly what hemming and hawing was, and now I knew—and felt a blush creep up my recently shaved neck. "I was right, as a Plexus Inspector General inspector, she in essence is a secret agent." So there.

"And Gus might even be in the top spot right now," sighed Rexann. "She's certainly a fast burner."

"She must take after her mother," I said. Of course, in the back of my mind I was worried to death about Sandy. If she was just playing along with them, she was in the midst of a barrel of thieves—and worse.

"You're worried about her, aren't you?" Rexann asked.

I looked down then up. "She's a good partner when you have to do a little breaking and entering illegally."

"Well, let's just see how she's doing."

"What?"

Rexann touched a keypad on her console. "Get me a Plex comm link, please. I'd like to talk to my daughter, Gusselwaithe."

"Yes, Rexann." The computer had a soft female voice. Rexann was the kind who was threatened by no other woman, and thus didn't need a subservient male voice.

Rexann looked expectantly at me.

"If you get through," I said, "perhaps it would be best if you didn't mention me? They might be monitoring her."

"All right."

Looking at the scarf of stars still in my lap, I recognized a little bit of myself. Dreamers are a special people. I could tell Rexann O'Clock McSpanish was a Do-er. Her daughter was a Dreamer and a Do-er both.

"Working," said the computer femme-voice. "Be advised she is not in quarters presently. We are patching through to her workplace. Standby, please."

"Bring up the lights," said Rexann. The room glowed into friendly life.

"She's been located," the computer reported. "Standby."

"Mom?"

"Hello, dear." Rexann adjusted the pickup.

I stayed out of the way. It was likely that all Sandy's communications were monitored.

Inspiration struck. I rose and went to the console beside Rexann, careful to stay out of the picture.

While they exchanged pleasantries, I typed onto the screen. TELL HER MARION ZERNICKE'S DATE SAID MAJ AND ED SEND BEST REGARDS. I hoped that would be sufficiently cryptic to escape eavesdroppers.

Rexann read it and nodded, her hair bobbing a bit, but nothing falling out of place.

"Gus?" said Rexann. "I'm visiting with Marion's date."

"Marion Zernicke of Sector Eight News Service?" Sandy's face went into immediate disdain.

Rexann looked the query at me and I nodded.

Sandy was still talking. "That groundhogging floo-zie—"

"Anyway, he says that Maj and Ed send their best."

"Oh." Her face changed from cloudy to a big, wide, happy smile which made me feel real good. *"Oh!"*

"Unfortunately," Rexann said, looking at me, "he's got a skin condition I had for about ten years and he can't really get out and about nowadays."

Sandy scowled. Then she brightened. "Well, okay, Mom. Tell him I said hi. Listen." Sandy appeared thoughtful and fluffed her shoulder-length hair. "I'm certain Betsy would be glad to hear that and tell him I'd bet Betsy would like to visit right soon."

Rexann lifted an eyebrow.

BETSY IS MY SHIP. GUS IS COMING HERE ON BETSY.

Rexann lit up like launching sequence lights on a starship. "Really?"

"Really," said Sandy. "I'll talk to Betsy right away, and get back to you."

"Call collect, dear."

"Sure, Mom. Bye."

The screen blanked.

Rexann stood and kissed me on the cheek. "I don't care who you are or what you've done. My little girl is coming home."

Sure, right here where the new mountain of a man named Alfredo was waiting.

18: GUS

Scheming is one of the things I do well.

After the comm link with Gus, our conversation centered on her forthcoming arrival. When, we didn't know. We could figure the time differential, or the computer could, flying Betsy from Galacticon Central to here, but we didn't know how long it would take Sandy to break loose from her duties. I was worried Roanoke's time was running out. Standard days are longer than T-hoe and Bristlebrush days, so I figured I still had perhaps fifteen of the one hundred days remaining.

During the conversation, Rexann's husband arrived.

He saw her first and smiled and walked toward her. "The tax assessor still isn't happy, Rex. I told him he could take it and—" His eyes caught me standing beside the bubble-windows against the night sky.

Elrod was a dapper sort, you could tell, for everything he wore, including a 'stache and slicked back black hair, was meticulously groomed and worn.

Rexann introduced us and explained my presence, condensing the story a lot more than I could.

Elrod was fourth executive vice president of Casino Casino, apparently outranked by his wife.

"His job here is dirpers," Rexann explained.

"Diapers?"

"No, no." Elrod shook his head. "Dirpers, like in dure purse. Director of Personnel for Casino Casino."

"Ah," I said intelligently, plans and schemes leaping into my mind.

"But disregard my duties," said Elrod. He admired his wife. "I've seldom seen you so radiant."

"El, I feel wonderful! Just because of Rusty, Gus is coming to visit."

"No!"

"We just talked to her."

"That is wonderful."

"Thank Rusty."

"Thank you, Rusty."

"You're welcome, Elrod."

He looked at me with a critical eye. "If there is anything I can do to ever repay you, please, please, please let me know."

Yours Scheming Truly decided I might need a little muscle, muscle indebted to me, in case of an Alfredo attack.

"Ah," I said. "It wouldn't be exactly a personal favor. But it might well be to your benefit."

"What is that?" he prompted.

"As we just told you, I, uh, um, encountered the Casino Casino upstairs security detail." Shorty and Toothpick.

"Private security help is hard to come by on T-hoe," Elrod said with a knowing glance. "People just are not overly antagonistic these days. I wonder why?" He shook his head. "So you take whomever you can get."

"I ran across a fellow that would do you proud; in fact, he's loyal and antagonistic to boot."

"Where can I find him?"

"His name is Mean Mike." I described him and told where he could usually be found. "Have your guys mention my name, it will facilitate matters."

"Consider it done." Elrod went over to the console and I joined Rexann. I was going to make my excuses and depart when the door swished open and this dapper little kid walked in.

The kid was maybe ten and had black hair slicked

back and wore a dapper three piece suit with a snap-closed vest. He looked more like his mom than his dad, but he certainly acted like his dad.

"This is my son. He's Gusselwaithe's half-brother. Rusty, meet Juan O'Clock McSpanish. Juan, this is Mr. Wallace." Rexann beamed proudly.

"How do you do, Mr. Wallace?"

"As little as I can, kid—"

"Juan," said the kid. This kid was meticulous, a neatnick, and immaculate. He needed to learn how to be a kid.

Rexann arranged a room for me on 143.

The next day Juan and I were sitting in PRSNL SVC RESTAURANT—OFFWRLD FDS sipping on double peanut butter milkshakes when I heard a mountain rumbling and the roof fell onto my shoulder.

"Ay!" rumbled the mountain, and his hand tapped me on the shoulder again. "Mr. Wallace!"

"Mad Mike," I said, grinning my happiness.

"Mean Mike," he rumbled.

"Right."

"Lissen, Mr. Wallace. I want to thank you for gettin' me th' job. Ay? I be grateful."

"Call me Rusty. You will more than earn your pay." I indicated Juan. "This is my friend Juan McSpanish."

"How do you do?" Juan said, looking up at Mountain Mike with total awe.

"Good, Juan. T'nk you very much. Hiyou?"

"Very well, many thanks." Juan had a milkshake mustache and reminded me a lot of his father, a condition which I was trying to do something about.

"Ay, what's those?" asked Mike.

"Double peanut butter milkshakes," said Juan. "Do you want one?"

"Sure. Smells good."

Juan ordered us refills and one for Mike.

"Make it two," Mike said, and Juan signaled the

waitress with a nod. Mike looked at Juan with appreciation. "This boy got pull around here."

"He does," I said. "Now if we can only get the kid to lighten up."

"You want I should do that, Mr. Wallace?" Mike asked.

"Call me Rusty, please. Sure, if you want the job."

"It be my pleasure."

After a couple of more milkshakes and a stain on Juan's immaculate suit, I think we were making progress.

We spent a lot of time together, Juan, Mike, and I. Our favorite pastime was in the special room in the Casino Casino gym, which was located on the sub-basement level 48. You could control gravity. Our game consisted of Mike and me tossing Juan back and forth at low or zero gravity. He'd roll up like a ball and splay out his limbs when thrown.

We only went down there when I determined the coast clear, because the guy in charge of Casino Casino's gym and exaerobic facilities was a giant named Alfredo.

I also spent much of my time in research trying to find a shuttle or any kind of space-worthy vehicle on or off the planet that I could beg, borrow, or steal to take me into orbit. From there I could get on a starship and beat the Bristlebrush ten-year rap.

Nothing. And twelve days left.

Atop the Casino Casino building, above even the aircar docking platform, sits an eatery called GRAND OVERLOOK AND SLOTS.

It's open air, although it's got safety bubble walls and, in inclement weather, they can activate a bubble-dome.

Juan, Mike, and I were sitting there at the "edge table" eating a concoction of my personal devising, peanut butter nachos, plenty of jalapeños, but shred some sharp cheese and maybe a little white cheese if you want to mute the hot peppers.

"Ay! These are great, Mr. Wallace," said Mean Mike.

"Call me Rusty, Mike."

Juan grinned and thought that was funny. A strand of melted cheese dripped from the corner of his mouth down to his chest. I didn't say anything.

Mike was shoveling nachos into his mouth like a piston into a cylinder, if they still use opposed engines anywhere.

The staff was respectful, most staring in awe at Mike's eating habits. A mutated dragon wouldn't have gotten as much interest.

However, as had become the case, when a new peanut butter creation occurred, a great many people observed with more than just passing interest.

"There isn't as much dbt to adj," Rexann had told me yesterday. "Casino Casino is doing the most business in its history."

"We've hired new people," Elrod put in.

They even had a new gaming table, called "Peanut Butter Gravy, Roll 5" which was a game I didn't understand all I knew about. It consisted of cards, reflective crystals, time frames, and a cube of actual flame. Not being a gambler, I didn't want to know anything about it. On the other hand, aren't all spacers gamblers? Either gamblers at heart or by definition, or both.

Several women at a table behind us were eating peanut butter nachos now, and apparently enjoying them. I'd seen it before. We'd eat a peanut butter (crunchy) dish, and if it was a good one, soon people would be ordering it right and left in a land-office rush. Sometimes it gets crowded. I'd continued to tentatively decline all royalties, though the amount of money was beginning to be attention-grabbing.

My contributions to Casino Casino had really spurred business. All the money might turn my head.

It was possible I might have to take 'em up on their offer if I could find a shuttle or ship to buy or rent.

The wind was blowing and it was overcast, but not raining. It was shortly after school and the three of us were having our customary after-school snack.

Below an aircar landed and a leg came out the wing door and— "Sandy!" I said, a little loud, but by the time the wind had blown the word away, I was down the ramp and hustling to the aircar.

When I was on the dock and Sandy was fully out of the aircar, I slowed self-consciously.

As I got near, Sandy saw me and a broad smile broke out on her face. It wasn't as beautiful as her mother's, but it sure was attractive.

"Rusty!" She grabbed me and hugged me. "Gawd, I'm glad you're alive." She let me go, probably as self-conscious as I was.

"I'm glad I'm alive, too. Why, I haven't been stunned by a friend in days and days."

"I saved your life."

"And fried my gizzard."

"It was the only thing I could do, stun you," she said. "When the gas started in, I had to make it appear like I was on their side."

"You *were.*"

"Not necessarily," she said, the old enigmatic look returning to her face.

I would have continued the argument, rather, discussion, had not Mike and Juan showed up about then.

"Kid, this is your half sister Gus. I call her Sandy."

"I will, too." The kid was straightening right out, what with my influence and all.

"Sandy, this is Juan O'Clock McSpanish."

"I know, I know. I might not have visited T-hoe, but aperiodically I've commed them."

"Oh, yeah." Where had I heard that word before? This was one screwy family.

"Me, Mr. Wallace," Mike said.

"Rusty, my name is Rusty."

"Yessir, Mr. Wallace."

"Sandy, this is our friend, Mad Mike—"

"Mean Mike," he grumbled and the most fleeting of looks flashed through his eyes. Could he have been pulling my leg all the time? I suspected people automatically underestimated him. The name business between us had taken on dimensions of ritual.

"Hi there, Mike," Sandy said. "Pleasure's mine." She held out her hand and took his. Old "Nobody touches me" had sure changed. Not only that, but she made a friend for life. Mike's return smile was beatific. See, Mike wasn't just big, he was ugly. As the old saying goes, beauty is only skin deep but ugly is bone deep.

"I think your mom would really like to see you," I said.

"Let's go."

We walked toward the bubblevator, Sandy and I in the lead, Juan and Mike behind, with Mike carrying Sandy's bag.

"Have you learned anything?" I asked.

She turned and looked into my eyes and got my immediate attention.

Finally, I broke the contact.

"When Mom called, I was getting ready for a trip to Laquinto."

That took a bit of pondering.

After all the hugs and kisses, reunitings, and so on, Sandy, Rexann, and I were sitting around Rexann's "kitchen" table.

Mike, Elrod, and Juan had diplomatically left.

I say "kitchen" because they didn't really have a full kitchen, since Casino Casino's many restaurants, cafes, and eateries (or is it eaterys?) would provide whatever they wanted to eat any time day or night.

Pushing and pulling, I was testing the concoction I was fooling around with in the portable synthesizer.

"What is that horrible *goo?*" asked Sandy.

"I'm trying to design a peanut butter chewing gum."

Sandy made a sour face.

Rexann told her about all my "creations" and the business they had attracted to Casino Casino.

"Pretty creative, don't you think?" I said.

"A shrink would come up with terminology like Compulsive Eating Disorder," Sandy said.

"Now, now," said Rexann.

I kneaded the mess and returned it to the synthesizer, checking the list of available additives. "The difficult part is getting the gum to be chunky. I think I can do smooth without any problem; but the real challenge is chunky. How come you blasted me with a stunner?" I was still angry.

We all knew it was time to get down to business.

"As I said, the only thing I could do when I translated into Merritt-Browne's home was to stun you— else I'd be tinit fodder along with you—"

"Thanks a ton—"

"So, I stunned you to make them think I was on their side. Also, maybe I could learn something." She absently took a spoonful of peanut butter and ate it.

"Don't get your germs in there," I said pointedly.

"The problem was," Sandy continued, "that Inspector General Kalhen was no longer the IG. Helen Merritt-Browne was in full charge and changed all the orders around."

Rexann took the spoon from her daughter and stuck it in the sterilizer and returned it to the table.

"Investigating the alien signal was suddenly taboo. I was assigned menial IG admin duties, sent here and there. I wouldn't do any of their dirty work. Did you notice how I saved your life by changing the destination code at the last second?"

"Um," I said uncomfortably, "I couldn't help but notice as many times as you've brought it up."

"Right, Rusty." She picked up the spoon and ate some more peanut butter straight.

I glared at her and her mom took the spoon and sterilized it again.

"While you were vactioning on Bristlebrush," she said, "another thing I did was to find my old boss General Kalhen. The reason he was forced to retire is that he was gathering evidence against Helen Merritt-Browne. It seems that early in her career, she had begun stealing funds. As she climbed her career ladder, she continued." Sandy fiddled with the synthsizer. "Likely, she never guessed she'd make it to the top. Now she and her trained security ape Churnenski are stealing on a larger scale."

Rexann was following this with interest. "Now that Merritt-Browne doesn't need the money, she can't stop skimming—or else wants to salt away an enormous retirement fund before someone inevitably exposes her past chicanery. It's common on T-hoe, no matter how well protected the casinos think they are."

"That's the way I figure it," Sandy agreed.

I rolled a wad of peanut butter between my fingers and was thinking about grilled peanut butter stuffed olives including the pimento when it hit me. "That's why they tried to kill me." I explained about the attack on the aircar landing and the bomb in the Plex beacon buoy. "I was directing too much unwanted attention to the Plex Net and might have gotten an investigation." I discarded a peanut butter-sauerkraut salad concept. "What did you do next?" I looked at Sandy.

"After a while, I decided I wasn't going to get the promotion to be the IG, and it was becoming evident they were diverting me, that they didn't trust me and had decided against inviting me into the inner circle."

"Maybe if I apply these tiny little chunks of peanuts to the *surface* instead of trying to mix them into the batch, that way the production process will be simplified and each stick of gum won't be so expensive to make."

"That's good," said Rexann. "All it needs then is a little layer of sticky stuff."

Sandy glared at us both.

"Peanut butter *is* sticky stuff," I pointed out. "That's my problem. So all the time I was shoveling tinit manure for Grandpa O'Clock, you were moping about the galaxy doing make-do work and nothing of stellar significance."

She crossed her eyes at me. "I checked my job description and nowhere therein does it say Rollingham Wallace has any input into anything I do or am supposed to do."

"Pardon me! Put me in my place," I added ice to my voice, *"partner."*

"So, I went and dug up Betsy from her hidden orbit and was planning a trip to Laquinto when I received Mom's comm."

"Laquinto being the only remaining cold trail to whatever it is we're chasing, the aliens or the missing Roanoke, take your intertwined pick."

"Exactly my thoughts," said Sandy.

"Weren't you afraid you'd lose your job?" I asked. "Your being on the job with the conspirators was the one big advantage we have—had."

"It wasn't paying off anymore." Sandy studied the mush coming out of the synthesizer. "I couldn't get promoted and I don't do anybody's dirty work."

"I knew it," said Rexann, looking askance at my bubbling mixture. She turned her attention to me. "I sort of held out on you. I knew some of what she was doing. I wasn't as ignorant as I seemed."

What were they talking about? I raised my eyebrows.

"The old IG, General Kalhen, was legitimate and we were able to nab and identify malfeasors," Sandy said. "Not so these new guys. Churnenski and Helen Merritt-Browne, in addition to a little embezzlement, are involved in other no-so-pure activities. You see, Rusty, while I did want to go out and explore the galaxy, I left T-hoe with a single goal in mind: I wanted to terminate forever the practice of exiling malcontents to unidentified and unlocatable planets.''

A lot of left-over things fell into place.

I mashed my mess around and set the synthesizer for less moisture. ''You've certainly a noble goal. You're to be congratulated—''

''Thank you, Rusty.'' She dimpled.

''You could have told me earlier. Why didn't you trust me?''

''It never came up.''

''The opportunity was there several times.''

Sandy crossed her eyes angrily again. ''It was something I'd hidden for years and years. I've never told anybody until now.''

''Oh.'' I was embarrassed. ''Ah. Thanks for confiding in me. It makes me feel, um, special.''

Rexann patted my hand. ''There. Now we're all on equal footing.''

I certainly hoped so. There had been too many layers to Sandy O'Clock, too many wheels within wheels. She was a schemer.

She kind of reminded me of me.

The mess was smaller and rounder and a lot drier.

Sandy reached over and took it from me. She dropped it on the table surface and it bounced.

''I thought so,'' she said.

''That has interesting possibilities,'' said Rexann. ''Let's have Juan act as a test market, what do you think?''

''I— Sure.''

''And another thing, Rusty,'' Rexann said with a cocked eye. ''Juan is getting sloppy. He won't clean his room any more. He used to do it twice a day. And Mike keeps calling him 'Kid,' and I don't know what to make of it all except that my child is changing.''

''Don't worry about it,'' I opined, ''it's probably just a phase.''

"Yeah, sure." She hit me with one final killer look and crossed her arms.

Finding it necessary to change the subject real quick, I addressed Sandy. "So you thought you'd take on Galacticon by yourself?"

"At least I did it the smart way, from the inside," she said haughtily. "Another person I know was doing the same thing head-on and bouncing off a lot."

"Um, how's Betsy?" I asked.

"Once I played her the recording of your authorizing me to pilot her, she was happy to cooperate with me. We get along well, thank you."

"No. Thank you." Suddenly I realized Sandy had come immediately to my rescue, as soon as she'd learned my whereabouts. Even when she hadn't known about the one hundred days. She'd come to T-hoe, a place she'd obviously been avoiding. "You've done quite a bit. No, make that a lot. No, make that more than humanly possible. What you were trying to do had to be terribly difficult—"

"You can cut the crap any time now," Sandy said, but I could tell we were friends again. She was enough like me that she knew how appreciative I was that she'd come to my aid.

Thinking about Sandy, I couldn't help but he impressed. A young girl, stuck on a gambling planet had decided and acted. She'd coldly worked her way into a position at Galacticon Central in the Plex Net's IG office where she could make a difference. I said as much. "It had to take guts and long, long dedication."

She nodded soberly. "I pursued my goal to the exclusion of all else. I had no time for anything, no social life, no real close friends—"

"Sort of like a spacer—"

"I *am* a spacer—"

"Like I said." Me.

"What was that?" Her.

"I forgot." Me.

Rexann was looking at us both strangely.

"At any rate," I said, "Major and Edna would be proud of you."

"Your dedication and self-sacrifice did pay off some, it appears," said Rexann.

"But now with this aliens business, we've got a new level of problems and some executives not afraid to use the dirtiest tricks afforded by the Plex Net." Sandy was reflective.

"There is one small fall-out of your years of sacrifice," Rexann said carefully.

"What's that, Mom?"

"Alfredo."

"Oh."

"Do not forget that the two of you are officially engaged."

"Oh."

I tried to be as quiet as possible and mostly succeeded.

Rexann was relentless. "You do still want to marry him, don't you, child?"

Sandy looked at the floor, her face unreadable. "I said I would, didn't I?"

"Is that a yes or a no?" I interrupted.

"Who asked *you?*" said Sandy.

"Nobody, but—" Me.

"But, nothing. Butt out." Her.

"Now just a minute—" Me.

"What?" Her.

"I'm not going off to Laquinto out in the wilds of the galaxy with a married woman—"

"Who said you're going with me?"

"Betsy is my ship, and you can't translate to the Laquinto system anymore since the Sundays sabotaged the relay beacon, remember?"

She gave me a hard look. "Be that as it may, you can't get off this planet and Betsy—nay, *Virginia*—obeys me now, too."

She had a point there.

Sandy looked at her mother. "Rusty is right, Mom.

I can't very well get married and go traipsing off. You know Alfredo hates space—"

"I knew it!" I said unnecessarily because somebody had already told me.

Sandy glared at me again. Pointedly, she looked back to Rexann. "I think I need to see this through to whatever's at the end of the trail. It wouldn't be fair to me or Alfredo."

"Have you seen him lately?" I asked. "Alfonso's a huge—"

"Alfredo," corrected Sandy.

"That's what I said." I stuck my nose in the air. "It's gross—"

"I spoke with him not long ago on a comm link," Sandy said. "I'm not totally unaware of certain, um, changes. Now he's really *big* and *strong*."

"Gimme a break—" I said.

Rexann interrupted. "Gus, you can't really leave Rusty here. He—well, to put it delicately, Juan has changed due to certain influences. Elrod is not happy over these changes, either. Being a father is not easy in these days, but with unfair competition—"

"What do you mean 'unfair'?" I asked.

"Fathers have to be disciplinarians, so Elrod is. You, Rusty, are not burdened with any of that, only the good stuff."

She had a point. "The kid's all right, Rexann. He knows what's right and what's wrong."

"For now."

"It's Mean Mike's fault, not mine." I turned to Sandy. "So you just up and quit the Plex Net IG?"

Her face softened and her eyes went from side to side. "Not exactly."

"Not exactly what?"

"I kind of just left and came here."

"You're AWOL?"

"I thought I might still need my credentials out on Laquinto and since there is no Plex link and thus no comm, I figured what they don't know out there won't hurt them."

"Good thinking. Too bad that's our only remaining lead."

"Yeah."

I had an idea. "Though the story in the Sector Eight news might have paid off by now."

"I don't suppose you're going to try and establish a comm link with that Marion Zernicke?" Sandy's voice was nasty.

"I am," I said, trying to put some haught into my own voice. "It'd be worth a try."

"Fat chance, red spotted underwear pants." Her.

"How could you know that?" Me.

"It's an old childhood saying." Her.

"I knew that." Me.

Rexann appeared exasperated. "Do it or not, just don't argue about it."

We did it.

I sat in front of the pickup and Sandy stood behind me, arms crossed.

Marion took the call in bed. It was night on her side of D'Earnhardt. Marion didn't turn on the lights. I saw a shaded outline.

Off to the side was a mishmash of glowing, intertwining colored streaks.

"I knew it," whispered Sandy. "Night-glow worms, too, all in a tank. Groundhogs, ugh."

"Rusty? Is that really you?"

"It's me, Marion. How are you?"

"I'm really fine. Well, not exactly fine. I miss you."

She did? Glancing around, I decided I'd damn well better be diplomatic. "Marion, listen. Have you received any response from the missing planet story? Or my interview?"

Nothing. Then, "Oh. I forgot. I shook my head and you couldn't see it."

Sandy snorted derisively.

"So nobody made any inquiries for more information?"

"Well, there was one. A spacer who said he was from Roanoke. His name, let me see, I put it in the data bank, let me recall it. There. Yakamura Yamasita Yoriken Yyllander—''

"I know him," I said. "He's a spacer from Roanoke himself. What'd he say?''

"He wanted to know if the story really was true. When I assured him it was, he told me he had another contract he had to fulfill and that if anyone could straighten it out, you could.''

Well, I hadn't been the only spacer away from home. Yakamura would have discovered Roanoke missing eventually. Briefly I wondered about the people on Roanoke. What were they thinking?

"Listen, Marion," I said, "lock onto this comm link code. If anything else comes up, call collect.''

"Thanks a lot," said Rexann. "Elrod will love that. He'll probably try to write it off our taxes.''

Sandy walked off. "Thanks a lot, Wallace. Just what I need. That bimbo comming here every fifteen minutes looking for you.''

"What was all that?'' Marion asked.

It was a good thing Sandy and Rexann had been out of the pickup area.

"Nothing," I said. "Just some noise interference. Look, I've got to go now.''

" 'Kay. Bye, Rusty. I'll dream about you tonight.''

Somebody behind me "humpfed'' real loud.

"Thanks for your help, Marion. I appreciate it.''

"I'll hold you to owing me," Marion said. "You will come back to D'Earnhardt again, won't you?''

"Well, I don't exactly know. See, I've got to find Roanoke first. I'm willing to sacrifice myself and my personal life and all—''

"Oh, Rusty, you're so noble.''

"If you say so. Gotta go. Bye now. Thanks for everything.''

"Bye, Rusty.''

Quickly I cut the connection.

"Well, that certainly kills that possibility," I said brightly. "A dead end, that.''

"Noble?!?" Sandy's voice held more disdain than one word could possibly express. But it did.

I didn't want to be catty. "Noble can cover trying to find your missing home planet just as much as it covers working hard to stop the Galacticon government from zapping people into exile, outcast, expatriation—"

"They're thinking of changing Casino Casino to Casino Casino And Peanut Butter Emporium," Elrod said.

"They could use Emporium Emporium," I said. "Or would that be Emporia?"

Sandy already knew me so she didn't look sour at my flippancy. Rexann tossed it off, but Elrod, serious as he was, thought about it.

It was later and we were all sitting around their apartment discussing the peanut butter crisis.

Elrod was worried about Casino Casino's tax position, so we decided to set up a "Roanoke Enterprises Tax Corp. Harborage" to receive peanut butter royalties. Affectionately, we called the company "RETCH."

"I'm going to establish a marketing section and man it and start selling peanut butter concoctions on the market, too." Elrod was serious about the RETCH enterprise.

Juan and Mike walked in.

Juan's mismatched clothes were muddy and disheveled. "Damn, Rusty, me and Mike had a ball at the game—"

Elrod said, "Juan!"

Sandy said, "Rusty!"

Rexann said, "Rusty!"

Mike said, "Mr. Wallace!"

Why me, Lord?

You see a problem and go out of your way to correct it and do people appreciate your efforts? I guess not.

Not only that, but Rexann got hold of Alfredo and

told him "Gus" had just arrived home and would visit him the first thing in the morning.

In the morning, I schemingly arranged for Mike and Juan and me to be below in the Casino Casino gym when Sandy was going down there to talk to Alfredo whom I'd managed to avoid so far. It's easy to make such arrangements when your friend, namely Mean Mike, is on the security staff with all its accesses.

While the time wasn't high noon, the situation was fraught with similar tensions and drama.

19: ALFONSO

You'd think a guy who, like most people, is frightened of space and Plex Net travel would *not* be agressive; you'd figger he'd be a pushover, an easygoing kind of guy.

Not so Alfredo.

Maybe it was the chemicals he had to take to mutate his body into cordwood he-man knots.

I managed to get Mean Mike and Juan down there early to play our daily game of "toss the Juan." Mike's security colleagues kept us posted of key personnel movement.

So we knew when Sandy left her suite and where she was going. We knew when she took the bubblevator way down to the subsubsubbasement where the guy was.

Not wanting to know what I'd find out if I were there when Sandy walked in and encountered Alfredo, I didn't go into that room right away. I gave them a few minutes to get reacquainted.

I found them in the weight training room. The place had all those fancy passive machines you just sit in or lie in and they work your muscles and presto, you're a body-builder. Surprisingly, there also were free weights in a far section.

With Mike and Juan trailing curiously behind me, I spotted Sandy and Alfredo standing near a wall in an open area. It was probably a place for exerobics since there was a mat on the floor.

Alfredo was even more impressive in person. He must have spent minutes a day in a tanning machine because he was bronzed, even his hair. Some people don't do things halfway. He wore a pair of exercise shorts and had a towel over his shoulder, one of those towels which release specially designed scents. I thought his eyes were little, beady, and sunken into their sockets, but that might just be my perspective.

Obviously, Mike and Juan knew something was up.

Juan caught up with me and tugged on my tunic. "You gonna whip him, Rusty?" His hair was a mess. Getting tossed around will ruin your basic slicked-back hairdo.

"No," I said disdainfully. "That's beneath me. Now let me see what's going on here."

Alfredo was saying, "You're *what?*"

I stopped beside them.

"Here he is now," Sandy said. "What a *coincidence.*" She gave me one of her "You're getting in my business again" looks.

"Hi," I said brightly. "We were just over playing 'toss the Juan' and saw you come in—"

"Sure you did," she said.

"*This* is the fellow you're going to fly across the galaxy with?" said Alfredo. Strained veins in his neck were making him look blue.

I don't think he liked me right off. "That's me." I stuck out my hand. "Rusty Wallace, Alfonso, glad to meet you."

He ignored my hand and the name-change. This wasn't beginning too auspiciously. From the corner of my eye, I checked to be sure that Mean Mike was hulking behind me.

"I don't think I like that at all," Alfredo said.

I glanced down at my still-outstretched hand self-consciously and left it stuck out there for another moment to milk embarrassing him for all it was worth. That didn't seem to bother him either.

"It's something I've got to do," Sandy said. "I've

worked years and years to get this far and I'll be dipped in spit if I'm going to stop now.''

Alfredo's shoulders fell just a degree. But there was nowhere for them to sink to, so I might have been imagining the gesture.

''I don't want you to go,'' Alfredo said just like he meant it. ''You left me once before and you promised when you returned that we'd get married. You swore you'd never leave me again.''

''It's very important to me,'' Sandy said. ''I've been working toward this forever.''

Alfredo seemed to pout. ''*My* entire life I've spent waiting for you.''

''It doesn't look like it,'' I said.

He glared at me.

I shouldn't have baited him, but I didn't like his whiny attitude.

''You stay out of this,'' Sandy said.

Trying to prejudice matters against him a bit, I said, ''Well, I won't have this hunk of meat stand here and *dictate* orders to you like he owns you.''

''I wasn't ordering—'' said Alfredo.

''You could have fooled me, Alfonso,'' I said.

His right eye paid a lot more attention to me than it had before. ''You've called me that twice.''

''Oh? I wasn't counting. Now you've proved *you* can count all the way to two.'' I felt his hostility directed at me.

Even Alfredo's ears looked like they had muscles. The right helix bulged. ''Shut up.''

''Me?'' I asked innocently.

''Rusty,'' said Sandy, warning in her voice.

''You,'' said Alfredo.

''Alfredo,'' said Sandy, warning in her voice.

''Well, I never thought much of single-named people,'' I said, surprised at myself and not exactly certain why I was pushing him so hard. My behavior could have been termed rude, pushy, childish, uncalled-for, and others.

''You probably never thought much at all,'' said Alfredo in a much milder voice, sort of like the predator who'd decided not if, but when, to devour his prey.

"Stop it," shouted Sandy. She put her hands on my shoulders and looked me in the eyes. "What's got into you?"

Guilt washed over me. I wasn't behaving very well. "Nothing. He just rubbed me the wrong way, bossing you around like you were his chattel. You're a woman who makes her own decisions, goes her own way, and this first-class macho jerk wants to tell you what to do for the rest of your lives. That's what's got into me."

"Oh." Her eyes turned a special kind of shiny. She dimpled. "That's the nicest thing you've ever said to me, Rusty."

"I also said you were real good at breaking and entering and there was the big fight with security at the ROAR offices—" My mouth was running to cover my feelings.

Over her shoulder, I could see rage burning across Alfredo's face.

Sandy had stepped forward toward me, folding her arms in.

Alfredo reached around her and pried us apart. "I've seen you around, Wallace. You strut like a spacer, like you're better than everybody else."

"I am better than you."

He pushed Sandy out of the way and reached for me.

"Mike?" I said hopefully, my plans coming to fruition and a happy thought at my ability to scheme far in advance. Adherence to the 7-P Principle pays off.

"What is it, Mr. Wallace?"

"Mike!" I said as Alfredo dragged me to him.

"You want me to take him down, Mr. Wallace?"

Juan cut in. "Rusty wouldn't do that. He fights his own fights."

"Nobody's ever fought over me before," said Sandy, eyes big.

As Alfredo folded me in his giant, rock-hard arms and up against his broad, hairless chest, I knew it had all been for naught. I couldn't disappoint Juan, not to mention Sandy, not to mention me. If only he hadn't made that crack about spacers.

I'd like to be able to report that his body odor overwhelmed me, that his breath was horrid, all the pejorative things I could think of. But it wouldn't be true. My face jammed into the towel and must have activated it, for a myriad of flowery scents immediately began to emanate from it.

The only thing I had going for me was that I was taller.

Oh, and one other thing. Being a proponent of the famous 7-P principle, I of course was wearing a most appropriate pair of fighting boots I affectionately referred to as "stompers." I'd looked up Shorty and Toothpick and had them direct me to a proper bootmaker.

I jerked my head free and slammed it alongside his neck where I thought his carotid artery had to be. They call it a carotid thump, it temporarily cuts off the blood flow to the brain and makes your opponent woozy or even unconscious for a second or two.

However, it didn't work. His neck was too thickly wrapped in muscle, all of which right now was rigid with his effort, straining to break my back.

All of my air expelled and I wondered if this was to be my death, an ignominious one at the hands of a groundhog no less.

My right stomper slammed into his left instep and while his scream was satisfying, it deafened my left ear.

I followed up with a well placed knee to his crotch which he attempted to replicate. However, the 7-P Principle still in my corner, I had thought to wear a protective cup and he only stunned me.

We fell apart, him gasping for air and bending forward in pain.

"Had enough, Alfonso?" I asked, working the words around the giant intake of air to replenish my squished lungs.

It might have been over had I not been so cocky as to use "Alfonso" instead of "Alfredo."

Well, nowhere in the 7-P Principle does it say you have to be smart, or even reasonably intelligent, or even just thinking logically.

His little beady eyes seemed to sink deeper into the folds of muscular flesh around his eyes. He spat and straightened, ignoring the pain. He grinned like he was already at my funeral.

So I faked with my left stomper and he had enough moxie to remember the boots were dangerous and went for the fake. While that was happening, I spun and slammed an elbow into his side and hurt the hell out of my elbow.

But it jolted him and he took in a ragged breath.

I continued my spin, coming back around the front of him and slammed an old Roanoke haymaker to his stomach.

He oofed again, not so loudly this time. I swear his eyes turned red and his front teeth sharpened into fangs.

Nothing fancy about him. He reached out and punched me in the chest and I flew about four body lengths.

As I was untangling myself, Juan shouted, "Get him, Rusty!"

A giant shadow occluded the light and Alfredo was in the air above me, gravity aiding his leap, feet slicing through the air right for my head.

Spacers are a quick breed, "lightning fast reflexes required" read most job announcements. And Roanokean spacers are better than most.

Spinning on the floor, I managed to avoid most of his feet. One kicked my shoulder as I dodged. The pain shot through my entire body and I thought I'd be paralyzed for life.

Shaking off the pain, I scurried backward as Alfredo stalked me.

He seemed distracted for a moment and reached up

and tore the towel off his shoulder and tossed it aside. Lavender wafted about.

He hadn't even dropped the towel yet.

But it gave me the moment I needed to regain my footing. I found my back against the wall.

Sandy was standing off to the side with her fist to her mouth, avidly watching the whole thing. Mike was making punching motions, as if trying to will me to do it his way. Juan was clapping and squealing with joy. He'd learn something this day.

And in a semicircle behind them were a dozen men and women just like Alfredo. Body-builders, all with huge biceps and quads and other muscles I can't name because I slept through that part of physiology class.

Alfredo was coming for me now, murder in his eyes, and up against the wall I had no escape.

"Come on, Alfonso," I taunted. When your back is up against a wall and you're going to die, do it with a flair. Maybe people will remember you fondly.

That jarred him enough to drop his concentration and I lashed out with a stomper and felt like I'd connected with solid rock. But his left knee buckled a bit.

Using that, I feinted to the obvious escape side and went the other way.

The ploy worked perfectly, if you don't count the stinging blow to my other shoulder. I was running out of shoulders to put between me and him.

Favoring my newly injured shoulder instead of the other one now, I spun, leapt and nailed him with two kicks and fell on my newly bad shoulder, rolled and kept rolling until I could gather sufficient momentum to flip to my feet, not easy with two shoulders on fire.

Alfredo was limping toward me.

"Had enough yet?" I asked with more confidence than I felt. I wished the 7-P Principle had given me the foresight to wear body armor.

My shoulders hurt too badly for me to be able to defend myself, so I attacked.

The move surprised him and I got some leverage

and was able to flip him aside, nailing his kidney with my knee as he tumbled out of my throw.

Not believing in being a gentleman during these kinds of brawls, I followed him with the full intention of kicking him while he was down. However, my lack of air wouldn't let me and I had to pause to breathe. Surely, I appeared quite the gentleman, not taking advantage of a downed opponent.

Alfredo was on his hands and knees and lunged at me. I wasn't prepared for that one, so his tackle worked and I went down with him crawling on top of me.

His sheer bulk held me down, especially his knees on my already maimed shoulders.

He grinned wickedly, clasped both his hands together, and swung them at my face.

My head dodged the first hammerlike blow. "Hey, fight fair!" I said indignantly.

Out of the corner of my eye, I saw Sandy moving toward us.

I had to do something. I couldn't let Sandy interfere. Not because I didn't want to be saved by a woman, but because I didn't want to be saved by her. I'd never hear the end of it—if I lived through this battle.

So before he could hammer another blow at my face, I spat in his eye, twisted under him, bucked, and managed to snag his head between my knees.

If you slap somebody directly on the ears with your hands, it hurts like the devil and you might even break his eardrums.

This maneuver is much more difficult using your knees from behind but in my panic I performed it very well.

His scream was short and high-pitched and *now* his breath smelled bad. But he ripped his head from between my knees.

His knees had become dislodged and my arms and hands were free. Even though my shoulders hurt when I moved, I was able to tattoo his chin and jaw with six quick jabs, not as effective because I was punching upward, off the floor and unable to generate a great deal of power.

He fell off me and I scrambled up. He rose groggily and came for me again.

Since the jabs seemed to work the best, I let him reach for me with his giant arms, stepped inside his reach, and hit him hard with three left right left combinations and wound up the right from below my waist and put my whole torso into the blow and cold-cocked him on the chin.

Except I missed and my right fist smashed his nose, which manifested itself by an explosion of blood and Alfredo went over backward, slamming into the mat and tumbling once, an awkward thing for such a muscled frame. Blood sprayed through the air and made a nice pattern on his face.

Sensing he wouldn't get up from this, I refrained from attacking and merely dusted my hands together, no matter how badly the movement hurt my shoulders.

A blow struck me from behind.

"Nice fight, Rusty," said Mean Mike, pummeling my back, making me wince. Since he'd used my first name, I might have just earned his respect.

Juan was dancing in front of all the muscled guys, lashing out with his fists. "C'mon, who's next?"

Sandy moved over toward me and Alfredo. Her eyes surveyed me and then him.

She knelt over him, got blood on her hand, and looked up at me. "Rusty! How could you?"

Let's see the 7-P Principle deal with that.

20:BETSY

Since Sandy was still in a huff, I told Betsy to put me out and I slept the whole way to Laquinto. It would also give my shoulders time to heal.

We'd taken our leave. Juan and Mike were sorry to see me go. Elrod and Rexann were glad to see me go on account of Juan.

Everybody was sorry to see "Gus" leave.

It wasn't as easy as that.

What actually happened was that Sandy translated to the orbiting Plex beacon and thence to Betsy. We all told her good-bye and saw her off, the whole nine yards of formal good-byes—though I did not think anybody was spying on us.

Alfredo wasn't present. I don't know if Sandy bid him good-bye privately or not.

They all hugged and kissed and Rexann was the last. "I'll miss you, Gusselwaithe Hortense O'Clock."

Hortense?

Curiouser and curiouser.

Sandy avoided my eyes and stepped into the station and was gone.

I made my own farewells and took an aircar and flew out over a lightly populated area.

I climbed for altitude.

At forty thousand, the automatic controls are supposed to override. By then, I'd rigged a bypass and the autocontrol override couldn't kick in.

Ten thousand higher, the aircar simply wouldn't maintain altitude.

Not to mention some nut behind a screen somewhere screaming at me for violating all kinds of rules I'd never heard of.

I'd already activated a transponder telling Betsy my location.

Shortly, Betsy swung low in front of my field of vision and I donned an oxygen mask and opened the wing door.

Now the air traffic control supervisor was really screaming. I killed that part of the comm and matched the aircar to Betsy's outstretched tunnel, swallowed real hard and jumped. It's different from when you do it from a buoy beacon in space because they mate, lock, and environmental support continues. In this case, I had to leap, hold on, and crawl (for safety) in an open-ended tunnel at Angels 50 with no environmental support, just a few minutes of portable oxygen. At least I'd remembered to wear gloves. My shoulders complained.

At any rate, I made it without losing more than ten or fifteen years off the other end of my life.

"Betsy, it's nice to be home."

"Long time no see, Rusty." She'd learned a thing or two from Sandy. I wasn't sure I liked that.

"Did you tell Betsy to set a course for Laquinto?" I asked Sandy.

"I did." The ice was still in her voice, colder than the atmosphere at 50K.

"How long will it take us?" I asked.

"If we get going right now, two days standard," Sandy said.

"If we don't get going right now, how long will it take us?" I tried to keep the pique out of my own voice.

When Sandy didn't answer, Betsy said, "Two days standard," not picking up on my sarcasm.

Sandy glared at me. "You didn't have to hurt him, you know."

"The poor baby," I retorted. "I wouldn't put it past you to have arranged the whole thing."

"Not on your life. I wouldn't give you the satisfaction."

"Hortense?" I said, letting a little zing into my voice. "On top of Gusselwaithe. You never told me that."

"It never came up," she replied.

"Rusty?" said Betsy. "I recommend we take appropriate action soonest."

"Why?"

"The entire world below is boiling with indignant ATC officers and their mounting threats. There are unmanned security interceptors en route our location."

"You've been listening to too many bureaucrats," I said, still angry.

"I'm waiting," Betsy said impatiently, with a definite inflection in her mechanical voice.

"You've been influencing her," I accused Sandy.

"Who, me?"

"Rusty, we have to do something now." Betsy didn't sound any different, but she was strung differently. I guess women do that to you.

"Yeah, yeah. Okay, get us out of here."

"Done."

Acceleration forced Sandy and me onto the couch and Betsy elongated it for us. My shoulders ached worse.

Sandy glared at me.

"Don't blame me," I said. "It was your mom who spilled the beans." I tried to push away from her but couldn't very well against the g-force. "You got any more hidden names?"

"I'm not ashamed of any of them." She wasn't answering the question.

"I didn't say you had to be."

"I'll never forgive you for humiliating Alfredo."

"Alfonso started it."

There was a lot more of the same and when Betsy

got clear of the planet and went translight, Sandy stormed off to her stateroom.

Me, too.

And that's when I had Betsy put me to sleep for the trip. Why waste that much time arguing and bickering with a woman who doesn't understand you?

When we got to Laquinto Betsy awoke me.

"What's Sandy been doing all this time?" I asked. My shoulders had repaired themselves.

"When she found out you were programmed to sleep, she had me put her out, too."

It's sort of a coldsleep, slows down everything and you don't age two days worth. Translight travel is tricky anyway, but I left all that stuff to the scientists. I was a spacer, not a theoretician.

I was getting my first fix of peanut butter under the guise of a warm peanut butter stew from a mug when Sandy came in.

"Hi." Me.

"Hi yourself." Her.

"I'm sorry." Me.

"Good." Her.

"I know names are personal things; it's never been my intention to make fun of yours—it's just that they're so, um, strange."

"Sure."

I had to dig deep to save this one. "It's just that you don't ever see such an attractive woman with such unique names."

That perked her up. "Do you really mean it?" Her look told me she wasn't stupid enough to be bought off like that but she appreciated me trying anyway and incidentally the thought was pleasing, thank you very much.

"Hell, yes, I mean it. Why do you think I got myself into a situation where Alfredo almost killed me?"

"That's true," she said demurely.

"Your mom likes me, too," I added.

"She told me. She said you'd make an awful father.'' Sandy shook her hair and I liked watching her do it.

"I bet Elrod made her say that.''

"Elrod's a bit on the ragged edge from all those tax problems,'' Sandy said.

"Excuse me?'' said Betsy.

I shot Sandy an angry look. "You've perverted my ship.''

"Me? Aw, shucks.'' She batted her eyes telling me that she owed me as much for giving her such a hard time about her names.

"What is it, Betsy?'' I said.

"We're hanging here in front of the Laquinto system. I need a destination.''

"System data,'' I said.

A systems schematic popped onto the wraparound screen.

"Forty-two inhabited planets,'' Betsy said, "and a dozen uninhabited. Total population one trillion one hundred billion rounded off at last databank update. Governmental system—''

"Is one of the planets the capital?'' I asked. Sunday A. Sunday had told me the same general info.

"It is. There is a strong government here, Rusty, one with idiosynchracies you might not—''

"Idiosynchracies? Who's been teaching you big words?''

"I know *all* the words, Rusty, I simply don't use them around you.''

"Intellectual elitism,'' I muttered. "Yeah, take us to the capital.''

Esfahan was a large planet and, while it had a lot of deserts, it wasn't a desert planet. There was plenty of water. A mountainous continent, normal stuff like that.

Betsy had warned us that the Laquinto system was run by strong, religious rule of some sort or other, and the government was consequently what you'd expect. To be in the one and only ruling religious party, you had to matriculate through their religion and become a tmalluh, a type of holy man.

We translated down from the buoy—Betsy was the only ship in parking orbit.

In two minutes, Sandy said, "I don't like this place a lot."

21: ESFAHAN

The main Plex fax was packed. I guess there was a lot of travel and freight shipments among the forty-two inhabited worlds. With the decommissioned relay buoy, they just couldn't travel outside the Laquinto system. Also, all the planets were centrally governed and controlled from Esfahan.

The Plex fax was huge and with all those people, you'd think bedlam would reign.

Not so.

Certainly, there was some noise, but it was surprisingly quiet. People weren't talking to each other, not a lot, and not loudly.

Sandy was banging me in the rib cage as we walked down the center corridor. Right away I knew we were dressed inappropriately. Usually, you just choose a neutral color jumpsuit and that fits in anywhere on most planets.

Not so here. It appeared that all men were dressed in military camouflage duds—BDUs, short for battle dress uniform combat clothing. The women wore dark colors.

Then I looked closer. You knew they were women because they wore long dresses.

And veils.

Men were staring at Sandy with undisguised hostility as if we were violating some taboo.

Five men in formation were cutting through the crowd toward us.

"Uh, oh, welcoming committee," I said.

They intercepted us shortly.

The one in front said, "You will come with us."

"Why?" I said testily.

Sandy nudged me. We didn't need to start off on the wrong foot right away.

"It is required."

"You could work for Galacticon. Who are you? What's your authority?"

They'd surrounded us by now and the human flow around us modified to account for the seven of us standing there.

The five were all dressed in olive drab and all had mustaches.

"We will take you to the security tmalluh, he will decide."

"Decide what?" I asked, anger rising in my voice. Were they picking us out because we were spacers? Did they want us to repair the inop Plex relay beacon? It didn't sound like it.

They crowded us and I shrugged, giving in. They marched with military precision through the crowd, not a bit of courtesy, and out into bright sunlight. We walked for ten minutes through a city of mostly square buildings no more than three stories high. Except for some odd buildings with domes and spires atop them I figured were temples or something similar. Not much creativity shown in architecture, styling, color. The place needed variety.

Of course, I realized with millions of inhabited planets in the galaxy, by definition some had to be the bottom of the barrel.

The tmalluh sat cross-legged on a rug in an otherwise empty room in a square building. He wore woodland camo fatigues and an olive drab squat turban which overshadowed his sallow face, mustache, and dirty beard.

Outside air blew in through open windows.

The spokesman said, "Your eminence, we present these strangers to you."

"I see," said his eminence.

"I don't," I said.

"Silence," said the spokesman and Sandy jabbed me again. I was going to have a bruise.

The tmalluh studied us. "Farangi?" A term for "foreigners."

"Thank God," I said.

"That could be true," said the tmalluh, "we consider ourselves a very tolerant people." He stared at Sandy and I got angrier, so I shut up. These people looked militant, but I thought that together Sandy and I could take all six of them if necessary.

Sandy shifted uncomfortably, but I noticed that when she was finished she was on the balls of her feet and her arms were raised slightly, ready to go into action.

"It is required," said the tmalluh, "that women wear dresses and chadri when in public."

"We are visitors," I said, holding in my growing anger.

He shrugged dismissal. "It matters not." He looked at me with renewed interest. "What is your relationship with this woman?"

"Friends," I said.

"Co-workers," said Sandy.

"You have no family relation?"

"No."

"Yet you travel together?"

"We're partners, we do that." I began to worry.

"It is sinful." He scratched his scrawny beard. "What is your business?"

Sandy looked at me. We hadn't prepared for this kind of inquisition. And from what had just gone on, it was possible that our answer would be the key to getting us deeper into trouble or helping to bail us out.

"We're spacers," I said carefully, because that was obvious and they could check it. "The Plex link with the rest of Galacticon is inoperational, so we came." I nudged Sandy. "At the insistence of Galacticon authorities. The *lady* represents both Galacticon and the Plex Net."

"Ah," the tmalluh said. "You have credentials?"

Sandy dug into a pocket. "I have a copy of my orders from Sunday A. Sunday, Sector Administrator, to repair and replace faulty relay beacons. Additionally, I have various pieces of identification. However, be advised that as a Galacticon representative I am not prepared to produce my credentials to the first lowly official who demands them." She waved a paper in front of him and replaced it in her pocket.

Several of the OD dressed guys simultaneously drew in breaths.

Surprise flickered over the tmalluh.

Since Sandy had brought it to a head, I had to play my part. "I think my personal friends, Sunday A. Sunday and Sunday B. Sunday would take umbrage at the treatment we're being accorded. We wish to talk to someone in authority, not some bottom-level bureaucrat trying to hassle every farangi he can drag into his little two-penny court."

More loud intakes.

The tmalluh looked like he wanted to explode and blow the turban off his head like a champagne cork.

Sandy was staring at me with unbridled admiration. I don't do stuff halfway.

An aircar delivered us to a taller building somewhere this side of the horizon. It was a big city.

The building was adjacent to one of the temples, festooned with golden domes, copper bubbles, and black steeples. From the foot traffic between the two, I figured they were connected and that this was one of the places where religion and government grew together.

The BDU was desert camo.

"There must be some significance in battle dress uniforms," I told Sandy. "Each level dresses differently."

"It indicates status, I'd say," she said.

Troops with desert camouflage uniforms led us into the presence of a bald man dressed entirely in black.

The security detail departed and I looked around.

The room was comfortable, environmentally controlled, and large. Modern accoutrements abounded. He had a command console and screen, a desk, modern chairs, and a Plex station.

The bald man's black clothes were billowy like pajamas. He had intelligent eyes and a black mustache.

He was shorter than both of us; nonetheless he rose and came around the desk to greet us.

"I am Abon Sel Murad. How do you do?" He shook my hand first, hesitated, then offered Sandy his hand, too.

She took it slowly and reluctantly.

"I don't know yet," I answered, keeping a trace of belligerence in my voice. "When I speed through the dangers of space on a mercy mission, I am not accustomed to a welcome of rude and arbitrary treatment as if I were a common criminal. If it were up to me, I'd recommend to my friends Sunday to allow me to not repair or replace the dysfunctional relay beacon and leave the Laquinto system isolated from the Sector and Galacticon."

Sandy was watching me with interest. She turned to Murad. "We came to help with no the intention of violating your customs. Our dress and behavior were correct as far as any part of Galacticon I've ever heard of or visited. Apparently some of your more officious and zealous personnel do not agree with me." She was being rather diplomatic. "We did not wish to offend."

"We should introduce ourselves," I said.

"I am G. H. O'Clock, special Galacticon Representative and Plexus Net Inspector General, on detached service to Sector Eight." She indicated me. "This is my pilot and technical advisor, Mr. R. Wallace." She looked curiously at me as if to ask what my middle name or initial was. I kept my face bland. She'd learned my real name, but not many people knew my middle name. It was on only a few documents such as Betsy's registration and so on.

Sandy had rolled that spiel off very well, improvising to fit the facts.

"May I inquire as to your position?" Sandy said, voice deceptively soft. "I would not ordinarily be so discourteous as to do so, but your overzealous underlings have volunteered no information."

I could tell that Abon Sel Murad was taken aback by Sandy and her commanding attitude. I was impressed with the authoritative presence she was projecting.

"Forgive me, Miss O'Clock—"

"Mizz," Sandy said.

"Of course, if you wish." His tone was a shade obsequious, telling me he'd accepted Sandy's story. "I am the administrative assistant to His Holiness, the Tollah."

According to Betsy's briefing, religion here was a business. Laquinto was a hierocracy. Tollahs ran things from Esfahan. They were religious leaders and their minions were the tmalluhs. And there were only a handful of Tollahs. Each Tollah was in charge of a separate section of government, sort of like ministerial portfolios in other types of government.

"Your Tollah oversees what sector?" asked Sandy.

"Please, sit down," Murad said, indicating chairs. He sat down along with us in a corner grouping. I liked that. He could have sat behind his desk and tried to lord over us.

We sat and a man dressed in leaf-brown camos brought in a teapot and cups. He poured for each of us except Sandy. He put the teapot in front of her and left.

Sandy glowered after him. She did not pour herself tea, figuring, I guess, that she would ignore the slight. On Esfahan, they did not think well of women.

"His Holiness is the Minister of the Exterior, if you will. His duties include liaison with Galacticon, and other functions to do with the remaining worlds in the Laquinto system."

Sandy stood. "We will see his holiness, then." The

way she said it, you knew she wouldn't have capitalized the title.

"But, but, you cannot." Murad leaped to his feet.

"I said I am a personal representative of the Sector Administrator. He has the affairs of millions of worlds which to attend. I have already wasted more time with you than he spends on any planet, any system. However, I suspect he will make an exception in your case."

"But, but, you do not understand."

I got to my feet, too. "We don't want to understand. So far all we've encountered is discourtesy and arrogance. May we use your Plex station?" I moved that way.

"Please allow me to explain." His voice was pleading. Maybe he'd forget to ask for our credentials.

"Well? Get on with it." Sandy was imperious.

"Once raised to Tollah status, *no one* can see him. It is so written."

This was interesting. "So how does he do his job?" I asked.

Murad looked down at his feet. "The Tollah expresses his wishes to me and I interpret them and implement them. Tollahs generally express themselves in terms of the Written Word, which is why they are known as His Holinesses."

Wouldn't it be their holinesses? I wondered.

"Very well," Sandy was saying, "we will deal with you. However, in the future, I suggest a little more honesty and openness up front. We will tell Administrator Sunday that you did not necessarily *mean* any offense to him or his good offices."

"It's the least we can do," I said helpfully. It sounded like Murad ran things for this Tollah.

Sandy sat down abruptly.

Murad dropped like he'd been shot. The only reason I could guess was that there was some local custom about woman not sitting in the presence of standing men. Aw. I draped myself back onto the chair.

The servant returned.

"May I offer you food or other drink?" Murad said.

"A peanut butter crepe would go awfully good right now."

"Nothing for me," Sandy said pointedly.

The servant left.

"Now—" Sandy began.

The servant scurried back in and whispered into Murad's ear.

Murad lost two shades of color. "We cannot. Peanut butter is proscribed. It is so Written."

"Disregard, then," I said, trying to look as if the whole thing bored me.

"I will take your full report back," Sandy said. "However, you may give me an oral summary so that I may save Administrator Sunday some valuable time."

"Summary of what?" Murad asked. "Do you wish to know of the public outcry of rage, of the riots attributable to the alien signal?"

"There's that," Sandy said, her eyes veiling, but I could read her well. Paydirt. "We must also relate to the Administrator how the citizens of Laquinto reacted, and are still reacting, to the loss of contact with the rest of Galacticon."

"As for the latter," Murad said, sitting back, "the people do not care much whether the Plex Net link to the rest of Galacticon remains or disappears. Laquinto is self-sufficient among all its worlds, and we do not need contact with Galacticon or any one else. It is Written that each man shall look within himself—"

"How about women?" I asked.

Murad shifted uncomfortably. "Women are not addressed." Quickly he resumed. "When the mass hysteria was occurring, it would have been well to have the Plex connection with Galacticon repaired and working for many of our people would have been reassured by the link and the possibility of succor and escape. However, since then, we have armed ourselves and are prepared for invasion."

More question than I could count were forming in my head.

"I assume the Plex Net malfunctioned simultaneously with the news of the aliens," Sandy said.

"That is correct," Murad said. "Actually, it occurred shortly thereafter, but for purposes of your question, the answer is yes."

So the Sundays had pulled the plug after hearing what the news about the aliens had done to the Laquinto system. My opinion of the Sundays continued to rise.

I really wanted to discover the contents of the alien signal; however, if we were indeed who we'd represented ourselves to be, we'd have full knowledge of the entire signal.

So, I took a chance. "You mentioned invasion by the aliens and that the whole Laquinto system is prepared for war. Certainly none of the message can be construed as immediately threatening."

Abon Sel Murad shifted uncomfortably again. "Unfortunately, the very existence of other-than-human lifeforms contradicts The Word. Nowhere is it Written; therefore, the very existence of intelligent beings is inimical to The Word, so spaketh the Tollah responsible for Reconciling The Word with Actual Events."

In other times, they called them party theoreticians.

I nodded as if I understood. "So in a mad rush of religious fervor, people rejected the quote very existence unquote of the aliens; and if the aliens were real, then the people were ready to repel the attack by these farangi non-entities."

"Exactly," said Murad. "I see your understanding is Universal. It is Written that Understanding is the First Step to Nirvana. Your intuitive grasp would assure you of Theopathy in short order."

"Excuse me?" said Sandy. "We can discuss Mr. Wallace's religious grasp and conversion another time. One of the things we have been tasked to investigate and evaluate is the inoperational Plex relay beacon. Since the relay malfunctioned approximately right after the message from the aliens arrived, I would like to know if your technicians found any evidence the two were somehow linked?"

Sandy was returning to the alien message. We already knew the Sundays had disconnected the relay by remote command. But Murad couldn't know that.

"The coincidentality of both events did not escape our attention. The Tollah who Interprets Occult Occurrences determined that both were manifestations of the same event; that is, that Now is the Time of Test of The Word. This becomes a fortuitous occasion in that it allows each and every one of us to Reaffirm our Faith and Pledge anew our Devotion to The Word."

"Is it possible that this general angst about travel, whether via space or Plex Net, contributed to the unrest?"

Murad sat upright. "That is possible, possible," he admitted. "Why, The Word even teaches that the massive open space between humans on different worlds should either be closed up or Disavowed."

Great. Just what we needed. Humanity was in bad enough trouble as it was without these religious freaks preaching to the internal fears and fanning the flames.

"Theologically speaking," I said wording very carefully, "could it not be that the very angst we now address helped give rise to The Word?"

"Indeed, indeed. Humanity cried out in Need; thus the Genesis of The Word."

So, The Word was merely another manifestation of this retreat of humanity. Perhaps it was akin to those elsewhere stamping the infinity symbol on their foreheads.

"With the apparent tie-in of the disconnection of the Plex link and the arrival of the alien signal, were there any other astronomical irregularities?" Sandy was sticking to the right line of questioning.

Murad shook his head. "The riots which I mentioned earlier performed as a catharsis for our peoples; therefore, certain Anti-Word activities halted."

Sandy nodded. "Because of the mass hysteria, the

rioters destroyed all scientific and observation apparatus which *delivered* news of aliens and possible other follow-up future signals.''

''You are quite perceptive. There is a stellar cloud out there,'' he waved vaguely upward obviously indicating Duke's Cloud, ''which is a galactic anomaly in that it contains many stars going nova, supernova; it also has several black holes, white dwarfs, red giants, and neutron stars. These phenomena gave rise to The Word as interpreted by the Tollahs.''

''But Duke's cloud has been there a long time,'' Sandy pointed out.

''It has,'' Murad agreed. ''The Word has bidden its time to Manifest itself to the Tollahs and, in turn, the people.''

''You must understand,'' Sandy said, ''that I've only seen copies of copies of the alien signal. Bureaucracy, you understand?'' Sent through the Plex comm link, all *anybody* would have seen would have been a copy. But Sandy was working on something. She continued. ''It would aid us in determining the point of inoperationality'' —she could indeed be a bureaucrat in her reach to obfuscate the issue— ''of the Plex link and, indeed, the very one individual relay beacon should we be able to trace the path of the alien message from point of origin to the databank through the Plex system to the point of infracture.''

I'd have to check with Betsy, but I doubted there was such a word as ''infracture.'' Sandy was flimflamming Murad with imaginary jargon to back him off.

Murad appeared puzzled for a moment, then The Word must have kicked in, for surely he wasn't going to admit he didn't know what a mere *woman* was talking about. ''You, ah, would, ah, follow the path of the transmitted signal with special equipment to determine the possible, ah, breaking down of the Plex link?'' he scratched himself self-consciously under his black pajamas.

"Very good," Sandy said brightly and Murad didn't get her sarcasm. She leaned forward confidentially. "There is a theory," she whispered, glancing around conspiratorially, "that the signal itself contained a hidden message which decoded itself once inside transmitting equipment of the Plex comm link which directed the equipment to disconnect or self-destruct in order to preclude relay transmission of same so that satanistically it could, by its very nature, isolate Laquinto from the rest of the galaxy and therefore make Laquinto more vulnerable and without further recourse, galactically speaking, of course; and perhaps even now the aliens are studying Laquinto as if the system were a mere object of curiosity. On the other hand, perhaps the aliens, again satanistically speaking, in their nefarious designs, have isolated Laquinto as a test case, one with which to toy, to invade and/or use at their *very* convenience."

Sandy was brilliant. I tried to communicate that thought through an admiring glance.

Murad was standing. "What you say is true!" He moved toward the Plex station. "I must get word to the Tollahs at the Holy City. Even as we speak, His Holinesses are likely considering your theories; surely they would like to be able to discuss it in the terms which you make very articulately. It is why we are all ready for war. The Word Calls. The Word Calls!"

"Wait," I called.

"Yes? What is it? What is it?"

"You could show your appreciation by directing that we be provided the access to which we were referring." I wasn't at all certain what *I* was talking about now, but that would cover everything.

"Well said," Sandy whispered.

Murad nodded his head. He went from the Plex station to the console, touched a keypad and spoke impatiently. "I must go see His Holinesses. Please accord our guests every courtesy and allow them access to which they refer.'' He snapped the connection and hurried to the station, touched a control and translated out.

I stood and turned to Sandy. ''That line about 'satanistically' was very well dropped. I doubt he noticed.''

''It certainly got his attention.'' She stood, too. ''Now they've a new conspiracy to prepare for.''

The door swished and a man dressed in tiger stripe BDUs entered. He gave us a friendly smile and went to the console. ''Abon Sel Murad directed, I execute.'' He worked the command console for a moment. ''I would inquire of the access to which you refer.''

''Our equipment is built into our ship,'' I said, and watched him shiver at the mention of a starship. ''What we want to do is trace, from the exact moment of acquisition and origin, the alien message, and the forwarding of it through the Plex Net comm link so that we may ascertain the exact point of systemic failure.''

The man's eyes glazed over and he said, ''If Abon Sel Murad so ordered, so be it. Give me your ship's code and I shall key it in for total access.''

I went over and typed it in myself, scarcely believing our good fortune. Well, we certainly were due some good luck.

''Thank you. Now if we may avail ourselves of your Plex station?''

The man shivered. ''If you must, but please allow me to withdraw first so that I do not have to witness the doing firsthand myself.''

''Sure.'' I was magnaminous.

Tiger stripe camo left in a hurry.

Sandy and I walked toward the Plex station.

She hugged me and whispered. ''We done good, Rusty.''

''We're a team, all right.'' In my enthusiasm, I hugged her back. She didn't seem to notice the familiarity of the gesture.

I set the destination code for the beacon buoy above Esfahan.

Finally, we were going to discover the contents of the alien message, the first human contact with a non-human intelligence.

22: THE MESSAGE

"The aliens could be on the other side of that boiling star cloud," Sandy said. "Or somewhere *in* Duke's Cloud."

"Let's wait until we read the message before we jump to conclusions," I said.

We were back in the safety of Betsy's womb. We moved off a bit from the beacon buoy, just in case. Obviously, there were no spacers on Esfahan. But with forty-two inhabited worlds, you never know. And I'd learned to be wary of these Laquintons.

Both seated on the extended pilot's couch, we were munching on a concoction I'd invented early in my life: peanut butter bran muffins.

At first, Sandy had been leery, but once she had a bite, she was converted. A tad of llamaornt cream, frozen and preserved from Roanoke, gave it the precise kiss of taste.

"I've got it all now," Betsy said.

I'd had her suck up everything from the Esfahan databanks, and then some.

"The riots are worthy of note," she said academically. She knew at times I was a student of history. "Observe, Rusty—and, Gus—"

"Sandy," said Sandy.

"Right, Sandy," Betsy said. "Did I miss a change of orders?"

"Never mind that," I said, "roll the stuff."

Sandy shot me an accusing glance.

The screen lighted and a turbaned somethingorother appeared. "News from The Word," Betsy said. "I'll cut to the unedited raw footage and show you a sampling."

"Do something," I said, licking my fingers to get the last bit of cream.

One thing we must have missed during our trip to Esfahan: town squares, city squares, great plazas where the Faithful To The Word gathered to Share The Word, or some such.

"They must do this often," said Sandy.

People were rioting and screaming and attacking what appeared to be specially reinforced walls designed to be attacked by mobs.

"The mass hysteria occurred shortly after a reference to the alien signal was made on a news broadcast primarily devoted to The Word." Betsy's voice had turned slightly didactic. She did that when required to condense and recap, probably trying to put me to sleep.

A montage whipped across the screen.

"These are bits and pieces from the different worlds in the Laquinto system," Betsy continued.

"Jeez," Sandy said, "they're *all* crazy."

The system was rather homogenous. The men all wore versions of the BDU we'd observed on Esfahan. The women uniformly wore dark dresses and chadri.

"What a real neat place for women," said Sandy.

"Observe the offices of the Galacticon and Sector VIII businesses," Betsy said.

Modern buildings offset from the squat square affairs of which Esfahanians were so fond. Smoke coming from their insides. Looters, rioters, plunderers.

Security standing aside and simply watching.

"Tacky," I said.

"You'll note," Betsy continued, "this. It occurred a few days before the report about the alien signal."

Another day's newscast, crowds of worshipers in the central squares and plazas.

"Only security personnel are wearing battle dress uniforms," I said.

"I will not bother to bring up the audio on the newscast. But it is a report from some Tollah in charge of Defense of The Word. He is making a call to arms."

"So they worked the people into a frenzy and hit them over the head with the alien signal." Sandy absently picked up another muffin and ate it *without* the all-important llamaornt cream. To each her own, I guess.

"Perhaps we can draw the conclusion that the alien signal was propitious for the hierocratic leadership." I wanted to reach over and add the cream, but that wouldn't be polite. "Maybe they have some pressing internal problem that they can push to the back burner by using the alien signal to rouse the people in a common high-profile goal."

"That's possible," Sandy said. "On the other hand, it could be that the leadership needs occasional new provocations to maintain a frenzy fever of religious adherence to The Word. This kind of thing helps those in power to stay in power."

"My analysis indicates Sandy's reasoning to be closer to the actuality that yours, Rusty." Betsy's tone was neutral.

"I was gonna say that next," I said. "The other possibility is that the guys in charge were afraid that the message would be construed to be The Word and took action to prevent that. What's the message?"

"We have been messing around too long and ignoring the big stuff," Sandy said, finishing her muffin.

"First you have to understand that it arrived in mathematical form," Betsy said didactically, "for that is the only way two separately-evolving intelligent species can initially communicate. I've duplicated the local Plex Net computations and concur with their reading of the contents of the signal."

"What's the message?" I asked again.

"Perhaps it is best put by showing you the initial report from Abon Sel Murad."

"Whatever, just do it." I wondered if Sandy had taught Betsy to pull my chain. Upon consideration, it

was on the order of high probability. Nonetheless, the
ship still smelled better for having a woman on board.
Even if I had to put up with a few inconveniences.

The screen changed and there was the report.

TOP SECRET EYES ONLY

TO: SUNDAY A. SUNDAY, SECTOR VIII ADMIN-
ISTRATOR
SUBJECT: RECEIPT OF ALIEN MESSAGE
FROM: HIS HOLINESSES' HUMBLE SERVANT
ABON SEL MURAD, REPRESENTING HIS HOLI-
NESSES AND THEIR 42 WORLDS OF THE WORD
DOCUMENT #: 1CYCLE5588, this subject
DATE: 88 STANDARD OF CYCLE 5588

Sir,
As no doubt you have possibly heard by now, the
Plex Net has received what appears to be a genuine
signal from an alien source. The entire text is contained in Appendix A, in accordance with Galacticon
reportage procedurals. It is as we originally received
it and the translation thereof by the Plex Net computer system is contained in Appendix B. The math-
ematics correlate properly, so the academicians are
certain of the correctness of the interpretation. At a
time in the Future, our Word academicians will apply
The Word and determine the proper Translation.

While we have no way of knowing what has actually
initiated this transmission from aliens, the academicians speculate that the Plex Net comm link has been
bleeding off and has not all been recaptured by our
out of the way Plex Net receptors, relays, apparatus, and other technical terminology about which I am
not articulate.

Consequently, Galacticon comm link transmissions
to Laquinto have been leaking continuously past us.
The experts theorize that these continuous transmissions happened to have reached aliens which possess
similar Plex Net technology. These aliens, upon de-
tecting our transmissions, have responded in kind.

Mr. Administrator, I make no guess as to what the aliens mean, for I cannot reconcile their message with The Word; even so, that is not up to me. All the computations are in the appendices. To the best of our ability, besides the establishment of a basis of communication by the math, the following is the entire *nonmathematical* text of the message:

WHO ARE YOU.

WHAT DO YOU WANT.

The significance and meaning is for you and your superiors to determine.

Submitted in accordance with procedure and The Word,

Respectfully submitted,

His Holinesses' Humble Servant,

Abon Sel Murad

"Well, hell," I said, stumped.

"Me, too," said Sandy.

"Me, three," said Betsy. She gets her humor from me.

"Betsy, you don't have any ideas?"

"None, Rusty. Alien interpersonal characterizations are outside my envelope of experience and knowledge."

"Mine, too," said Sandy.

"The lack of interrogative at the end of the statements must be significant," I said. "It kind of smacks of, say, a calculated aggression."

"Calculated aggression, that's good," said Sandy at my insight. "That rather describes the whole thing."

I stood and pushed aside a fernlike leaf that was growing on a ball of fur I'd picked up on some world I couldn't remember. "The slightly arrogant and threatening nature of the message could well have been what set off the mass hysteria—"

"After some holinesses had stirred them up," said Sandy.

"Right." I paced the bridge. "What with the general human entropy, it wouldn't have taken much to set them off, and the Laquinton religious fanaticism pushed them over the edge."

"That explains a lot," Sandy agreed.

I sat down next to her again.

She looked at me.

I looked at her.

"So that's the message," she said.

"That's it," I said.

Neither of us wanted to address what came next.

"What comes next?" Sandy said.

"I was afraid you were going to say that."

"Somebody had to," she said.

We'd been anticipating the contents of the aliens' message so long, we'd both kind of assumed it would contain an answer or two.

Nothing. No tie-in.

No Roanoke.

"That leaves only two options, I think," Sandy said.

"That's the way I see it. Betsy?" I said. "Is there any way to determine the origin of the signal?"

"Sure. It's way and the hell and gone."

Sandy glanced at me. "You've changed some of her programming." Sandy was not exactly accusing me, but the idea lingered there between us.

"It was done in an effort to repair someone else's tampering," I shot back.

"Well, squeeze the spit out of me," she said.

"Maybe one of these days."

"If I may?" said Betsy. "To determine the origin of the signal, we'd have to employ the entire Plex Net computer system, using the data it has picked up out here and the comm link transmissions to here that have bled off and the energy differentiation between what was transmitted and what was received—"

"You could work for Galacticon," I said dryly.

"Could we pop in and out of Duke's Cloud?" Sandy

asked hopefully. She didn't know about the one hundred days, only nine of which were left as close as I could figure.

"Forever," said Betsy, "without finishing the task."

"You're assuming that's where the signal came from," I pointed out.

"Oops, the star wall doesn't necessarily have to be the origin," Sandy said. "You've a good point."

"Which leaves us the final alternative," I said. "Some Sundays."

"That's about it," Sandy said. "Except it is possible that Hyman Bookbinder has turned up something in his search."

Hyman was going to search to find if anyone would profit from Roanoke disappearing.

"I don't hold much hope for that route," I said, "considering everything we've been through and learned in the interim.

"There's the conspiracy at the top level of Galacticon and the Plex Net," Sandy pointed out.

"There is that," I agreed. "They could be concealing the alien contact for their own purposes, maybe with some machinations like their holinesses did on Esfahan. Or the opposite. They could be concealing the truth because they *fear* a repetition. Think in terms of jillions of people going crazy like they did in Laquinto."

"I've been thinking about it. That 'calculated aggression' fits right in, doesn't it?" Sandy lounged back and cupped her knee with her linked hands.

"It does. There appears to be a message within the message. The manner in which the message was put— and delivered, are worthy of attention. If they've intercepted our comm link, then they know generally of our current racial psychology. They've read us well, you can tell, from the way they worded their message."

"But they sent math," Sandy pointed out, "not our language."

"That's explainable. If the signal came in Galacticon English, then it could have been construed as a hoax, no matter the strange delivery system and the direction from which it came." I paused. "The math proves it is not a hoax. Right, Betsy?"

"Right, Rusty. It is definitely nonhuman in origin."

"Also," I went on, "the bleed-off the aliens received might have been too weak or even distorted by the mess in Duke's Cloud, so that they can't figure out our language yet and wanted to respond anyway."

"That's the best explanation yet," said Sandy. "Have you considered the aliens might not want to bother with our language?"

"Anything like that could be likely, depending on their psychology—and their physiology."

"There are too many possible scenarios," Sandy said. "We'll never know until we ask them—and we can't do that until we locate the origin of the signals."

Much food for thought.

I stopped in front of Sandy. "I keep coming back to the key link, the one link which is involved at both ends, here and Galacticon. Sundays."

"You've a feeling?"

"Sunday A. Sunday, and his brother B., denied knowing anything about anything. They tried to divert you and me both by sending us off to find an inop relay beacon. Each acted not very intelligent. Each was bland, a born bureaucrat."

"You're beginning to make sense," she nodded.

"Each, to run a Sector and a big part of the Plex Net, must be on the ball. They do the work, Galacticon is overwhelmed by bureaucracy. You can't just administer millions of planets and be a bland bureaucrat of average intelligence."

Sandy unwound herself and took my hand. "Does it matter? We've found no connection between the alien signal and the disappearance of Roanoke."

I was excited. It must have transmitted through my hand to her. "That's the thing, Sandy. You said it yourself long ago. Two anomalies, both improbable to the zillionth order. The seeming disinterest of the brothers Sunday. No, now I am certain that the alien signal and Roanoke are involved in some fashion.'' Spacers have good intuition. While the possibility existed that the two occurrences were not connected, I couldn't admit it. I would have nowhere to go, no trail to follow.

"If Betsy is correct," Sandy said, brows furrowed with thought, "then consider. She said that it would take much of the Plex Net's resources to identify the origin of the alien signal.''

"I said that," Betsy said.

"Which Sunday involved in this thing could command said resources?'' Sandy asked, squeezing my hand.

"B." I thought for a moment, watching Sandy watch me. "Remember Sunday A. Sunday's top secret eyes only message?''

Sandy nodded.

"It did *not* mention Roanoke. They've obfuscated the disappearance. And Sunday was concerned with your presence, pointing out obliquely that you were interfering—in what we don't know. Immediately thereafter, your boss, the Inspector General—''

"General Kalhen," Sandy said and withdrew her hands and held them to her chest.

"—got unceremoniously dumped," I finished.

"It could be that or the embezzlement he was tracing," Sandy said. "We're coming up with more unanswered questions than when we started.''

"Yep. But we've one thing now we didn't have before, and that's direction." I slammed my fist into my palm. "You know, Sandy, you don't have to follow through with this any more.''

"But I do." She stood in front of me and pushed the fernlike thing aside, too. "I'm a renegade, don't forget, just like you.''

I hadn't forgotten. "There are criminal charges from the ROAR office B and E. You could have been tagged a rogue agent by now.''

"You're right. I'm AWOL and they never did trust me. But be that as it may, I've lost my opportunity to change the system from within. Any fool can tell that the situation with the aliens and Roanoke is in the process of blowing wide open, and might well provide me with leverage enough to accomplish my goal."

"You could work for Galacticon."

"I do," she said, her green eyes gleaming.

"Oh, I forgot." I stepped back since she was crowding me. There was a lot here to think about. Another reason I wanted to return to D'Earnhardt: nine days left and that was our only trail.

"We've got to return to D'Earnhardt," Sandy said. "The Sector VIII capital seems to be the center of the mystery."

"And a couple of Sundays," I said.

"And no newsy floozie," said Sandy.

"Marion Zernicke?" I said. "I'd forgotten about her—"

"I'll bet," Sandy said.

"Maybe she can help," I said hopefully. "She has resources and she's bright—"

"Not if I can help it," Sandy said, stepping back from me, green fire erupting from her eyes. "Wake me when we get there." She stormed off to her stateroom.

"What'd I say?" I asked nobody.

23: SUNDAY BRUNCH

I t took us a standard day and a half.

"If we don't come back," I instructed Betsy, "you go find another Roanoke spacer and play all the tapes for him or her." I remembered Marion Zernicke of SNS, Sector News Service, had said that one of our spacers had checked with her. "Like Yakamura Yamashita Yoriken Yyllander—"

"Or ex-Inspector General Kalhen on Chalan Kanoa," said Sandy. "He would be a good one to tell."

"Is he afraid of space?" I asked.

She shook her head. "He's just been around a long time and doesn't go out much anymore."

We were hanging over D'Earnhardt near the beacon buoy, ready to go over and translate down.

However, there was a small matter of getting an audience with one or more Sundays.

"When in doubt, try the front door," said Sandy.

"Good idea." I commed the Sector Administrator's office and got a low level flunky who was a receptionist's assistant in the front lobby of the building.

"You want an appointment with the Administrator?" The guy giggled. On his forehead was an infinity tattoo, more evidence of human decay.

Four levels higher, a woman told me, "If your business is so urgent, then you would already possess the comm code thankyouverymuch," and disconnected.

I tried Sunday B. Sunday, Plex Fax Mgr for D'Earnhardt and Sector VIII.

Soon, it became quite obvious that we'd never get through via normal channels.

"Can you work some of your magic on the Plex Net and get us the destination code?" I asked Sandy.

She nodded. "Probably. But, remember, these guys are surrounded by security. We'd get stopped before we reached them. *We* have to give them a reason to talk to us. We can approach them all day and part of tomorrow, but they still don't have to enter a dialogue with us."

"Yeah, you're right. Hmm." Time for some of the famous Wallace scheming. "So the important thing is to make *them* want to talk to *us*."

"You've a way with the obvious," said Sandy.

I glared at her. We still weren't speaking to each other very much. We'd both had Betsy put us to sleep for the real time it had taken to reach D'Earnhardt from Laquinto.

Just to get a shot at her, I pulled up the SNS headlines on the screen and idly read a few.

Sandy favored me with a frosty look, fully aware I was paying her back—for which supposed offense, I wasn't altogether certain of right then.

"Betsy, see if you can get me Sector VIII Internal Security, the highest officer you can raise." Turning to Sandy, I asked, "Internal Security is tasked with head-of-state protection, meaning Sunday A. Sunday, correct?"

She nodded, her eyes suddenly interested. She knew my penchant for scheming.

I bullied through a couple of levels higher than Betsy could raise and wound up with a colonel.

"What is it?" he demanded.

"Colonel, I'll lay all my cards on the table. I need an audience with Sector Administrator Sunday—"

"Call the receptionist," he snapped.

"That's it," I told him, "you know I'd never get through."

He started to reach for his disconnect keypad.

"Wait, Colonel. Give me some credit. I knew enough to go through you, didn't I?"

Appealing to elitism never hurts when dealing with public servants, and especially military types.

"You've got twenty seconds," the colonel said. People keep threatening me like that.

"It's important enough," I began, "for me to go through security channels. Tell Administrator Sunday that Rusty Wallace—" I glanced at Sandy—"and Agent G. H. O'Clock—" Sandy gave me an appreciative look telling me I was redeeming myself in her eyes— "from Galacticon wish to talk to him. The specific message is as follows: We have been to Laquinto and we know all about it."

"That's it?" The colonel sounded interested.

"I'll discuss the rest with the Administrator," I said.

He shrugged and blanked the screen.

"Now we wait," I said.

"That was good," said Sandy. "Laquinto and an enigmatic message that can cover a multitude of sins. It's the perfect mix to jump levels of bureaucrats."

"If our speculation is right, it ought to get their immediate attention." Sitting back in the command lounge, I took a bite of popcorn upon which I'd added a liberal amount of powdered peanut butter and parsley sprinkle.

Sandy was giving me that look which said I was eating the equivalent of tinit manure from Bristlebrush.

So I said, "You Bristlebushers have no room to look down your noses, considering tinits and—"

"Bristlebrushians," she corrected automatically.

"Never mind." We'd been starting to get along well there for a moment.

"I think you do stuff like that on purpose, Rusty Wallace, just to get under my skin." She crossed her arms.

"Me?"

"You."

"I'm not the one so touchy about his names—"

"Oh?" Her eyelids shot up a mile. "What is your middle name?"

"Um, I ain't tellin'." Me.

"Why not?" Her.

"None of your business." Me.

"You know *my* names." Her.

"*Some* of 'em. Your mom told the Hortense one." Me.

"Leave my mother out of this." Her.

"Not to mention the bulky Alfonso." Me.

"Alfredo, and you're jumping off the subject." Her.

Suddenly, I shot her a grin. "I don't know what I'm going to do without you. One day I won't have anybody to give me a hard time."

That got her angry. "Well, Wallace, you just go your own way then. See if I care." She pouted. "When this is all said and done, we'll see who eats whose dust."

"When all is said and done, there's more being said than done." I smiled at her again. It was that or let my own frustration overflow and I'd probably comm Marion Zernicke down below and get in a ton more trouble. Besides, I kind of enjoyed fencing with Sandy.

She stuck her tongue out at me.

I grinned again. "You know we sound a bit like Major, Senior, and Edna."

"You leave my grandparents out of this."

"Besides," I said slowly, "I wouldn't trust anybody else in the galaxy to be partners with during this final run for the money."

"Really?" Her eyes batted innocently.

"Really, and you know it, too."

"Well, I—"

Betsy interrupted. "I have the Administrator's office. Would you care to call a truce and get on with business?"

"*I* never taught her sarcasm," I said, and looked accusingly at Sandy.

She beamed. "Your humor *is* unsophisticated."

"Well, hell, squeeze the spit out of me and forgive me—"

"That's my saying," she said. "Put them on, Betsy."

The front screen lighted and a woman I recognized from Sunday A. Sunday's outer office sat waiting. "Captain Wallace?"

"You remembered," I said and regretted the attempt at humor. It was time to get serious.

"Not at all," she said smoothly. I guess you don't get to work directly for somebody like the Sector Administrator without being pretty sharp. "We understand you'd like to talk with Mr. Sunday."

"I would. So would Agent O'Clock."

"That would be Ms. Gusselwaithe H. O'Clock?" She pronounced Gusselwaithe correctly.

"It would and is."

"Can your audience be addressed over this comm link?" she asked.

It probably could, but I doubted if it would work out that way. "No," I said, "definitely not. It would also be better if we could talk with Sunday B. Sunday, the Plex Net Manager."

"Mr. Sunday and Mr. Sunday are having brunch together right now. Would you and your wife care to join them?"

Sandy pushed into the pickup zone. "I'm not his wife."

"Ah, so."

"Yes, we would like to join them," I said, nudging Sandy aside. Her shoulder was hard and soft at the same time.

"I've programmed the beacon station with the appropriate destination code," the woman said.

"Thanks."

"They will expect you immediately."

I cut the connection and looked at Sandy. "Well, partner, this is it."

"If you're waiting on me, you're backing up," she said.

"Hey, I thought that was my line?"

"Whatever," she said heading off the bridge.

We took the tunnel to the beacon and stood on the target plates.

Zap.

Security intercepted us as we stepped out of the Plex station.

They searched us, took our weapons, and the two comm relays I had for Betsy to record whatever happened. I'd expected no less. The Sundays were thorough.

It was obviously a private home or two.

As a security detail led us down a hallway, Sandy said, "Hold it," and stopped at a wall unit. "May I?"

The second of three security guys—and I was thankful they weren't wearing jungle camo BDU's or anything similar—said, "Why?"

"I want to call up an outside shot of where we are," Sandy said.

"Sure," said the guy. I liked him already. This was no high pressure situation. "I'll do it for you." He moved to the unit and hit a sequence of keypads. "I'll just show you it from a security camera viewpoint."

The screen lighted and from away, probably a low flying aircar patrolling a perimeter, came the shot. We were in a large castlelike structure. There were turrets and balustrades and balconies and parapets and other architectural oddities I didn't know the words for.

The guy pointed. "We're heading for there." The castle made a giant U and in the center of the U was a large patch of green and blue.

When we got there, it turned out to be a series of lawns and ponds used by a couple of dozen children as pools. Which the ponds were probably designed to be, but disguised as ponds.

All but the head security guy peeled off. He led us through plants and shrubs and lawns and children playing to a section right in the middle of the U and consequently directly in the center of activity.

Sandy nudged me. "Do you see anything peculiar about those kids?"

"They all look like the same family," I said. "But they're too many."

The security guy stopped, pointed, and left us.

Where he'd pointed was a little knoll ahead. People sat and stood on the knoll.

We climbed, perhaps half again my height, and came to the flat place atop the knoll. Four men and one woman were there, all the exact same.

"Quintuplets," I whispered to Sandy remembering that Sunday A. Sunday had said he was one of quints.

"No," said Sandy.

Ignoring her cut, I walked forward, not knowing whom to address.

All of the quints were wearing shorts and sunshirts, each one a different color—I supposed for children or security to identify them from afar. Red, blue, green, peach, and yellow on the woman.

Red shorts came toward me. "Captain Wallace, Mizz O'Clock. It is my pleasure to see you again." He shook hands with us.

"Mr. Administrator?" said Sandy.

"I am. Forgive us, I know it is difficult." He indicated a muscular man in blue whom I figured was B. Sunday since the Plex Fax Manager had worked out during most of my earlier interview. "My brother Sunday B. Sunday, I think you remember." He indicated one after another. "My brothers Sunday C. Sunday, Sunday D. Sunday, and our sister, E. Sunday Sunday." Green, peach, and yellow.

"Welcome to our home," said Ms. Sunday.

The Administrator was still standing there watching us. "I see they're beginning to understand a bit."

I was, and by her glance I could tell Sandy was, too.

We'd been invited to their home, amongst children

and pets and clutter. These powerful people who could crush us in a split second were sending us a message.

"You're disarming me with charm and hospitality by inviting me into your home," I said. "I do not feel threatened in any way." I put steel and ice into my voice. "Yet Roanoke is gone, disappeared, and you know where." I was stabbing in the dark, but my suspicious mind was following my spacer's intuition. "And you know why." I waved my hand including all their castle. "These grounds, this home which you use as a weapon, cannot dissuade me. Where is Roanoke?"

"I don't get bought off either," said Sandy.

The Administrator of Sector VIII grinned a friendly grin. "You are under control of professional security. The creeping malaise has not infected these special women and men. You are both wanted on criminal warrants stemming from incidents at Galacticon Central. And yet you have the gall to dictate to us?"

"We are not dictating," Sandy said.

"We're demanding," I said.

The Administrator squinted up at me. "You certainly are. You are aware I could have you translated to Nowhere? Exiled?"

"I've been that route," I said.

"Those are a few of the things I'd like to straighten out about Galacticon," Sandy said.

"So would we." The Administrator reached into his pocket and tapped on a portable unit. The unit purred and a plastic strip emerged. He tore it off and handed it to me.

I took it and read it. It was a sequence of numbers. "Coordinates?"

He nodded. "You will find Roanoke and its sun there."

"In one piece?"

"Unharmed, people and planet and star, all."

"Just like that," I said, dazed.

Sandy threaded her arm through mine, sensing my

disorientation. She gave me strength, though it took me a moment or two longer to regain control.

A little girl ran up the knoll screaming. "Roll me, Uncle." She could have been a daughter or grand-daughter of any of the Sundays. She wore a one-piece bathing suit and was wet. She leapt at the Administrator and he caught her, swung her around, set her down on the ground, and, like a log, rolled her downhill. She squealed the whole way and tumbled into a pond. I didn't want to know what these alphabet Sundays named their children.

Sandy's look told me we had to do some reevaluation here. People with these kinds of values were not inimical to us and the galaxy. Or so I hoped.

The Administrator rose and faced us again. "I suspect its time for explanations. You've both certainly earned them." He indicated the ground. "Please, sit down."

"I've things to do," said one of the Sundays, the one in peach.

"Me, too," said C. or D. and two brothers and the sister walked down the knoll, leaving the Administrator and the Plex manager with Sandy and me atop the knoll.

Well, it was about time we got some answers.

However, I wasn't certain whether I'd like those answers or not. You just don't relocate a planet and star for good and moral reasons, and hide the fact to boot.

They had just *relocated* Roanoke, hadn't they?

Sure, I had what the Administrator *said* was the right coordinates for Roanoke. Did I trust them? Did I trust the Sundays?

Giving me the new coordinates meant the world and the star had actually changed location in one fashion or another.

I never heard of a planet moving, relocating, whatever. Much less a star. Much, much less a star and a planet together.

Planets and stars, while always in motion relative to

each other, the galaxy, and so on, don't change locations of their own accord.

Somebody—or some*thing* had caused Roanoke to be gone from one place and be currently at another. I never heard of that happening, nor was I aware of technology which could accomplish that feat.

"I'm not sure I'm gonna like this a lot," I muttered.

"Me, either," said Sandy, and tightened her arm within mine.

24: WHY

We were sitting cross-legged on the top of the knoll with Sunday A. and Sunday B. Sunday.

My heart was now slowing down. My family was still alive! My friends.

And Virginia Bavarro.

Sandy removed her arm from mine as if she knew what I was thinking. Or maybe, more charitably, she thought I no longer needed her support.

The Administrator, Sunday A. Sunday, was sitting like we were, comfortably across from us. His brother, Sunday B. Sunday, the Plex Fax Mgr, was sitting rigid in a variation of the lotus position and I wondered how he could bend his legs like that.

"How can you *move* a planet?" I asked, questions bubbling out of me.

"How are the aliens connected?" asked Sandy.

"Why did you move Roanoke?" I asked.

"Where are the aliens?" asked Sandy.

"Me first," I said.

"Why?" she said.

Then we both looked at each other sheepishly.

"Forgive us," I told the Sundays. "We're spacers. I'm sure you understand."

"I don't," said Sandy.

"I do," said the Administrator.

"To the taxpayers," said the Plex Sunday, "my brother's time is worth more than a million credits a day. I'm certain you can divide that by the number of hours or minutes and understand the value of this conversation.''

"Wow," said Sandy.

"How much did it cost to move Roanoke?" I asked.

"He gets right to the crux of the matter," said the Administrator. He took his unit out and touched a keypad. "Clear my calendar for two hours, please." He clicked it off without waiting for a reply.

"I have to agree that the 'why' question is most important." Sandy leaned against my shoulder, the extra pressure showing her heightened anticipation.

"We moved Roanoke, quite simply," said the Administrator, "in order to position it at the outer edge of the galaxy."

"Again, why?" I asked.

The Administrator looked at his brother.

The Plex fax mgr took a deep breath and answered. "We're going to send Roanoke to another galaxy."

I froze.

Against me, Sandy froze. "Boy, when you answer a question, you answer a question."

"You're going to *send* Roanoke to *another* galaxy?" My initial paralysis was wearing off.

"That's what he said," said Sandy.

"We are," said the Administrator.

"That's what I thought you said." I looked into the stark blue sky. My home world. My family. My—fianceé. My friends. An entire planet.

Sandy's right arm was around me for support. "I can add two and two, too. I don't suppose you're going to tell us that the mysterious aliens have anything to do with all this."

"They do," said the Administrator, adjusting his red shirt.

"Nobody's *ever* been to another galaxy—" I started to say.

"It is a long way," said Sandy.

"—much less a world," I finished.

"What galaxy?" continued Sandy. "Not to mention intergalactic space is quite wide."

"Very wide," said the Administrator. "Galaxies, even as we speak, move away from each other—some of them at up to eighty percent of light speed, if I remember."

The Plex Sunday nodded. "Galaxies moving away from each other as the universe expands, that's called the rate of recession."

"Thanks," said the Administrator. "The name of the galaxy to which we refer is something scientific, like LZ-948. Among ourselves, we call it the Hostile Galaxy."

For a moment I thought about that. "You're sending Roanoke off to some galaxy which you term *hostile?*"

He nodded. "We are."

"Great, just great." I shook my head. "I don't think I want to know any more."

"I do," said Sandy. "Has anybody, any human, been to this galaxy?"

Both Sundays shook their heads. "We're looking forward to it," said Sunday B. Sunday and I misunderstood his statement. I thought he was speaking generically. "It'll be an adventure, don't you think?"

"An adventure?" I shook my head with more verve this time. "A riot. A barrel of laughs. An adventure? Maybe you ought to check with those citizens on Roanoke and see what they think."

The Administrator's face turned hard. You could tell he was into his command mode. "When you were on D'Earnhardt before, you were heard to say repeatedly that nobody cared about fifty thousand people. Recall that?"

"I do."

"Well, what did you discover?"

This time I shook my head minutely. "Just what I thought. Nobody cares about fifty thousand people."

"That's right," said the Administrator. His voice turned as hard as his manner. "I did not ask any of those fifty thousand if they wanted to go; I decided for them."

"Well, at least he's honest," said Sandy, leaning away from me and dusting her hands off.

"What evidence do you have that that galaxy, those aliens, are hostile?" I asked. Sandy's presence was comforting while I was being assaulted by these revelations.

"Their message appeared hostile to us," said Sunday the Plex man.

"We labeled it 'calculated aggression,' " I said.

For a moment there was silence. D'Earnhardt's sun seemed colder.

The Administrator wiped his brow. "We hadn't used that term, but I like it. I like it."

"So do I," said his brother. "We also see you've managed to read the message. That tells us you are very resourceful."

The whole thing was beginning to percolate through my mind. "You are just labeling this galaxy 'hostile.' You don't know for sure?"

The Administrator shook his head. "No. We've only the evidence of the one message from them upon which to go."

Sandy nudged me. "Hon? They don't know anymore than we do."

"We don't."

"I didn't think so," I said. "We've discussed it and we think they sent us the message worded as it was to characterize themselves to us. They want us to think they're tough, aggressive."

"We've come to the same conclusion," said Sunday B.

"If these aliens are, in fact, hostile," Sandy said, "then we don't think they'd have sent the message as it was. We thought that they were trying to put us off, keep us at bay, or start public panic like they did in the Laquinto system."

I said, "Who knows how they operate? Their philosophical approach to life and relations with other species. They could have experience with other intelligent races; *they* could be more than one alien race. The only certain bet is that they *do not* think as we do.''

The Administrator's smile broke through his hardened demeanor. ''We have come to many of the same conclusions. Consequently, that is why we decided to send Roanoke.''

''Which consequence?'' I asked. ''Laquinto? Or the alien's aggressive message designed to keep us away from them?''

''All of those reasons and others,'' he said. ''We suspected that they were afraid we'd discover *them* and come looking. Perhaps by Plex comm link bleed-off, much the same as they likely encountered their first evidence of us.''

''Furthermore,'' said Sunday B., ''the very fact of the panic reaction in Laquinto stirred us to action.''

''It also stirred us to keep the existence of the aliens secret,'' said the Administrator.

''Why?'' demanded Sandy. ''A free society means not concealing newsworthy events, especially something as significant as the first intelligent nonhuman contact.''

''It does,'' he replied, thrumming the hem of his red shirt. ''However, I've the public safety to consider. I wish to avoid repeats of riots, pogroms, suicides—''

''That was in Laquinto,'' Sandy said. ''They're religious fanatics and not your normal run of the mill people.''

A. Sunday's face hardened again. ''You're talking about people who are frightened of their own shadow. They don't go into space any longer.''

''Travel frequency on the Plex Net is at an all-time low,'' said B. Sunday.

''We saw a report about population growth trending downward,'' I said, remembering the missing report at the ROAR office at Galacticon Central.

The Sundays looked at each other.

''That confirms Sector VIII statistics,'' said the Administrator.

"I understand you struck illegally into the heart of Galacticon," said Sunday B. Sunday, smiling. "Do the terms 'wants' and 'warrants' mean anything to you?"

"It couldn't be near as felonious as kidnapping and exiling fifty thousand people at once," I said, half-flippantly.

"The point is," said the Administrator, "Loquinto with one point one trillion people reacted to the news of aliens horribly. And they are a warlike people. How do you suppose people who are fading back into their individual shells will react? Many of them are frightened of *human* spacers. Imagine how frightened they would be of *alien* spacers."

"I can visualize it," Sandy said.

What they were saying was true, I knew. I thought about it. Then my scheming mind kicked in and the big pieces fell into place.

Finally getting my chance to nudge Sandy for a change, I did so. "You've more in mind than simply sending emissaries, albeit fifty thousand emissaries, to the aliens, don't you?"

The Sundays looked at each other again, this time surprise showing on both identical faces, with identical signs of surprise, also.

Sandy watching me with heightened attention, I went on. "The very fact that humanity is entering an entropy stage, full of anxiety about the vastness of space and this galaxy, tells me you're up to something. They don't hire sector administrators and Plex managers because they can't think ahead."

"What are you trying to say, Rusty?" asked Sandy.

"It's the 'calculated aggression' business," I said. "Think of what their—rather, his holinesses did in Laquinto."

"They whipped their people into a fighting mood," Sandy said, her voice telling me she was figuring it out, too.

"Exactly. Four or five far-seeing Sundays have decided the human race needs a spark, something to move it forward again, and out from under the collective rock it's been hiding under."

"You realize," said the Administrator very slowly, "that you have just signed your death warrants?" His voice was soft and the zephyr touching the knoll almost carried his words off. He was fingering his unit.

"Maybe," I said, uncomfortably aware he could do that thing right there in the middle of their home in the middle of their family. You don't get to be in charge of a few million planets without enough ruthlessness to kill people. And we'd already established that he'd arbitrarily decided the fate of fifty thousand and was playing with the destinies of zillions. "Maybe, that is, you'd kill us for what we now know—if we didn't agree with you and want you to succeed."

Sandy nodded. "I've had it with people discriminating against me because I'm a spacer. I'm sick and tired of people using me to frighten their kids."

The Administrator relaxed and I wondered if there were snipers in the castle with weapons trained on us or would the Administrator do the deed himself with his unit. I decided I didn't want to know the answer to that one.

Sunday B. Sunday took up the story. "We are trying to walk a fine line here. While we do not wish to have people die in riots and pogroms and panics, we do wish those same people would change their attitudes. We cannot simply announce what we're doing, for lives, economies, even whole societies would be lost from the mass hysteria. The catharsis the human race needs shouldn't be a catastrophic upheaval, an Armageddon, a Rollback, a disaster. We're trying to *save* humanity and what humanity has accomplished, not kill it off prematurely."

"So you hope Roanoke finds the aliens and, because Roanoke's population is comprised of mavericks, pioneers as it were, puts a tougher face on humanity than it in fact possesses. Roanoke is not representative of other worlds, but you'd have the aliens think so." I stopped for a moment. "Then, according to your projections, we'd start a dialog with the aliens and, you hope, generate sort of a friendly competition between our two races."

Sandy stretched her left leg, grabbing my attention as usual. "Obviously you are betting that same friendly competition gathers up our race and drags it out of its ennui."

"We want to get people, worlds, whole populations moving again," said the Plex Fax Mgr.

"You could have selected an exile planet," I said.

"You *are* resourceful," said the Administrator. "No, the exiles might have been the choice had not Roanoke been there and available. You see, the exiles are actively anti-something. We couldn't one hundred per cent trust them. Additionally, the exile planets wouldn't have been as easy to move as Roanoke. Most had other planets in their systems, whereas Roanoke was a single planet system. For the trip we need a sun to keep the world alive; thus any other planets in the system would die were we to remove their sun. Logistically, we didn't want to move more than one star and one planet."

"I'll be dipped in spit," said Sandy.

We were unconsciously holding hands now, excitement traveling between us like electricity.

"You could have told me when I was here the first time," I said.

"We could?" asked the Administrator. "You went to the press anyway. You didn't know about the aliens then. Remember, we had a choice then, and our decision was not to inform you and bring on what troubles I can only guess."

"*Nothing* and *nobody* will interfere with our plans," said his brother.

I believed him.

"There's another thing," the Administrator said, "we were afraid that if the word got out before Roanoke actually began the trip, the public *and* governmental reactions would preclude contacting the aliens, to retreat once again.''

It occurred to me the Sundays were taking one hell of a political chance.

"By governmental, you mean bureaucratic,'' Sandy said. She looked at our joined hands, seemed to realize what she was doing, and gently disentangled her hand from mine.

To cover my regret, I laced my fingers together and straightened my arms to stretch.

"Your inquiries here in Sector VIII,'' said the Plex Fax Mgr, "led us to discover some parts of the story had seeped out—''

"That's when Inspector General Kalhen picked up the rumors.''

The Administrator shrugged. "It could well be. I talked to the Executive Administrator of Galacticon. We have his tentative approval for our plan. But nothing in writing. Ostensibly he knows nothing about this. However, he did take corrective action at Galacticon to squelch rumors which were beginning to circulate.''

"So the actions of the Galacticon Plex Net boss-lady—'' I started.

"Helen Merritt-Browne,'' said B.

"And her Chief of Security, Churnenski,'' finished Sandy.

"What actions?'' asked B.

"Attempting to kill Rusty. Stopping the investigation. Sweeping me out of the way.'' Sandy was almost indignant.

"I thought I was telling this,'' I said. "Excuse the spit out of me.''

Sandy rolled her eyes.

"So they're not tied in with Roanoke,'' I said. "We sort of figured that.''

Sandy gave me one of her looks. "Are you finished now?''

"I am.''

"General Kalhen found a pattern of embezzlement

and fraudulent billing through Merritt-Browne's career in Plexus. It cost him his job, and likely mine, too. Rusty hit them with a spotlight and Merritt-Browne through security chief Churnenski tried to knock him off. The exposure threatened them on top of General Kalhen's investigation.''

"I see," said the blue-shirted Sunday.

The Administrator looked at his brother. "Perhaps we can help rectify that problem?''

Sunday B. Sunday held up his palms. "I think we shall. We already have the ear of the Galacticon Executive Administrator.''

He sounded truthful and I believed him.

Sandy looked happy again.

The Administrator massaged his throat. "I'm thirsty. Would anyone like refreshments?''

He held out his unit. Each of us said what we wanted and they all looked at me like I ordered green slime when I spoke. The Administrator said into the unit, "You copy?''

"Aye, aye, sir.''

The administrator pocketed the unit.

Sandy was staring at me, trying to tell me something. She stood. "I've got to stretch a minute.''

"Me, too," I said, catching on real quick.

Soon, all four of us were standing.

I could tell Sandy was ready, for she shifted slightly to the balls of her feet. Her arms hung loosely, but ready.

"You know, Rusty," she said, voice calm, but I could tell she was in a state of heightened alertness, "they talked about having us killed ''

"Or killing us themselves," I pointed out.

"Whichever," she said. "This Sunday is worth more than a million credits a day, yet he spends a long time explaining things to a couple of interlopers.''

I knew what she was thinking. I'd been trying what they said on and it didn't fit exactly. There was something else involved here.

"What is it?" asked Sandy.

"They *need* us," I said. "They need us for something. You and me. They didn't need us before when we were chasing down leads. Something has changed, something in their plot has gone askew."

25: HOW

Sunday B. Sunday, the physical fitness buff, noticed Sandy. "You must be aware that any threatening move on your part will be instantly fatal?"

"I figured as much," she said. "I just don't trust you-all that much." She was showing the Sundays a lethal proclivity.

The Administrator actually smiled. "Come, come. We are friends here now. No need for that kind of behavior."

"What's the answer?" I asked.

"It's quite involved," said the Administrator. "However, to sum it up. When we moved Roanoke, we used all of the Navy assigned to Sector VIII—which itself is dying by attrition, as are many other institutions. We shut down the Roanoke Plex beacon so that neither transportation nor comm link remained to upset our plans. We moved Roanoke to its present location—"

"How?" asked Sandy.

"I'll get to that in a moment," he said. "It was a surprise move on our part. I knew full well that a world of individualists like Roanoke, while they'd agree with the necessity for doing what we were doing, would refuse to be the ones arbitrarily designated to do so, to be sent to another galaxy. So, I had the Navy capture any and all starships at Roanoke. The Navy surprised them and did so. We moved Roanoke and its sun. At its new location, someone on the planet's surface must have been thinking, for they did the one and only thing they could conceivably do to fight back.''

"Understandable, really," said Sunday B. "For a world of individualists." His blue shirt flapped in the wind.

"What'd they do?" I demanded.

"They had GLMs," said the Administrator.

"Ground launched missiles," I said. "A matter of conversion of unmanned probes. The Roanoke leadership would think they were being attacked in some outlandish manner—which they were."

"That is correct," said the Administrator. He smiled ruefully. At the last moment, we tried to convince them, but it was too late and they didn't believe us. In fact, they were boiling mad. While the Navy ships were deploying some special beacon buoys and thus not as alert as they should have been, came the GLM sneak attack. They rather decommissioned the entire Navy fleet—''

"Three ships," put in his brother.

"Which leaves you without a Navy," I said.

The Administrator turned to stone again. "It leaves us without a starship to position the Plex buoys necessary to send Roanoke off to the Hostile Galaxy. It leaves us without a starship to transport our families to Roanoke." His arm made a sweeping gesture incorporating the entire castle grounds.

"You're going with Roanoke?" Sandy asked.

"Our brothers and sister are," said B. Sunday. "And most of the children and grandparents. Not the two of us. We must remain to face the music as surely as it must come, and to carry out our plans." That's what they'd meant earlier with the comment about looking forward to the trip.

"Plans which need an occasional boost," said the Administrator, "for we must carefully manipulate what the public knows, when they learn it, and how it is released in order to stem the rising angst of the people."

"Well, you just swept away my concerns," Sandy

said, relaxing. "If you are going to send your families with Roanoke, then you are dead serious."

"They wouldn't miss it for anything," said B. "What a fascinating voyage."

"There's one thing missing," I said, trying to reason it through. "Just send 'em to Roanoke via the Plex Net." I snapped my fingers. "Got it! Somebody figured part of it out. A spacer would determine that Roanoke was important for someone to go to all the trouble to move it. They needed leverage, bargaining power. It stood to reason that the one instrument through which everything would occur would be the Plex Net beacon orbiting Roanoke. You tried to talk to them. They figured you needed cooperation. They hit it with a missile, too, didn't they?"

"They did," said the Plex fax mgr.

I continued. "Not only did they take out the beacon buoy to gain some power of their own, but they thought that it would be a red flag to any Roanokeans offplanet who wanted to translate back home or comm Roanoke. It's something my grandfather would think, and it's something he would do to send a signal to me."

B. looked at A. "What he says sounds reasonable."

"Whatever you were going to do, they put a kink in your plans by destroying the beacon." I was proud of my fellow Roanokeans.

"That they did," said A. ruefully.

"You need us, then," I said. "To deliver Plex buoys. To deliver a bunch of Sundays. And one more thing."

"That's true," said B.

"They need *you*, not me," said Sandy.

"They need me, so they've got to take you, too," I said.

"Aw," she said.

I turned back to them. "You need me to convince them to not blast any more beacon buoys so that you can go ahead with your plans."

"Yes," said A. "The GLMs destroyed some of the special Plex buoys." His voice and face hardened once again. "We had some preliminary discussions with leaders of Roanoke, so they know what's going on. We are going to do it regardless of their cooperation. You can perhaps discern that fact?"

"I can."

"So, your job is to convince them to be cooperative."

"There's got to be more to it than that," Sandy said. "Once again, something is missing."

B. Sunday nodded sadly. "We're running out of time. If we don't do it soon, our opportunity will be lost for a long time. Perhaps a generation or two."

"It figgers," I said. The one hundred days Dad had referred to. I'd been worried that something outlandish would happen in a hundred days, like Roanoke exploding from alien mines or an alien virus needing to be cured or a million other possibilities. I had certainly not come up with the most outlandish scenario of them all; the Sundays had. Seven days now, I thought, and a bit left over.

A servant came up the knoll with an honest-to-God tray balanced on his upturned hand.

My steaming mug of melted peanut butter sherbert warmed my hands and drew stares of awe. Well, hell, I needed something strong to pep me up, considering the circumstances.

"There's a world I read about yesterday," said the Administrator, "which has brought peanut butter cusine to new heights and, consequently, is generating much new commerce and tourism. A gambling world—"

"T-hoe," Sandy told him.

"That's it. I assigned a team to study the situation in case there were economic lessons to be learned."

Sandy looked at me and I shrugged. It wasn't important.

Watching the servant go back down the hill, I said, "Which all leads us to the method which you used to move an entire world—and its sun, no less—from one place to another. It ain't something you do everyday."

B. gave a hand signal and another servant trotted up with four floating chairs. We all sat and I watched a few boys jumping off a ledge into a pond. A squirmy, slinky, furry animal squirreled along after them. Splashes and squeals drifted up the knoll. It was a calming scene. These people trusted us, me and Sandy, with their kids. And they had enough confidence in their own decisions to send their own children along with Roanoke to a far and distant galaxy. Something never before done. Bringing us here to their home to discuss Roanoke and the aliens was a calculated move on their part. They had to convince us, especially me, first, so that they—or me—in turn, could convince those on Roanoke to cooperate. It was a brilliant move on the part of the Sundays.

"Right now, the timing is the problem," said B. "Since we've initiated the action, we can't stop. We are committed. The engine we're using to provide the energy to translate an entire star system, albeit it only one planet and its sun, from one galaxy to another is a supernova and it's reaching the critical moment in the explosion process where we must harness the energy and use it."

I began to understand. The one hundred days were almost up, meaning the Sundays' collective back was against the wall.

The Plex Sunday finished his frosted glass of fruit juice. "There was a nova, not a supernova, in the neighborhood of Roanoke—"

"Over past the black hole," I said. "I noticed its energy was gone when I was searching for Roanoke."

"We placed special beacon buoys," said B., "to tap its energy. We located other beacons around the Roanoke system, harnessed the energy from the nova, and translated the planet and sun, the solar system, together, maintaining the proper locations and distances—"

"You needed the sun to keep the planet alive," said Sandy.

"That is right. We zapped the whole kit and kaboodle to the edge of the galaxy closest to the Hostile Galaxy and on the far side of a wall of stars—''

"Duke's Cloud," I said. "It precluded any astronomical observation of the newly arrived star."

"—and near to the forthcoming supernova," he finished. "It was a good test of the project. Prognostications say the method will in fact deliver Roanoke to the other galaxy."

"I guess sending a starship on the intergalactic voyage wouldn't have the impact a planet and a star would," Sandy said. "Hit them between their metaphorical if not physical eyes with our technical ability."

"I thought the same," said the Administrator. "Translight travel is not as fast as Plex travel. We could have sent a starship as we intend dispatching Roanoke, but I decided against that option. Additionally, it might take a long time to locate the intelligent beings within the Hostile Galaxy. We might well be talking about a generation or two before actual contact is made— meaning a planet is the best form of transportation in this case."

"Doubtless, you thought you'd make a stronger point by sending fifty thousand maverick humans to respond to their calculated aggression." I looked at my empty mug. The melted sherbert had been good. Sundays had a good cook—or synthesizer.

A. Sunday rewarded me with a wide smile. "That did occur to me. Earlier you correctly stated that we don't know the psychological bent of the aliens; the converse is also true. We expect them to think of the Roanokeans as typical humans, representing the race. I'm trained in problem solving and experienced therein—"

"There is *nothing* small about his thinking," said B. proudly.

"I couldn't have done it without your technical expertise," A. said. He turned back to us. "It took the Plex Net a while to determine the approximate origin of the alien signal. And," he glanced around confidentially, "it will require the entire Plex Net computer capability to send off Roanoke when the time comes. We'll take the system off the line for a couple of hours under the guise of 'technical difficulty.' "

"That will get the attention of everybody in Galacticon," said Sandy, nodding.

A. grinned. "We will." He tipped his glass upside down to prove it was empty. He flipped it in the air and casually aimed his unit at it and the glass disintegrated in midair.

"I'm glad we're on your side," I said admiringly.

Sandy looked at me. "If you say so, partner. It sounds like they've sold you."

"How about you?" I asked, panic streaking through me.

"You're going to make the trip to the Hostile Galaxy?" she asked, her face controlled.

"I, um, assumed I would." I was going to feel empty if she turned it down. Then I'd have to do some rethinking of my own.

"If you can convince the Roanokeans to cooperate," she said.

"I'll try. The Sundays and their vision have sold me. Somebody's got to do something about this onrushing human entropy. And I'd like to be part of that effort."

The Sundays favored me with identical smiles of appreciation.

"Besides, think about it, Sandy. It will be one hell of an adventure. A different galaxy. A seemingly *hostile* galaxy. We'll need spacers and all the help we can get."

"You make an attractive offer," she said haughtily, like only she could be haughty.

"What'd *I* say?" I said.

She didn't answer.

I swear, I'll never understand women.

I got mad. "Well, hell, Gusselwaithe Hortense O'Clock, think about it. If you want to go along, you're invited."

She shot me another look. I'd missed her first point, but her scheming face told me I'd pick up on the next point. Slyly, she looked at the Sundays. "I think my friend Rusty might not want to go—or even cooperate under these circumstances."

They both straightened in their seats, frivolity gone.

"There's a small matter," she said seriously, "of a few exile planets."

I caught Sandy's train of thought. "On the other hand, I might be too upset to go to Roanoke and help you-all out."

"After your enthusiastic pitch of a moment ago?" asked B.

"Yep. However, if you address Ms. O'Clock's concerns, I might change my mind and sign on."

"You've power," Sandy urged, "enough to stop the exile to unknown and uncharted worlds."

"We'd be fighting the bureaucracy of many worlds," said the Administrator, concern written all over his face.

"Not to mention sectors and Galacticon itself," I put in.

"Think of it this way," Sandy said with a gleam in her eye. "You need people, malcontents and rebels, in the worlds of Galacticon. They'd infuse new life into the populations. Dissent is important. It would contribute significantly to stemming the decline of our galactic society. I'm thinking in terms of reinvigorating, not just stemming tides."

They looked at each other.

"She has a valid point," said A. "I'd considered ideas along those lines. Anything of the like would have to be done deftly—"

"Which is one of your strong points," said his brother.

"You could stop the Plex Net from sending people to those destination codes," Sandy told B., "and totally abolish the kill code which translates someone into space until the boost energy of translation runs out."

Something tickled my brain but I couldn't put my mental finger on it.

B. Sunday looked sour. "It is a curse we've inherited. I have never myself dispatched anyone to the destination with no station or beacon buoy to capture them. The code known as Nowhere."

"Nor have I," said the Administrator. "However, your point is valid. You have my—our—word that we shall do our best to eliminate that policy." He cleared his throat. "I've the Executive Administrator's ear nowadays, what with my Roanoke project, and thus have a leg up on the other sector administrators. Intramural politics, you understand."

"What if you thought in terms of *returning*, that is, repatriating the exiles to their planets of origin?" Sandy had obviously given a lot of thought to this.

"That would certainly hasten the process we're discussing," said B. He nodded to his brother. "It would allow us to attack the problem on different fronts, a combined offensive to give it a description."

"We can try," said A.

"Your word is good with me," Sandy said and beamed. No wonder she was happy. Her goal had been reached. Her lifetime effort to stop the exiling of dissidents had come to fruition. She looked at me and I smiled, sharing her good fortune. Her face froze and she turned away. What the hell was wrong with her? Her moment of crowning glory and she was giving me the cold shoulder.

"I'm happy for you," I said and meant it.

"Thank you," she replied.

"Will you make the intergalactic voyage on Roanoke now?" I asked.

She thought soberly for a moment. "I'll tell you what. I'll help until the time for Roanoke to blast off comes."

I felt glum. "If that's the best you can do," I said sourly.

"It is."

"Thanks. Thanks a lot. It's big of you." Me.

"You're so magnanimous." Her.

"Whatcha tryin' to say, O'Clock?" Me.

"Nothing. Not a thing." Her.

The Sundays were interested spectators.

I felt worse than glum. I felt like I'd just been zapped to Nowhere.

That was it!

I turned to the Sundays. "Speaking of sending people off into *nowhere,* how do you go about sending a planet to a location, even if it is in another galaxy, without a beacon at the end, or a station—a receiver—and the necessary destination code?"

The Plex manager sat back. "Ah, you've got us. It was easy to plant a beacon where Roanoke is now for the intermediate trial trip upon which we sent Roanoke. But not in a far galaxy. And we cannot depend on the aliens having beacons we could track—"

"You wouldn't want a planet and star popping out in the middle of a black hole or a planetary system, would you?" I said.

"Not at all. We can translate Roanoke and its sun, we've established that. In a stasis field, it just takes the tremendous energy we're going to steal from the supernova. Within that stasis field all will remain the same, relatively speaking. You can fly about in your starship *Virginia*—"

Sandy shot me a dirty look.

But I was glad to hear that—I don't think I'd go to a strange galaxy without Betsy.

"—so long as you stay within the field. One of your tasks will be to drop relay beacons along the way so that we can establish a permanent link." B. looked at A. "This new adaptation of Plex technology can be fun." He addressed Sandy and me. "After extensive Plex Net computations, we've determined you can go to the exact edge—or lip—of the stasis field and simply drop off the relay beacons. This is possible because the stasis field is also a magnetic field, a gravity field which has different properties than if you simply zapped people and freight in a normal translation from one station to another. The beacons interact between the Plex stasis field and the gravity field. Additionally, they can harness the star Zira's energy to keep the Plex 'engine' going after the initial burst from the supernova. By the same computations, we figure the beacons generating your stasis field can tell you when you're translating through the proper part of the Hostile Galaxy we've identified as near the origin of the signal; at that time, you simply drop another beacon much the same as you've dropped the relays, and key in that destination code and pop into regular space to that beacon.''

His words had come in a rush and I thought I understood. ''That final beacon will also carry an observation package to determine whether that part of space is safe enough to plop down an extra planet and an extra sun.''

''That's what our figures tell us.''

Sandy stood. ''At that time flags and alarms should start going off if our aliens possess anything like our Plex Net technology, meaning instant communications and transportation.''

''Yes,'' said both Sundays simultaneously.

I stood and spoke. ''At that moment is when the citizens of Roanoke have to be ready to face your 'hostile' aliens.''

''I think,'' said the Administrator, ''that I would put it in terms of making first contact and representing the human race.''

''Or fighting,'' I said ominously.

26: ROANOKE

The three-day trip was a circus, what with Betsy's belly full of Plex beacons, relay and other special buoys, and her passenger section full of Sundays. Children running everywhere, knocking into plants and eating all my peanut butter. I wondered what Betsy thought of it all. Sandy was distant the whole time, but that might be attributable to the pandemonium on board.

We ran out of peanut butter and some of the ingredients to synthesize a respectable batch.

We popped out of translight and into normal space. Right there was Roanoke and Zira, sitting peacefully where they shouldn't be. Briefly, I worried about the delicate balance of the universe and our galaxy in turn. Perhaps there was some physical law which held everything in its place and accounted for all celestial bodies. If one moved unnaturally, what would happen? Chaos? Nah. That theory wouldn't account for comets and stars turning into black holes or going supernova, and so on. I hoped.

"Starship, ID yourself," squawked the comm.

Someone on Roanoke's surface was paying attention.

"Betsy?" I said.

Sandy and I were on the bridge with Sunday D. Sunday.

"Rusty," said Betsy, "remember you had me deactivate the ID transponder when we went from T-hoe to park over D'Earnhardt.''

"Reactivate.''

"Done.''

"Move toward orbit and gimme a comm link.''

"You have it," said the ship.

I cleared my throat. "Hello, Roanoke Control. This is the *Virginia.*''

Sandy made a rude sound.

Sunday D. Sunday looked at her as if she were an alien.

"Roger, *Virginia,* I have your ID squawking now. Confirm. Gee, we're glad to see you, Rusty.''

"Thanks. Listen, Roanoke Control, can you patch me through to my dad?'' There wasn't a Plex beacon to channel normal comm traffic. Roanoke had taken it out with a GLM to scramble the plans of whoever had moved their planet.

"Roger. Standby.''

"Betsy, give me video, too.''

The screen lighted and ping, up came my father. "His name's Red," I told Sandy and the fourth of the Sunday quints. "All the Wallace men have red hair.''

"Rusty! By God, it's about time you got here.''

"I'm glad to be home, too, Dad.''

"You know we've missiles trained on you now,'' he said matter of factly.

"I figured. But you won't catch me and Betsy off-guard like you caught the Navy.''

Sandy stirred beside me.

"No, I don't think we would. State your case or prepare to be fired upon.''

"What the devil is going on?'' asked D. Sunday.

"He doesn't trust anybody, even me. Somebody could be holding me against my will and he is just making sure.'' Although we had a code established and I'd have already used a key word telling Dad I was under a weapon. Still, Dad wasn't taking any chances. In a galaxy of less assertive people, there wasn't much chance of someone overpowering me for nefarious purposes—but you never know. So, being from Roanoke, we don't take anything for granted. Maybe that's one of our characteristics which the Sundays were counting on.

"Also," said Sandy, "you mentioned how they took the Navy, so obviously he's figured out you've consorted with whomever conspired to shift Roanoke to this location."

"Come into the pickup zone, Mr. Sunday."

D. moved over to stand behind me and Sandy.

"He's my bonifides, Dad."

Dad was quiet. "That's convincing, but not enough, son."

"Betsy," I said, "show some scenes of the kids down in the lounge."

Betsy cut in with live shots of Sunday children.

"While that could be prerecorded," Dad said, "I'll grant you a shipload of executive bureaucrat children is not an ominous threat. Go ahead and land, son. We have to talk."

"Are you still Managing Director?" I asked.

"By the skin of my teeth, last vote of confidence."

Losing your world will do that to your political popularity.

"Good," I said. "I'd like your permission to drop a Plex beacon and we can translate down."

"Nope. Don't trust them. I don't know what will happen next, but—"

"It's a special beacon," I told him. "It's totally controllable from Roanoke. Have Roanoke Control check it out when I deploy it." We didn't want an ordinary beacon above Roanoke. This one had been designed for the trip to the Hostile Galaxy with total control exercised from either Betsy or Roanoke Control. That way in case the aliens could use our beacon, at least we could select who and when.

"Just a minute," he said and the screen blanked.

I took the opportunity to run scenes of Roanoke.

Sandy and D. watched with interest, especially Sandy.

Glaciers fingering out from both poles.

Broad oceans.

Three major continents and a number of minor ones.

The land was mostly highlands, from which raw mountains stabbed the skies. Snow on peaks and slopes. Green plains and valleys. Cliffs and magnificent waterfalls. Towering trees as old as five thousand years, standard. Great carved valleys, results of roving glaciers. Swaths of land cut by smaller glaciers moving different directions at million year intervals; so much so, much land appearing like a devil's playground with mountains virtually sheared in half. A geological nightmare.

Toward the ocean, our continent swept out, giving us sufficient lowlands to grow food crops.

"On developed worlds, you miss this kind of scenery," said the fourth quint.

"It reminds me of Bristlebrush," said Sandy.

Dad cut back in. "We're ready."

"Betsy, deploy the beacon." She could do it herself or I could go down and manhandle the thing out.

"In progress, Rusty. Done."

"Activate it."

"Done."

"It's active, Dad. Have your guys give it an ops check."

"Working," he said, his head turned, obviously watching a monitor on the side. After a moment, he faced the camera again. "What you said is true. You've clearance to disembark and translate down to the surface."

"On the way."

"Good. Your mother has been alerted and I'm certain she's making peanut butter tacos in celebration." He eyed me suspiciously. "You've quite a lot of explaining to do, young man. I can assume that you've things well in hand?"

Sandy nudged me. "He assumes you've solved all the problems and overcome whatever force it was that translated Roanoke to here?"

"Sure. Why not? I'm his son."

"Talk about chutzpah." She folded her arms.

"You, a Bristlebusher, have the nerve to accuse *me* of—"

"Bristlebrushian," she said automatically.

"Tunnel to beacon is in place," Betsy said.

"Thank God," said Sandy. "It's too stuffy inside here."

"What'd I say now?" I said.

"We talked to Virginia a while ago," Dad said. "She's grabbing an aircar and will arrive as soon as she can."

Uh, oh.

Ginny.

Mix that with one each Gusselwaithe Hortense O'Clock and what do you get?

Probably the late Rusty Wallace.

"Who's this girl Sandy?" Dad asked. He's a big guy with the family curly red hair and seems to sprawl wherever he sits. He's not as caustic or enterprising as his father, Rebel Wallace, whom I call Granddad. Nor is Dad as brash or impudent as I am. He's a lot more thoughtful and, while you can't tell it, he's a schemer like me—or vice versa. These are probably the reasons he quit spacing and became Roanoke's Managing Director. That's when I came of age, got Betsy, and took off.

I was eating a crunchy peanut butter mustard pizza and talking to Dad.

We'd cleared the kids out of the family room in the sprawling ranch style Wallace family house. There were always people going and coming, family and friends and traders, that we'd built a big, long and wide, one-story home to take care of everybody. Mom was In Charge. Dad did his Managing Director stuff from an office in the west wing. Granddad ran the family business from the office in the west wing. I did most of the work from Betsy. It was a total family effort and wouldn't have functioned without each one of us.

The family room overlooked the bay into which this tiny penninsula stretched. The ocean out there, the Hotlantic, was roaring. Up and down this coast were dozens of small-to-large penninsulas, each one of which housed one family. We colonials like our privacy. We called the sound between us and the next penninsula to the north Albermarle Sound. Others were fjords, bays, whatever. Since we didn't live in close proximity to each other, we didn't really have cities. And we were too young a world to have any political boundaries. However, since the Wallace house contained several members of the Roanoke Board of Directors including the Managing Director, it was the de facto capital.

"Um, Virginia is on her way over *here?*" I asked intelligently.

"That's what I said." Dad made a face. He doesn't like to repeat things. "About your new young lady?"

"Sandy? Sandy's all right, Dad. She's a spacer and—"

"Your grandfather likes her." Dad shifted position and covered the couch with an outstretched leg.

Finishing my slice of pizza, I said, "When they get here, I'll tell—"

"Tell what?" said Granddad coming in through the hardwood double doors arm-in-arm with Sandy.

"Everything," I said.

"It's about time," grumped Granddad. "Also, I want your balance sheet. You'd better be showing a profit—or have a new discovery or two to make up for it."

"Ah, um, Granddad? I've been kind of busy."

"*You* say," he said. "Have *Virginia* comm me the figures."

"Who's Virginia?" asked Sandy.

"Yessir," I said. "Have a slice of pizza, Sandy."

She picked one off the platter. "Um, good. Your mom's an excellent cook."

"Trained her myself," said Granddad. A tinge of

gray had hit the red on his temples, but he moved as if he were my age.

"Who's Virginia?" asked Sandy again.

"A family friend you'll meet later," I said lamely. "Now, we've got to talk."

Both Dad and Granddad gave me curious looks. Sandy was sharp enough to pick up on it.

Damn.

"It was like this," I said, "I popped out of transpace and Roanoke wasn't there any longer."

"We already know that," said Granddad sitting in a hardback chair. "We were on Roanoke, remember?"

"What was it like?" I asked, curious about the first translation in a stasis field where you remain whole and actually *experience* the experience.

Dad sat up. "It began with a sneak attack. The Navy emerged from translight and nailed the ships in orbit. There was some give and take. Since they controlled the Plex beacon, we couldn't use the Plex comm link, so I began sending a non-Plex message, when came a quick moment of disorientation. On the night side of Roanoke, the view of the neighborhood star field disappeared. Instrumentation, probes, and observations told us that our entire planetary system, sun, planet, and surrounding space, was cut off."

"I figgered it out, Rusty," Granddad said. "It was the only answer."

"It's a good thing that our citizens are hardy," Dad said. "We had some panic as it was. Fortunately, nothing significant happened on the surface and life went on as usual."

"Cut to the chase, son." Granddad stood and waved his arms like he always does. "A few days real time later, suddenly we're back in the galaxy we know again, but way in hell out on the edge past this star wall full of activity blocking our view of most of the galaxy."

"They had killed the Plex beacon," Dad continued, "except for the comm link, which, as I said, they controlled and would not allow us to comm out. We had a quick war council and decided we didn't like what was going on.''

"They translated Roanoke before you completed the message,'' I said.

Sandy looked at me. "What message?''

I explained. "So that's another thing that worried me. A hundred days standard—''

"You didn't trust me.''

"I did. I just forgot.'' I was defensive again.

Fortunately, Dad continued. "We'd been told that in the preliminary discussions with the Navy. That is the critical juncture when Roanoke is to be translated out of the galaxy.''

"Four days left,'' I said.

Sandy pouted.

"I should've told you,'' I admitted.

"You should—''

"I thought up the idea of knocking off the Navy,'' Granddad said proudly. He's the most bloodthirsty and warlike of the clan. Obviously.

"We did that thing,'' Dad said.

"Too bad,'' said Granddad. "It's not often you find boys and girls who like space—''

"Not anymore, you don't,'' agreed Sandy.

"Their escape boats worked. We got 'em freezing their butts off out on the island.'' Granddad jerked his thumb toward the Hotlantic. Maybe a hundred miles out was a small island in the middle of an arctic current flowing south. "They didn't know much,'' Granddad continued, "and if they did, they wouldn't tell.''

"Then is when the Board of Directors met and decided to take out the beacon,'' Dad said. "It was the obvious thing to do. Not only did it give us a stronger position in whatever was to come, but it sent a message to whoever, and finally, it bought us time. Time enough, we hoped, that perhaps someone like you would come along and—''

"Not someone *like* him,'' Granddad interrupted,

"him in particular. We had faith in you, boy. Now tell us what the hell is going on."

I did. Sandy helped.

Then we called upon Sunday C. Sunday, Sunday D. Sunday and ther sister, E. Sunday Sunday.

When we finished, Granddad said, "Let me get this straight. You want us, the world Roanoke, to traipse off to some hos*tile* galaxy as representatives of the human race?"

"In essence," said D.

"And your brothers sent you three and a passel of kids, sort of as hostages, to show their good intentions?"

"In essence," said C. Courteously, they were wearing color-coded clothing so we knew which was which.

"However," put in his sister E., "it is a challenge and an adventure which we'd have wished to accompany at any rate." From her language, I wondered what bureaucratic office she worked in—or, rather, managed.

Dad stood and walked over in front of me. He locked onto my eyes. "What do *you* think, son?"

"I'm for it." I surprised myself by not hesitating.

"I can see you've thought it through."

"I have."

Granddad snorted. "You're probably ascribing your decision to noble motives."

"Well, I—"

"That's what I thought," he said.

Dad stepped back.

"Um, Granddad?" I said. "It had occurred to me that if we pull this off and establish a Plex link between us and the aliens, that *somebody* will profit *hugely* by being on the ground floor of the initial trading."

Dad's eyes glinted and swiveled to Granddad.

'Hmmmmmmmmmmm," said the old man, and I could see him counting his skyrocketing bank balance. "There *are* certain aspects of this situation which require in-depth review and consideration."

"We'd be the ones establishing the initial trading," I said. "The word *windfall profits* surges to the top of my thoughts."

"That's two words," Sandy said automatically.

Granddad moved over to Dad. "Look, Red. I been gettin' sick and tired of bein' sick and tired. We need something interesting, something out of the ordinary. I'm for it. Let's do it."

"I've a lot of thinking to do," said Dad. "There are people who won't want to go."

"They don't have much choice," said Sunday D. Sunday.

"They just might," I said enigmatically.

"That's what I've been thinking," Sandy said, nodding. Again, we were thinking alike.

"We'll call a meeting of the Board of Directors," Dad decided. "Then we'll have a public debate and I'll call a referendum, a binding referendum."

"That's fair," said E. Sunday Sunday. It was amazing to me how the same features on four of the five quints, the males, looked so entirely different on her. Her hair was long, framing her face and cascading down her back. She had a flash of a smile none of her brothers had. But I suspected, she had the same drive, the same intellect, the same ambitions.

Her brother, C., had been looking at me. "What exactly did you mean when you said the citizens of Roanoke who didn't want to go had a choice?"

The hardwood double doors flung apart and there stood Virginia Bavarro.

"Rusty!" she said breathlessly. She threw out her arms and rushed to me.

27: VIRGINIA

Next to me, Ginny Bavarro looks real young—probably because she is. She's several inches shorter than I am. Her hair is always cut short and swept back like wings, but hangs well and doesn't give that bad of an impression as short hair does on some girls.

Where Sandy is angular, Virginia is soft. Virginia has big, wide brown eyes that can melt you. The rest of her is gorgeous and shapely. Most of the young men around here have proposed to her.

To no avail. Ever since she was a couple of years old, she'd known she would marry me—even though I was eight years older than she. When she was six, she'd told me that we were going to get married and I strung her along like you do young kids. When she became a teenager, I was gone a lot, just starting out as a spacer.

Every time I returned to Roanoke, though, she was more beautiful than the time before. Now she was "of age" and ten times more attractive than ever.

"Uh-oh," I muttered and stood.

Virginia hit me running at half speed. She came against me, her arms wide, and I overbalanced and we fell onto the couch. It didn't seem to bother her. She kissed me quickly and hugged me until I was out of air.

"Here, let me help," Dad said, and pulled us up, Virginia still clinging to me.

I tried to disentangle myself self-consciously, and finally managed.

Sandy was standing now, watching us with a hard look on her face.

The Sunday brothers and sister withdrew diplomatically, albeit with knowing smiles.

Dad was concerned in his studious way.

Granddad was hugely amused, a smirk smeared across his entire face.

Ginny looked at Dad. "Hi, Pop." She smiled at Granddad who could always be bought off by the smile of a pretty girl. "Hi, Grandpop." Her voice was crisp as a bell, and you wanted her to be lyrical.

She turned to Sandy. "Who's this?"

Nobody said anything so I thought that the protocol was that I had to do the introductions.

"Um, Virginia Bavarro, I'd like you to meet, ah, Sandy O'Clock."

"Hi, Sandy," said Virginia, not catching the undercurrents flowing about the room like hot lava.

"How do you do, Miss Bavarro," said Sandy, her voice telling me she'd seen how young Ginny was.

"Fine," Ginny said, standing beside me and putting her arm around my waist.

Granddad's jaws must have been ready to explode trying to keep a straight face, the old codger. He spoke to Sandy. "Virginia is Rusty's fianceé. They're going to be married."

The room temperature dropped maybe a hundred degrees. Frost popped out on Sandy's eyebrows and her voice was only a degree above absolute zero. "You're engaged?"

Everybody looked at me, especially Virginia in that way she has that says she adores me.

"Um, ah, well," I thought furiously then came up with what I thought was a brilliant response covering every contingency. "I guess, when I last left we were."

Virginia smiled happily. "We've been engaged for eighteen years."

I groaned.

Sandy looked aghast. "Most people aren't *married* for that long." She shook her head. "You can't be *eighteen*."

"We started kind of young," I said lamely, "besides it hasn't been official for that long." I was feeling rather awkward. Well, not rather. I was feeling tremendously awkward.

Virginia squeezed me again.

"You never told me you were engaged," Sandy said.

"You never asked," I shot back.

"I, I kind of assumed you weren't," she said.

"It's not something I go around wearing on my sleeve," I said.

"It's not?" Ginny snapped. She stood back. "What do you mean by that, Rollingham Wallace?"

Uh, oh, I was in deep trouble now.

"Ah," I said grasping for a lifeline, "it's just something that doesn't necessarily arise in normal everyday conversation."

"*You* could be a bureaucrat and work for Galacticon," Sandy accused.

Virginia was adding things up. "Just exactly *who* is this woman? And, for that matter, why are you trying to appease her?"

Granddad was grinning from ear to ear.

Dad had moved away as if embarrassed. Likely, he was.

"I ain't appeasing nobody," I said. Something Granddad had taught me came to my aid. A good defense is to attack. "Besides, why is everybody yelling at me? What'd I do?" I stepped over to the table and picked up a piece of peanut butter pizza. I chose the one which had the mustard mixed well with the cheese.

"How many women are you stringing along, Rusty Wallace?" demanded Virginia.

Granddad laughed. "Pretty soon it's gonna be none."

I shot him a dirty look. I tried the offense again. "Look, this is supposed to be a happy homecoming.

Let's not argue.'' There. Take the high ground, I always say.

"Happy homecoming for whom?'' asked Ginny, tears welling out of her big, brown eyes. It almost ripped my heart out.

"Um—'' I started.

Virginia continued. "First somebody kidnaps everybody in the world and send us to this godawful nowhere in the galaxy, now my knight in shining armor comes to rescue me from a fate worse than death, only he shows up with a blonde tootsie just drooling all over him and—''

"Tootsie?'' Sandy sputtered. You'd think she was choking.

Not knowing what to do next, I took a giant bite of pizza and almost choked myself.

"Not only that,'' Virginia continued, "but my knight on his rescuing charger still has his filthy habits—''

"Peanut butter is *not* filthy,'' I objected.

"Obsessive,'' Ginny accused. "That's what it is. It shows an unstable personality, probably as a result of nutritional deficiencies and imbalance brought about by space travel—''

"Give him hell, kid,'' said Sandy smugly. She does smug so well she ought to patent it.

"I'm not a kid.'' Ginny smacked her fist in her palm. Tears continued to roll down her shapely cheeks. "I've waited and waited for Rusty my whole life, darnitall. He was a shining knight to me years ago, saving me. So I dedicated my whole life to learning how to be a good wife to him and he shows up with an older woman on his arm, ignoring the very fact that I'm twenty-one now, and legal age, and ready for a lifetime in the shining tower on the hill of blissful life and even having his children—if they don't have eating disorders, too, that is—and trying to break him of his revolting and disgusting eating habits—''

"Whatd'ya mean older woman, kid?'' Sandy looked dangerous.

"And a *spacer* to boot," said Virginia, her clear voice turning hard.

Which, of course, changed things immediately. My Dad was a spacer, as was my Granddad before him. They still are, just a bit inactive. And me and Sandy were spacers, too.

Sandy drew herself up, changing her attitude even as I watched. She spoke slowly. "I *am* a spacer, at your service, madam." She bent low in a parody of a bow.

Ginny's right hand went to her lips and pressed hard. Her tears were still coming, but not as many and not as serious.

"And proud of it," said Sandy.

Virginia Bavarro looked up at me, her big eyes going right to my soul. "Rusty?" It was a plea.

I didn't know what to say.

I didn't know what to do.

I can make decisions aboard a starship at translight speed, but this was far out of my area of expertise. Not only that, but I didn't think I'd done anything to deserve this grief.

I was thinking of a way to diplomatically defuse this situation when Virginia cried out and bolted out the doors.

"Uh, oh," I said.

Granddad grunted. "Damn, boy, you sure got a way with words."

"Rusty?" Sandy said. "Can we get on with this so we can finish our tasks and I can get back to the real galaxy and go about my business?"

A vision of the first time I'd stepped into a pile of tinit manure assaulted me. I could even smell it.

Well, I'd stepped into it again.

Why me, Lord?

28: TREACHERY

The referendum passed by a 60-40 margin. Even on Roanoke some people were affected by the creeping heebie jeebies, and the prospect of traveling a lonely route between galaxies didn't make things any better. Some of the forty percent against were probably just angry that we didn't have much choice in the matter: Either remain stranded out here at the galactic edge or cooperate with the Sundays and take the trip to a new galaxy.

And the time was getting close. The supernova was building. Three days and counting.

That's when Sandy and I sprang our surprise on the Sundays.

Of course, we first cleared it with my father.

"It's a good idea," he told us. "It is a shame about the planets of exile."

"We've some leverage," I said, "and I don't think the plotting Sunday brothers will argue too much." Having only three days left was plenty of leverage.

Sunday D. Sunday, Sunday C. Sunday, and E. Sunday Sunday said they had to coordinate with their brothers on D'Earnhardt.

Dad arranged for the Plex beacon to give us a comm link to the Sector VIII capital.

We hitched in with both parties, realizing that what we said might be intercepted or in some way compromised. So we had to speak in general terms.

After the preliminaries, I acted as spokesman.

"Not having a lot of other options," I said, "we've agreed to your proposition. We've taken a vote, and the proposition carried 60-40."

"We're very glad," said the Administrator. "We hadn't heard anything from you and we were worried."

"The problem is the forty percent," I said.

His eyebrow raised an inch and he glanced at what had to be another screen with a separate connection to his brother at Plex Fax.

"What we'd like," I continued, "is to translate as many of those forty percent who don't want to take the trip."

"Where?"

"Bristlebrush, and other similar planets," I said, my meaning obvious that I was referring to the other planets of exile. So the Sunday program would remain under wraps.

"We'll consider it," said the Administrator.

"Additionally," I said, "all those Bristlebushers who—"

"Bristlebrushians," said Sandy.

"—want to accompany us, they can. Establish an outgoing Plex station and send 'em here. Roanoke is practically empty and we've lots of room."

E. Sunday Sunday leaned forward. "Brothers and I have discussed it and think their plan has merit."

"Can you maintain the comm link for a while?" asked Plex mgr Sunday.

"Certainly," I said, "but be advised there are a few other individuals we wish to invite as well."

"Understand."

After a while, they came back on the link.

"Your suggestions are acceptable," said A. Sunday.

They weren't suggestions, but I hadn't used the implied threat, either, to fail to cooperate with them.

"As long as those who wish to leave Roanoke before the fact," said B. Sunday, "understand they must remain on Bristlebrush until the project is, ah, made public.''

"Done," I said and sat back. I nibbled on my frozen peanut butter rice cake.

Our Plex fax was a small one near the public meeting house nearby. It was the start of what would become continuous usage. The pax fax would be expanded, and the freight fax was to be enlarged.

They let us bring individuals before shipping out those of our forty percent minority who decided to leave.

Major, Senior, and Edna O'Clock were first. They came through the Plex station bickering and we put them up in the southeast wing.

"This shore beats shoveling tinit manure, boy," Major said as he shook my hand. "I knew you'd amount to something."

"And I'm not even a Bristlebusher," I said.

"Bristlebrushian," he corrected. He missed my sarcasm.

"Whatever."

Sandy was hugging them to death all the while. She hadn't seen them since she was very young.

Juan O'Clock, Rexann, and Elrod McSpanish were next. Along with them came Mean Mike and, surprisingly, Shorty and Toothpick. They all trickled out of the Plex station at noon.

As usual, Mike pummeled my back and Juan dripped peanut butter gravy all over the place.

Rexann got reacquainted with Sandy while I talked with her husband, Elrod McSpanish.

"You've got troubles, Rusty," Elrod said to me.

"Why is that?"

"Remember the company we set up to merchandise peanut butter products and collect the royalties?"

"RETCH," I said, remembering it stood for Roanoke Enterprises Tax Corporation Harborage. "What's the problem?"

"The T-hoe and Sector XI and Galacticon tax authorities want a few words with you." He smiled strangely and dapperly. "I think it was the Famous Recipe Peanut Butter Chili which really brought in the trade and got their attention."

"Oh, great. Thanks a lot, Elrod."

The dapper fellow looked at his filthy, peanut butter-bespeckled kid, and said, "It was nothing."

Now I *had* to go to the Hostile Galaxy. Or to jail for the tax shenanigans Elrod had done.

One good thing about the McSpanish family and the O'Clock grandparents being present for the trip was that it put some pressure on Sandy to go along, too.

But she remained adamant.

And she still wasn't talking to me.

Neither was Virginia Bavarro.

My grandfather was enjoying himself immensely at my expense.

Then things got hectic.

We began the people transfer between, at first, Roanoke and Bristlebrush, then the other six exile planets. We weren't exactly bursting at the seams, but we had to put together an even larger Plex fax, more stations and one which could accept the necessary freight and supplies.

The Sundays helped find the few Roanoke spacers out and sent them here.

Hyman L. L. Bookbinder turned us down. "But," he told me, "if you ever return, look me up. You've a promising future as an Obfuscator."

I was glad somebody wanted me. Though I considered the bureaucracy, with which he continuously dealt, mindless amebae with the moral imperative to change human effort into metaphoric solid waste.

From D'Earnhardt, Professor Egbert Owens Girrard Simpson, doctor of history and geography, and now the Director of the Roanoke branch of the Galactic Geographical Society, came reluctantly.

"We need a geographer and an historian," I said.

When he arrived at my invitation, I'd briefed him. He'd come initially to visit the "missing planet."

"You know," he said, "there's a parallel between here and the original Roanoke. Some of the New World colonists opted to stay in Roanoke and some decided to return to England."

"That's nice," said Sandy.

"Many of those colonists who remained in the New World disappeared."

"Great," I said. 'That's really reassuring. Are you with us or not?"

"Well, I'm not one for space, but . . ."

"You're on the ground now, doc. The whole planet will be a spaceship."

"Well, in that case. You say aliens? I get to meet aliens?"

"And personally record the history of the first contact," Sandy put in.

"I'll do it," Professor Simpson said. He turned to me. "By the way, Marion Zernicke of SNS said to give you her best."

"Uh, thanks, doc."

Sandy favored me with one of her glacierlike glares.

What with all my troubles, I wondered if I wouldn't be better off by extending an invitation to Marion. But she was a hardcore groundhog, albeit a very attractive and nice one, and she was totally against space and those who frequented it.

With less than two days until the critical juncture, Sandy and I placed all the special beacon buoys around the star going supernova. We were in the process of dropping new beacons around Roanoke and its star as backups in case of technical malfunction. Betsy placed the final buoy and we jumped back to Roanoke orbit.

As we prepared to disembark through the tunnel, Betsy's alarm went off.

"Proximity alert," she said.

I went to the command console. "It's not a ship I

recognize," I said. "Its transponder is deactivated. Betsy, give me a visible."

"Visual," she corrected. The ship appeared floating alongside the buoy.

"That's an old Galacticon warship," Sandy said. "I trained on several of them."

I nodded.

She looked concerned, which beat the hell out of her current attitude. I should be calling her Frosty, not Sandy. But I didn't need anymore trouble than I already had.

"They've established a comm link with Roanoke Control," said Betsy.

"Tap in and let's see what's going on."

"That is illegal, Rusty," said Betsy.

"Command override," I said.

"Done."

Sandy gave me a hint of one of her former admiring looks.

The screen split.

On one side appeared my father. "Yes, *Thunderchief*," he was saying. "I am in charge, if you will. I am the Managing Director."

On the left hand side of the screen appeared the bridge of the other starship.

Sandy's quick intake of breath said she recognized them a second before I did.

Helen Merritt-Browne.

And her security chief, Churnenski.

"Director Wallace," dash Browne said, "it is my understanding that your world is lost?"

Dad obviously didn't know how to answer. "It was. What is your interest?"

"I am the Chief Executive Officer of Plexus Net," she said. "And this is my assistant, Inspector General Churnenski. We've been looking for you." Churnenski had been promoted. No wonder Sandy hadn't gotten the IG position.

"Oh?" said Dad, still being cagy.

"I understand Roanoke is becoming, in essence, a starship."

Dad still didn't know what to answer, nor would I. "That could be," he nodded.

Merritt-Browne must have seen the Plex comm link traffic, not a problem in her job, and if she had the Plex computers under her command, she could well have been apprised of all the personnel movements between Roanoke and the planets of exile. Thus she knew what was occurring and could have easily traced the activity to the new code of origin that was Roanoke way out here on the galactic edge.

"In that case, and since your world is both missing and a de facto ship, I hereby invoke Galacticon Salvage Regulations and claim Roanoke as our personal salvage claim, subject to our disposition."

"Wow," said Sandy.

Dad turned aside. The female Sunday moved into the pickup and whispered to him.

Dad turned to Merritt-Browne's image. "I'm informed only civilians can claim salvage. You are Galacticon employees."

Merritt-Browne grinned. "Not any more. We were fired yesterday."

E. Sunday nodded. "That's what my brothers hinted at when we talked earlier. There was the financial misconduct. You were too inquisitive, too ambitious. They were going to get the Galacticon Executive Administrator to help unseat you."

Merritt-Browne shrugged. "It no longer matters. I'm going to be fabulously wealthy now." She grinned mirthlessly. "And I'm in control. If you or someone fails to provide us with a great amount of money, I will stop this project. Furthermore, I will publicize it and the existence of the aliens. If you do not accede to my demands, there will be a galactic-wide catastrophe."

"Revenge, money, and power, the greatest motivators," said Sandy.

It was extortion, pure and simple. We were supposed to pay them off. "Extortion, plain and simple."

"Blackmail," Sandy corrected.

Merritt-Browne continued. "We have one final demand. That is Churnenski and I be cleared of any charges of financial misconduct. You must understand we mean business. The *Thunderchief* is armed and at any sign of missile launch or other aggressive move, we shall destroy the Plex beacon and carry out our threats. Do you understand?"

"Only too well," said Dad.

Everything ruined.

"You know," said Sandy thoughtfully. "She's really angry. I think she will take the money and expose this conspiracy anyway. After that, I'd bet they'll blast the special beacons and ruin the whole thing."

"It sounds like something she'd do," I said. "You know them better than anybody else. She must think she can get away with it."

Sandy said, "She never discussed it in my presence, but I'd guess she intercepted something and ferreted out their plans somehow, maybe via the ROAR secret files. And likely has been monitoring the comm link traffic. Anyway, I suspect all along she had her own agenda to take advantage of the Sunday plan. Instant megawealth. No more felony charges, so no threat of judicial punishment. And power. Now toss in revenge for her untimely dismissal, and you've got a neat package." Sandy looked at me, eyes full of—meaning? something else? "And you know whom she blames, way down deep. You and me."

Exposure would cause millions of deaths in catastrophic upheaval and perhaps even the cancellation of our mission—if the special beacons remained intact. And now that I was signed on and committed to the project, that made me angry.

"It is your responsibility now," dash Browne said. "Be advised that if we have to destroy the Plex beacon, that there will most likely be people translating to or from Roanoke at the time and that will result in their deaths.''

Sandy shook her head. ''All that work. A few people trying to save the race from dying of its own accord and now this. All washed away in one woman's greed and revenge.''

Everything ruined. And we had only a couple of days left. Anything dash Browne did would cause us to miss the key period of the supernova.

29: THUNDERCHIEF

"**I** will not accept this," I said. That something special in Sandy's eyes spurred me to action. And right damn now was the only opportunity we'd get.

Helen Merritt-Browne's image turned slightly. "Another thing, Director Wallace. The starship *Virginia* is close to us and connected to the Plex beacon. Should the *Virginia* make one hostile move, we are prepared to fire upon it and the beacon simultaneously." Our transponder was now squawking our ID.

Sandy was looking at me.

"Betsy's a she, not an it," I said.

The shot of Helen Merritt-Browne expanded and showed Churnenski at a fire-control command console.

"My associate," said Merritt-Browne, "is monitoring the situation. If the starship *Virginia*—" Sandy didn't even blink— "begins any activity, we shall know it in plenty of time to take our action."

Of course Betsy was armed. Not like a Galacticon warship, but sufficient for a trader, explorer, and courier in these days and times. I'd practiced with her weaponry, but never really used it in battle—well, maybe *one* little battle, but that's another story.

Dash Browne was correct, though. A Naval warship could pick up emanations from us like radar lock-on, sonarand, flexar, infrared tracking, weapons' ports operating, missile system activation. All they needed was a split second.

Browne looked our way as if through the bulkhead. "We need little excuse to attack the *Virginia;* I believe Captain Wallace and agent O'Clock were instrumental in our being here." She started to frown and didn't.

Sandy made a sour face. "They don't like us a lot." She sounded like me now.

I didn't think Browne could know who was aboard Betsy, but it was an easy guess.

"Betsy," I said. "Are we closer to them than the Plex beacon is?"

"Yes, Rusty. We have drifted around the buoy."

"Good. Keep our drift heading their way."

"Yes, Rusty. Be advised the tunnel is attached and locked."

"Sandy, I'm going out there. If they notice me, stall 'em, do anything."

"What are you thinking of doing?" Her voice showed concern.

But I was already running. Through Betsy's systems, Sandy could monitor my actions and, as smart as that Bristlebrushian was, she'd figure it out in a D'Earnhardt minute.

Donning and ops checking my spacesuit didn't take but a few minutes. In the cargo hold, I manually opened an access door on the opposite side of Betsy from dash Browne's ship. They might also be monitoring visual or have a configuration-change alert program.

With no gravity, it was simple to manhandle one of the special Plex beacons out the cargo door. Only its size made it awkward.

My problem was that they couldn't help but notice me soon. Proximity alarms being the state of the art and all.

I tacked around a few curves and got to Betsy's other side. I attached the monofilament line to the eyehook on one of Betsy's big guide-flanges. The reel was attached to my suit. Instead of using my powerpack, I pushed off from the flange. They'd be able to detect the energy from the powerpack.

Now having time, I keyed in my comm to Betsy's central, so I could follow everything she was monitoring in addition to being able to receive comm from her.

I didn't dare talk to her or Sandy, though, because a Navy ship surely had the equipment to detect and intercept anything we said.

And Churnenski, as a security guy, would surely have the technical expertise to operate those systems.

Fervently I hoped I'd aimed properly, because I certainly couldn't afford to use the powerpack to correct my track. However, I didn't need to be exactly on target. I had only one correctional move.

I was certain I was now out of Betsy's shadow—and that of the Plex beacon to which she was moored with the extended tunnel.

They had to see me soon.

"Madame Merritt-Browne?" The question squawked in my ear. Sandy was calling.

I didn't bother to turn on the tiny magnification-augmented video. I needed to watch what I was doing, that is flying toward the vicinity of the warship holding onto a buoy beacon.

"Go ahead, *Virginia.*" Merritt-Browne's voice.

"Be advised, I am disconnecting the access tunnel to the Plex beacon at this time."

Was Sandy trying to keep the woman's attention off of me and the special buoy?

"Why?" demanded Merritt-Browne.

I wanted to know what Sandy was doing, too.

"It's quite simple," said Sandy. "If you blast the beacon, we don't wish to be connected."

"Go ahead, then, *Virginia,*" said Merritt-Browne, "but no hostile moves."

"Roger." Sandy's voice was curt. I wondered if she were angry from the constant use of *"Virginia."*

After a moment, Merritt-Browne's voice came back. "*Virginia,* what's the object? You have five seconds to answer or we'll fire."

Uh-oh. Caught redhanded. And not close enough to their ship yet.

And about to be fried.

"Go ahead and blast it if you must," Sandy said matter-of-factly. "It is our portion of the tunnel extension. Upon retraction, something failed and it sailed away from us."

Sandy had figured out what I was doing and had even come up with a plan ahead of time to explain away logically what I was doing. She was brilliant.

On the other hand, she'd nonchalantly told Merritt-Browne to "blast" me.

"However," Sandy continued, "you must be aware that if you do blast the tunnel section, then those trigger-happy Roanokers below might misconstrue your actions and open fire and we've all lost."

Silence answered her and I held my breath.

"Additionally," Sandy's voice turned stone-hard, "once firing commences, I will join the battle. The *Virginia* is well armed." Sandy didn't choke over saying "Virginia" that time. And she was poised to fight. If I knew her, she'd already have agreed on a program with Betsy that would include quick maneuvers, the only advantage Betsy had over the *Thunderchief*'s firepower.

I was within a mile or so of their ship now. My reel was starting to go faster, telling me it was running out of linc.

Time.

I estimated angles and directions and distances. I'd ridden over with the buoy in case my original aim hadn't been good enough. In fact, that was the case. As a last corrective maneuver, I pushed off from the buoy and the motion caused it to change direction slightly. I hoped it would be good enough. I touched the control and the reel locked and reversed, beginning the takeup process drawing me back to Betsy. Roanoke spun lazily beneath me, greens and blues and grays.

Merritt-Browne came back on. "Hello, Roanoke Control."

"Go ahead, *Thunderchief.*"

"You've been following our conversation so you know about the tunnel?"

"Roger."

"Tell your people that I am going to blast the tunnel in forty-five seconds and please do not fire."

"Why?" demanded Sandy.

"It is approaching the *Thunderchief,*" Merritt-Browne said, "and I don't trust you, O'Clock, I never did."

Her proximity alarms must be going off.

Sandy came on immediately. "I warn you not to start something, *Thunderchief.* Nobody will win." Her tone made you think of glaciers and volcanoes at the same time.

"I'll try," said Roanoke Control, probably not knowing what was going on but taking Sandy's lead. She has this presence which inspires people to follow her.

"Thirty seconds," Merritt-Browne said.

I touched the reel control to egg the last bit of speed. I was flying toward Betsy.

"Twenty-five."

I was feeling a definite chill. If she fired, I'd be in the blast-wash zone and turn into ashes.

"Twenty."

And the special beacon buoy needed to be closer to the *Thunderchief* to work. That's how I'd manually set the area to be affected.

"Fifteen."

I was a whole lot colder than I was ten seconds ago. I looked longingly at Betsy, probably more than twenty seconds away.

I wasn't going to make it.

"Ten."

Sandy's voice came on. "*Thunderchief,* you'll be firing in my direction and I don't trust you, either. I

say again, any weapons fire on your part will be returned.''

Sandy was sacrificing everything for my safety. Or
so I thought. Brinkwomanship if nothing else.

"Five seconds."

I could picture Churnenski's fingers already having
removed the "safe" switch covers.

"Three."

Uh-oh, was there time? Was the buoy close enough
yet? No time remaining to wait.

"Betsy," I shouted, unable to control my voice.
"Power up and activate the buoy now."

"One and zero," said Merritt-Browne, overlapping
my commands.

"Done, Rusty."

I was watching *Thunderchief* at the time. Automatic
ports opened. I think I saw the wink of weapons locking onto the buoy I'd kicked their way.

I imagined—felt Betsy rumble with a generation of
power and zap it to the buoy.

Then the scene in front of me shimmered like waves
off pavement on a hot day and the background stars
blurred for a moment and I felt a brush of nausea and
Thunderchief and the beacon were no longer there and
I slammed into Betsy's flange, twisting at the last moment so that my feet took the impact.

"That's Roanokeans," I scolded Sandy. "Roanokers sounds like something tinits do."

Browne at Mary Churnenski...

30: HISTORY

"**B**ut they're not dead?" Dad said. He was always concerned about people, good or bad. He considered that philosophy to be central to civilized behavior. Me, I agreed with Granddad. Some people are better off assuming room temperature.

Dad and I were walking from the southwest wing toward the family room.

The house was pretty well filled up.

"Churnenski and Merritt-Browne are no more dead than we will be when we shove off for the Hostile Galaxy," I answered.

"But," he pointed out, "we have a method of self-stopping our Plex travel, they don't."

"Well, I didn't have time to arrange everything," I said. "It was a miniature stasis field. What you have to understand is that unlike regular instantaneous Plex Net travel where you are not aware that you're in transit to another location, the stasis field sends you whole and able to go about your normal activities—within the structure of the field itself."

He stopped and grabbed my arm. "You're telling me, son, that the woman and her accomplice will simply continue to be in translation forever?"

"Yep," I nodded happily. "In the restrictive confines of their ship, they're stuck with each other for eternity."

Dad caught my small white lie. "That much travel

would require additional power, just as we are going to need power. They won't have a star to tap."

"That's true," I said. "However, Betsy assured them sufficient power for the buoy to keep translating them for a couple hundred years. They'll be circling the universe long after they've died of natural causes."

He walked away shaking his head. "You always were a schemer."

I turned and went toward the family room. I recalled Helen Merritt-Browne telling Churnenski and Sandy to kill me by sending me to Nowhere. And I remembered Churnenski forcing Sandy to set the Nowhere code. They tried to toss me off a landing and to bomb me. And I remembered the two of them trying to blackmail us and the Sundays in our effort to save the human race and contact the aliens.

No, I had no remorse whatsoever.

It also tickled me—and Sandy, too—to no end that dash Browne and Churnenski were stuck with each other and no one else for the rest of their lives. I'd done them no favors. Two such as they would likely be at each other's throat in a matter of weeks. And they had decades and decades to spend together.

Approaching the family room, I heard voices.

The doors were ajar and I slipped in, it being night and I not wanting to interrupt someone else's privacy.

The lights were off, and two people stood at the bubble overlook, backs toward me and watching the phosphorescent froth fly off waves as they beat against the rocks below.

I was feeling pretty good, having just talked to Rexann before running into Dad, and wanted company.

Something made me stop back in the shadows.

Granddad and Sandy were the two watching the bay and the ocean roar and attack this penninsula.

"What do you mean, 'obligated?' " said Sandy.

"Virginia always considered herself morally obligated to Rusty," said Granddad soberly.

"I've heard that he saved her from something when

she was a child," Sandy said. "But I still don't understand."

"It was this way," Granddad said. "When Rusty was ten and Virginia two, they were in an aircar driven by Virginia's uncle, going someplace or other. The Bavarros were our nearest neighbors at the time, and that was far, far away. At any rate, they landed to check out the sighting of an animal or some damn thing and an earthquake hit and a mountain fell on them."

"Uh, oh," said Sandy.

My feet were rooted to the floor as I remembered. Atavistically, my body reacted by trembling and turning cold.

Granddad shifted position. "We didn't find them for three days. The mountain had fallen and killed the uncle immediately. Just cut the front of the aircar right off. Which must have saved the two children, for the aircar crunched almost all the way, but not enough to kill Virginia and Rusty. However, they were trapped, laying side by side, unable to move around. Rusty's legs were pinned and Virginia lay against his torso." Granddad shook his head. "It's still unbelievable."

I remembered the horror of those three days. My head throbbed just thinking of it. After that, nothing would ever frighten me as much.

"You've seen the scar on Rusty's lower lip?"

"I have." Sandy leaned back against the upper part of the couch.

"See, he couldn't move much. But he could cradle the toddler. Virginia. The crying got to him first. After about a day, he thought Ginny was dying. So he worked up saliva and pushed it into her mouth, giving her sustenance."

"For another two days?" Sandy said. "My God!"

"No, only occasionally. He was dehydrated himself. When he could no longer raise saliva, he bit his lip and the sucking reflex still in Virginia took over. She sucked blood and moisture from his lip. When he could take the pain no longer, he bit into his fingers and let her nurse from them like teats." The old man sighed.

It had taken a year for me to return to my normal healthy condition, with repaired fingers and all. But my lower lip retained its scar.

"This natural disaster bonded the two of them together; as they grew, Virginia decided that fate had destined them to be together. Naturally, she decided they would be married and live happily ever after."

"And," Sandy said, "she grew into a beautiful young lady."

"She did that. As growing children, they had much in common. Nowadays, though, Rusty is a spacer and she's, um, ah—"

"A groundhog?" Sandy volunteered, but without the obligatory spacer's rancor in her voice.

"Exactly," said Granddad. "Some people got space in their blood, some don't. Interestingly, Ginny acted as a stabilizing influence on Rusty as he grew up. He wasn't as wild as he could have been, but then again, he wasn't as conservative as his father."

"So," said Sandy slowly, "it was always assumed that when Virginia reached age, she and Rusty would marry and settle down together."

"Yep, except Rusty's been gone a lot." I could envision Granddad grinning now. "Us Wallaces sometimes drag our feet down the aisle." He was referring to his own wedding with his late wife Zira.

"Each felt linked to the other," Sandy went on. "And the romance kindled, its genesis being a false feeling of obligation."

"Geez, girl, you got a way with words." He paused. "On the other hand, I've seen many marriages beginning with less in common, and with less bonding, thrive."

My head was still buzzing from the memories.

"Thanks, Rebel," Sandy said.

"I'm glad you asked," he told her. "I hadn't thought about that episode for a long time."

"I asked—Oh, my God!" Sandy's voice was full of alarm.

I stepped forward.

"What's wrong?" asked Granddad.

"It's Virginia. Ginny Bavarro."

"I know that," he said.

"I just came from the Plex station." Sandy was standing straight now. "Ginny Bavarro was there, waiting her turn to translate to Bristlebrush and I was so smug I wasn't going to tell Rusty. Don't you see? It's why I asked about the two. Now I know and I must tell him."

A freezing pit had exploded in my gut and I was running full speed before I straight-armed the double doors open.

"Rusty!" Sandy shouted from behind.

I hoped I wouldn't be too late.

The local population was so spread out, we had plenty of room around the big building we used as a meeting place. The original Plex station was there, too. So when we needed to expand it to accept larger shipments from D'Earnhardt, that was the logical place.

Time was running out and the Plex stations were operating around the clock. It was close to the moment when we would be propelled across intergalactic space. The supernova wasn't on a schedule we could postpone.

I slewed up to the Plex station in an aircar. Lights probed into the night skies. People hurried here and there. Others, with power equipment, were moving giant pallets of supplies and equipment. People were queuing up to the personnel translation stations.

I had the wing-door up before the aircar reached a stop. I jumped out when it was still six feet off the ground. A couple of miners shouted at my lack of courtesy and disregard of safety.

Sprinting toward the line at the station, I searched it.

Nothing.

No Ginny.

I remembered her growing up. Always following me around. Getting in the way a lot. Adoring me.

Frantically I ran along the line. People were walking into the station and zapping out to Bristlebrush rapidly.

My breath was coming fast and in gulps and I couldn't find her and it was as bad as when we were in the crushed aircar and I thought we were going to die and had to fight the panic rising—

"Ginny!"

She was off to the side, waiting alone.

I saw her parents standing near the head of the line.

She saw me and her face lighted for a moment. Then it turned to a shadow.

BAVARRO appeared on a display above the station.

Ginny's parents moved toward the station.

Ginny walked toward them.

I ran to her.

She stopped.

"Why didn't you tell me?" I demanded as I stopped in front of her.

"It's too late for us." Her mouth was determined.

"No," I said, desperate. "Not this way."

"Yes, this way, Rusty. You don't love me and you know it."

"I always thought I did."

"Me, too," she said.

"You what?"

"Virginia," her mother called.

"It was contrived, all a figment of a girl's imagination," she said.

"No." My words were sure. "It might have started that way, but that's not the way it ended up."

She put her hand on my arm. "You're a victim of the illusion as much as I am. You've always felt a responsibility for me, ever since the accident. That was your crutch. Mine was a big-eyed adoration of the boy who'd saved me."

"Virginia Bavarro," her father shouted.

She squeezed my arm hard, hugged me and stepped back. "I find I do love you, Rusty, now, but not like I always thought I did."

"You don't mean—"

"No. Don't say anything else. You know we've not enough in common now. I'd always be frightened for you off in space. And I know that you'll be the first to face these dangerous aliens—it's in your blood." She wasn't weeping like she'd done the other day. Her eyes were dry and strangely bright. "I'm glad it's going to be you to meet the aliens for us, Rusty."

"Ginny—"

A voice from a loudspeaker chanted, "Last call for Bavarro." Only one day and change remaining, and they had no Plex time to waste.

Virginia looked at me one last time. "Go back to your spacegirl, Rusty. Now we can both make a clean start."

"Ginny!" her mother screeched.

I had no power to stop her.

She did not look back.

Ginny Bavarro walked over to the station, joined her parents on the target plate, and zap they were gone.

31: DEJA VU REVISITED

It didn't get any better.

After finally getting to sleep, I was rudely shaken awake.

Granddad stood there in the glaring lights he was using to help wake me.

"You better get to the Plex station, boy. Your girl is leaving."

"Ginny left last night."

"I ain't talkin' about her. I'm talking about Sandy."

I hurt myself dressing so fast. I took the time to make sure I had the right jumpsuit on, the one in which I'd cached the things I'd been carrying around for what seemed forever.

Again, I slewed up to the Plex station. Again, I leapt out, even higher this time.

Again, the girl was just ready to enter to the Plex station.

"Sandy." I grabbed her arm and tugged her away a bit.

"What is it you want?"

"You can't leave. Your mom. Your grandparents."

"Oh?"

"Me."

"What about you?" she said, eyes angry.

"I don't want you to go."

"You've never said so."

"Um—"

"You've had plenty of opportunity, but you never,

ever told me how you felt about me and asked me to stay here and go with *you* and this planet to another galaxy.''

"I didn't?'' I was ashamed. "I'd, er, just kind of assumed that we'd, um, together—''

"Assumed, assumed,'' Sandy said. "But you never formally asked. Just a backhanded 'invitation', that's all. Even when you had your big chance at the Sunday Castle on D'Earnhardt. You never, ever asked.''

I remembered the conversation. Sandy had gone strange on me. Now I understood why.

I got angry myself. "Well, hell, Gusselwaithe Hortense O'Clock, I had Virginia Bavarro to consider and you had Alfonso—''

"Alfredo, and I dumped him.''

"You did?'' I asked. "You never told me that.''

"You never asked me.'' Her.

"I didn't want to pry into your private life.'' Me.

"You say.'' Her.

"I say and I meant it.'' Me.

"You've never made an effort to prove it.'' Her.

People were standing around watching us. The chill of the predawn had fallen and I felt it to my bones. I didn't want to lose this woman. I dug into the pocket of my jumpsuit.

I held out my hand. "Here's proof.''

The small gemstones tumbled into her hand. "My star-stones.'' Her voice turned soft. The facets of the river stones reflected the industrial lighting around us. The foggy-clear one was especially glowing.

"I brought them from Bristlebrush. Your grandmother told me you used them to dream about space.''

"I did.'' Her eyes were moist.

I dug into my pocket again.

"Here.'' I held out the scarf with the field of stars that I'd pilfered from Rexann McSpanish's apartment at Casino Casino.

"Oh, Rusty.'' Sandy was standing close in front of me, clutching her long-lost treasures.

She folded into my arms and the night chill went away.

"Do you want me to ask you formally to stay on Roanoke and go to the Hostile Galaxy with us?"

"And other things," she murmured.

"Last call for O'Clock," said the loudspeaker.

"I love you to death," I said, "please stay with me."

"O'Clock, to the station."

Sandy waved her hand and came up for air. "I'm not going."

Some of the people watching applauded.

We began walking away.

"I was all happy last night," I said. "I'd talked to your mother and learned why you were named Gusselwaithe Hortense—"

"I could have told you that."

"You could?"

"I could," she said. "But you never asked."

I shook my head. I swear I had asked—somebody anyway.

"What'd she say?" asked Sandy.

"She said that she wanted *her* daughter to be unique amongst the jillions of people in the galaxy. She did a computer search and could find no others named Gusselwaithe Hortense O'Clock."

"That's what she tells me sometimes," Sandy said enigmatically.

"What do you mean, *sometimes,*" I demanded.

"Why'd they choose Rusty as your nickname?" Sandy said changing the subject.

"Because of my hair. And it was also the nickname of some hero out of antiquity."

"They couldn't use Rolly?"

I stopped the aircar. "Ugh." I shivered. "I had some fights as a kid growing up over that one. It helped make me tough." I was glad Sandy didn't know my middle name yet. When she learned it, I'd probably never hear the end of it after all the grief I'd given her over Gusselwaithe Hortense.

"Your granddad told me," she said, coming into my arms again.

"What?" I said. Dread climbed up my spine.

"*Your* middle name."

"Oh, no."

"Beauregard." She was smug again. She does smug good.

I shook my head. "Boregard."

"Beauregard?" Her.

"No. Boregard." Me.

"Jeez." Her.

"Why me, Lord?" Me.

"Rollingham Boregard Wallace. It has a certain ring to it." Her.

"I was thinking in terms of a peanut butter and mustard and spinach casserole to celebrate with." Me.

"I can think of other ways to celebrate." Her.

"Or a mesquite barbecue peanut butter soy patty." Me, with other things on my mind.

"How about this?" Her, with glowing green eyes.

"Mmmm."

EPILOGUE: THE SCENTERS

"Completed as of now have you the form for approval of the establishment of a Planning Commission to review and approve the temporary location of the world termed Roanoke?" said the alien.

I called them "the Scenters" and the nickname stuck.

After a couple of standard years traveling in our stasis field, we found a nice quiet corner of their galaxy in which to stop.

We'd all had much apprehension about what the effects would be. No higher tides occurred, our shards of moons didn't sling off into space, and the sun continued to provide solar energy.

In two weeks, three alien starships showed up and approached Roanoke.

Dad, Granddad, Sandy, Professor Simmons, one Sunday, and I trucked out in Betsy to greet them. It was safer, Granddad said, and Dad said it was better protocol. Whatever, we went.

Betsy matched their frequency and soon we were looking at each other.

They'd already synthesized Galacticon standardlingo, having worked on it since receiving the bleedoff from Plex comm links.

Their ships looked like pregnant pyramids, but whatever it took was all right with me. I couldn't design a starship myself, so who was I to complain?

They looked like pregnant pyramids of flesh, maybe that's why.

Like any civilized race I knew about, they wore a sort of clothing. Actually, their garb was uniform, like a giant muumuu designed for pregnant pyramids. And they had several appendages which stuck out and waved and acted as arms and fingers and tentacles and everything else you could think of to manipulate things. They appeared to move about on fleshy stumps just below the bottom of the pyramid. I've yet to figure out how they do it.

The first meeting, while nice, was rather anticlimactic.

I spoke the first words over the comm link with their ship.

"We're called humans," I said answering their question of long ago, "and we don't know yet what you've got that we want."

Everybody had looked at me strangely. "A little calculated aggression on my part," I explained.

Later, we discovered they were crafty traders—which Sandy and I privately agreed was the genesis of their "calculated aggression."

Now we were gathered together in Roanoke's Plex station area. Dozens of Scenter officials were here, all semi-squatting, or whatever they do, in front of high flat surfaces I'd call portable desks.

The Scenters were on average a shade shorter than humans, but their desks are higher because of their appendages, I guess.

The Cultural-Interface team led by Ms. E. Sunday Sunday had worked around the clock and now we understood each other sufficiently to maintain a dialog with enough common references to get along.

My first concern was that the Scenters were carbon based and air breathers. Boy, were they air breathers.

Now I understood the bulky pyramidal body structure. They were mostly lungs. The xenobiological team led by Sunday D. Sunday was already speculating that they'd evolved thus to breathe different atmospheres of different composition. Why that is, they don't know yet.

But each of the aliens maintained six to twelve patches on the front of his/her/its muumuu. They'd touch one and a light scent would waft about. They'd pause, sniff, nod, and go about what they were doing. The smells ranged from semifamiliar like burning wood and garliclike to unfamiliar *alien* smells. With many aliens present, the air was laden with overlapping scents, a conglomeration it took getting used to.

Sandy poked me in the ribs. "Hurry up, will you?"

"Yes, dear. But I'm not really proficient at filling out forms."

The Scenter at the desk in front of me grunted, sniffed his/her/its personal fragrance, and grunted. "Please, it is please finish. Input when we into computer, it will correlate to our symbology, no sweat sir. You must must the form complete."

"Bureaucrats," I mumbled.

"What is that, sir sir?"

I shook my head. "You're going to get along great with the Galacticon government employees."

"Ah, that is so I hope is good, sir sir."

I glanced at the form Sandy was filling out. Somehow the special clement making up the form would automatically input into a computer system when scanned and convert, perhaps phonetically, into Scenter script.

Then the discontinuity struck me.

I leaned over and looked closer. "Prunella? Gusselwaithe Hortense *Prunella* O'Clock Wallace? Pruncy? You never admitted that, not even on our marriage forms."

"You never asked."

"I did."

She looked beleaguered. "Listen, fella, you don't think that out of the gazillions of people in Galacticon that a three-name name would be unique?"

"Well, I—"

"Even a computer search through Galacticon records for four-name names is difficult." Rexann must have done all this after they reached T-hoe.

"Pruney. You never told me."

She gave me her special warning look and I grinned a chummy grin and that disarmed her. I wondered how many more names she was withholding.

At the next desk, Dad was working on filling out applications for temporary residence within what the Scenters called their "Form for Being and Linear Organization." Must be their government.

Granddad had refused to fill out a form for their Soil Classification Bureau and was wandering around watching all the rest of us filling out Scenter government forms and grumbling. "What's in the next galaxy over, anyway?" he asked an alien.

"Sir sir?" the Scenter responded.

"Phew!" Granddad said, waving his hand in front of his face. "You're a stinker, aren't you?"

Dad gave Granddad a blowlike look. "Some diplomat you make."

I agreed more with Granddad.

I pushed the plastic sheet toward Sandy. "Here, you do it."

"Me? Me? *I* am not on the Board of Directors." Her.

"But you're good at obfuscatorial matters." Me.

"Says who?" Her.

"You used to work for Galacticon." Me.

"So what does that prove?" Her.

"I don't know nothing about bureaucrats and Preliminary Planning Commissions to plan planning commissions," I said. "Anyway, you wanted to come along, so make yourself useful."

"I haven't been useful?" Her voice took on a threatening tone.

"Ah, um, why, sure, but—"

"Could you have done without me?" Her green eyes were shaded, but inviting.

"Not for a second, but—"

She waved Granddad over. "Rebel, Rusty says I haven't been useful. Do you reckon that's true?"

"Hell, no, girl, we couldn't have done without you."

"See," said Sandy, "I told you so."

The Scenter was trying to follow this, but he just shook his little pointy head.

Sandy took the stylus and began slashing about the plastic sheet like she didn't care what she put down.

Maybe she had a point.

In reflex, I pulled out a stick of peanut butter jerky and took a bite to soothe my nerves.

Suddenly there was a strange silence. All the aliens were looking directly at me and, while not disconcerting, it wasn't an experience I was used to. "What'd I do?"

The Scenter in front of me moved around his table, jostling it and stopped in front of me.

Others were coming this way and soon Sandy, Granddad, and I were surrounded.

"Rusty," Granddad said, "I shore hope you haven't plucked the duck."

"What the hell does that mean?" I asked.

Sandy was watching closely. "That hard stick of peanut butter. That's it. That's what they're doing: they're smelling it."

A murmur of alien sounds came from them, and a lot of swishing from waving and rubbing appendages.

"I think they haven't ever smelled the like," said Sandy.

The Scenters were crowding around us closer now, all forms forgotten.

I broke off pieces of the peanut butter jerky and handed them around. I pulled a couple more from my pocket. "Here, try these, I have plenty more where they came from."

Until that point, I'd never envisioned a look of euphoria on the features of aliens I couldn't picture anyway.

Until then.

"I think we can come to a mechandising and licensing agreement," I said scanning the crowd for Elrod McSpanish who could take care of the details.

Sandy shook her head. "Why me, Lord?"

"Hey, that's my saying." Me.

"Well, so what?" Her.

"You allatime accuse me of stealing your 'dip me in spit' saying." Me.

Granddad pushed his way through a clod of Scenters. "You know, *two* galaxies just ain't big enough—"

DAW

Epic Science Fiction Adventures
C.S. Friedman

☐ **IN CONQUEST BORN** (UE2198—$3.95)

Braxi and Azea, two super-races fighting an endless campaign over a long forgotten cause. The Braxaná—created to become the ultimate warriors. The Azeans, raised to master the powers of the mind, using telepathy to penetrate where mere weapons cannot. Now the final phase of their war is approaching, when whole worlds will be set ablaze by the force of ancient hatred. Now Zatar and Anzha, the master generals, who have made this battle a personal vendetta, will use every power of body and mind to claim the vengeance of total conquest.

☐ **THE MADNESS SEASON** (UE2444—$4.95)

He'd had many names over the centuries. Now he was Daetrin, a name given to him by the alien conquerors of humankind, the Tyr. Three hundred years ago, the Tyr conquered Earth, isolating the true individualists, the geniuses, all the people who represented the hopes and discoveries of the future, imprisoning them in dome colonies on poisonous worlds. There the Tyr, a race which itself shared a unified gestalt mind, had left these gifted individuals to work on projects which might reveal all of humankind's secrets. Yet Daetrin's secret was one no one had ever uncovered, for through the years he had buried it so well that he had even hidden his real nature from himself. But, taken into custody by the Tyr, there was no longer any place for Daetrin to hide. Now he must confront the truth about himself—and if he failed, not just Daetrin but all humans would pay the price.

DAW

Charles Ingrid

THE MARKED MAN SERIES

☐ **THE MARKED MAN** (UE2396—$3.95)
In a devastated America, can the Lord Protector of a mutating human race find a way to preserve the future of the species?

☐ **THE LAST RECALL** (UE2460—$3.95)
Returning to a radically-changed Earth, would the generational ships aid the remnants of a mutated human race—or seek their future among the stars?

THE SAND WARS

☐ **SOLAR KILL: Book 1** (UE2391—$3.95)
He was the last Dominion Knight and he would challenge a star empire to gain his revenge!

☐ **LASERTOWN BLUES: Book 2** (UE2393—$3.95)
He'd won a place in the Emperor's Guard but could he hunt down the traitor who'd betrayed his Knights to an alien foe?

☐ **CELESTIAL HIT LIST: Book 3** (UE2394—$3.95)
Death stalked the Dominion Knight from the Emperor's Palace to a world on the brink of its prophesied age of destruction. . . .

☐ **ALIEN SALUTE: Book 4** (UE2329—$3.95)
As the Dominion and the Thrakian empires mobilize for all-out war, can Jack Storm find the means to defeat the ancient enemies of man?

☐ **RETURN FIRE: Book 5** (UE2363—$3.95)
Was someone again betraying the human worlds to the enemy—and would Jack Storm become pawn or player in these games of death?

☐ **CHALLENGE MET: Book 6** (UE2436—$3.95)
In this concluding volume of *The Sand Wars*, Jack Storm embarks on a dangerous mission which will lead to a final confrontation with the Ash-farel.
